BEST KIND
OF
Trouble

ANGELA CASELLA

BEST KIND OF TROUBLE

A SPICY ROMANTIC COMEDY

BABES OF BREWING

ANGELA CASELLA

ALSO BY ANGELA CASELLA

Apple Ridge

Falling for Mr. October (September 2026)

Catching Mr. Mistletoe (November 2026)

Hideaway Harbor

The Holiday Hate-Off

Babes of Brewing

Best Served Cold

Worst Nanny Ever

Best Kind of Trouble

Worst Faking Idea (May 2026)

Unlucky in Love

The Love Fixers

The Love Bandits

The Love Losers

The Love Destroyers

Spin-off Standalone

The Thief Who Saved Christmas

Finding You

You're so Extra

You're so Bad

You're so Basic

You're so Vain

You're so Phony (coming soon!)

Fairy Godmother Agency

A Borrowed Boyfriend

A Stolen Suit

A Brooding Bodyguard

A Reluctant Roommate

Bringing Down the House (Nicole and Damien's story)

Highland Hills

(co-written with Denise Grover Swank)

Matchmaking a Billionaire

Matchmaking a Single Dad

Matchmaking a Grump

Matchmaking a Roommate

Matchmaking a Player (novella) by Angela Casella (May)

Bad Luck Club

(co-written with Denise Grover Swank)

Love at First Hate

Jingle Bell Hell

Fraudulently Ever After

Matchmaking Mischief

Asheville Brewing

(co-written with Denise Grover Swank)

Any Luck at All

Better Luck Next Time

Getting Lucky

Bad Luck Club

Luck of the Draw (novella)

All the Luck You Need (prequel novella) by Angela Casella

For those who dare to dream.

CHAPTER ONE

BRIAR

I hate conflict so much that I continued seeing a therapist I disliked for a year before I managed to ghost her after a scheduling mishap. It's no wonder I'm twitchy as I wait for Cleet and Ross to report to my father's office at Silver Star Brewery. It's a Sunday, less than three weeks before Christmas, and I'm about to fire them.

Not because I want to, but because my father threatened to fire five employees if I don't choose two to fire and do the deed myself. I tried convincing him it would be heartless to fire anyone before the holidays, and in retaliation he announced to the already-dissatisfied staff that there would be no holiday bonuses this year and it was all my fault.

He sounds like a sadist, right?

He *is*, and proud of it.

According to him, his ability to "think beyond others' feelings" is a key ingredient in his recipe for success.

I suppose he would know. My father is a wildly successful businessman who has developed and sold half a dozen businesses since I was born. Print-on-demand photo albums. Fake chicken he would never eat himself. Kombucha, right on the cusp of it becoming the next big thing. An inappropriate gummy candy he and my mom prefer not to talk about.

My mother thinks so highly of his recipe for success that she had it burned into a slab of maple. It hangs in their dining room.

Identify a rising trend

+

Think beyond others' feelings

+

Give the people what they want

=

Success by any measure

I sit in the literal shadow of my father's success every week when I have dinner with them, knowing his recipe will never work for me because I don't have all of the ingredients.

Which is bad news for me, because I'm the heir apparent of Silver Star Brewery, my dad's latest success story.

Silver Star is one of the nation's few fully organic breweries, and we age all of our sours and some of our saisons in oak barrels in our barrel room.

It must be acknowledged that my father knows how to stand out. He always has, but none of his other business efforts have mattered to me personally.

Silver Star does.

I've loved this brewery from the moment my father sent me photos of the empty warehouse a few years back. I can't explain why it stood out for me other than that the space seemed to tremble with possibilities. And now it's a place of literal transformation, where grain, yeast, and hops are turned into gold... well, golden beer.

Even though my parents and I aren't close, and I was busy running a small business at the time, I'd helped my dad make some important early decisions. We'd discussed how to decorate the tasting room, which beers his brewer should focus on, and even his decision to go organic.

I'd given this brewery a piece of myself. So when my life imploded just under a year ago, my father knew exactly how to reel me into his world.

Give the people what they want.

Instead of patting me on the back and telling me it was going to be okay, he announced he'd *give* me Silver Star Brewery if I moved back home, worked at the brewery for a year as an "ideal employee," and attended family dinners every Friday night.

"You can even bring a guest to dinner," my father had said as if he were granting me a massive concession.

I knew there'd be dozens of strings attached, but I'd wanted it badly enough to sign on the dotted line.

Yes, there was a contract—an extensive one—and the one-year period is up in a couple of months. The brewery will finally be mine.

But my dad doesn't believe in making anything easy. For the past few months, he's been putting me through "Briar Boot Camp"—a series of increasingly obnoxious challenges designed to test my mettle and prepare me to run the business.

I hate the tests, but my God, I want this brewery.

So I've decided to show him I *do* have what it takes by firing Cleet and Ross.

When I told my friend Hannah about the firing challenge, she said I should axe the two least popular staffers, not the worst, but my sense of fairness wouldn't allow it. So I picked Cleet, who wears the same hoodie every day and stinks of cheap pot, and Ross, who tried to look up my dress last week when I was lifting something off a high shelf.

(He also did not offer to help.)

Choosing them was the right thing to do. Still, firing two

people back to back would destroy my soul, which is why I asked them both to meet me here, in my dad's office, so I could do it at the same time.

I *really* don't want to go through with this. I'm tempted to sneak out the back and join my friends at Big Catch Brewing, where Hannah works. She's throwing a holiday party for the staff (and her friends) there tonight, and within fifteen minutes, I could be drinking mulled wine. It would be worth the effort of having to dodge the inevitable mistletoe like it's poison ivy.

I can practically see my father shaking his head. *If you weren't the product of IVF, I'd doubt you were my daughter...*

I'm still stewing about what to do when Cleet raps his knuckles lazily on the door. He and Ross come in without waiting for a response, trailed by a cloud of pot stench. If it had a color, it would be the purplish gray of ennui.

I wait until they're sitting in the visitor chairs and then slip behind my father's heavy desk. I stay standing, because sitting in my father's chair would feel like stealing a king's throne. I'm also worried his asshole aura would rub off on me.

"Thanks for taking the time to meet with me," I tell them. "You guys are great. So great."

"We are?" Cleet asks with understandable doubt as he plucks something from his nose and flicks it onto the floor.

I try not to cringe as I tug a tissue out of the box near my father's computer and hand it to him.

He looks at it in confusion. "What's this for?"

"You're *great*," I repeat, my tone frantic now. I definitely should have done more yoga this morning. I'm as zen as a Wall Street trader during a market crash.

"You already said that," Ross points out, a corner of his mouth hitching up. His gaze rakes over me. "And I'd love nothing better than to show you how great I am, *in detail*, but what's this about? Are we getting some kind of raise?"

"Uh...no."

"An award?" Cleet asks, perking up. "I never got an award before."

Panicking, I blurt, "No! There's no easy way to say this, but we're going to have to let you go."

Cleet's mouth gapes open.

Ross hikes up his eyebrows so high they get lost in his mussed blond hair.

Before either of them can say anything, I add, "I've emailed you a list of open jobs you can apply to. I'm sure you'll find something in no time. There's lots of seasonal work right now, and—"

"You fired us at the same time, *Rapunzel*?" Ross says in a mocking voice. I've heard plenty of people call me that in whispers, as much because I'm "daddy's little princess" as for my waist-length blond hair. "Is this the respect you show your staff?"

"I'll give you both positive references," I continue, falling back on the script I wrote and memorized.

"Well, lah-di-dah," Ross says with a snort. "The princess will give us a positive reference. Did *you* need any references to get this job, or did your daddy just give it to you?"

"He gave it to me," I say through a tight throat, "and I've done everything I possibly can to earn my place."

It's true. Since moving back to Asheville, I've devoted most of my time to learning about beer and breweries. It's become my special interest, I guess you could say. Even my best friends are connected to the brewery world—Hannah is at Big Catch Brewing, and Sophie used to work at Buchanan Brewery and came up with a new nonalcoholic drink line for them.

And, sure, the *real* reason I met Hannah and Sophie was because all three of us, along with a fourth woman, were unknowingly dating the same beer distributor—Jonah Price—but I'm trying not to dwell on my failures.

Ross snorts, turning to Cleet, and says, "We're lucky we're getting out of this dump. Bubba has it right. If she's taking over, it's going to hell in a handbasket."

I bite my lip. Bubba is the head brewer. I had a feeling he wasn't my biggest fan, but I was hoping that was just paranoia.

Truthfully, I'm worried he's right about the handbasket. My father isn't a caring boss, but there's no denying he gets things done. The one time *I* ran a business—the online jewelry store I started with my then-friend Theresa—it was initially successful and then crashed and burned.

Hannah would probably have toasted marshmallows in the ashes; *I'd* come home to daddy.

Ross makes a disgusted sound, but Cleet sniffs and leans forward in his seat. There's a mystery crust attached to the string of his hoodie. "Now that we're not working together," he says eagerly, "maybe you'd like to get a beer with me sometime?"

"Oh...*oh*." My chest feels tight. "I'm so sorry, Cleet, but I don't date anymore."

Ross snorts. "That's her princess way of saying she's not interested in *your* hairy ass, Cleet. Take the hint."

"It's nothing but the truth," I insist hotly, even though I wouldn't date either of them if we were the last three people alive. "I'm focusing on work. No more dating until next summer at the earliest."

After the Jonah debacle, I made a vow to myself to stay single for an entire year. One year with dating off the table. It's been refreshing, honestly, and I have Hannah and Sophie to keep me company. Sure, both of them are newly in love and busy with their own lives and business ventures, but they're always there when I need them.

"Can I borrow a pen?" Cleet asks.

I hand him one, hoping it'll get him out of here sooner.

"And a sheet of paper?"

I grab one from the printer and slide it across the desk, then watch as he slowly and painstakingly writes on it.

"That there's my number," he says, tapping it with the pen. "I'll wait for you, Briar. As long as it takes."

Ross snorts again, shaking his head at his friend. "You'll be waiting forever, you fool."

Cleet pockets my father's expensive pen, but I don't have the heart to call him on it.

"Uh, thanks," I say, folding the paper and sliding it into the back pocket of my jeans.

My father forces all staffers to relinquish their phones at the beginning of their shifts, like a Boomer math teacher on a power trip, so I return Cleet's and Ross's phones with a tight smile and then follow them out of the office.

I'd expected them to take off immediately to pursue job leads—I'd spent five hours compiling that list for them—so I'm discomfited when they instead bypass the exit and trudge down the hall toward the two short steps leading up to the tasting room.

I trail after them and then follow them through the door, which swings shut behind me. Surely they can't intend to...

But they do, because they approach the bar.

"You're staying?" I ask them in disbelief.

Ross gives me a wounded look. "We just got fired, sweetheart. Of course we want to grab a drink with our friends. Would you begrudge us that?"

"Of course not," I stammer, trying to figure out if I'm being unreasonable. "The first one's on the house."

"Thanks, Briar," Cleet says, beaming at me. "Want to sit with us?"

I back up so quickly, I nearly bring down a wire display filled with Silver Star stickers. "I have to get back to work."

"Must be nice to have a job," Ross comments.

I don't have a response for that, so I head into the back, hoping they'll down their drinks quickly. But I check on them fifteen minutes later, and they're still sitting in front of beers, talking to the bartender. The guy notices me and gives me a stare of death from behind the bar.

I feel it then: the goose walking over my proverbial grave.

AN HOUR AND A HALF LATER, I peek into the tasting room, and they're still there, looking pissed. The other staffers must have heard the whole story by now. They're going to be upset, and they'll blame me for being the bearer of bad news.

Hannah would probably say I'm making this up, but I can feel dark energy leaching into the brewery, filling all the nooks and crannies like a cursed English muffin.

I try to keep busy by doing inventory in the stockroom, but the feeling only intensifies. So I'm not surprised when Bubba interrupts me a few minutes later and announces there's going to be an all-hands-on-deck meeting by the vats. "That includes you, Princess."

I've tried to like Bubba. Really I have. But he's a big guy who tries to use his size to look down on everyone he thinks is weaker. My great aunt has always said eyes are the windows to the soul, and Bubba's deep-set dark eyes that have about as much human kindness as a couple of raisins do.

He's not even a very good brewer. Hannah's brother Liam is much more talented.

Not that I'm surprised my dad went for Bubba instead of trying to poach Liam. Bubba makes a big act of being deferential to powerful people (i.e. my father, not me), but Liam would never put on a show. He's an amateur boxer, and no one with any self-preservation would attempt to bully him. He's tall and broad-shouldered, and everything about him screams *I have a Y-chromosome, and I'm not afraid to use it!*

Liam's beer is top-notch, though. Worlds better than Bubba's. Especially the beers Liam brews in his downtime, since everything is standardized at Big Catch.

I've thought about offering him a job once Silver Star is mine, but I'll have to build up the brewery first. Make him a sweet offer he won't want to refuse. Someone with his talent wouldn't work at a place where he's forced to hand over his cell phone and where there are no chairs in the break area.

"Did he say what this meeting's about?" I ask Bubba, trying not to sound defeated. These meetings have been nearly constant since Briar Boot Camp started, because everyone knows nothing kills the soul faster than pointless meetings.

Bubba just grunts and lifts his chin to indicate I should join him.

I fall in behind him, worried I'm not demonstrating good leadership qualities but well aware that it would be worse if I tried to "steal" the lead.

We join the others already assembled in the open area next to the beer vats, and I glance around, surprised, because everyone on staff is present, even the people who aren't working today. Not including Dad and me, there are twenty Silver Star employees now that I've let Cleet and Ross go. My father is currently standing in the middle of them, a bemused look on his face.

"Isn't anyone in the tasting room?" I ask.

Bubba gives me a dark look with his raisin eyes. "You know what? Cleet and Ross are out there. So we're good. They'll help anyone who shows."

Now that goose is tap-dancing across my grave.

I glance at my father. "What's all this about, Mr. Sterling?"

Yes, at Silver Star Brewery, I refer to my father as sir or Mr. Sterling. My request. I get enough disrespect without running around calling for Daddy.

"Bubba's the one who called this meeting," he says pointedly. "So why don't *you* tell *me*?"

He might as well have said, *You want the brewery? It's your problem.*

I turn to Bubba, who smiles at me for the first time ever and pulls out a cell phone. My father grumbles something under his breath, because, yes, technically the phone should be in the tub in his office with the others. But I'm not going to tackle this six-foot-two man and try to confiscate it.

Bubba lifts the phone. "We figured we all wanted our phones back. So we sprung them. You know this is the only brewery in town where employees are forced to give up their phones?"

"I missed a dental appointment because of you," someone calls out from the back, provoking other murmurs of agreement.

"But we're done playing by your arbitrary rules," Bubba says, glancing from me to my father, who looks amused by their rebellion. Probably because he's already checked out, and it won't impact his life for better or worse.

Bubba fiddles with his phone until a Christmas song starts playing. *"You better watch out. You better not cry..."*

Giving me an arch look, he says, "Santa's always watching, Briar. We all know what you did to Cleet and Ross."

"I didn't try to keep it secret." I can feel my cheeks flushing. Damn my pale skin and its failure to keep my moods secret.

"You didn't even have the decency to fire them one at a time. And this is after you cut our holiday bonuses."

The song keeps piping out around us, oddly cheerful, as the

staffers nod and mumble in a show of solidarity. My father continues to watch the revolution with passive interest.

"And you keep changing the schedule," someone says from the back of the group.

"And rejecting time off," another person yells.

"You've insulted every single tropical IPA I've made over the last six months," Bubba steams. "And you took away the seating in the break area."

I want to point to my father, to say *he* did all of those things, or I did them on his orders, but he still has another couple of months to yank the brewery from me. If he does that, the last ten months of torment will have been for nothing.

So I stay silent.

"I quit," Bubba says with a determined nod of his heavy, stubbled chin. "And I've warned every other brewer in town not to accept a job at this dump." Grinning, he turns and nods to the rest of the group, and I swear to God, they must have choreographed this ahead of time. Because while I stand there, incapable of saying anything other than *"But you can't,"* they come up to me one by one and quit too.

The last person, an intern who's not even on the payroll, throws a bottle cap at my feet as a final insult. All the while, that awful song is playing in the background. The song finishes and restarts, adding insult to the injury.

I look up from the bottle cap at my feet and stare in dismay as the whole staff leaves en masse, pouring out into the cold through the back.

At least they're not hanging around for beers the way Cleet and Ross did.

I look at my father, hoping he's going to fix this mess he coerced me into making with him. But he gives me a broad, satisfied smile and pats his belly. "You know what, I'm going to give you the brewery early, honey. We'll sign the papers tomorrow morning. If you can make it back from this one, I'll know you're a real Sterling after all."

Then he leaves too, and I'm left a huddled mass of a person. I want to curl into a ball and pretend none of this ever happened. But this problem is mine. This brewery is mine.

But there's no brewery without a brewer. If Bubba has been bad-mouthing me, no brewer will want to work with me, let alone a talented one who could turn this business around.

No one will want to work for me, period.

I stumble into the tasting room, briefly thankful that at least Ross and Cleet have finally left. No one else is around, so at least the staff warned the customers before they up and quit.

My only conscious thought is that I need to leave too. I need my friends. I only stay long enough to flip the sign to CLOSED and lock up. Then I head toward Big Catch Brewing, my mind in a haze.

Unless a miracle happens, I'm screwed.

CHAPTER TWO

LIAM

"Mr. Miracle, huh?" asks a gangly, curly-haired guy I've never seen before. He gestures pointedly at my name tag.

Hi! My name is <u>MR. MIRACLE</u>, and I like to <u>WOULDN'T YOU LIKE TO KNOW.</u>

I grin, patting the name tag, a "gift" from the new retirement-age floor manager at Big Catch Brewing. I like him as much as I like anyone, especially since he's friendly with my sister, Hannah, but he needs to lighten up. So I've taken it upon myself to help him out by messing with the name tags he forces everyone to wear.

He even brought them out tonight, for a party, so he was basically asking for people to revolt.

"That's not actually your name, is it?" the curly-haired guy presses, raising his eyebrows.

A grin spreads across my face. "It's my preferred nickname. I also answer to Sir Miracle."

"Or 'asshole' will do too," suggests Travis, Hannah's boyfriend.

My grin stretches wider. I actually like this boyfriend. I hope he doesn't screw up with Hannah and force me to tear him from limb to limb.

"It's just a little joke between me and the new evening floor manager," I explain to the new guy, who isn't wearing one of the name tags.

"Oh, you mean my dad," New Guy says, glancing around the crowded space for his father, one Eugene Peebles.

Huh. No shit. It's a good thing I didn't say any of the other crap I have on my mind. Like: Big Catch is boring as hell, and we have to make our own fun. Or: I got sick of working here before I started, and that was four years ago.

Four long, tedious years.

Boring is good, Hannah would tell me, even though she does *not* think boring is good. None of us Moroneys do. We were born with a wildness at our core that nothing can fully satisfy.

What Hannah would mean is that boring is good for *me*.

I suppose she has some say in the matter, given that my sister is the only reason I'm employed right now. Yup that's right. I was given this job as a favor to her. Hannah was working as an evening floor manager at Big Catch at the time, and I'd just lost my job at Mountain Morning Brewing for beating up the owner.

Trust me when I say he deserved it.

Other people did not agree with me, unfortunately. I got arrested and condemned to a year of probation and a round of anger management classes. In all likelihood, that's what *I* deserved, although it would have made it hard for me to find a job if Hannah hadn't pulled some strings for me.

Can't say the classes did much for me. I met my buddy Mick at one of them, though, and he introduced me to boxing—the one activity in life where punching people is allowed and even encouraged. He owns a crappy little gym that I go to several times a week.

It's boxing that's helped me maintain an even keel. Boxing, and having Hannah working here at the same brewery. We're used to keeping an eye on each other. We've been doing it our whole lives, ever since our mom walked out on our family.

New Guy is still looking my way expectantly, and I realize I must have zoned out midconversation. So I give him a nod. "And you are?"

"I'm Cormac, Sir Miracle." He nods to Travis. "And not to be creepy, or whatever, but I know who you are."

I laugh. Travis laughs. *Cormac* laughs.

It's a pretty feel-good moment, truth be told. We're all picking up on the cheerful energy in the room, which is infectious compared to the way this place has felt for the last few months.

For me, it has nothing to do with the holiday decorations or the free-flowing beer. It's all thanks to my sister.

Hannah quit in late summer, which was my fault, but she's finally back. I still hate this place, but I hate it a hell of a lot less than I did while she was gone.

"I know who you are too," Travis says pointedly, waving a finger in the direction of Eugene. "My girlfriend's the one who set up your dad and—" Travis's eyes widen, and he turns away. "And—"

"And the woman my sixty-six-year-old father is making out with in full view of everyone," Cormac says wryly. "Yeah, I noticed that too."

Damn. Maybe it's the alcohol, or the high of having Hannah back at the brewery again, but I like this guy too. That's gotta be a new record for me.

Travis laughs and then looks for Hannah in the crowd, a

lovesick expression stealing over his face when she blows a kiss at him. "She's pretty proud of the way Eugene has embraced public displays of affection."

"Don't take a page from his book," I warn, hiking up an eyebrow. "I might know you're sleeping with my sister, but I don't want the evidence shoved in my face. There's only so much a man can take."

Travis lifts both of his hands, and Cormac snorts a laugh.

"Actually, though, I know your band," he says, smiling at Travis. "Garbage Fire."

Travis's smile gets strained. I pat him on the back before saying, "Sore subject right now."

Travis's friend Bixby, the former bassist in the band, stabbed him in the back, and they had to boot him out. They'd already been looking for a new rhythm guitarist to replace a guy who'd moved out of town, so they were left with just Travis on the drums and his pal Rob as the lead singer and only guitarist.

Two people do not a band make.

I offered to play with them for a while as the rhythm guitarist, but I'm not interested in sticking around. I'm not what you might call a team player. I'm trying to sweet talk Mick into taking my place. He can be a bit of a dick—we both came by those anger management classes honestly—but he's good people. He'll do right by them.

Cormac makes a face he probably thinks is sympathetic. "Yeah, I know. Actually...I was wondering if you were maybe looking for a new bassist."

He's acting aw-shucks embarrassed, which is hilarious. Travis and Rob had to cancel a bunch of shows after losing Bixby. At this point, they would happily invite a serial killer to be their bassist, so long as he could lay it down with his guitar.

"You're a bassist?" Travis asks, his face lighting up.

Cormac nods but says quickly, "I haven't been in a band before, though. I play alone."

A weird instrument to play alone, if you ask me, but no one did, so I just grunt.

As predicted, Travis doesn't seem to care about the hows and whys. He scans the crowd, his eyes darting wildly, then blurts, "Wait a sec." He disappears, presumably to find Rob, or to light a candle to whatever deity he believes in.

Now that Travis is gone, Cormac and I are left in silence. Cormac rocks on his heels a couple of times as if searching for the optimal standing position, then says out of nowhere, "What's your biggest problem as a brewer?"

No need to think that one through. "Talking to people."

He surprises me by laughing. "That's my biggest problem as a person. I'm told you're supposed to ask questions to form a dialogue."

"Silence is good too. Silence is underrated." I'm just giving him shit, though. He's funny, this son of Eugene's. Maybe he doesn't mean to be, but I'm willing to accept him at face value.

He smiles at me. "It would be a stretch of the imagination to call this silence."

That makes me laugh, because we're surrounded by bustling activity, people talking, and the low hum of Christmas music. The song that's playing at the moment is, ironically, "Silent Night."

A few seconds later, Travis comes back. Twisting his mouth to the side, he says, "I can't find Rob. But he'll want to have a conversation."

While we wait, we talk music. Cormac knows his shit, and it's obvious Travis is excited. I'm pumped, too, because once Travis and Rob get him settled in, presuming he can play anywhere near as well as he talks about playing, I can bow out and leave them to it.

The front door opens to admit a late arrival, and I glance over—

And feel like I've been frozen in spot from the cold air wafting in.

It's a woman with long blond hair, down past her waist, wearing only a T-shirt and jeans despite the cold. For a second, my eyes linger on that hair—feet and feet of it, the shiny gold of a perfect lager. It seems to catch the low lights and radiate them back. Then my gaze finds her face.

Her eyes are big and light brown and full of misery. She looks like one of those princesses in the movies my sister's friends liked to watch growing up. The ones that always made Hannah roll her eyes.

It takes me half a second to register that this is Briar, one of Hannah's new friends.

I don't really know Briar, although I know the story of how Hannah met her and Sophie. The three of them, plus another woman, were all unknowingly sleeping with the same guy— Jonah, a spineless piece of shit whose brother, Rob, happens to be the front man of Garbage Fire.

Rob and Jonah don't get along, which is good, because once I found out what Jonah was pulling with my sister, I threatened to kill him and hide his body if he ever came near her again.

Now, Hannah, Sophie, and Briar are friends.

Sophie's dating Rob, Hannah's seeing Travis, and Briar... well, I don't know much about Briar other than that she works for her rich father's brewery, which is infamously one hundred percent organic. A pointless gimmick, if you ask me, but I suppose there are enough breweries in this town that you've got to stand out somehow. Might as well stand out for something stupid.

I've only seen Briar a few times, exchanged probably two dozen words with her, at least three of them hello, but I've seen enough to know she's usually more put together than this. More aloof. A princess in a tower. Tonight, she looks desperate and on edge—a different kind of princess entirely.

My instinct is to stride over and ask who did this to her so I can punch them. Or, if it's a woman, hand the situation over to my sister. But I made a promise to Hannah that holds me back.

The reason my sister left Big Catch this past summer is that I started casually sleeping with one of her friends, Margaret, who was also on staff. We'd agreed to no-strings sex—a way to scratch an itch—but after a few weeks, Margaret asked when she could move a toothbrush into my apartment.

The only toothbrush that's ever going to be in my apartment is mine.

When I told her so, she accused me of being emotionally unavailable.

After what happened to me, yes, abso-fucking-lutely.

Next, she accused me of cheating.

An interesting accusation, given we'd never agreed to be exclusive. Even so, I wasn't seeing anyone else. I've never had any interest in juggling women.

Didn't matter. She was pissed, and she threw all of my boxing gear into one of the vats at Big Catch. Which meant all the beer had to be thrown out.

The brewery took a thousands-of-dollars hit, and Hannah had to fire her friend, which led to my sister losing most of her other friends. They'd stupidly sided with Margaret. Hannah was pissed enough at me to temporarily quit Big Catch, even though she'd been here longer than me and actually liked her job.

Last month, she agreed to forgive me for my screwup, thank God, on one condition. I had to promise not to mess around with any of her other friends, and also to grant her two favors. Anything she wants, anytime she asks.

Quickest agreement I've ever made.

Hannah's already come to me for one favor: helping Travis out of a bind involving his band. The second is yet to be determined.

But I meant what I said. I'm never going near any of her other friends. Because being at odds with my sister or our little brother is unacceptable to me.

So I just stand there, ignoring the magnet-pull of Briar as she stands in the doorway, looking lost and beautiful and cold.

Crap, she's *cold*.

I'm about to stride forward so I can at least offer Briar someone's coat—there's a rack full of them by the door—when my sister and Sophie hurry through the crowd and flock around her.

I'm surprised by how relieved I feel, but more so by the hint of disappointment that I didn't get to be the one to help her.

Seconds later, Rob comes over to us, and Travis wraps an arm around his shoulders. "Cormac is a bass player," he gushes, acting like a zealot who worships at an altar with a bass guitar on top.

"No shit?" Rob says, his gaze following Sophie as she and Hannah hurry Briar away from the door. No doubt he's interested too. Sophie *is* his girlfriend.

"What's going on there?" I ask, nodding toward the front.

"Don't know," he says, shoving his hands into his pants pockets. "But I've got a feeling Hannah and Sophie are about to find out."

This makes me laugh, though it doesn't lift the uneasiness pressing down on my chest.

The others start talking about music again. I leave them to it, slipping away to check in with Eugene and make sure we don't need to tap another keg yet. Through it all, there's a metaphysical itch at the back of my neck—the need to find out just what the hell is going on with Briar. It's not my problem, though, and Hannah will surely deal with her friend.

When I come back, Rob and Travis are God knows where, and Cormac is watching a woman with a short dark bob and a no-nonsense expression.

"Creeping on someone else, Eugene Junior?" I ask.

I meant it as a joke, but he jolts as if I'd slapped him. "Oh, no. That's Nora. I don't like her."

The name rings a bell, and I realize I know who this woman is. She's the brewer at The Ginger Station, and good old Jonah's fourth secret girlfriend.

Well, damn.

This town is big enough, but it can feel as small as the one in *The Andy Griffith Show*. Except with more secret dating and old grudges.

I whistle through my teeth. "Tell me how you really feel."

Cormac adjusts his glasses on the bridge of his nose. "You know my dad's girlfriend? That's her daughter. She probably doesn't even remember me, but we went to school together."

"Small world." My sister's going to have a field day with this one, no doubt. "She uptight?" I ask sympathetically.

"Something like that. She ruined my science project our senior year."

I laugh again, finding this guy plenty entertaining. "Must have been a hell of a science project if you're still pissed about it."

"It was. But that was twelve years ago. She probably doesn't remember."

"But you do."

He shrugs. "I put a lot of work into it. It was one of my first inventions."

"You're an inventor?"

He looks uncomfortable, like I just gave him a wedgie. "It's a grandiose word, but yeah, I guess. I like taking things apart and putting them back together better. And building things to solve problems. But my day job is in coding."

"Solving problems. I like that. You might have just solved one of ours." I cock my head to study him. "Say, why'd you take up bass guitar if you mostly play alone?"

"The bass is what holds the music together. It's the backbone. You wouldn't get very far without a backbone."

I nod, liking the analogy. "Damn straight."

"And then there's the way it feels. You can feel the vibration inside of you."

"You sound like Travis when he's talking about his drums."

I'm distracted by an officious tap on my shoulder, and I turn to see Hannah and Travis. She's practically buzzing with energy, the way she gets when she sucks down too much sugar or is high on an idea that will either make or destroy someone.

"What's up?" I ask, my mind flitting to Briar. "Something wrong with your friend?"

"Yes," she says. "You and I are having a super-secret meeting in the storeroom. *Right away*."

"What about Travis?"

"He's coming as my Emotional Support Travis."

"Are you good with that emasculating description?" I ask him, trying to break the tension. Maybe get a hint at what they're up to.

"Yup," he says, squeezing her close. Her curly hair must be tickling his nose, but he shows no sign of discomfort.

"Well, by all means. Let's pack into a tiny space together, because that's not at all suspicious."

Travis laughs, and Hannah jabs him playfully with her elbow and says, "Just be cool, and it'll be fine. If anyone asks, we'll say someone puked in the bathroom and we're getting cleaning supplies."

I nod to Cormac. "You good?"

"Yeah," he says, "I think I'm going to head out." He gives Travis a hopeful look. "But I'll be in touch about the band?"

"Yes, *please*," Travis says, giving him a fist bump.

Then Hannah's shuttling both of us toward the storeroom. She's five foot two, and Travis and I are both over six feet, but no one can say my sister doesn't have hustle.

A couple of minutes later, we're all sealed into the small space together, Hannah still radiating nervous, excited energy. I feel the buzz of it in my own veins. Hannah's like that, capable of transferring her excitement to others. It's a gift you have to accept, like it or not.

"What is it?" I ask.

"That other favor you promised me," she says slowly, nearly breathless. "You meant it, didn't you?"

My heart beats harder in my chest. "You know I did."

She looks at Travis, a silent communication passing between them.

"Hannah?" I say, never much of a patient guy. "I didn't come in here to watch you make out with your boyfriend. Aren't you going to tell me what this is all about?"

My sister looks me dead in the eye and says, "I'm calling in that other favor."

CHAPTER THREE

BRIAR

"It's going to be okay," Sophie says, her voice upbeat, her smile fixed. "Hannah has a plan. I know she's not usually a planner, but she really seems to be onto something this time. She had that look she gets in her eyes."

Sophie and I are sitting on a couple of chairs in the big warehouse at the back of Big Catch Brewing—no decorations, no food, just a bunch of kegs, a few scattered chairs, and the muted sound of other people's fun. As soon as Hannah and Sophie saw me, they pulled me back here and dressed me in a sweatshirt Hannah grabbed from the merch section up front. I'd told them my sob story through chattering teeth. Every word made me feel more pathetic, reminding me of how little I've changed since I was first sent to boarding school as a six-year-old.

The second week of first grade, a girl named Melly stole my American Girl Felicity doll, and instead of demanding that she return her to me, I watched in silent misery as she gave Felicity haircuts and had tea parties with her. The worst part was that Melly was supposed to be my friend. My mother and father had told me to *stick close to her like glue*, because she was the daughter of one of their best friends, a real estate developer who always gave Dad the "good deals."

Good people, my mother said. *I know they raised her right.*

I did get my doll back eventually, but only because my house mother finally figured out what was going on and forced Melly to return her to me and apologize. It wasn't much of a victory, though. Melly's apology was insincere, and my relationship with Felicity never recovered. From that point on, I only ever saw accusation in her hollow green eyes.

I've tried to *work on myself* for years. There's been yoga, therapy, meditation, and art. But at my core, I'm still that frightened little girl who wasn't daring enough to ask for her doll back.

I know without asking that Hannah would have punched Melly in the face, or maybe stolen her teddy bear to give her a taste of her own medicine. I want to be strong like that, but I feel my father's recipe for success hanging over my head—always poised to crush me. Now, the weight of the brewery is on my shoulders too.

I have the building. The supplies. The beer. The profits. But I have nothing else.

If you can make it back from this one, I'll know you're a real Sterling.

But I'm *not* a real Sterling in any way that matters.

I'm a thirty-one-year-old failure, who's tried to play the game, several times, and only gotten through the first few rounds.

Sophie starts rubbing my back again. "You'll see. Hannah seemed really confident."

She's right. After dressing me and prying my story out, Hannah practically launched herself out of the room, insisting she was going to hire more staff for me.

Tonight.

She must have been talking about Liam, right?

I hope to God she was, because the only thing that will save me is if I find a brewer good enough to pull everything together.

I also hope she *wasn't* talking about Liam, because if Hannah convinces her brother to work for me, I'll be a nepo baby twice over—my father gave me the brewery, and my best friend gave me—

"I *can't* let her give me her brother," I cry out, tears tracking down my cheeks.

Sophie cocks her head, and I feel the telltale flushing of my cheeks again. "I mean...she obviously can't give him to me...he's a grown man. He's six foot four, maybe even six foot five. But he'd do anything for her, you know he would. What if she asks him to come work for me, and he only does it because she made him, and then the brewery is a huge failure—"

"No one can make anyone do anything," Sophie says firmly. "Let's do more of that yoga breathing."

We've been doing it off and on since Hannah left the room.

I learned Dirgha breathing when I was a kid from my great-aunt Sky. For a month every summer, I stayed with her in her cabin in Georgia, where we used to pick wildflowers and do yoga together. Sometimes she would take me to her art collective studio so I could learn from the different artists.

My great aunt is probably the only reason I made it through childhood. She'd spent so much time teaching me ways to calm my anxiety. But the most useful has probably been how to breathe through stress. I can practically hear her whispering to me in her soft, musical voice: *inhale deeply into your belly, then rib cage, then chest, and exhale in the opposite order.*

She'd insisted Dirgha breathing was magic, and she may have been right. I can already feel the weight on my shoulders lessening.

The snick of the door opening at the back of the warehouse

catches my attention. It lets in a spurt of noise from the staff party—someone laughing, followed by strains of that hateful song about a stalking Santa.

Oh, I'll never listen to "Santa Claus is Coming to Town" again without thinking about Bubba's hostile raisin eyes.

I turn toward the entrance, expecting Hannah, but Liam walks in, shutting the door behind him.

Yeah, he's *definitely* six foot five, with broad shoulders and thick arms. He has auburn hair and a short, trimmed beard that gleams red and gold or brown depending on the lighting. His eyes are brown, not a dancing green like Hannah's, and even though they're light—the color of our amber ale—they're not warm and welcoming. They remind me of a wolf's eyes.

He nods a greeting as he walks over, his movements brimming with confidence. Something is tucked under his arm, but my overloaded brain can't make sense of it. My heart starts racing like a scared rabbit's. It's that confidence of his, that *swagger*. He walks like he owns the world.

I nearly gasp when he comes to a stop in front of us, because there's a sticker on his shirt that says,

Hi! My name is **MR. MIRACLE.**

I needed a miracle, and I came here. Perhaps I'm being foolish, but this feels an awful lot like a sign.

"We have to talk privately," he says, his words giving me an electric jolt.

"Why can't we talk here?"

He raises his eyebrows. "Hannah said you want to poach me. You've got some pretty big balls if you want to discuss it at my place of employment."

My cheeks burn as I get to my feet, needing to show some agency, even if I'm suddenly hyperaware of my tearstained face and mussed hair. I had it in a ponytail earlier, but somewhere in the middle of my crisis the scrunchie must have slipped off.

I search his face but can't tell whether he's pissed, annoyed, or bored. I can't read him at all, other than his confidence. If Hannah's an open book, he's a firmly closed one. Actually, he's like one of those lockable diaries every girl is given at some point, with a key that gets lost after a week.

It's hard to imagine two more different siblings.

"Where's Hannah?" I ask.

"I don't want her anywhere near this," he insists. "She works here too. People don't look kindly on poaching employees."

It feels like he just punched a hole in my chest with a rusty office implement. Hannah's risking her job for me.

If she asked Liam to quit, and their boss finds out...

"Okay," I say. "We'll go to Silver Star. No one's there." Those words nearly pull another sob from my chest, but I hold it back through sheer force of will.

"People are going to find out about the mass walkout," he says gruffly. "I can't be seen at your brewery until we get this settled."

I swallow down fresh panic. "Okay. Then maybe..."

My mind whirrs. Other than Silver Star and the tea shop that my friends and I love, what do I have? What places in this town are mine?

There's always my apartment. But I can't take him there. It would feel too intimate. And my cat, Karma, hates nearly everyone, sometimes even me.

"I have someplace private we can talk." He gestures at the back door. "Let's leave out the back."

Sophie gives me an encouraging smile. "Good, this is good! We'll meet at the tea shop tomorrow to run through everything. I'm sure Dottie will have tons of ideas."

Dottie is the sweet older woman who runs Tea of Fortune.

Even though she has a huge extended family of people she's "adopted," she still found space in her heart for Hannah, Sophie, and me. She reminds me of my great-aunt. Her aura of kindness ripples outward, touching everyone in her presence. Just being around her makes you feel like you're getting a warm hug.

"Am I invited?" Liam asks. The only sign that he's teasing is the corner of his mouth lifting slightly, maybe two millimeters.

"Of course," Sophie says. "But we all know you're not going to come."

He laughs, the sound low and deep, almost like the growl of a wild animal. "No," he admits. "Not really my scene."

I give Sophie a quick hug, then wrap my arms around my body for warmth as I follow Liam to the back door of the warehouse.

"It's good that I didn't take the bike today," he says conversationally as we reach the back door. "I don't have an extra helmet."

"You ride a bicycle to work?" I ask, bracing myself for the burst of freezing air.

He gives me an incredulous look, his lip curling, and I feel like an idiot.

"A lot of people do," I mutter.

"A lot of people are idiots," he replies. He tries to hand me the thing that's been tucked under his arm, and I realize it's a coat. "Put it on, and let's go."

Offering me a coat is thoughtful, but he's being condescending. I decide I don't want to go anywhere with him, Mr. Miracle or not. I'm tired of being treated like a pretty imbecile.

"I'm not stupid," I say heatedly.

He takes a step toward me, and suddenly we're standing inches apart, both of us right next to the worn wooden door. I can feel heat radiating from him. He's wearing a long-sleeved black shirt that clings to his thick arms and makes him look even more intimidating as he peers down at me. "You would be if you rode a bicycle in the dark in twenty-degree weather with ice on the roads."

"Yeah, that would be pretty stupid. Kind of like considering leaving your job of four years for no better reason than that your sister asked, so you can work for a woman whose entire staff just quit."

To my surprise, he laughs again, and this time his eyes crinkle at the corners. "Yeah, but you're the one who said you're not stupid. I never made that claim about myself."

He holds out the coat again.

"If you give me that, you won't have one," I object.

"And I've got probably a hundred pounds on you. I'll be fine."

I can tell he's not going outside with me unless I put on the coat, so I do, my hands trembling slightly. So much has happened at once, and I'm still reeling. The coat smells a little spicy and is warmer than the hoodie. Once I've got it on, Liam opens the door again and leads the way to a run-down blue-green truck.

His mouth inches up into a half-smile as he unlocks the passenger-side door, using the actual key, not a key fob, and opens it for me. "It's all yours, Princess."

The nickname puts a bitter taste in my mouth, but I climb in without comment. Liam gets into the driver's side and puts the truck into drive, leaving Big Catch behind. He maneuvers through the crowded streets of downtown Asheville, cursing liberally as pedestrians casually stroll across the street in front of the truck without waiting for the crosslights.

I expected Liam would want to talk business once we were on the move, but he doesn't say anything. He just turns on the radio, finds Christmas music on two of the stations, and then turns it off with another curse.

I'm the one who finally breaks the silence. "I have lots of ideas for the brewery."

"That's great," he says. "Do you want to keep it organic?"

"Yes. It's one of the main draws."

He whistles through his teeth. "If that's the main draw, you've got a problem on your hands."

"There aren't many fully organic breweries."

"Because it's BS, and most people know it. There are better ways to stand out."

"Like what?" I turn in my seat to look at him, not entirely convinced he's not trying to piss me off.

He gives a careless, one-shoulder shrug. "We'll talk about it some other time. Once we come to an agreement."

"If you don't want to know what my plans are for the future, what *do* you want to know?"

"Let's talk shop when we get there."

I want to ask *where*, but something tells me he wants me to ask so he can be withholding. I've experienced enough turmoil for one day, so I don't say anything. We just sit in strained silence—strained on my part, at least. He seems perfectly at ease. I look out the window at the lights we're drifting past, trying to comb my hair with my fingers without looking like I care about my appearance.

Finally, after pulling onto the highway and then off on Tunnel Road, he parks in the lot of a brick building with no lights on inside.

He turns toward me, his profile illuminated in a way that makes me half tempted to trace my finger down the bridge of his nose—slightly off-center, suggesting it's been broken at least once—and says, "We're here."

"We could have just talked in the car," I point out.

"Not the way I prefer to do business."

He gets out of the truck, and I do the same, following him to the front door of the building. There's a weathered sign above the door that reads: Ring Your Bell Boxing Gym. It looks like a brisk wind would send it flying.

"Why are we at your boxing gym?" I ask in confusion.

But Liam just busies himself with unlocking the door, which unleashes another question in my mind—why does he have a key?

Inside, he flicks on the light switch by the door. The reception area smells musty and a bit like feet. There's an ugly red-and-gold-patterned carpet on the floor and a front desk with an ancient desktop computer parked on top of it. Several award plaques hang on the wall behind the desk, and a couple of old, doughy-looking armchairs sit in the corner. They might have been white once, but now they're slightly beige.

I shrug off the coat and hang it from a tilting coat rack.

"We can sit in those chairs," I suggest, gesturing to them. Immediately hoping he says no, because they look like they could be the source of the smell.

He shakes his head and walks to the opening behind the desk, flicking on another fluorescent light as he goes.

"You don't believe in open communication, do you?"

He glances over his shoulder with a smirk. "Is that important to you in an employee?"

"*Yes.*"

I'm surprised by how steely my voice sounds, but my former business partner's betrayal cut deep. I'd had plans then, too, and my life had been blown apart by her dishonesty. I'd barely pulled any of my pieces back together before they were blown apart again by Jonah's dishonesty.

So, yes, integrity is important to me.

I only wish I were better at identifying it.

My mind whirling, I follow him down a short hallway that opens into a large room lined with blue mats. A couple of boxing rings sit in the middle, and heavy bags—long, solid-looking blue cylinders—hang from the ceiling on either side of the gym. Smaller speed bags, mounted on swivels, line the back wall.

Liam pauses in front of a floor-to-ceiling rack stacked with worn-looking gloves, then surprises me by taking my hand. A shiver of awareness jolts me as he traces its shape and then carelessly drops it. He frowns and then pulls a pair of gloves off the bottom shelf.

"Here," he says, trying to hand them to me. "These are probably still too big, but they'll have to do."

"Do for *what*?" I ask, refusing to take them. My voice sounds harsh and grating in the open space.

To my surprise, Liam smiles. "I know what a person looks like when they need to hit something. You, Princess, need to hit something."

I gape at him. "No, I'm not angry. I'm..."

Sad. Defeated. *Broken*.

He plops the gloves into my hand. "Maybe you *should* be angry."

"Anger is a dark emotion." I shove the gloves back at him. "I don't want any part of it."

"It's only a dark emotion if you let it take root inside of you." He pushes the gloves back at me, the corner of his mouth hitching up. "Look at that. You just got six months of anger management classes for free. You're welcome."

"You took anger management classes?"

His half-smile widens. "I'm surprised my sister didn't tell you the whole story. She loves giving me shit."

"All she told me is that she loves you, you're the best brewer in town, and you're an asshole."

Not entirely true. She also said he's emotionally unavailable and never dates a woman for longer than a few weeks. She made Sophie and me promise never to date him, particularly since his casual relationship with one of her former friends imploded in a messy way.

But I don't think he'd appreciate it if I brought any of that up.

"Well, there you go." He's full-on smiling now. "I *am* an asshole. That's why I took anger management classes."

"And they told you to punch someone?"

"The best way to avoid blowups is to let it out. I have a feeling you've been carrying everything in here." He taps his chest with one hand, holding the gloves with the other, and my gaze follows the movement, transfixed. He has so much more physicality than anyone else I know. He's all muscle and movement. "My sister told me what Bubba and the others did to you at Big Catch. How they humiliated you. Your father watched and did nothing to stand up for you. Doesn't that piss you off?"

Tears burn in my eyes. "You and Hannah were both right. You *are* an asshole."

"Can't say you weren't warned," he replies, his smile softer as he offers me the gloves again.

I ignore them. "Will you stop messing around and tell me if you're really willing to consider working at Silver Star? I know Big Catch offers better benefits, but we've been turning a healthy profit, and I was thinking I could offer you—"

"I'll take the job because my sister asked me to." All the humor has dropped from his face. "I don't need another reason. But if you show me you've got some fight in you, then I'll be a hell of a lot less pissed off about being told what to do."

CHAPTER FOUR

LIAM

Briar wraps one hand around her hip, capturing a few locks of her long golden hair. My gaze follows the motion before I manage to tear it away.

"Aren't *you* telling *me* what to do right now?" she asks.

I hold back a smile. Whether she realizes it or not, she's giving me what I wanted by challenging me. Showing me she's capable of holding her own. Which is good, because I meant what I said—

I'm not letting my little sister down again. I'd take this job even if it were for the McDonald's of breweries.

Which, honestly, might be a step up from Silver Star—the pretentious plaything of Don Sterling.

Yeah, I know a bit about Briar's father, and what I know doesn't impress me. He opened Silver Star knowing jack about beer, and it shows. Fully organic beer? Please. It's not like they're selling vegetables from a farm stand. Organic beer is a buzzword, a gimmick. A marketing ploy aimed at big city people, who can be tricked into paying more for the same thing.

But if Princess wants to keep her beer organic, we keep it organic. Hopefully she'll be more open to some of my other ideas than the corporation in charge of Big Catch has been. They value consistency over creativity, which has made working there an endless slog of the same, the same, the same. So much so that it was actually exciting when someone spotted a rat racing through the back room a few weeks ago.

I'm more than ready to catch a curveball. And from the look on Hannah's face when she spilled the whole story of Silver Star earlier in that closet, she knew it.

Briar shifts her weight from foot to foot like a prizefighter, making me smile. "There, I knew you could get pissed off if you tried. Your old man deserves it. He didn't stand up for you the way he should have."

Eyes bright with anger, she replies, "You don't know anything about my relationship with my father."

"Nope. But can we both agree that he's an even bigger asshole than me?"

Surprised laughter gushes out of her, causing her hair to dance around her face, and she lifts one of her hands to her lips in wonder—as if it's the first time she's ever laughed. I remember what that hand felt like in mine, small and soft. Too small for the gloves I'm carrying, but they're the closest the gym's got.

Her laughter has faded, but her face still wears the imprint of it. Her brown eyes are warmer now, and her cheeks are flushed from coming in from the cold. She looks...

Nope, not going there. It doesn't matter how she looks. She's going to be my boss, and while learning from past experience isn't my strong suit, Hannah has made it clear our truce is toast if I touch another of her friends.

There are billions of women in the world, and most of them don't know Hannah exists. It shouldn't be a hard rule to follow.

I focus my gaze just beyond Briar, on one of the heavy bags hanging from the ceiling. My finger drops to my wrist, and I snap the elastic band I keep there for refocusing my attention.

"I shouldn't have laughed," she says with a soft smile. "He's...well, I wouldn't call him an asshole. He'd say one of his strengths is thinking beyond others' feelings. It's part of his recipe for success."

I snort. "Sounds like the kind of thing an asshole would say."

"You'd know, I suppose, but there's no arguing with success."

I shrug, finally looking back at her. "Sure. Seems to me he's so successful his whole staff quit, and he passed the brewery on to you so it wouldn't make him look bad."

"It's not like that," she says earnestly, taking a step toward me.

I take a step back on reflex, and her cheeks get pinker.

"I wasn't going to, like, throw myself at you. I just..." Her blush deepens. "Oh, I'm making a horrible impression."

"I don't make a practice of caring what people think of me. Couldn't recommend it more."

"I *have* to care what people think of me," she says, folding her arms. They form a shelf for her perfectly shaped—

Look away, you idiot.

I focus on the heavy bag behind her again. "No, you really don't. If someone doesn't like you, fuck 'em. Why waste any energy on a person who doesn't like you?"

"I'm going to be the boss," she says. "I have to care what people think of me."

I snort again. "You think your father gives two shits what *anyone* thinks of him? He's so unlikeable a brewery full of people just quit on him. And no offense, Princess, but if all this energy you've put into being likeable were working, they wouldn't have walked out on you either."

I let myself focus on her then. Her features have hardened, and her chin is pointed up. Good. If she's going to succeed in this industry, she needs to learn to look and act tough.

"Maybe I don't like *you*," she says.

"That's fine. As we've established, I don't give a shit. Hannah asked me to work for you, not become your new best friend."

Her pretty pink lips fall open.

If Hannah were here, she'd laugh and say, *Making friends, Liam?*

"Now, are you going to hit something or not?" I ask.

"I have half a mind to hit you."

I grin at her. "Now we're getting somewhere."

She scowls at me and then pads closer. For a second, I think she's going to round up and punch me in the chest. It would be kind of cute if she tried, and I wouldn't hold it against her. We could both agree I'd deserved it. Instead, she snatches the gloves from me.

I hold back a smile as she pulls them on.

They're too big, but she doesn't complain. I get the sense this woman doesn't complain about anything, other than me.

"How's the fit?"

"Terrible," she says. "Now, what do I do?"

"Turn around."

Her eyes meet mine, and fear flickers in her gaze for half a second. "You want me to put my back to you?"

She might as well have gripped my throat and squeezed.

"Did someone hurt you?" I ask, my voice harsh. Not because I'm pissed at her, but because I'm filled with the need to destroy whoever did.

"A lot of people have hurt me," she says, her voice soft but crisp, and the roiling feelings inside me dial up from ten to an impossible thirteen.

"I mean, did someone...take advantage of you?"

"Not in the way you're probably thinking."

"But something *did* happen." I didn't mean for it to come out as a growl, but I don't like the thought. Don't like it one bit.

"It was in high school," she says, rubbing her arms as if she's suddenly chilled. "It's no big deal."

"Oh, it's a big fucking deal."

She tips her head, looking at me with surprise. "It's okay, Liam. It happened, like, twelve years ago. Maybe longer."

I press my lips together in displeasure. "I talked to this guy at the Christmas party who was still pissed off because a chick he knew in high school ruined his senior-year science project. *Twelve years ago.* I'm guessing whatever happened to you is worse than that. You're allowed to have feelings about it."

She nods. "Okay, thank you. I don't want to talk about it, though."

Suddenly, it's all I want to talk about. I want to know what this person did to her, and also where they live. It's not a logical thought, but there it is.

I pluck the elastic band on my wrist again.

"We won't," I say after a long moment. "But, just so you know, I wasn't going to do anything while your back was turned. That's not my style. The heavy bag is behind you. That's where we should start."

She nods, but before she can turn around, I stride forward to stand beside her. I'm a hell of a lot taller and broader than her, and I don't want her to feel physically intimidated. Fear is only something I covet from my enemies.

Her hair is still down around her shoulders, her waist. Fucking everywhere. I deny myself the urge to "accidentally" brush my hand against it. While I'd like to know what it feels like, it wouldn't be a very intelligent research project.

"Do you have something to tie your hair back with?" I ask.

"No. My scrunchie fell out."

"That's okay. I've got something you can use." I pull the hair band off my wrist and hand it to her.

"But..." A startled expression fills her eyes. "*Oh*. No, thank you. I don't want to use some other woman's—"

Laughter spurts from me. "Oh shit. You think I stole this off some woman after sleeping with her? Now I'm really wondering what Hannah's told you, but no. It's mine. Snapping it against my wrist helps me shift my focus when I need to. Feels better than a rubber band."

"Oh. Thank you, then," she says, sounding embarrassed.

I hand the band over, our fingers brushing, and I watch with fascination as she picks up all of that hair and easily twists it into a loose bun at the base of her neck.

My mouth goes dry, and I force myself to look away, wishing like hell I still had the band on my wrist so I could snap it.

I clear my throat, then say, "Are you right-handed?" She nods tightly. "Left foot in front of the right, then bend your knees."

She takes the position, just as I described it, and glances back at me for guidance. "Lift your other hand up to protect your face."

"You think the heavy bag is going to hit back?" she asks dryly. This time she's joking intentionally, not being naïve the way she was about the bike.

"Might do, if you hit it hard enough." I pause, studying her stance. "I'm going to touch your arm now, Briar. Is that okay?"

She turns her head, her gaze fiery. "Don't start treating me like I'm made of glass. If you do, then I know I'm in trouble."

I nod in agreement and adjust her arm, careful not to let my hands linger.

"Okay, one last step..."

I pull out my cell phone.

Her eyes round when she notices what I'm doing. "Let me

guess, you're going to take a video of this so you can show Hannah and make fun of me later."

"Nope," I say, "but that's not a half-bad idea." Then I play "Eye of the Tiger" on my phone.

Her laughter sounds delighted this time—and I'd bet everything I own that this particular sound has never filled this particular space before.

"It's a rite of passage," I explain. "It's played on everyone's first fight at Bell's. Owner's rules."

"And my first fight is against a bag of sand?"

"Nah, that thing's full of cut-up shirts and fabric scraps from the lost and found."

She rolls her eyes as she pokes the bag. "It isn't."

"It is. Maybe a few mouse carcasses. Now, put your whole body behind your punch. The strength comes from your core, not your arm. You want to twist your hip and rotate your shoulder as you strike. Give it your all."

She scrunches her nose, which is cute as hell, then rounds up and hits the bag. It moves about four inches.

Her eyes widen, and she jumps a little on her feet. "I hit it, and it moved."

I nearly laugh, but she's so damned proud of herself I'm not going to piss on her parade. "You're a regular Rocky. You want me to keep the music on for round two?"

She glances at the phone, considering, and nods. "Yeah, I've always liked this song."

I'm smiling as she positions herself to throw another punch. This time, the bag moves five inches.

"You hit it harder," I point out.

She beams at me. "I did, didn't I?"

The song ends, and I restart it, getting a smile from her.

After she does another rep, I point to her other hand. "How about we switch it up?"

I help her get situated, and she practices a few rounds with her left fist. When I catch her thinking a bit too hard about it, I say, "Harder. Imagine my face is printed across the bag."

She's laughing as she punches fictional me in the nose.

She pulls back from the bag and smiles broadly at me—and I can't do a damn thing to keep myself from smiling back. "You broke my nose."

"You think?"

"At least a sprain." My grin spreads wider. "Let's keep going."

She seems to be hitting her stride, and it doesn't take long for me to guide her into a rhythm of alternating between hands, jab and cross, jab and cross, breathing with each punch. As she attacks the bag, I sense something changing in her. She's feeling less broken by what happened to her tonight, more motivated. It's...well...I've got no desire to look away.

"What do you say, slugger? Are you ready to pack it in?"

She takes the gloves off and flexes her hands, which are pink across the knuckles. I turn off the fourth rep of "Eye of the Tiger" and pocket my phone.

"An ice pack will help if it bothers you," I suggest. "Or a bag of frozen food."

Briar holds the gloves in one hand, her big eyes peering up at me. "Thank you for being so nice to me, Liam."

All I can do is laugh. "Princess, if this is what you think good behavior is, you need someone to show you a good time."

I didn't mean for it to sound like that, but from the way her expression shifts, she heard the innuendo too.

"I meant you should have higher expectations, that's all," I clarify.

"Thank you," she says again. "This is exactly what I needed tonight."

"Does this mean I get a raise?" I ask as I reclaim the gloves from her.

She smiles up at me. "You don't even know what I'm offering to pay you."

"So you can lie and tell me I'm getting a raise. I'll never know the difference."

"I'm going to be nothing but honest with you," she says, her expression serious. "Something tells me you value that."

"I do," I reply softly. I know I should move, but I feel rooted in place, unable to take my eyes off her. It's like she saw past all of my bullshit, down to the core of me.

But no man likes to feel weak in his favorite gym, so I get it together and lead the way back to the supply shelf. I wipe down the gloves and shove them in their place.

"Now, what else do you do when you've had a bad day? Drink with your friends? Would you like me to bring you back to Hannah and Sophie? You've probably got a dozen messages from them on your phone by now. I should warn you, though, my sister might be a half-pint, but she can drink most grown men under the table."

She considers the offer for a moment before shaking her head. "No, I think I'd like to go home, if that's okay. Can you drive me to my car?"

"Let me guess, it's parked at my future place of employment?"

She nods. "Should we talk about the brewery on the way over?"

"No, Princess, there'll be time for all of that. For now, there's something else you should know about being the boss."

She gives me a wry look. "Oh, really? And you would know this from personal experience?"

"That attitude will get you everywhere," I say, leading her out to the dumpy lobby area.

I hand over my coat when we reach the coatrack, and she puts it back on, rolling her eyes.

"Before you hire anyone else, come up with a plan for how you want to run the brewery," I continue. "Then we can talk about my ideas and Tom, Dick, and Harry's ideas."

"Why do you think I'm only hiring men?" she asks, wrapping the coat more tightly around her as we step out into the night.

I grin at her. "There you go, assuming poor Tom, Dick, and Harry aren't women."

She gives another surprised laugh as I hustle her into the truck.

We don't talk much on the way to her car, but when "Eye of the Tiger" plays on the radio, she makes a little cooing sound like she's a damn dove. I turn up the volume.

I park behind her brewery, across from the spacious outdoor beer garden, and check out the only car still in the lot—a red Mini Cooper I probably couldn't fold myself into.

She shifts in her seat, clearly intent on making some kind of pronouncement.

"Don't thank me again," I insist. "I've reached my daily quota."

Smiling, she pulls the hair band out of her hair, freeing the gorgeous waves of gold across her shoulders. Then she shrugs off the coat, folds it, and leans over to put it in the tight back seat.

My mouth goes dry again as she finishes by presenting the hair band to me. "Goodnight, Liam. I'm glad we'll be working together."

"Me too, Princess. You tell me when I'm getting started, and I'll pull the trigger and leave Big Catch. I've been looking forward to quitting this job for four years."

"You've only been there for four years," she says, laughing.

It's a light, tinkling sound, like a damn jingle bell. I had no clue a human being could sound that way.

Shaking off the thought, I say, "Then you can imagine how beat up I am about leaving."

"I don't know if working at Silver Star will be much better."

I arch my eyebrows. "Not with that attitude it won't. Make your plan for the brewery. I look forward to hearing about it."

She smiles one final time before she gets out of the truck and steps into the night, heading over to her tiny vehicle.

I lift the hair band to my nose and sniff like a chump. It smells like lilacs.

I slip it around my wrist, feeling like this favor Hannah asked me for is going to be a hell of a lot more than I bargained for.

CHAPTER FIVE

BRIAR

Text conversation with Hannah

Liam didn't try to seduce you, did he?

He's been warned, but I'll cut off his balls if he
so much as looks at you the wrong way.

No, he brought me to his boxing gym.

Ugh. That place smells like feet.

It does.

He thought I needed to hit something.

He was right.

Shit, I should have thought of that.

Did you deck him in the face?

I saved my aggression for the heavy bag.

It felt good, to be honest.

Want to get tanked? The party's over, but
Sophie and I are still here with the guys. Don't
you dare say you're getting up early to do
yoga.

I'm getting up early to do yoga.

Of course you are.

OK, we're meeting Dottie at the tea shop
tomorrow at FIVE P.M. Don't be late. We're
going to work everything out, you'll see.

Thank you, Hannah. THANK YOU. I love you.

I can't tell you how much this means to me.

Liam might be the only person who could help
me save the brewery.

I think he needs this too.

Good luck at work tomorrow.

Thank you.

I love you too, BTW. You're a badass bitch.
That's your new mantra. Chant "I am a badass
bitch" in the morning while you fold yourself
into a pretzel.

The next morning, after I finish my yoga session, I sit on my mat and try to do as Hannah suggested. She saved me, and in return, I intend to give her every single thing she ever requests. Even if that means chanting "I'm a badass bitch" to myself like a total weirdo.

Who knows? Maybe it'll even work. I could use a confidence boost—I'm meeting my father at his lawyer's office this morning to sign the papers that will make Silver Star mine. So there's no better time to start believing I'm a badass bitch. Or at least tough enough to sit across from him without showing any signs of emotion.

Still, I feel kind of dumb saying something like that out loud, especially since the only "person" around is Karma, my Siamese cat, who gives me a withering look whenever I do stupid things. He also enjoys leaping onto me while I'm doing bridge or wheel pose, as if I've formed a useful table shape for him to rest on.

I love him madly.

Then again, I have a history of falling for emotionally aloof men's BS. Jonah wasn't the first, but his betrayal hurt the worst, because I'd really thought all the yoga I'd done and hours of therapy I'd endured had gotten me somewhere. I'd promised myself that I would never fall for someone else's lies, the way I had with my business partner and past boyfriends.

Great-Aunt Sky once told me that I have a natural instinct for reading the energy people put out into the world, but that I ignore my better judgment because I'm too accommodating and let other people paper their version of the world over my own.

Lo and behold, she was right, because I'd dated an engaged man for months, totally oblivious.

It's mortifying to think about the promises we exchanged, which meant nothing to him and everything to me.

Jonah was supposed to help me run Silver Star Brewery. I had the creative vision, and he'd use his talents to get the brewery's beer into all the right places and keep my staff and customers satisfied. He'd claimed his people skills were superior, and let's be honest, he was obviously right. He's so good with people he convinced four women to believe they were his one and only.

I'd certainly believed in the vision he'd created.

I'd thought I *loved* him.

I've spent a lot of time over the last six months wondering why Jonah went to all the trouble of lying to us. Was it only for an ego boost, or had he been forming tidy little backup plans? Separate lives waiting for him in case he decided he wanted or needed to slip into them.

Sometimes I wish I had a backup life—an existence separate from the one I have as Briar Sterling, my parents' greatest disappointment. My mind drifts to those alternate lives whenever I try to meditate. I imagine myself as a barista in Seattle, or a musician scraping by in New York City. An artist in some tropical place where everyone walks around drinking alcohol out of pineapples. Anything but me, here.

"You're a badass bitch," I remind myself. My gaze drops to Karma, who has padded up to my thick yoga mat. He gives me a look that says, *Please, who do you think you're fooling?*

I suppose he has a point.

"Should we move to Seattle?" I ask out loud. "I know it rains a lot, but maybe that means there are perpetual rainbows."

He meows.

"I am a *badass bitch*," I make myself say one final time before getting up and rolling up the mat.

I get another doubtful look from my cat. He nudges me with his front paw—an *are you for real?* gesture if ever there was one.

"Yeah, yeah, I'm feeling sorry for myself, but I'm going to stop, because...drumroll, please...I am a badass bitch. Hannah says so, so it must be true."

He looks dubious, but I really felt like a badass bitch last night. It was satisfying to beat that bag with my fists at the boxing gym. My knuckles are still sore this morning, but sore in a good way. Sore from being used.

My mother would have an aneurysm if she knew I'd been to a boxing gym. She'd definitely insist I bathe in sanitizer after putting on those dirty, scuffed gloves. Then again, my mother has never known best. Practicing at the gym made me feel the kind of bone-deep enjoyment I get from spending time with my friends, from doing yoga, and from planning my upgrades for the brewery.

Could I join a gym like that?

I mean, surely it's not just for men...

My next thought, I'm ashamed to admit, is to wonder what my parents and their friends would think if they found out I'd joined a boxing gym with a bunch of burly, sweaty men.

Liam wouldn't ask a question like that.

He also wouldn't daydream about being someone else.

He's such a big man and sticks out in any crowd, but he's comfortable in his own skin. No doubt. No fear. No second-guessing himself.

What would it be like to live like that?

I'm guessing Liam would never let anyone else put up the wallpaper in his internal room. His reality is his, and his alone.

I want that for myself. I yearn for it.

My mind flashes back to last night. To him saying, *Princess, if this is what you think good behavior is, you need someone to show you a good time.*

His words sent a tremor through me, but it wasn't because *he* said them. He was right. I've been living on the razor's edge for months, waiting for my father to finally give me the brewery or snatch it away like a child's toy. Other than my hangouts with Sophie and Hannah, I haven't let myself have much fun.

My favorite escape used to be making jewelry. Twisting the wire to hug the stones used to fill me with the satisfaction of making a small addition to the world's beauty. But that joy seeped away when my jewelry became tied to failure. Aside from a set of crystal pendants I made for Sophie, Hannah, and me, I haven't created any jewelry in over a year. People had loved my jewelry. I probably could have figured out a way to continue the business, despite what Theresa had done, but I'd lost the spark and didn't know how to bring it back. No beauty can be made without at least a speck of joy.

I give Karma some more love, then stow my yoga mat and get ready to go to the lawyer's office. Dealing with my hair takes the most time, as it has to be brushed in sections.

I've let it grow too long again. I know I should trim it, but cutting my hair will never be a simple act for me. Not after what happened to me in high school.

"I *am* a badass bitch," I murmur to myself as I brush it.

Maybe if I say it often enough I'll believe it.

Or maybe, a voice in my head suggests, *you can find a way to prove it to yourself.*

THE RECEPTIONIST LEADS me into the conference room at John Joy's, the law firm my father has used for the past thirty years since he and John Joy, otherwise known as "Uncle John," are golf buddies. My father has already arrived and is sitting at the table in the unremarkable black-and-white conference room —windowless, to make it more depressing. His hands rest on his belly as he grins at his lawyer, seated beside him. John is wearing a slick suit, his thinning hair combed forward to create the illusion that he's unstylish rather than balding.

My father's grin stretches wider when he sees me, and he taps on his phone. Seconds later, "Santa Claus is Coming to Town" flows out from the speaker, tinny and aggravating.

I dig my nails into my palms.

My father made his no-phone ruling at Silver Star after reading an article that indicated cell phone use made work-forces at least twenty-five percent less effective. But he's never cared about following his own rules. Other people have to fall in line; he's the one who *draws* the line.

I press my bruised knuckles with the pad of my finger, reminding myself of what it had felt like to hit that bag last night. Keeping my expression stoic, I say, "Very funny, Dad."

He chuckles as he stops the song—*thank God*—and I take a seat opposite him and his lawyer, as if we're on opposing sides of a custody battle. It feels like it.

"Let's get this settled," I say as the receptionist leaves us and closes the door behind her.

My dad nods to Uncle John, who gives me the sympathetic smile of an unskilled actor. "You'll get the building and all the supplies, of course," he says, nodding. "You and your father have already agreed on all of that, and he's also giving you an operating budget that will last you through the end of the year."

My mouth falls open. My gaze bounces between them before settling on my father. "The end of the year? That's less than three weeks away."

There's a hard glint in his eyes that tells me he won't be moveable, but I still have to try.

"I thought...you said you'd be giving me all of the brewery's resources. Shouldn't that include its bank account?"

My father shakes his head. "I'd be doing you a disservice if I made it too easy. *I* wasn't given any of the advantages you've had. I made a man of myself. I want you to do the same."

Another reminder that he wanted a son—a carbon copy of himself.

I take a deep breath, hold it, and then slowly release it. "All of the staff quit. It'll take at least until the end of the year to replace them. The new hires will have to turn in their notices. We won't be able to open until New Year's Eve, at the earliest."

"Then I suggest you have one helluva New Year's party," he says with a grin.

"I've found a brewer, but—"

"You did?" my father asks. He leans forward in anticipation, as if Briar Boot Camp finally became worthy of his attention in its last sorry episodes. "Who?"

"I can't say yet. He hasn't resigned from his current job."

"Someone interesting?"

I think of Liam watching me punch that bag. Liam with a hair tie on his wrist and a history of anger management classes. Liam, who makes the best beer I've ever tasted.

"Yes. Someone *very* interesting."

"You'll bring him to our next family dinner," he says, making it clear it's not a request.

"But the next one is practically on Christmas."

I hope that'll pacify him.

We usually have dinner every Friday evening, except it's not happening this week because my mother is getting a chemical peel. That's not the official reason, but it's the real reason.

The Friday after that is December 22, two days before Christmas Eve. What are the chances Liam will even be in town? I know for sure that Hannah will be traveling for the holiday. For all I know, Liam might be going to New York City with her. With any luck, he is, because I do *not* want him attending any family dinners at Sterling Manor.

Yes, my parents *named* their house. There's a sign out front and everything. They also serve dinners that require multiple sets of silverware. Something tells me Liam would laugh his ass off if asked to identify a salad fork.

No, he'll never respect me if he comes to one of those tedious family dinners. I'll always be the little rich girl with the silver last name, the silver brewery, and a proverbial silver spoon in her mouth. Briar Sterling, sitting beneath the wooden recipe for success that will probably fall down and crush her someday.

My father clicks the annoying Christmas song back on, laughing to himself as he bobs his shoulders to the beat.

"I'll ask him," I say tightly.

"There's one more stipulation," Uncle John says.

My father grins as he shuts the song off again. "You'll like this one. Your old friend Melly's back in town. She's one of those influencers. You know, with 'social media'"—he makes air quotes with his fingers—"and she's doing some freelance writing on the side for *The Asheville Gazette*. She's agreed to write an article about the changing of the guard at Silver Star as a favor to us. Isn't that sweet?"

I feel my hands start to tremble, but I straighten my back. "Yes, but there's no need. I'd rather she didn't."

His merry expression takes a hit. "You and Melly went to boarding school together for twelve years. You lived in the same dormitory."

No need to remind me. I'll *never* forget her.

My parents don't know what she did to me, but something tells me my father would have asked me anyway—as a test of my mettle.

"It's part of the deal. Take it or leave it, honey," my father says. "This is the offer. My *final* offer. If you walk away now, I'll sell the brewery."

It's obvious he views himself as a game show host offering a couple of exciting last-minute twists to entertain the audience.

The next time I'm at his house, I have devious plans for his Wi-Fi router. He's so technically unsavvy, it might take him weeks to fix it.

"Well?" Uncle John asks.

I clench my teeth and nod. "I'll sign."

I loop the letters across the page, feeling every bit like I'm selling my soul.

I GO STRAIGHT from the lawyer's office to the bar across the street.

Unfortunately, it's closed. They're *all* closed, because it's not even noon on a Monday. So I walk a few blocks farther and head into Sunshine Diner, which has an enthusiastic name but is a bit disappointing inside—plastic cushioned booths that probably squeak if you sit on them, a red jukebox with worn buttons, and a droopy Christmas tree with sad plastic ornaments. I seat myself at one of the small off-white tables, and when a server comes by, I refuse the food menu and order a double whiskey.

"Are you sure?" the middle-aged server says, wrinkling her nose as she adjusts her frilly half apron. "It's not very good."

"It's good enough for me."

I'm already feeling sorry for myself. Why not give myself another reason for self-pity?

"Suit yourself," she says with a shake of her head, then steps away from my booth.

I press the bruised area on my knuckles, thinking about how it felt to sink my fists into that heavy bag last night. Then I pull out my phone and text Hannah, letting her know what happened and also that I might not be able to make it to Tea of Fortune this evening. If I go, I know they'll make my problem theirs.

I want to be the one who comes up with a plan for keeping the brewery open. I need to be. I'll accept help from my friends, but only after I do the legwork. Being a nepo baby twice over is bad enough—I won't accept another unearned favor. Not unless I have something of my own to offer.

Before I put my phone away, I send one last text:

> I'm going to figure out a game plan, and then I'll get in touch.

"I *am* a badass bitch," I mumble under my breath.

My phone buzzes, but I don't check the screen.

Instead, I pull out the BIG IDEAS notebook I've been carrying around since listening to a podcast about the habits of highly successful people.

One of the habits they recommended was to write down all of your "big ideas." So far, the only idea I've jotted down is to offer special dinners in the barrel room. I want to decorate it with soft lighting, flowers, and a plush rug to create a unique romantic experience.

Liam would obviously scoff at the idea, but this is exactly the kind of thing that will bring in more money. Besides, he doesn't care what other people think, and he said I shouldn't either.

"I *am* a badass bitch," I repeat, my pulse quickening as I open the notebook and flip to the first empty page.

The server returns with my double whiskey, plus an egg and cheese on a biscuit.

"I didn't order this," I say, baffled.

"It's to make up for the bad whiskey," she insists, her expression making it clear she's not going to budge. "I've got kids your age. I won't let you drink without eating, doll."

To my horror, I feel heat burning my eyes.

"Thank you," I say, glancing at her name tag. "Thank you, Sharon."

She shocks me by squeezing my shoulder.

"I'll tell you what I wish someone had told me twenty years ago." Her blue gaze is fierce. "He's not worth it. The ones who make you drink never are. A beautiful girl like you could have any man you want. You don't need to settle for someone who's gonna jerk you around and play games."

She walks away before I can tell her it's not about a man.

Except...it *is* about a man, and he *has* been playing games. Ever since I was born, it feels like.

I've always lost, but I'm not going to lose this time.

I want this brewery.

I want to prove myself.

I take a sip of the whiskey, cringe, then take another, my mind churning. My father said we'd have to put on an impressive event to keep the brewery open. He played it off as a joke, but it's factual. If I want to keep Silver Star open, I'll have to put on one hell of a New Year's Eve party.

But it has to feel like a big deal. He said Melly would write about the changing of the guard, and that's exactly what this needs to be: out with the old, and in with the new.

The quickest beers to make are pale ales and wheat beers...

I've done enough research over the past year to know it would take about two weeks for Liam to make a beer like that.

On New Year's Day, we could have our first new beer.

If Liam's willing to start immediately.

If he's even willing to take the job, given the new curveballs my father just threw.

CHAPTER SIX

LIAM

On Monday afternoon, my sister tugs me back into the storeroom at Big Catch, where she changed the course of my life last night. It's her first day of work, she's obviously hungover from the staff party last night, and someone has already puked in the women's restroom. Still, something tells me Hannah's not nearly as worried about her own problems as she is about Briar's.

That's my sister for you. She'll do anything for the people she cares about.

The good news is that Hannah doesn't really need to focus on her job in order to do it. She worked the evening shift for years, so she has this daytime floor manager gig in the bag.

But while the job's a cinch for her, it's got to be boring. Hannah's like me: we live for trouble. But her new boyfriend has a seven-year-old kid, a kid she loves, and she'd rather be around for him than have a more interesting job.

"Couldn't you just go outside with me for a cigarette break instead of bringing me in here?" I say, rolling my eyes at her as she switches on the single bulb in the cramped room.

"Neither of us smokes."

"I've been thinking of taking it up to get more breaks."

"Very funny," she says, because we both know she'd figure out a way to kick my ass if I started smoking again. "Have you heard from Briar?"

I stop myself from snapping the hair band on my wrist. It still smells like her.

Not that I've been sniffing my wrist constantly like a weirdo. I just noticed, is all. I don't usually walk around smelling like flowers.

"No," I say gruffly. "I thought you told me you didn't want me messaging your friends."

She growls at me.

I lift my hand as if tapping out of a fight. "Look, I told her I'd take the job, and I will. But we're not suddenly friends who text each other. She'll let me know when she's ready for me to start working, and we'll go from there."

She glances around at the shelves anchored to the walls and stacked with supplies, as if she thinks there might be someone else in this tiny-ass room with us. When she reaches the obvious conclusion that we're alone, she says in an undertone, "She texted me an hour or two ago. Her father's only giving her a budget to last until the end of the year."

I whistle, and she shoves me for making noise, then bites her lip.

"Look, in light of this new information, I'm not going to make you take the job, Liam. It's a risk. I can find her a different brewer."

Laughter rips out of me. "Oh, so now you're trying to give away the job you 'made' me take? How were you going to *make* me take it, anyway?"

"I know you're ticklish," she says pointedly. "What if I

tickled you in public, right before a boxing match? Wouldn't that be embarrassing?"

"Nice try." I smirk. "It would be helpful, if anything. The other guy would underestimate me, and then he'd be the one feeling embarrassed after the ticklish asshole smashed his face in."

But my smile fades as I consider the latest development in the Silver Star drama. Odds are, Briar's cooked. A few weeks of budget, no staff. That's a lot to turn around, and over the holidays too. She'd be lucky to make it halfway through January.

I'll be damned if that doesn't make me curious to see what Princess Briar pulls out of the think tank between her ears. Because I saw her hit that bag last night. That woman might be green, but she's tougher than she seems.

Challenges light me up, and I got a feeling she's the same way.

"You don't have to do it," Hannah says again, although I can tell she still wants me to. She's feeling guilty is all. She'll feel guiltier if I'm unemployed in a month.

Would I give her shit about it? Would I ever. But only because it's the Moroney way. I've never loved anyone as much as I love my sister, our dad, and our little brother, Connor. Never will. That's what happens when you get thrown into the deep end and have to save each other.

Our mother walked out when Hannah was little and Connor was a baby. Something like that happens, you either get close with the people left to you, or you leave everyone behind forever. We chose each other, thank Christ.

"I'm not going to let you down," I insist. "If the brewery kicks it, I'll get another gig. We won't be able to work together anymore, which sucks—"

She huffs in protest.

"But I won't mind having a new challenge," I continue. "It's felt stale around here for a while now."

She plants a hand on her hip. "Stale? How *dare* you. Eugene just started a couple of months ago. How could it feel stale with me and Eugene as the main floor managers? This place is hopping."

In the distance, I hear someone calling *Code V*, which means there's more puke. I lift my eyebrows at her.

"Oh, come on. As if there won't be puke there too."

"I'm giving you what you want, Hannah, but what about you? Don't you think the GM is going to get a little suspicious when I go to work for your best friend?"

She laughs. "You think Frodo knows who my best friend is? He barely knows which end of the bottle the beer comes out of."

She has a point. We call the general manager Frodo because he spends the majority of the day anywhere but the brewery—*Look yonder, Frodo left on another quest*—and also because he loves to talk about the Super Bowl ring he bought off eBay. It's a fake, but he's a dick, so I'm content to let him make a fool of himself.

"Okay, but stop doing suspicious shit, just in case."

"Like pulling you into storerooms in the middle of the day for private meetings?" she asks, clearly amused.

"That makes the list, sure."

"Why'd you take Briar to the boxing gym?" she asks, her forehead creasing.

"I could tell she needed it," I say, feeling the hair on the back of my neck prickle, as if sensing an electrical storm. "And we needed somewhere private to talk. I don't want to be seen at Silver Star until everything is settled."

She gives me a frosty-ass look. "You're not going to hit on her."

"We talked about this already, didn't we?"

"Just make the promise again for my neuroses."

"I'm not going to hit on her," I agree. I snap the elastic around my wrist without really intending to.

I'm *not* going to hit on Briar, obviously, but I wish Hannah would shut up about it. She's as contrary as I am, so she should know she's only planting ideas in my brain.

"Okay, great," she says, patting me on the arm. Then her eyes brighten. "Hey, Travis told me Eugene's son is going to practice with the band tomorrow."

This makes me smile, because Cormac is an oddity I enjoy. "Yeah, he's a bit strange."

"You get the son, and I get the father."

"You're a bit strange too," I say, shaking my head. God, it feels good to be on good terms with Hannah again. It was a dark time indeed when she was pissed at me.

"Come on...you know what I mean." She waves a hand and nearly knocks over a broom propped against the wall. "Eugene's my platonic soulmate, and setting him up with Mrs. Applebaum has basically been my life's work."

"Yep." I reach for the door to leave, then pause and turn back. "You know I'm not staying in your boyfriend's band, right? It was just a temporary thing. A favor to Travis for not being a dick."

I also wanted to keep an eye on him in the beginning so I could make sure he was good enough for my sister, but I don't need to tell her that. Odds are she knows.

"Yeah, I figured," she says, sounding kind of sad about it. I'm probably supposed to ask her why—women love to be asked why they're upset—but if she's not gonna call it out, I'm not poking.

"Mick's probably going to join, though. He said he'd come to Cormac's audition with me tomorrow."

She wrinkles her nose.

"Oh, come on. Mick's a good guy."

"If you say so. But you can never let him know that Travis accidentally glitter-bombed him."

"How can you *accidentally* glitter-bomb someone?"

"The artillery was meant for me," she says with gravitas.

"So Mick robbed you of your weird sex game?"

She shoves my arm. "Gross. And yes. I wanted that glitter."

"I can guarantee you Mick didn't."

The code for puke gets called out again, more urgently this time.

I grin at her. "They're playing your song, Red."

She rolls her eyes but grabs my hand. "Come to Tea of Fortune this afternoon. Five o'clock. We're going to figure out the rest of the staffing for Silver Star."

"You think you'll manage it in one afternoon?" I say with a whistle. Frodo sometimes keeps job listings up for weeks with no bites.

"In one afternoon," she repeats firmly. "Because if she's going to pull this off, she needs to reopen next week."

🍺

MY PHONE BUZZES HALF an hour later, while I'm sitting in Frodo's office being talked at. I'm curious enough to pull it out immediately, even though my boss is passing on some directives from on high (i.e., the suits at the corporation that owns us). Couldn't be less interested in what he has to say, and soon I won't have to pretend to care.

"Liam?" he asks, stiffening in his chair. I ignore him and open my messaging app.

I have two texts from the same number.

Can you mete mee? I'm at the dinr on Pack
Square. Theo silver one. I have a plan.

This is Briar. Hannah gave me yor numbr.

Interesting. She's either drunk or dyslexic. Given the news she got this morning, I'm going with drunk, but I'll have to sober her up quick if she's supposed to make big decisions this afternoon.

"Liam, this is *outrageous*," Frodo says.

I glance up from my phone but don't pocket it. He's glaring at me from behind his desk, his eyebrows furrowing so hard they've formed one quivering, furry line.

"Yeah, I'm gonna have to take off," I tell him before it occurs to me that I should probably offer an excuse. "I've got this beer idea. I bet the suits will like it."

"But..." His lips open and close repeatedly without any words coming out, until he lands on, "But we're in the middle of a conversation about what BevCorp wants. I'm *telling you* what they want."

"You were the only one who was talking, really. Why don't you let the assistant brewer know what's up, and he and I will discuss it? Or you could record yourself talking, and I'll totally watch the whole thing later."

"No." He pushes out his lips unhappily. "No, we'll discuss it now."

"It'll have to wait," I say, getting up. "Inspiration strikes. I wouldn't be doing my job if I pushed it away."

He gets to his feet. "You may be talented, but I can find another—"

"Are you going to fire me?" I ask, more interested than disgruntled. Honestly, it would be pretty convenient if he did. I wouldn't have to give notice, and I'd probably get a couple of weeks' salary.

His face turns red, and he twists that not-a-Super-Bowl ring around on his finger three times.

I gesture to it on impulse. "You know that's fake, right? You got hosed. The font's all wrong. Devil's in the details, man. Next time you should insist on getting proof before shelling out."

His eyes widen, and he clutches a hand to his chest.

Shit. I didn't just give the guy a heart attack, did I?

I might not be Frodo's number one fan, but I start mentally reviewing everything I know about emergency medical care (not much, but we do have a yearly staff seminar arranged by Hannah), when he pokes a stubby finger at me.

"You...you..."

I lift my eyebrows. "Me?"

"You're fired. Leave. Get out of my sight."

"Don't you have to check in with your superiors before you trigger the nuclear option?" I ask, knowing he does—and that pointing it out will piss him off.

"No." His face is an even darker shade of pink now. "I have complete autonomy. Go."

I shrug, feeling like some lucky star must be hovering overhead. This is fantastic news all around, because my decision to join Silver Star is much less likely to be blamed on Hannah.

"Well, all right, Merry Christmas to you." I pause, deciding I need to act at least slightly upset for my sister's sake. "This is obviously incredibly difficult for me. Will you let me be the one who breaks the news to Hannah?"

His face softens slightly at the mention of Hannah. Everyone loves my sister, quite rightly (though he might feel less fond of her if he found out she's the one who came up with the Frodo nickname while drunk off her ass at a staff party). He nods once in agreement.

I take off, whistling to myself. It feels like I'm getting away with something, which I suppose I am.

There's no sign of Hannah on the floor, and I don't seek her out. I really don't want to get her into trouble, so it would be better to fill her in later, when we can talk privately.

In the meantime, I've got a business meeting to get to with my new boss.

CHAPTER SEVEN

LIAM

I spot her as soon as I walk into the diner. Of course I fucking do. She has golden hair down to her ass and the face of an angel. I could pick her out of a lineup of ten thousand people with only one eye open.

I don't have a thing for her—she's just objectively beautiful.

A warm chuckle draws my gaze away from her. An older woman with white-streaked brown hair and an ugly pink apron is standing practically in front of me, waving her hand to get my attention.

"Get in line, son," she says. "We've had young men mooning over that girl all day. She hasn't spoken to any of them yet."

I clear my throat unnecessarily and shove my hands into my coat pockets. "But she asked me to meet her here"—my gaze dips to her name tag—"Sharon."

Her expression turns icy. I'd know. I have a history of pissing off women without trying.

"It's you, then," she says with displeasure.

"Does my reputation precede me?"

"Go along," she responds frostily, shooing me. "But if you hurt that young woman any more than you already have, I'll give you a good wallop. The kind your mother should have given you."

I can't help but laugh. "You know, I'm flattered you think I could score with Princess over there, but it's not that kind of a meeting. If you can find my mother, though, feel free to tell her off for both of us."

I head on back, aware of Sharon's eyes staring at me from behind. It's surprisingly disconcerting.

"Briar?" I say as I near the table, because she's writing feverishly in the notebook set out in front of her. A nearly empty glass of whiskey sits beside it, and she smells like she drank the whole bar.

Getting her sober might be more of a challenge than getting fired was.

Briar glances up, her big eyes full of excitement. "Liam! You came!"

I smile without meaning to. It's not every day a man scores a greeting like that from a woman like her. Particularly not when he's a six-foot-five bearded man with a broken nose. Plenty of people aren't too happy to see me coming. It's rare I get a one-person parade.

"Yeah," I say, pulling out the chair across from her. It's small, and I know before I sit down it's going to be uncomfortable.

I lower into it, biting back a sigh as it digs into me.

Yep, damn near excruciating. I stretch my legs out to ease the discomfort, and my knee brushes against Briar's.

"I heard your news," I say.

She drops the pen, and her shoulders slump.

Sharon approaches our table eagerly. It's a few minutes past two, and despite its expensive downtown location, this place isn't exactly buzzing with activity. I'm guessing it's got a month or two, tops, before it gives up the ghost and is replaced by a business selling liquified wheatgrass or patchouli incense and tarot cards purchased off Amazon.

Sharon pauses a half step from our table. I'm tempted to offer her a seat for the show, but she might actually take me up on it.

"Anything else, love?" she asks Briar.

"Oh, I'll have some more of that awful whiskey," Briar says. "It's not as bad after the first couple of glasses." She waves an unsteady hand at me. "And a glass for my guest."

I shake my head at the server. "We'll both have black coffee. She needs to sober up. We'll take the bill too."

"You don't have to talk about me like I'm not here," Briar says, picking the pen back up and waving it at me. "I'm right in front of your face."

Sharon hurries off, probably realizing the hot drunk girl is more intoxicated than she thought. No one wants a Code V.

"You are." I wrap my hand around hers and slide the pen out of her grip, provoking an enraged gasp. "I don't want to lose an eye," I add.

Briar angles her head to study me, some of her hair tumbling over her shoulders. "You'd look like a pirate if you had an eyepatch. Maybe it would look good. Do you think it would look good, Sharon?" She snaps her fingers. "You'd be like that Redbeard guy. Or is it Bluebeard? Maybe Sharon knows." She glances over her shoulder, looking for her.

"She went to get the coffee," I say, smiling. "You're acting shit-faced."

She clenches her jaw, and I figure I'm about to get blasted. Maybe she'll pull a page out of Frodo's playbook and tell me I'm a shitty employee—obviously—but instead she lowers her gaze to her glass. "I might have had more than I intended. It was a difficult morning."

I nod. "You had some bad news, but you don't have to let it

break you. You remember what it felt like when you punched the heavy bag last night, don't you?"

Her big eyes seem to grow even bigger. "*Yes.* I've been thinking about it all day." She places her hand over mine, nearly bowling me over with her unexpected touch. Her fingers are soft but warm against my skin, rubbing gently across my flesh.

She's drunk. She's just drunk, and as my father told me when he first taught me how to brew, drunk people are either touchy-feely or punchy-fighty.

Briar Sterling is a touchy-feely drunk.

"This challenge isn't going to own you," I say, prying my hand away. "You're going to take it on. You're going to punch it like that heavy bag."

Briar grins at me, practically blinding me with her white teeth.

"I'd like that." She picks up the notebook and waves it, then drops it unceremoniously, nearly knocking over the mostly empty glass of bad whiskey. "Oopsie-daisy."

I give her an incredulous look before turning to search for Sharon. Thank Christ, she bursts out of the back with a carafe of coffee and beelines for our table. Within seconds, she's got both of our mugs full. The coffee smells like what you'd find at a 7-Eleven at three a.m., but at least it's caffeinated.

"Okay," Sharon says. "Two decafs."

"Decaf?" I blurt in disbelief and, yes, horror. "What's the point of decaf?"

Sharon's gaze is full of the same disapproval I used to get from my high school principal. "She asked for it earlier."

I fix a quizzical stare on Briar.

"Too much caffeine disrupts the body's natural balance," she says primly. "I like to be in touch with my inner self."

"Something tells me drinking your weight in whiskey does

the same thing." Turning to Sharon, I say, "Yeah, we're gonna need some real coffee."

She sniffs and gathers the mugs she just filled. "Fine. But I'll have you know I *have* been feeding her."

Briar sighs. "Everyone talks about me. No one talks *to* me. I'm not a child or some plastic doll like Felicity, you know. I'm a full-grown woman."

"No one could mistake that," I say, then instantly regret it. It's too much like flirting, and there are two very solid reasons I shouldn't flirt with her, on top of the fact that she's wasted. Reason one, she's my new boss. Reason two, Hannah will cut my balls off—with a butter knife for maximum agony.

"I'm thirty-one," Briar says, holding out one finger.

"I would have guessed thirty-five," I lie.

She and Sharon both scowl at me, so I lift my hands. "Joking. You barely look legal to drink, let alone run a brewery. I'll bet you still get IDed to buy drinks."

For some reason, this deepens Briar's scowl. "They ID everybody."

"Sure they do, Princess."

Sharon walks away, clucking her tongue and murmuring something about men. Moments later, she's back with the real-deal coffee.

Briar doesn't even seem to notice the coffee set in front of her. She's playing with a long lock of her hair, and it takes me a few seconds to tear my gaze away from her.

"What am I going to find in that notebook?" I ask, forcing my eyes to focus on her nose. "Drunken bullshit, or do you have an actual plan for the brewery?"

"I told you I have a plan," she says, sounding disgruntled.

"Is that plan drunken bullshit?" I ask, picking up the book and starting to thumb through it.

"No!" She glowers at me, which looks cuter than she probably wants it to.

I start reading. The last couple of pages *are* drunken bullshit.

Silver beer?

Ooh, star-shaped glasses!

Dottie. Herbs. YES.

Sophie, decoration.

Hannah. I LOVE Hannah. Have I told Hannah how much I love her?

Suppressing a smile, I flip to the beginning.

New Year's party: Drink us dry.

Midnight: Reveal of first new beer.

January: Weekly parties to launch new beers

I look up at her sharply. She was twisting a few straw wrappers together in an intricate design but now drops them.

"You want a new beer by New Year's?" I ask. "That's less than three weeks away."

And the feeling in my gut...

It's excitement. I haven't been challenged for years. What she's asking for...it would be nearly impossible to do it well, and that's exactly what makes me want to pull it off.

"I know," Briar says. "Hannah probably told you, but my father only gave me enough money to last through the end of the year. So we need..." She waves a hand around. "What's that thing people say?" A finger snap follows. "Butts in seats. And soon. I'm hoping I can hire enough staff to reopen the tasting room next week."

"So Hannah said."

"We can take longer to hire the bottling people. Sales reps. That kind of thing. But we need to serve Bubba's beer until it's gone. On New Year's, I was thinking we could lower the price on a few of the old beers as midnight gets closer—you know, start at five dollars a pint, then four, five, three, two, one."

I smile at her drunken slipup, especially because despite having downed a ton of whiskey, she's come up with a bold idea. An *interesting* idea.

"And we'll reveal your first new beer on New Year's Eve at midnight." She tries to snap her fingers again but fumbles it. "A free midnight toast."

"Even if it sucks, they'll love it if they're already tanked," I say with a smirk, a bit carried away by her vision.

I can see this working. It'll be a big show built around my beer. A beer I'll only have a few weeks to make.

Can I do it?

Damn straight I can.

"Yeah, I thought maybe that would help," she says, prompting me to laugh.

"It'll have to be a pale ale or maybe a wheat beer."

"I know. I was thinking we could do something similar to the Easy Drinking Ale you made this summer. Hannah gave me a bottle. Maybe with a couple of variations to make it more exciting..."

It's obvious she knows her beer. She hasn't been sitting around doing her nails, waiting for her daddy to hand her the keys.

"And then, I was thinking..." She splays her hands dramatically in the air, nearly knocking over a water glass. "Weekly reveal parties for the new beers. Obviously the dark beers will have to come out later. It'll be...the publicity...it'll be great. People will want to see what we're doing. How do you feel about herbs?"

I laugh at her non sequitur. "Herbs in our organic beer, you mean?"

She taps my arm with her hand.

"Was that supposed to be a punch?" I ask, laughing harder.

She responds with a headshake, a few strands of her hair whipping around and catching me in the arm. "A nudge for a noodge. I was thinking herbs and fruit. I want something different. Something special." She smiles again, her whole face lighting up. "I want those reveals to blow their minds."

"I think we can come up with something." I have about a hundred ideas for flavor combinations that BevCorp would never let me mass-produce. Ideas that have been weighing down my brain. Recipes I wrote years ago and have made only for myself and my friends. Here's my chance. "I've got a few different beers I'd like you to try. As soon as possible. Which makes it pretty inconvenient that you're wasted."

"I am *not* wasted," she insists, frowning at me. "Would a wasted person be able to do this?"

She stands up, her posture perfect, and presses the bottom of her little booted foot to her inner thigh. My eyes track every movement, even as I stand up, preparing to catch her when she inevitably falls.

"And what, exactly, are you doing?" I ask.

"Tree pose," she says with a frown, probably because she looks like a tree caught in a windstorm. "See, I can definitely do it. I practice every day."

A second later, she topples.

"Timber," I murmur as I catch her. For just a second, she's pressed against me, warm and smelling of bad whiskey, and then she pulls away with a pouty look on her face.

"It's the floor in here. Don't tell Sharon, but it's not level."

It's cute that she thinks Sharon gives half a shit about this place just because she works here. It makes me think that Briar could run the kind of business people *do* care about. Which is definitely what I should be thinking about, not the way my sister's friend felt pressed up against me.

But my mind has never been very good at obeying anyone, myself included, and that's exactly what I'm thinking about.

Then again, it's been a long time since I've touched a woman—months and months. It was Margaret, Hannah's *other* friend.

I shake off the memory as Briar resumes her seat and plants her elbows on the table, cradling her head in her hands.

"I might be a little tipsy," she finally concedes as I sit across from her.

I lean back in my chair, watching her, feeling an unwelcome awareness. "Hannah's making arrangements, you know. She says you should be at the tea shop at five, ready to make some decisions on staffing."

Her eyes widen in alarm, and she lifts the coffee and takes a big sip. She sets it back down and stares at the mug as if it betrayed her. "It didn't work."

I laugh. "It'll take more than a single sip. It'll take time. We'll walk in the cold too. That'll help. We can head over to Silver Star so I can check out the equipment."

"But you need to start working on the new beer." She sounds a little panicked now, as if she's beginning to realize her plan is impossible or sitting squarely on impossible's doorstep.

"I do," I agree. "And the first step is making sure we have the equipment and supplies I need. Your organic-only rule is going to make that harder."

She idly taps her lips with her fingers but then sits up straighter, not even wobbling much anymore. "It's staying organic."

"Whatever the boss wants, the boss gets," I say. If my gaze follows her fingers as they tap her lips again, at least she's too tipsy to notice. "But we'll need to work quickly. If everything's in order, I'd like to get that beer fermenting today."

"Today?"

"Today. Yesterday would have been preferable. Last week would have been even better."

"I have plenty of barley and hops, but I don't have a time machine."

I grin at her. "More's the pity. As for the other brews...we can do a taste test of some of my small batches. Maybe tomorrow afternoon." Then I remember the whole Cormac-slash-Mick audition and swear under my breath. It's further proof I've got no business trying to be in a real band. "Make that Wednesday. We'll see what else we can get started."

"Oh no, Liam," she gasps, her eyes going wide. "I forgot about your job. You need to quit. Do you think they'll make you put in a two-week notice?"

She starts pulling on the straw-wrapper creation, which resembles a Chinese finger trap.

"It's your lucky day," I say. "I've already got that taken care of. I got fired this morning."

She gapes at me, then glances around, making her recon attempt so obvious she would have gotten us iced if we were spies.

"What did you do?" she whispers.

"I hit on my boss."

She leans forward a little. "You *did*?"

"Yeah," I say. "He told me we could only be together if I wasn't working for him anymore, so I said to hell with it. Fire me so we can be together."

"*Really?*"

"No," I say with a snort. "If I were gay, he's the last man I'd go for. I walked out on him in the middle of a meeting so I could come here."

She surprises me by reaching for my hand again, squeezing it, her eyes on mine. "You're like Hannah. You use humor as a coping mechanism."

"Did you learn that term in therapy?" I don't move my hand, because I honestly don't feel like it.

"Yes, but I didn't like my therapist, and I don't think she liked me either. Have you ever thought about that? How therapists must only pretend to like some of their patients?"

"Can't say I've given it any thought, no."

"I guess you wouldn't care if your therapist didn't like you," she says dreamily, her fingers moving softly over mine as if I'm an animal she's petting. "Because you don't care what anyone thinks."

"Wouldn't go to a therapist," I say. "Why talk when you can punch something instead?"

She gives me a slow smile that grows to encompass her whole face. "You think you're such a tough guy, *tough guy*."

"You still sound drunk, you know."

"I know," she agrees, her hand not budging from mine. "I want to go to that gym again. I really liked it when you helped me punch that bag."

I should tell her no.

I should tell her it's a bad idea for us to spend any time together outside of professional situations, but I saw what punching that bag did for her. Even though she's drunk, it's still doing something for her now. She worked up the confidence to fill that book with notes. That's something. It's more than what she had last night.

I'll figure out another way to keep my distance.

"All right. We'll go again sometime," I say noncommittally, finally pulling my hand away.

"Did you really lose your job?"

One corner of my mouth lifts up, as if it's decided to cut ties with the other. "Yeah, Princess, I really did. I lost it for you, if you want to know the truth. I want to do this with you. You have me convinced."

"But I haven't even told you about the percentages yet!" she says, looking worried.

"Percentages?"

"I'm going to meet your old salary," she says. "Our benefits plan sucks almost as much as the whiskey in this place—sorry, Sharon." Sharon's nowhere near us. "But I *can* offer you a percentage of the business. Ten percent."

"Ten percent," I repeat in disbelief.

This woman is nothing if not surprising.

"And, look, I totally realize it might be ten percent of nothing," she says quickly, as if she thinks I'm objecting to the concept. "My dad says you should never accept an offer like that, and he'd know. He has that foolproof recipe for success, remember? It's engraved in maple, so it can't be changed."

"That's stupid. Recipes can always be improved."

She grins at me, and I'm soaking in her smile as Sharon comes around with our bill.

"What do you say?" Briar asks, leaning forward. A lock of her long golden hair tumbles onto my arm, and it's soft as silk. Smells like the hair band on my wrist too.

Speaking of...

I pluck the elastic on my wrist like it's a guitar string, hesitating even though I've already decided. I decided the second Hannah asked for a favor.

"Honey, don't keep us in suspense," Sharon says to me, her hand on her hip. She doesn't have the slightest idea what we're talking about, but it's obvious she's been swept up in Briar's tide.

Truth is, I feel swept away too. For the first time in a long while, I have no idea what next week is going to look like. Or next year. The future is a blank canvas.

Maybe it'll end up looking like a drunk person decided they're Picasso and attacked it with a brush. Or maybe it'll end up looking rosy.

Either way, I'm more than ready to risk it all.

Even if I'm a lot more attracted to Briar Sterling than I'm willing to admit to anyone. Myself included.

"Like I said," I tell Briar with a grin. "I got fired this morning. I'm all yours."

Sharon looks a little put out by this big reveal. Like maybe she's thinking Briar deserves better than an unemployed pirate look-alike.

But Briar squeals and jumps unsteadily to her feet before running around the table and hugging me again.

Dammit, I wish she'd stop doing that.

CHAPTER EIGHT

BRIAR

Great-Aunt Sky always says that positive thinking can create ripples in the real world.

So maybe I can think myself sober.

You're sober, I tell myself silently as Liam and I walk toward Silver Star, his arm hovering just behind mine as if he's ready to catch my potential fall again. *Sober. So-ber.*

My yoga teachers would have been ashamed of me for falling out of tree pose, which is one of the easiest balance poses. So easy a toddler could probably do it.

I can still feel Liam murmuring *timber* in my ear. He must have been smiling too—that smug, manly, *I know better than you do* Liam smile. Why, I'll bet he's doing it right now...

I turn abruptly to face him, nearly slipping on a slick patch of sidewalk.

"Yes?" he says dryly, and there it is. That horrible, beautiful smile.

"I *knew* you'd be smiling at me like that," I say, only realizing after the words come out that I must sound like a psychopath.

"Would you prefer it if I frowned?" He tugs me out of the

way so a couple of people with sour-lemon expressions can pass us.

"I don't think so. You're a bit scary when you frown."

"I take that as a compliment," he says, then wheels me around so I'm facing the right direction. I feel like a doll again, being set onto a path.

"Of course you do," I mutter sulkily.

Somehow his arm ends up woven through mine, and since I'm still unsteady on my feet, I don't complain.

You're not drunk. You're just slightly tipsy. It'll pass. Everything passes. Think about a river flowing along. The water—

I stumble over a shriveled slice of pizza lying in the middle of the sidewalk.

"At least it wasn't dogshit," Liam reflects as we continue walking. "That happened to me on a date when I was a teenager. I was looking into her eyes, the way Hannah said I was supposed to, and I stepped into dogshit in the middle of the sidewalk and slid and fell right onto my ass. She fell with me. *Into* the dogshit."

I laugh in surprise. "Why are you telling me this?"

He shrugs, but I think I already know the answer. He's trying to make me feel better about drinking myself silly on bad whiskey.

Warmth fills me, and I feel stronger. Though not more sober, if I'm being perfectly honest. I think I must have had three or four glasses of whiskey.

We walk in silence for another couple of minutes, passing a sad-looking Santa Claus, to whom I give a dollar, and a busker playing Christmas music. Then Liam surprises me by asking, "Do you like your father?"

"Excuse me?" I ask, shifting my head to look at him.

"Eyes forward, boss. Remember what happened to me on that date all those years ago. We learn from our mistakes."

"Do we?" I ask with a bitter laugh.

You'd think I would have learned my lesson after Melly took my doll. But then Theresa and Jonah came along, proving I hadn't.

"We do," Liam says firmly, pausing on the sidewalk and meeting my gaze. "You've learned from them whether you realize it or not."

"I don't know if I agree with that," I mumble, hugging myself against a sudden chill. "But to answer your question about my father...I don't think he's the kind of person people like."

He gives me a knowing smile that makes me angry for reasons I couldn't begin to guess at.

"I can tell what you're thinking, and that's not what I meant," I say, exasperated. "He's...impressive." I wave a hand. "He's got that recipe."

He steers me to the edge of the sidewalk, close to the building storefront, so a group of people can pass us. I lean against the cool stone, and he leans right next to me, his big body blocking the wind.

"The recipe that never changes?" he says from several inches above my head. I wonder if I'd hear an echo if I leaned in and pressed my ear to his chest.

Looking up into his brown eyes, I say, "It's a pretty good recipe. He's made a lot of money using it."

"Money's not the only thing that matters."

"It is to him." I hesitate, remembering my father's dinner invitation. "He wants to meet you."

He smiles. "You're already telling your parents about me?"

Startled, I nearly lose my balance, but I realize he's just giving me a hard time. A Moroney family specialty, it seems. I guess it's kind of nice that he feels he can adopt the same friendly, teasing dynamic that Hannah and I share.

"Yes. He wants you to come to dinner next Friday, but I'm going to make up some kind of excuse."

"Oh no," he says easily. "I'm definitely coming. I've got to see that recipe for myself."

"You don't want to come," I gush.

"Why not? I hate cooking, and it sounds like I'm going to be pretty busy making beer. I'll need a break."

I remember that I have no idea what he's doing for the holidays. What if he planned on taking a long vacation?

"Oh, no," I say. "Are you celebrating Christmas?"

He gives me an incredulous look, hesitates, then says, "No."

"Oh," I say, feeling guilty now. "You should. Of course you should. What do you usually do?"

"It's my favorite day to get drunk. So I'll definitely be free for your family dinner."

"You probably don't want to meet my parents. My mother's not the kind of person people like either."

"That's an interesting way of saying *you* don't like them," he remarks.

I cross my arms over my chest, suddenly cold down to my bones. "I didn't say that. I *wouldn't* say that. They're my parents."

"You didn't ask them to be," he points out. "They're the ones who decided to have a kid."

"I never thought of it that way." I shiver, either from the thought or the chill breeze sneaking into my coat. "But I still don't want you to come."

"Which only makes me want to come more." He nods in the direction of Silver Star, which is only a couple of blocks away now. "Let's keep going. It's cold out here."

I doubt he's cold, although it surprises me that he'd care that I might be.

Neither of us says much for the rest of the walk, but Liam

catches my elbow a few times to keep me from slipping or bumping into someone. The places he's touched are covered by my sweater and jacket, but the skin there practically buzzes with awareness.

When we reach Silver Star, a strange feeling tears through my chest. It's a mixture of pride—*it's mine*—and fear—because *oh no, it's mine*—and the shameful memory of what happened here last night.

Liam gives my arm a gentle squeeze, startling me. My gaze meets his, and he smiles. "I'm not going to tell you it's going to be okay. This situation will probably go tits up soon enough."

"Thanks for the pep talk," I mutter, all at once feeling sad and mostly sober.

"But you're really going balls to the wall, Briar. I respect that."

There he goes again, surprising me. I peer up into his eyes, a much deeper amber than the whiskey I spent my morning drinking, and I'm hit with a bolt of awareness of him as a man.

Not that I was totally oblivious to him before. I've always known he's big and strong, and that his features suit him. His crooked nose is balanced by those big, brown eyes, and his short beard brings attention to his perfectly sculpted jawline. His strong throat. And then there's his hair, too red to be brown, too brown to be fully red.

No! a voice in my head shrieks. *No men for a year!*

And not this man, ever. Even if he weren't already completely off limits because he's both my employee and my best friend's brother, there's no way I'm blowing up my life, again, for a man who isn't interested in a relationship.

Like Liam said, we have to learn from our mistakes, or at least try.

Amusement is dancing in his eyes again, almost as if he can hear the thoughts I would never give voice to.

"Thank you," I say, trying to sound indifferent. "Now, come inside and see what you own ten percent of."

His smile fills his eyes. "Which ten percent is mine? The bathroom? The basement? Details matter."

"Would you like to bring out a tape measure?"

"Oh, there's definitely no need for that, Princess," he says with an easy grin that sends a shock wave through me.

I poke an accusatory finger into his chest. "Hannah warned me about your wily ways."

He shrugs, a smile still playing on his lips. "Probably for the best."

We're quiet for a couple of minutes before he says, "You're being more than generous, you know. Even if my share ends up being ten percent of nothing. I'd rather own ten percent of nothing than spend another year working at Big Catch."

I squeak out another thank you, feeling self-conscious, and lead him toward the entrance of Silver Star—the door with the glass window I painted a sunburst on—just as Hannah comes bursting from around the opposite corner.

"*There* you are," she says.

Liam and I exchange a glance.

"Which one of us are you talking to?" We say it at practically the same time. I'm tempted to laugh, but I feel metaphysically dizzy from everything that's happened in the last twenty-four hours, not to mention the fact that Hannah's here at the brewery.

"We've been drinking in the bar next door, waiting for you to show up."

"Is it five already?" I ask, glancing at my fitness watch, which informs me with a frowny face that I'm behind on my fitness goals. I flick it in annoyance.

"Who cares what time it is," Hannah hisses, glaring at her brother. "You didn't tell me you were going to taunt Frodo into firing you. Do you know how hard it is to act sad without any warning?"

"You work for a hobbit?" I ask in confusion.

Liam looks like he's holding back a laugh.

"It's not funny," Hannah says, shoving his arm. "But good thinking, obviously."

"What are you doing here?" He gives her a pointed look. "You should still be working."

"I pretended to be emotionally distraught about my pain-in-the-ass brother, and Frodo gave me the rest of the afternoon off," she says with a lift of her chin. "So what gives? Neither of you were answering your phones."

"I asked Liam to meet me at the diner to discuss some..." I search for the correct word, my brain blipping—"percentages."

"She was shit-faced," Liam says as he leans against the brick wall of the brewery. He looks effortlessly cool.

I frown at him, annoyed without really having any reason to be.

"Still is, a little," he continues as Hannah pulls me into a sideways hug. "But it's nothing some coffee and freezing weather won't eventually cure."

I'm about to correct him when I start hiccuping, so I settle for saying, "Mildly tipsy. I need some water."

Liam and Hannah exchange a knowing look, and then Hannah waves to someone behind me.

I turn to see a small knot of people approaching us—sweet Dottie from the tea shop, Sophie, and Sophie's cousin Otis, who's wearing a beanie cap shoved so low it almost covers his eyes and carrying a wilted bouquet of flowers.

"What's this?" I ask, bewildered.

"Your welcoming party, dear," Dottie says with a smile, engulfing me in a hug that smells like cinnamon. I close my eyes for a second as I burrow into her, soaking in her calming spirit.

Hannah would roll her eyes, and Liam would definitely laugh, but I *feel* it. Her energy is just like Great-Aunt Sky's. Soft and soothing, like warm water lapping at your feet in summer. "I heard the good news, of course. I couldn't be happier."

"*Good news?*" I repeat as I pull back.

"The best," she insists as she pulls off her knitted cap, revealing freshly dyed lilac hair. Dottie must be in her eighties, but she's living her best life. She owns a tea shop, lives with the man she refers to as "the second love of my life," and only works when she feels like it. Most of her time is spent with her family and her even bigger family of friends, including the club of senior citizens she refers to as the Wise Elders Group. It includes both Eugene and Sophie's great-aunt. "I felt moved to do a tarot reading for you last night, and when I pulled the Ten of Cups card, I *knew* you'd finally be getting your castle."

"Doesn't a person need to be present for you to read their tarot?" I ask, my brain sluggish.

"Oh, I don't let things like that stop me."

Hannah grins at her, shaking her head. "You let nothing stop you, and that's why we all love you."

"Takes one to know one, my dear," Dottie says with a smile as Sophie swoops in and wraps me into a hug.

"It's all going to be okay," she whispers into my ear.

When I release her, Otis steps forward and shoves the flowers at me. They look a bit shriveled, but I smile at him. He's a sweet kid.

"I left them in the car all morning," he says in a rush of words, "but Sophie told me they were still pretty."

Sophie grimaces beside him.

"I just wanted to say that I'd be so honored to help you, Briar," he continues. "I'll do anything you ask. *Anything*. I can work in the tasting room or whatever. Clean the place. You name it, I'm your guy."

Sophie's grimace turns into a frown.

"That's really sweet, Otis," I say, clutching the flowers to my chest. "But Sophie probably needs you."

They've already soft-launched their new crafting business, The Crafty Monster, with pop-ups around the city, but they plan on opening a brick-and-mortar location within the year.

"Oh, it's fine," Sophie says quickly. "We can work our pop-up schedule around it. He really wants to help."

So why was she frowning?

I'm still too impaired to figure it out, so I just smile at him. "Thank you. I'm probably going to take you up on that."

He beams back at me. "You don't even need to pay me if the budget is a problem. Doing you a favor is all the payment I need."

"You'll definitely be paid," I insist. "Everyone who works for me will be paid." Even if I have to sell off every gift my parents ever gave me. eBay was invented for a reason, wasn't it?

"Let him work for free," Hannah says breezily with a wave of her hand. "We'll see how much he likes it after a single shift of people spilling beer on him and telling him long, pointless stories." She slides her attention to him. "To be clear, Otis, it will be me doing both of those things. To prove you should never price your worth at zero. There, that's a lesson for the ages."

He lifts his hands up. "Someone else can wait on you. Not it."

Liam laughs under his breath, Hannah calls them both rude, and I fish out my keys.

As I unlock the front door, I suck in a deep, frosty breath that burns my lungs. This is going to be a defining moment—the first time I step into Silver Star as the owner. Maybe it won't last long, me being in charge, but I want to enjoy it while it's still mine.

Steeling myself, I push the door open and walk in. It looks just the way it did last night—empty, with pretty, high-gloss picnic tables, a couple of booths, and a tinsel Christmas tree wedged into the corner. The shiny walnut-wood bar is lined with twinkle lights, which I'd insisted on, and a pine garland.

I expected to feel something. Fulfilled, maybe. Scared off my ass, definitely. But I wasn't expecting the smell.

It smells *rotten*.

"Oh, that's interesting," Otis says, scratching his head as he follows me inside, right on my heels like an overeager golden retriever. "Is that...it's an *earthy* odor. Some people really like earthy things. Is that because it's an organic brewery?"

Liam, who files inside last, exchanges a glance with Hannah.

"Yeah," Liam says. "Someone must have stuck a fish in your radiator on their way out."

"Why would they do that?" I sputter...and then remember the way everyone looked at me last night, their eyes mocking and full of disgust.

A bitter taste fills my mouth. They really do hate me. They hate me enough that they wanted me to walk in here this afternoon and smell dead fish.

"Why do people do anything?" Liam replies. "No big deal. I'll hunt it down for you. I bet Oats here will even fry it up for us."

"Oh...er...sure," Otis says. "I've been cooking at home more. Haven't I, Soph?"

Sophie gives Liam a reproachful look and straightens her ponytail. "Stop messing with *Otis*. I know how guys are, and I'll tell you right here and now, there will be no hazing of any kind."

Liam lifts his hands, flashing her an easy grin. "My mistake." He nods to me. "Balls to the wall, Princess."

"You should work on your motivational speeches," I say, but suddenly I'm smiling.

Hannah scrunches her nose. "Yeah, so I think we're going to have this sit-down next door. "No offense, Briar, but this place is rank."

"Not to worry," Dottie says. "We'll clear that right up. I have just the thing for nullifying bad energy. My Wise Elders club already promised they'd help me with a psychic clearing later today. But in the meantime, next door would do just fine. They have that lovely brandy drink. The one with the milk and the egg whites."

My stomach lurches, and I run toward the bathroom.

"Oh, God," Hannah groans. "Not another Code V."

Someone follows me inside, and the next thing I'm aware of is a strong, capable hand pulling my long hair back into a knot. Shame curdles inside of me even before I vomit.

Because I know it's Liam who's holding my hair back.

CHAPTER NINE

BRIAR

Half an hour later, I'm sitting in the bar next door, Great Escape, at a table with Dottie, Sophie, Hannah, and Otis.

I'm mostly sober, having doused my face with freezing cold water after puking in Silver Star's bathroom. My stomach is still a little queasy, but saltines and black tea have helped. Hannah and Sophie are drinking tea in solidarity, and Dottie, thank God, decided against the hideous milk-brandy concoction and is drinking tea too. It's nothing like Dottie's tea, obviously, but at least it's strong.

Otis, the sole tea-holdout, went for a beer.

"All better?" Dottie asks me.

I nod, sighing, still mortified that Liam saw me vomit. He's still at Silver Star, looking for the fish. Once that's been dealt with, he's going to collect everything he needs from the storeroom to get going on the pale ale.

"Can we talk about staffing now?" Sophie asks. "Because Otis and I have this crafting event to get to at five."

"Want to come?" Otis asks me with a sweet smile as he tugs his hat down even lower on his forehead. "We're making papeier ma-chay pots. It's French."

"No, thanks."

"Oh…" He gives Sophie a hesitant glance as she sips her tea. "Well, I could probably sit out of this one, if you need help at the brewery. Or some company."

"That's it." Hannah smacks the table so hard all of our cups jump a millimeter. "I'm signing this kid up for Tinder. Right now. Immediately. No is no longer an option."

Otis rolls his eyes at her. "Seriously, Hannah? I'm already on Tinder. Everyone I know is."

"Really?" Sophie remarks with interest. "I've never seen you bring a girl home, but you *do* have an awful lot of condoms. When do you do it? Do you wait until your grandmother is at one of her club meetings?"

"And if everyone you know is on it," Hannah adds, "have you ever had one of those awkward moments, where you, like, know the girl who works at the comic bookstore is kinky, and she knows you like food play?"

He swears under his breath. "Could we please not talk about this right now?"

"Oh, don't stop on my account," Dottie titters as she stirs her tea. "There's no shame in searching for love. Or having fun while doing it. Of course, they didn't have Tinder when I was your age. Back then, you met through friends or at community hall dances and hoped for the best. But after my partner Beau died, my friends did encourage me to start dating again. One of them even created one of those accounts for me."

"They did?" Hannah asks, her eyes full of fascination. "Tell me everything. No detail is too small."

Dottie laughs, tapping her spoon against the side of the teacup before setting it down. "Nothing came of it. I wasn't ready to so much as think of dating again, until Bear convinced me otherwise."

"How'd he do that?" I ask, swept up by the story.

Although I fully intend to stick to my no-dating plan, possibly forever, part of me still yearns to find someone to share my life with. I've seen what it's done for Sophie and Hannah.

I find joy in life—in my friends, in the peace from doing yoga in the early morning with Karma padding around me, and in watching the sun rise and set over the mountains with a mug of tea. But I don't feel the kind of joy I know my friends do.

"Oh, the dear man. He made me a tea blend that spoke his intentions as clearly as any handwritten note. There was chamomile for relaxation, ginger for courage, and rose hips for love. I drank down every drop, even though it didn't taste very good. And he declared himself in front of all of our friends. It was *beautiful*. I hadn't intended to fall in love again, but his love lifted me over every barrier. How could a woman help falling for a man like that?"

"Wow, that must have taken a lot of effort," Otis says. "Would you have gone for him if he'd just, like, asked you to hang?"

"*Otis*," Sophie chastises, her eyes full of disappointment. "You wouldn't."

Hannah slaps the table again. "And that, my friends, is why he never has any girls over."

"Hanging what, dear boy?" Dottie asks brightly.

"Not hanging pictures, I'll tell you that much," Hannah says with a snort.

Otis tugs off his hat. "Look, not that it's any of your business, but I go to their places. That's what girls like to do to make sure you're not a serial killer."

Hannah shakes her head as she sips her tea. "What's to stop you from serial-killing them in *their* places?"

"I don't know." He runs his hands through his hair. "Maybe

they have mace or brass knuckles or something. Some of them have dogs."

"Is that how you got bitten by a dog last month?" Sophie muses. "I thought it happened on one of your odd jobs."

"Look. I'm not really comfortable with this conversation," he says desperately, darting a pleading glance at me as he lifts his beer for a sip.

"Leave him alone," I say, feeling protective of Otis, and maybe a bit of myself, since Hannah's constantly trying to get me to sign up for online dating. "He has every right to keep his dating life to himself. It's none of our business who he 'hangs' with."

I reach out and squeeze his hand, and he instantly drops his drink into his lap.

"Oh my God. Are you okay?" I ask.

He makes a strangled sound before setting his mostly empty glass down and reaching for the mass of napkins in the middle of the table. He presses the handful to his lap. "I'm fine, but I have to use the restroom."

He walks off with the wad of napkins pressed to his crotch, just as our server, a pretty blonde girl around his age, comes by to ask if we have everything we need.

"Napkins," Hannah says, gesturing toward Otis, who still hasn't reached his destination. "Our friend there will need more of them. He had a little...accident."

"He spilled a drink on himself," I rush to explain, but the server walks away tittering. I turn toward Hannah, lowering my voice. "I'm glad I wasn't one of your brothers."

"Teasing is my love language," Hannah says. "And Liam definitely gave as good as he got."

I smile slightly, because I'm quite sure he did.

Then I remember that Liam just held my hair back while I

threw up. He'd done it so calmly, like it was no big deal. But it *was* a big deal.

Groaning, I bury my head in my hands. "Liam's going to think I'm so unprofessional."

Hannah pulls one of my hands away. "You've got nothing to worry about. He literally orchestrated his own firing today. And he nicknamed our boss Frodo." Her brow furrows. "Actually, you know what? I might have done that. Anyway, you're good."

"But he held back my hair while I puked."

"It *was* gallant of him, wasn't it?" Dottie says. She pauses to sip some tea. "But a man should do such things. It's what any true gentleman would do."

Hannah laughs, but Sophie keeps casting concerned glances toward the restroom.

"Are you worried about Otis?" I ask. "I think he was just embarrassed, talking about his dating life with a bunch of older women."

"It's this crush he has on you." She nudges her teacup with the tips of her fingers. "I keep thinking he's going to get over it, but it only seems to get worse. Maybe it'll be like a trial by fire if he helps out at the brewery for a while."

"Crush? What are you talking about?" I protest. "I'm practically old enough to be his mother. He's...like...a little brother. *Your* little brother."

"But he's not yours," Sophie says. "Have you honestly not noticed the way he's always mooning over you?"

Hannah, who just took a sip of tea, nearly sprays it out. "No," she chokes out, "because it's the same way literally every man acts around her."

"No, it's not," I insist.

I shoot Sophie a questioning look, but she shrugs, her smile sheepish. "She's kind of right. You're...*you*. Don't you ever look in the mirror?"

A sigh spills out of me. "Look, I know I'm pretty. It's the only thing my parents have ever liked about me. But plenty of people are pretty. You're all pretty, too. We don't have to make a big deal out of it."

"I don't think you realize *how* pretty you are," Sophie says seriously.

"I really don't want to talk about this. I just look the way I look. But if you're worried about Otis—"

"There's no need to worry," Dottie says, her voice ringing with certainty. "Otis will find his great love when the time is right, and so will Briar. I'm quite certain they're both on the correct paths."

I sit up straighter. "Correct paths for what?"

"For you," she says with a sweet smile.

"Is this a good time to say you should be on Tinder too, Briar?" Hannah says. "If we make a profile for you, we can creep on Otis."

"How is that going to help him get over his crush on her?" Sophie scoffs. "You'll give him false hope, all because you're bored."

"Bite your tongue," Hannah says. "How could I possibly be bored? I have a neurotic man to keep me busy, the best kid in the universe, a brewery to run, and another to help relaunch. My life is *on point*. I just want Briar's life to be on point too."

Dottie pats my hand. "It would be...amusing to see what this Tinder is all about."

"Oh, not you too, Dottie," I moan.

"But this isn't the time," she continues, thank God. "We were going to talk about staffing."

"Yes, *please*."

Dottie beams at me. "A couple of the other Wise Elders want to help. I was the floor manager at Buchanan Brewery for decades before I started my tea shop, and Ann and her dearly departed husband ran a restaurant together. Constance is leaving on vacation with her family soon, but she hates being left out of the fun, so she'll help us in the beginning. Eugene, of course, has the most brewery experience other than me, but he's bound to Big Catch and can't offer much help. But the rest of us are going to handle your tasting room and events management until you find replacements, dear. And we won't take a cent from you. We'll only be fill-ins until you have time to properly restaff."

"But I meant what I said to Otis," I say, taken aback. "Everyone's going to get paid. I can't let you work for free. I *can't*."

"We'll be getting something out of it too." Dottie pats my hand from across the table. "Of course we will. What fun and excitement we'll have, watching you young people save the brewery! We can start whenever you'd like us to. The tea shop is fully staffed, and we're all officially retired."

"Dottie," I say, tears in my eyes. "I don't want to let you down. I'd feel terrible if you put all that work in and nothing comes of it."

"The only way you'll disappoint me, my dear, is by not accepting our help."

"I can't just leave this open-ended. We'd need to set an end date. New Year's."

"The end of March," Dottie counters. "You should have plenty of time to get established by then, and my newest grand-baby is due in April."

Sophie smiles at me and lifts her cup of tea in salute. "You'll be accepting help from all of us, by the way. I'm going to help you redecorate."

"Nora wants to help too," Hannah gushes.

"Nora, who?" I ask, even though I only know of one Nora. But surely she can't be talking about *Jonah's* Nora.

After Sophie found out Jonah was cheating on her with me,

Hannah, and Nora, pretending he was exclusive with each of us, she sent out a bunch of texts. Hannah and I met up with her that very morning. Nora...didn't. She ignored Sophie's messages, but after Dottie had a heart-to-heart conversation with her, she helped us get back at Jonah.

The four of us tricked him into attending a concert where Sophie, Hannah, and I told everyone exactly what he'd done to us. He was publicly humiliated, booed, and he lost his job distributing to breweries. Now, he works for his father, and according to Travis, he's gotten twitchy and started chain-smoking.

Maybe I should feel guilty about that, but I don't.

"*The* Nora," Hannah confirms. "I can't believe I forgot to tell you last night, but she was at the party at Big Catch. She's Mrs. Applebaum's daughter. Boom. Can you believe it?"

"Mrs. Applebaum? As in the woman you set up with Eugene?" I marvel. "Nora's really her daughter?"

"Aren't the workings of the universe fascinating?" Dottie asks. "I knew Nora would reconnect with you girls at some point, but I didn't know *how*."

Hannah lifts a finger. "All the credit goes to Eugene. If he hadn't been so surprisingly interesting, I wouldn't have been able to set him up with anyone."

I smile at Hannah. She'd never admit it, but she sees the best in everyone—the seed of possibility nestled inside each person's soul.

"Anyway," Hannah says. "Nora said she wants to help you get the business going. I'll text you her number later."

"She's a dear girl," Dottie interjects. "She's had some poor luck in love, but haven't we all?"

"Maybe *she* should join Tinder," I mutter.

"You think she would?" Hannah asks excitedly. "If we

looked at Otis's profile from her account, he probably wouldn't think anything of it."

"So your plan is to hang out with her for the first time and immediately back her into signing up for Tinder so we can spy on Sophie's cousin?"

Sophie smiles at me over the rim of her teacup. "Nora might as well figure out what we're like now."

Warmth fills me, and I'm hit with the realization that while I'd thought I needed Jonah to help me with Silver Star, I was dead wrong. These are the people I need—the other women he betrayed.

And Liam, a little voice whispers in my mind.

"I had another idea," Hannah says. "Sophie and I were thinking we could get the guys' band to play at the brewery sometime after you reopen. Eugene's son is auditioning for them tomorrow afternoon, and obviously that's going to go great, so soon they'll have a bassist again. They already have an agent waiting for them to get their act together. Maybe the new-and-improved Garbage Fire's first show can be at Silver Star. People will definitely show up for that."

"What about doing it on New Year's?" I ask, then tell them about my crazy plan for the party.

Hannah grins like the Cheshire cat. "Hell yeah. I'm glad I got Liam to take the job. He must be beside himself. This is exactly the sort of shit he lives for."

"But I'd need him to work that night," I say. "He wouldn't be able to play with the band."

I start playing with a lock of my hair, nervous energy zipping through me. Because it just dawned on me that my whole plan centers around Liam. Is it a mistake to let my plan hinge on one person?

But his beer is good. It's *great.* And he seems so unshakable. Like a mighty oak.

"You don't need to worry about Liam," Hannah says with a shrug. "He already admitted that he was only filling in with Garbage Fire to help out. Honestly, he did it because he wanted to get the goods on Travis. He thinks he's *so* smart, but I have eyes in the back of my head."

"The third eye is on the front of the head, actually," Dottie says. "But an eye in the back of the head *would* be quite convenient."

Behind her, a big guy emerges from the bathroom, shaking his head. Otis follows him out with a splotchy wet spot over the crotch of his pants. "I wasn't doing anything wrong, man," he calls out. "It's just water."

The big guy picks up his pace, rushing away, and Otis makes his way back to the table and plops into his chair with a sigh. "I was trying to use the hand dryer. That's what it's there for, right? Drying things."

"But it looked like you were humping it?" Hannah guesses.

"Well...yeah," he admits. "I guess I kind of was, but only to get closer to the heat source. Jesus, I need a drink."

He lifts his glass, peering sadly at the quarter of an inch of beer in it before shrugging and downing it. "What did I miss?"

"We had a super-long discussion of your sex life," Hannah jokes, earning the playful shove he gives her.

"Actually," she amends, "we were mostly talking about staffing at the brewery." Glancing back at me, she says, "You'll probably need more servers and stockroom workers, but my brother can rope in a couple of people from his gym to do any heavy lifting." She grins at Otis. "And maybe Otis can use his amazing Tinder skills to recruit employees, since he's obviously super talented at convincing unsuspecting women to invite him home."

"Hey." He snaps his fingers to point at her. "That idea's not half bad."

Tears fill my eyes. "I love you guys," I say. "I...I can't tell you how much this means to me. How much all of you mean to me. Last night, it felt like the world was ending, and right now...it feels like I'm on the cusp of something wonderful."

"You are, my dear," Dottie tells me, capturing my hand in a warm clasp. "You are. And it will be *remarkable*. Now, let's go help Liam make the champagne of beer."

CHAPTER TEN

LIAM

Code V and I are well acquainted. Drawback of the trade. When you make beer, you get used to watching people get wasted off it.

So I wasn't fazed by seeing Briar puke. Or by pulling a half-rotted fish that looked like a zombie Billy the Bass out of the radiator. If anything, it was an upswing from sitting in front of my old boss while he twirled that fake ring around on his manicured finger—thinking he was looking impressive when he was really just advertising how much of a fool he'd been.

But when Briar walks back into Silver Star an hour later with my sister and Dottie, it's obvious *she* cares about being sabotaged. She's quiet and subdued. I don't even get a laugh when I tell them about the zombie bass. Maybe it's partly the smell—I propped the door open, but the brewery still smells like a Southern boil three days after the fact.

"Did they sabotage anything else?" she asks quietly, and something about the way she asks it, arms crossed defensively over her chest, makes me think of last night at the boxing gym.

Someone hurt her.

They fucked her over good, and she carries it with her.

The thought makes me curl my own hand into a fist.

But my sister's watching me, and I know better than to ask questions that will lead to more questions. So I just shake my head. "No sign of that, but I should do testing on all of the in-progress beers tomorrow to make sure everything's as it should be. There's empty space for the pale ale, and the amber looks like it's ready to be racked. That'll make space for another new beer, but right now, most of the equipment is in use."

"Maybe we need more equipment," Briar says, tugging on a lock of her hair. That simple act is enough for me to remember what it felt like in my fist, the heavy, silky mass of it woven through my fingers.

Nope. Not thinking about that. Especially not while my sister's studying me, her hand propped on her hip.

"What we need is for the beer to ferment faster," I say. "But the monks couldn't figure out how to hurry that shit up, and we're not much further along all these years later."

"Well...at least there's space for the New Year's beer and another new one," Briar says quietly.

"I found everything I need in the storeroom."

"So let's do it." She nods to her friends. "Sophie and Otis have to leave soon, but the rest of us will help."

"Hannah can't have anything to do with it," I insist.

My sister pins me with a scathing look. She's preparing a devastating rebuttal, I have no doubt. I glance out the window, temporarily distracted by a cluster of folks in heavy down coats heading down the sidewalk.

"You can't," I repeat, shifting my attention back to Hannah. "Frodo may have the brains of an inbred sheep, but even he's gonna figure out something's up if you're seen over here."

"Oh please, no one's paying attention," she scoffs.

As if her words invited them, the group that was strolling

down the sidewalk literally walks into the unlocked brewery, ignoring the oversized CLOSED sign in the front window.

One of the new arrivals, a man with bushy brown hair and a pair of clunky, oversized glasses, says, "Ooh, is that fish and chips I smell? Is anyone else hungry?"

Otis grips his stomach and rushes toward the bathroom, but I'm not about to hold *his* hair.

"We're closed," I say.

"The door was wide open," Glasses Guy says, like he can argue us into serving him and his friends. One of his pals grabs his arm to pull him back, but he doesn't budge.

He might have a shitty sense of smell, but he's brave. I'll grant him that.

"Sorry, but the brewery's not actually open. And we don't serve food, unfortunately," Briar adds. "Just beer and packaged snacks."

"You might want to get on that," a woman says.

"Yeah, I'll be sure to add it to my list," Briar says dryly. "Buchanan Brewery is a short walk from here."

Then, no shit, she gives them directions. *Detailed* directions.

Hannah leaves the brewery while they're tied up, either because she realized I have a point or because it's excruciating to listen. Glasses Guy doesn't seem to know his right from his left, and Briar's had to repeat herself at least five times.

A few minutes later, she follows them out, waving, and I trail out after her. I can't help but ask, "Why didn't you just kick them to the curb? They were rude. I could have scared them off."

She looks up at me, hugging her arms across her chest as an icy wind whips her hair. "No scaring off customers. That's going on *our* recipe for success, Liam."

For a second I'm floored.

Our recipe.

Ten percent.

I smile at her. "I hope you don't intend to uphold the family tradition of engraving your recipes in wood, Princess."

"It'll be written on a piece of paper." She edges the slightest bit closer. "So it can be updated and changed. I think we should start our recipe today. Actually...I envision it as more of a list." She gives me a sidelong look, a gush of icy wind rustling her hair. *"Don't puke in front of your employees* is going to be number one, just so you know."

"Surely that belongs farther down."

I want to tuck her hair behind her ear, but my hands can't go anywhere near her. If I let them, they'll end up liking the feel of her. Yearning for it.

"Oh, no, it's definitely number one," she argues. "You're the one who told me I should learn from my mistakes."

I grin. "Do we both get to make additions to this list?"

"Yes," she says. "But you can only write in pencil. That's an important rule."

"Will I get a company-issued pencil?"

"That can be arranged," she says with a small smile.

"And where will we keep our master list?"

"I thought we could tuck it behind that photo of my father that he propped up behind the register."

"Wouldn't you prefer to take that down?" I ask, amused by her dry humor.

"No. We're giving him a front-row seat so he can watch us turn this place around."

"Well, all right," I say, extending my hand to her for a shake. Her fingers are icy as they grip mine, and for a second I'm nothing but pissed at myself for not realizing she was getting cold again. Then she gives my hand a firm shake, and a smile spreads across my face.

Here it is again—proof that this woman is tougher than she knows. Tougher than she has any right to be.

"It's going to be a pleasure doing business with you, boss," I say.

And the way she smiles at me, her whole face getting in on the action, makes me wonder if I'm launching straight into my next big mistake.

THE NEW YEAR'S beer is fermenting.

Briar helped from start to finish, even though she probably wanted to go home and sleep it off. Sophie and the kid left after an hour or so. Dottie headed out, too, only to return with a couple of other old ladies—one a Black woman with oversized rainbow glasses, and the other a pale as milk white lady with a wonky orange and red handmade scarf. Rainbow Glasses is Ann, and the lady with the ugly scarf is Constance. The three of them took out a big bundle of sage that looked like a joint and lit it, waving it around the whole brewery as it belched out scented smoke in eye-watering bursts that at least smelled better than the rotten fish.

They chanted under their breath too.

It was a bunch of hocus-pocus bullshit, if you ask me, but they all seemed very pleased with themselves, and when they finished, Dottie pronounced the energy in the place "clean."

I was informed that all three of them would be working in the front of house until Briar hires permanent staff, which isn't a half-bad idea. Those little old ladies sure love to talk, and they'll keep guests here long enough to have several rounds of Bubba's mediocre beer.

When Briar and I finally finish cleaning up, we order pizza to celebrate.

Dinner is surprisingly enjoyable, probably because I don't have to say more than a few syllables in response to the steady flow of conversation. My attention keeps bobbing in and out, my thoughts wandering to which beers I'm going to have Briar taste. I like imagining how she'll react to each of them.

While we're cleaning up after dinner, Dottie wraps Briar into a hug and whispers something to her. Seconds later, Dottie's pulling me into a damn hug too. "We'll leave you to lock up, my dears. I'm so honored to be part of your journey."

Briar and I watch them shuffle out of the door, and I can't help but laugh.

"What is it?" Briar asks, and I inhale sharply as she wraps her hand around my arm.

So she's handsy even when she's not drunk.

I like it, which is exactly why I tug my arm away and snap the band at my wrist.

Wake up, Liam.

"Neither of us has a car here, do we?" I ask.

She laughs, her nose wrinkling. I make a point of looking away.

"No trouble," I say. "If you don't want to walk, we can order an Uber."

"No," she says, "let's walk. Exercise always does me good." Her gaze turns thoughtful. "But first we need to do something. Wait right here."

"The anticipation is killing me," I say as she disappears into the back. She returns to the tasting room a few minutes later with a pencil and a sheet of printer paper.

I can't help smiling as she scrawls at the top of the page, in perfect handwriting:

Liam and Briar's Recipe for Success.

"A humble list," I tease.

"A humble beginning," she replies.

I take the pencil from her, our fingers brushing, and sit down to write.

She leans in, her soft cheek nearly pressed to mine. Despite a long day of drinking and working, she smells good, although maybe my senses have been burned by the sage smoke.

When I finish writing, I look at her and find her face only inches away. Her lips curve upward. "I can't read a single word you wrote. Your handwriting is god-awful."

"Look closer."

She leans in further, near enough that her hair brushes the side of my neck, and then starts laughing.

Sage incense attaches to everything. Never again. Ghosts aren't so bad.

She's still laughing as she meets my gaze. This close, I can see the band of lighter brown in the middle of her irises, and a tiny mole next to her eyebrow. Her lush, full lower lip is pushed out the slightest bit as she laughs. But then her laughter trails off, and in the silence between us a new feeling comes to life—an awareness that we're alone in here, faces tilted together, laughing. Planning. Trying to build this place up, brick by brick.

I've never shared a dream with anyone before. While I had been invested in the success of Mountain Morning Brewing, it had never felt even one percent mine.

Without intending to, I lean in, drawn to her and the promise of our shared dream, but then reality hits me like a punch to the solar plexus. I made a promise to Hannah—a promise I need to keep.

So I pull away and stand up abruptly, the sound of the chair screeching back assaulting our ears. "Let's go. It's getting late."

She nods without speaking.

We step into the night, Briar pausing to lock the door behind us.

"What do you think about all of this?" she asks as she steps up next to me.

I hope to hell she's not asking about what just happened inside.

I don't have an explanation for why I almost kissed her. Maybe I'm just contrary, the way Hannah has always said, because there are billions of women on this planet that I'm allowed to kiss. Briar Sterling is one of the only ones who's off limits.

It's only the energy of the day, I tell myself.

It's natural to feel swept away by it.

We start walking, strolling past couples and a few drunk people howling with laughter and smelling of beer.

"Which part were you asking for my opinion on?" I finally say. "The cultist ladies with their sage?"

She laughs softly, the sound blending with the bells a corner Santa is ringing as he collects funds. "Working here with me. Do you really think we can pull this off?"

I feel a tugging in my chest, maybe a tearing. I come to an abrupt stop.

Briar stops with me, turning toward me expectantly.

The streetlights gleam down on us, making her long golden hair appear covered with frost. Her face is tipped up to me, like a question waiting to be answered.

"This is *your* brewery, Briar. I'm just an employee. Ten percent. We can say the bathroom's mine."

"I puked in the bathroom, so now it's partly mine."

I smile but don't say anything.

She reaches into her pocket and then pulls out a key, placing it in my hand, which I don't remember stretching out.

"This is yours," she says. "Part of your ten percent. I figure you might need to come in at odd hours. To check on things, I mean."

She pulls her hand away, her fingertips leaving little streamers of sensation on my skin. Again with the fingers. A simple touch that stays.

"Yeah," I say roughly.

Briar watches me as if all the mysteries of the universe might be solved if she studies my broken nose for long enough. "Don't you want to make your mark on the brewery?" she finally asks. "Or is this just a for-now thing?"

I consider her question as she looks up at me with those beautiful brown eyes, her breath warming the night between us.

"I don't know," I finally say. Then I decide to do the smart thing and draw a firm boundary for us both. "But it's just a job for me. It's your brewery, not mine."

For a second, I see the wounded look in her eyes, but the next second it's gone. Papered over. "You're right," she says. "I guess I'm scared to do this on my own. I didn't think I was going to have to. Jonah, my ex—"

"Oh, I know all about him," I say, flexing my fist.

"Yeah, I guess you were mad at him for lying to Hannah."

"That's one way of putting it."

I'd had to content myself with only threatening to do Jonah Price bodily harm. Plenty of people wouldn't believe it, but I have learned a few important lessons from my past mistake. Learned them good.

But I have to be honest with myself. At this particular moment, I'm not thinking about how that fuckhead messed with my sister. I'm thinking that he put his hands all over this woman in front of me, all while lying to her. He took advantage of her trust and used her. Even though Briar's not mine, and I'm mostly sure I don't want her to be, I find that deeply offensive. In fact, I'd prefer it if he didn't live in the same state as her, let alone the same zip code.

"It's just...he promised he would help, and—"

"I'm going to stop you right there," I say. "Rule number three, Princess. Don't share personal information with your employees. You're the boss. It's none of my business who you've slept with and what pretty lies they told you."

She flinches, a stricken look filling her face. I meant to sound like an asshole, and I did, and I can't let myself regret it. I need to stay on my side of the line I just drew. It's the only way this is going to work.

If I let myself get too close...

Well, I can't, and not just because of Hannah.

Briar is tough, more so than she realizes, but she's soft inside. More marshmallow than person. I won't be the man who turns her hard.

She stiffens her spine and meets my gaze, her expression closed-off now. "I'll find my own way home. I assume you can do the same."

I grunt and nod, wanting to take the words back, even though I know they've already made their mark. I tell myself it's for the best and only half believe it.

"I'll tell you where to meet me tomorrow to sign your employment contract," she says coolly.

"You got it, Boss." It's not the first time I've called her that, but it doesn't have the same playful ring as before.

It's like I just traced that line separating us with a permanent marker.

I hang back and watch her walk away from me, but I fall into step behind her, trailing her the several blocks to her car to make sure she's safe.

CHAPTER ELEVEN

BRIAR

Liam made it very *clear* what he thinks of me, so I resent the way he intrudes on my thoughts the next morning while I'm pretending to meditate.

I keep seeing the smug tilt of his chin, the quirk of his mouth when he told me he didn't care to hear which men had lied to me. And I keep reliving the half second in the Silver Star tasting room when our faces were an inch apart and I was certain he was going to kiss me—or worse, that I was going to kiss him.

It would have been the biggest mistake of my life, obviously. Not only did I promise Hannah not to date him, but he's my new brewer. I'll have to see him every single day. Kissing him would be the most foolish mistake I could make. Well, almost. The ultimate disaster would be sleeping with him. Especially knowing his dating history.

I've never been the kind of woman who can sleep with a man and have it mean nothing. For me, sex has always felt like giving away a piece of myself. Sometimes only a teaspoon of my heart, sometimes heaping cups of it. Heck, I don't even have to sleep with someone. Sometimes I find myself giving pieces of my heart to near strangers—the mailman who has a limp because his son accidentally ran over his foot, the woman who runs at the same time as me every morning and belts out sad Taylor Swift lyrics.

It's a personality failing, and I've tried to cure it over the past year by retreating into myself. But it hasn't worked. Obviously. First there was Jonah, whispering all of his sweet promises and lies. Then Sophie and Hannah. Dottie.

And now Liam.

He's been sweet to me several times over the past couple of days, which only makes this new feeling worse. He's like a Sour Patch Kid of a person, only inverted. First he's sweet and then he's sour. Everyone knows you don't want to *end* on sour.

Karma bats me with his paw, which feels metaphorically resonant this morning.

I draw in a deep breath, pushing down the conflicting feelings that kept me awake last night, then slowly let the air ease out.

"Today is a new day," I tell Karma, who meows and glances at his food bowl. "I *am* a badass bitch."

He gives me a glance that seems to say, *if you say so. Now, be my food bitch.*

My phone buzzes several times from incoming texts, but I ignore it. My stomach is quicksand as I fill Karma's bowl, getting several paw swipes because I'm not fast enough. Finally, I run out of excuses to avoid the outside world and grab the phone off the floor beside my mat.

I don't know which person I'm more afraid to hear from, but I'm guessing it's not going to be great news.

There are two sets of messages. The first is from Melly:

> Congrats on the brewery!

> Your dad is SO sweet to give you a job like that.

> Can't wait to hear all about it, but I promise I'll stay away from the scissors. [Laugh emoji]

> We all did some dumb shit when we were kids, amiright?

> When do you want to meet to discuss?

My skin prickles. I feel like I did as a teenager—a frightened animal cornered by a larger beast.

Unfortunately, my father told me I needed to give her access to the brewery, so I can't say no.

I reply:

> I'm reopening next week. You can come by any day between twelve and ten.

> I'm busy next week.

> We're having a New Year's Eve party.

> How quaint! I have plans for New Year's Eve, obviously, but maybe I can pop by earlier in the evening.

I take a deep breath, hold it, let it out, then respond:

> That's generous of you.

The second set of messages is from a number I don't recognize.

> Hello, Briar. This is Nora.

> Sorry if this is out of the blue, but Hannah passed along your contact information.

I'm the brewer/half owner of The Ginger
Station, and she thought you might like to
connect since you're assuming ownership of
Silver Star.

I'd be happy to help in any way I can.

Karma ambles over, and I give him a pat-down, letting his soft fur soothe me. The cautious part of me isn't sure I should give Nora the time of day. She ignored us for months; what could she want now? But I also want to pick her brain. The Ginger Station, a brewery that makes only alcoholic and nonalcoholic ginger beers, has been wildly successful.

I fire off a quick response:

Can you meet for lunch tomorrow?

Then, thinking better of it, I add:

Actually, Hannah would murder me if we met
up without inviting her. Sophie would be
disappointed to miss you too. Can you meet all
of us?

We agree to grab lunch at Tea of Fortune the following day, and then I text Hannah, Sophie, and Dottie and fill them in on the plan.

I get to the brewery a half hour before I told Liam to meet me this morning, and the first thing I do is make an addition to the list we started yesterday and tuck it back behind the frame:

Don't share personal information with your employees.
They might get the wrong idea.

Tuesday morning passes quickly, moments bleeding together, powered along by adrenaline and enough processed sugar that my mother would get a pimple just by looking at it.

Liam comes into Uncle John's office with me in the afternoon to sign the contract but makes no effort to read through it before scrawling his messy signature, which makes my pulse pound. I study the ugly swirls on the paper for half a minute, feeling a wrenching sensation inside of me that I don't fully understand, especially since I looked over the agreement. It all seems fine and aboveboard. Even so, he should know what he's agreeing to.

We head back to the brewery in silence, but when our hands glance off each other, I could swear he brushes his thumb across the back of my hand. I steal a glance at him, but maybe I imagined the whole thing, because he's staring pointedly ahead, his gaze on the horizon.

Later that afternoon, another couple of tourists try to enter the brewery, one of them nearly breaking the locked front door in a misguided attempt to open it. Liam collapses a huge cardboard box and writes CLOSED on it in red Sharpie, adding beneath it:

Enter at your own risk.

"Do you think they'll still try to get in?" I ask.

He gives me a crooked smile. "Everyone likes a challenge."

It's the last thing he says to me all day, but then again, he keeps busy. A few of his friends from the boxing gym come in to help him keg the amber ale, and they're more talkative than he is.

I keep busy too, making arrangements. I work out a schedule with Dottie, who will be coming in with Otis later this week to train the five part-time workers he found for the tasting room.

Tinder is apparently the recruiting tool everyone should be using to hire employees, because that's how he found them all.

I give Sophie a call too, to talk through my vision for the barrel room. My plan to hold upscale chef dinners there is risky, considering my budget is less than shoestring, but I'm determined to make it happen. I've already made a few exploratory calls around town to see if anyone's interested in partnering with me, and I found a New American restaurant a few blocks away that wants in on the idea.

Sophie and I spend an hour picking out décor for the barrel room, finding cheap materials that I can order for overnight delivery, and a possible set of inexpensive but stylish furniture.

Before I go home for the night, I check the list behind my father's photo. Liam has added something to it—

Don't act like an asshole. People might get the right idea.

It makes me smile, but only for a millisecond, because he's probably just humoring me. Either way, it would be foolish to ask him about it. It's important to keep things professional from now on, something he clearly signaled to me last night. I suppose I have a lot of work to do given I nearly puked on him, then nearly kissed him, and then gushed about my silly hopes.

I don't have any right to be angry with him. I *know* that. It's only...

I felt this kinship growing between us like a wild vine. A connection, new but strong. And it's like he picked up a giant pair of pruning shears and sliced it in half.

I can practically hear my mother sighing. *Oh, Briar, you're so overdramatic. It's exhausting.*

"Oh, shut up, Mom," I murmur out loud, which only makes me feel more overdramatic.

WHEN I COME in the next morning, Liam's already there, sitting at a table in the tasting room with a notebook in front of him and the pencil I gave him. His hair is damp, suggesting he's freshly showered.

"Something's off," he says. "Might be the yeast Bubba had wasn't good. I have to repitch the beer with fresh yeast. We'll lose a day, maybe more."

I swear under my breath.

He smiles and then swipes a hand over his mouth as if to wipe it away. "Better than losing the whole batch. Let's hope it works."

It's starting to feel like this whole enterprise is built on a wish and a dream. Instead of solid construction materials, we're working with sugar spears and gumdrops, and it's all going to collapse around us.

"This is crazy," I mutter and lower into the seat across from him.

"It is," he agrees. "It's either going to blow people's minds, or it'll be fucking terrible. Either way, it'll be interesting." He spreads his legs wider, his knee brushing mine under the table. We're both wearing thick pants, but I feel his touch, spiderwebbing across my skin.

I yank back abruptly.

"Yeah, thanks," I mumble.

He rises from his chair and his chin tilts up, as if he's forming some kind of resolution. "We have to figure out what I'll be working on next. There's space for one more beer, and Bubba's brown beer is going to be ready to keg in a couple of days."

My impulse is to smile and tell him I'll let him make the call, but I don't want to revert to our friendly, casual dynamic. Not after what happened the other night. I straighten in my chair and say, "I suppose you have some ideas."

"Naturally. But you're the boss."

"I am. Did you bring in those samples for me to try?"

His mouth quirks into a crooked smile. "You got a thing for drinking in the morning?"

"We'll do it this afternoon," I say, straightening. "And we'll include a few other people."

I can ask Sophie and Hannah to join me after lunch. Maybe Nora, if everything goes well. It'll be easier for Liam and me to spend time together with other people around. Less...intimate.

He runs a hand over his stubble, and I notice his knuckles are chafed. My gaze flits to his face, and I notice a small bruise on his cheekbone.

Has he been at the gym? Did he get that while sparring with someone?

The thought pisses me off, because he said he would take me back to the gym, and now I know he never will. Maybe this is unfair, but it feels like another promise made to me by someone whose word is as solid as piecrust.

"Shouldn't be a group decision," he says, leaning back against the wall.

"I'll decide how to run *my* brewery, thank you very much."

His smile spreads wider, which pisses me off enough that I get to my feet.

"Am I dismissed?" he asks, his eyes dancing with mirth.

"Is everything a joke to you?" What I mean...what I can't say, because I couldn't handle the answer is—

Am *I* a joke to you?

He gives me a cryptic look. "Sure. It's better to laugh if you can. I'll grab the beer samples when I'm out."

I'm about to walk off, frustration and annoyance simmering in my blood, when I remember Hannah's suggestion about Garbage Fire playing at the New Year's party.

I tell Liam, and he nods once. "She already checked with Travis, and they're up for it. Cormac's officially joining as the bassist."

"Is he good?"

He tips his head. "Very. Way better than that shithead they had before."

"That's great. Yeah, that guy always seemed kind of shifty."

"Shifty, huh?" he asks, his lips curling in amusement.

He's amused by me, obviously, not with me.

Maybe he'll talk about me behind my back, just like he did with Frodo. *Oh, that Briar is totally pathetic. I made the mistake of being nice to her, and she practically threw herself at me.*

I lift my chin. "Yes, shifty. He stared a lot."

"Well, of course he stared at *you*."

My cheeks heat. "What do you mean by that?"

He gives me a wry look, like, *you can't not know what I'm talking about, Princess*. His hands are buried in his pockets, so his arms aren't flexed, but his biceps still look thick and muscular, like they're straining the limits of his shirt. My eyes keep settling on them, as if to say, *People can't stop looking at you either*. My fingers want to dance over them.

Finally, he shrugs. "You said your parents aren't the kind of people others like. But you are. And you're definitely the kind they like to look at."

The heat from my cheeks spreads through my body, and I shove down the urge to fan myself. I have no idea what to say. He's the one who wanted to keep things professional, and here he is talking about how I look.

I swallow, then say, "You won't be able to play with the band at the party. I'll need you to introduce the beer."

He leans back, getting comfortable. Really settling in against that wall. I feel my muscles twitch in annoyance.

I remind myself that I have no reason to be upset with him. He never promised to be my friend, my confidant. He only said he'd help me, and he *has*.

"Won't be a problem, boss," he drawls. "I'm not in the band anymore."

"Did you quit this time, or did you trick them into firing you too?"

He grins. "Too many loose ends. I quit after finding someone to take my spot. My friend Mick, who owns Bell's. You know...Ring Your Bell Boxing Gym."

Part of me wonders if that's what he's planning to do here. Get me going and then find someone else who'll be willing to step in. But I don't ask.

"All right. Well..."

"Am I dismissed?" he asks with a twinkle in his eye.

That twinkle makes me want to shove him. Instead, I stand taller, calling on every last etiquette lesson my mother forced me to take, and say, "*Yes*."

A FEW HOURS LATER, I'm standing outside of Tea of Fortune with Sophie and Hannah. We arranged to meet ahead of time because Hannah seemed to consider it essential for us to present a united front for Nora.

Now, though...

"Don't you think Nora will be overwhelmed if we descend on her like a bunch of vultures?" I ask, idly rubbing a lock of hair between my fingers. "She'll probably try to escape out the back door."

"Ha!" Hannah says. "Then she'll find out the hard way there is no back door."

"Isn't there?" Sophie asks with a frown as a man dressed like a clown pushes past her. I've learned not to look twice. There's a comedic bus tour, Lazoom, with daily runs through town. They plant costumed people along their route—nuns on bicycles, clowns like this one, you name it. "If there isn't, we should talk to Dottie about it. It would be a major fire code violation."

"Of course there's a back door," I say. "It's through the kitchen. But, seriously, I don't want to freak Nora out."

"Well, *I'm* going in," Hannah says, and since I don't actually want to stand out here in the cold, I follow her. Sophie too.

The second we enter the tea shop, Dottie hurries toward us from her seat at the table closest to the door. She was sitting across from a woman with short, tidy dark hair, red lipstick, and hazel eyes, dressed in a blazer over a black sweater and jeans. Nora. I've seen her a couple of times from a distance. She's also easily recognizable from all the local articles about The Ginger Station. Last night, Hannah sent a fresh batch—*research*, she called it.

Nora started The Ginger Station with her business partner, José Perez. They're each half owners; she brews the ginger beer, and he runs the business end of things. The opposite of Liam and me, I can't help but think.

She stays seated, looking uncomfortable but determined.

"She's here," Dottie says in an undertone that everyone in the continental United States probably heard.

"It's okay," Nora says in a low, amused voice. "I know I'm here. I don't think that's the kind of thing we need to keep to ourselves."

"Of course not." Dottie clasps her hands together, smiling so wide it probably hurts. She looks like a child who's just tried cotton candy for the first time. "It's just such a joyous occasion to have all of you girls here, together at last."

We settle in around the table. Dottie refuses to sit back down, saying she wants the "full experience" of the tea shop today because she'll be away for a while, so I take her seat, across from Nora. Hannah is in the chair next to mine, and Sophie is beside Nora. The chairs are all charmingly mismatched—mine has a bouquet of roses on the upholstery.

Quiet descends on the table. Hannah, of course, is the first to break it. "So, Travis saw Jonah a few weeks ago, and apparently he took up smoking."

"Good," Nora says wryly.

"I was hoping he'd get gangrene of the dick," Hannah continues, "but I'll settle for karma smacking him with lung cancer."

Nora smiles. "Mom told me you were...colorful."

"Hannah's perfect," I say tightly. Maybe because "colorful" is the sort of thing Liam would say with a knowing grin.

"I meant it in a good way," Nora says before focusing on Hannah. "I'm grateful to you." Then she glances around at the rest of us. "So. You're probably wondering what my deal is."

"Oh, we want to know everything about you," Hannah says. "Seriously, everything. I especially want to know what it was like growing up with Mrs. Applebaum as your mother. Was she strict? Or is she, like, this secret softie? I have visions of her being a secret softie like Eugene. I swear, that man has never met a shade of beige he didn't like, but his soul is definitely maroon."

Nora's smile stretches wider. "Maroon. I like that. I like him too. Mom has a good heart, but she was strict. Had to be. My dad was hardly ever around."

She runs her finger gently over the rim of her teacup before continuing. "I feel like I owe you all an explanation. It's not easy for me to discuss personal stuff, but given the circumstances..." She shrugs and gives her attention to Sophie. "I need you to know I had no idea that Jonah was engaged. None. And when you texted me saying you were his fiancée, I believed you were someone else. Someone who'd been messing with me."

"Tell me more," Hannah says, leaning forward enough that the wood table scoots a fourth of an inch closer to Nora and Sophie.

"Okay." Nora blows out a breath. "Here goes. I'm not sure if you know this, but I started The Ginger Station with my friend—"

"José," Hannah interjects.

Nora's lips part a moment before she says anything. "Did my mother happen to tell you about him? She's not his biggest fan."

"No." Hannah waves a hand. "We did a deep dive on you."

Sophie laughs and shakes her head. "That makes it sound like we hired a private investigator. We just read a few articles about the brewery."

Nora nods. "Okay. Well. José and I used to be...together." She lifts a hand. "Briefly. We tried it for a few months, decided we were better as friends, and broke up a year and a half ago."

"And you still run the brewery together?" I ask, my heart speeding up. Because surely, if I needed another message from the universe that it would be utterly insane to think about kissing Liam, this is it.

"Yes." She tucks her hair behind her ears. "But it's okay. Really. José's still my best friend. We just...get each other. There wasn't any awkwardness."

"Until he met someone else," Hannah guesses.

Nora takes a sip of tea. "That obvious, huh?"

"And she was sending you threatening texts?" I guess.

"I'd gotten a few of them before I heard from Sophie," she says. "They were sent in the middle of the night, from an unknown number. Things like *stay away*, and *I know you're a slut*. Creative, right? Jonah knew about the messages, so he knew exactly what to say after you exposed him as a cheater. Obviously I feel like an idiot now. What's worse is that I showed José the anonymous messages."

Hannah whistles.

"Yeah," Nora says with a low laugh. "You can imagine how well that went down. He didn't believe his dear, sweet girlfriend would ever do something like that. He blamed Jonah and said he didn't want Jonah coming around the brewery anymore. As if he suddenly got to decide. He was acting almost..."

"Jealous," Hannah finishes.

Nora shrugs. "Yeah. Although he's the one who's *so in love*, so maybe he was only being territorial. We had this big fight about it, since his girlfriend basically lives at The Ginger Station. Anyway. After that, I met Dottie, who confirmed Jonah was a sleazy asshole, although not in those words, and here we are. I'm sorry. I fucked up. I should have admitted it months ago, but I was embarrassed. I meant what I said. I'll do anything I can to help you. All of you." Her gaze settles on me. "Hannah told me a little about your brewery."

"Yes, it's a disaster," I say, letting the most intrusive thought in my mind escape without a fight. I tell her about the mass walkout and my plan for redemption.

She listens, nodding in the right places, and then says, "It's a good plan. If—"

She bites her lip as if to cut herself off.

"If it works," I say, my voice quavering.

"If it works," she agrees. "Which means you need a plan B in case it doesn't. Always have a plan B."

Dottie, who's been gone for a suspiciously long time, returns at this mention of a plan B. "Have you finished your tea?" she asks sweetly, even though Nora's the only one who has drunk any.

"She's going to want to read your tea leaves," Hannah warns. "But she doesn't need to. I can tell you right now what she's going to say. You're going to fall in love, and it's going to be so amazing, and your whole life is going to change forever and ever."

Dottie smiles at her with a twinkle in her light-blue eyes. "And didn't it, my dear?"

Hannah barks out a laugh. "You know what, she has a point. If I were you, I'd hand over the teacup."

Nora smiles at them both but shakes her head. "No, thanks. I'd like to keep the future a mystery. If it's all the same to you."

"It's not," Hannah says. "She's not going to give up."

"Then we're at a stalemate," Nora says. "Because I don't know how to give up either."

CHAPTER TWELVE

LIAM

Conversation with Cormac

Thank you so much, man.

I can't believe I'm going to be in the band.

Can we meet up for a drink sometime?

Wait, do you drink? Or would that be like
mixing business and pleasure?

I think you'd be hard-pressed to find a brewer
who doesn't drink.

It would be like being a chef who hates food.

I think I'd hate food if I had to cook it all day.

Yeah, we can get a drink sometime.

When would be good for you?

I'll get back to you on that.

I tuck my phone back into my pocket after sending that last text, feeling like a bit of an ass. Because I'm not sure I meant what I said.

I like Cormac. He's good people—interesting, which most folks aren't—but I don't want to encourage him to think of me as a friend. I've got too much going on, and I'm no good at connecting with people.

I sigh as I move another bag of grain in the storeroom, verifying that this label bears bad news too, which is when someone starts knocking on the front door of the brewery loud enough to wake the dead. I ignore it at first, figuring it's someone else who can only selectively read and has chosen to ignore the CLOSED sign.

I'm dealing with a serious situation.

I know Bubba, the former brewer at Silver Star, from a few homebrewer competitions around town. Guy's an idiot who doesn't know how to run a tap room, let alone a brewery, so it came as no surprise that the supply room was disorganized. After digging in deeper today, I have confirmation of a suspicion I formed that first day, when I noticed the labeling on the supplies we used for the pale ale. There's something else in this brewery Bubba screwed up good.

Briar isn't going to like it, but it's my job to pass on the bad news, like a doctor telling a patient the lump they've been worrying about really is cancer.

Shit, she's going to give me that same unimpressed look she gave me this morning after accusing me of having a sense of humor.

Hell of a thing. Women have always liked when I make them laugh, until they don't. Of course, I know what the real issue is. I said something shitty to Briar the other night, and she's still pissed about it.

Maybe she doesn't understand why I felt the need to define

the line between us. Just because I feel a tug toward her doesn't mean it goes both ways. That asshole Jonah is a pretty boy who wears fancy suits and probably gets weekly manicures. He practically pissed himself when I told him I'd kill him if he got within five feet of my sister again. I enjoyed it then, and I enjoy the memory even more now. But if *that* is what Briar likes in a man, there's no way she'd ever be interested in me.

Sure, there was a definite moment between us the first night, but she was probably still tipsy. High on her plans for this place and on what is basically high-stakes gambling. Win big or lose it all.

The knock lands again, and I wipe my hands on my jeans and make my way to the tasting room, grumbling about whoever's dumb enough to interrupt me at a moment like this.

When I reach the front door, the kid from the other day—Sophie's cousin—waves at me through the glass with a goofy grin on his face and a couple of bulging boxes in his arms. He's wearing a red knit hat.

Will he keep grinning like that if I leave him out in the cold?

I point to my makeshift CLOSED sign, and he laughs as if he thinks I'm joking. I'm not. However, Briar is already pissed at me, and I know this kid is supposed to work in the tasting room. I have no real reason to keep him out.

Sighing, I unlock the door, and the kid trips on his way in, dropping the top box. It explodes open, silk flower garlands spilling out like it's a magician's snake trick.

"What's that?" I ask darkly.

The tasting room is already decked out with holiday garlands, twinkle lights, and that tinsel tree in the corner. We don't need it to look like a preteen girl's bedroom.

"It's a surprise for Briar," he says as he tries to stuff the garlands back into the exploded box.

"Looks like an underwhelming surprise."

He gets to his feet, leaving the destroyed box behind. "She picked out all this stuff with Sophie. They both have great taste."

I grunt.

"Briar asked Sophie to help her decorate the barrel room. She has this idea to host pop-up dinner experiences in there. Didn't she mention any—"

"No," I grumble, annoyed with myself more than Briar. I've effectively shut down our channels of communication, so no wonder she didn't tell me she was moving on her idea.

"Well, she picked out this stuff, and since she's so busy, Sophie and I figured it would be nice if I could get everything set up while they're out to lunch."

"What about furniture?" I ask. "She get a table and chairs for this dinner experience, or are the rich people going to spend hundreds of dollars to eat on barrels?"

Right now, the barrel room has nothing inside but barrels of aging beer, both on racks and on the ground. No windows. Sounds like a miserable place to have dinner, but I'm curious to see where Briar is going with this. Balls to the wall, again. She's good at that.

The past couple of days, I've watched her go about her business, making phone calls, taking meetings. Muttering to herself and playing with that long, silky golden hair.

I've been snapping that hair band on my wrist plenty. Taking in its smell of flowers until it stopped smelling like anything but me. I tried not to be disappointed about that.

"The furniture's out in the car," Otis says, practically chewing on his cheek. "I was wondering if you would maybe..."

"Lead the way, Oats."

He gives me an uncertain look. "Sophie asked you not to call me that."

"What about you? Are *you* asking me not to call you that?"

I'm not just giving him a hard time because I'm an asshole. A man needs to learn how to stand up for himself, especially around bigger men. It's a lesson my dad taught me, but clearly this kid hasn't learned it yet.

He swallows, his Adam's apple bobbing in his scrawny throat, then says, "Yeah. My name's Otis."

"Well, all right, Otis." I reach for his hand and shake it. "Show me the way. We'll get everything set up for her."

"You're going to help?"

"Yeah, I guess I am."

Maybe it'll make up for the bad news I'm about to unload on her when she gets back from lunch.

"Oh, that's so great," Otis says, his face lighting up.

I grunt in response and open the door. We walk outside together, the cold hitting me in a good way. Waking me up.

"Aren't you, like, cold?" the kid asks. "Or do your muscles keep you warm? I read that somewhere, that someone with a lot of muscles doesn't get as cold. I was wondering if it was bullshit."

"Most things are bullshit."

I follow him to an illegally parked green Subaru with a taped-up bumper. A small table is attached to the roof of the car upside down, like a bug flipped onto its back, and two chairs are arranged on its underbelly. The ropes are twined around so many times it looks like someone was trying to make a mummy.

"I take it you never worked for a Christmas tree farm," I say with a sigh.

"No, why?"

"No reason. I'll be right back."

I run back inside to Silver Star's basement and return with a pair of shop shears.

"Oh, no, we can just unravel—"

I cut the rope. "I'll teach you how to tie a proper knot later.

If you want to finish this while Briar's at lunch, we have to get moving."

"Right," he says, perking up. "I can't wait to see the look on her face."

He obviously means it. This kid would probably give up his right nut for Briar Sterling. Maybe the left one too, if she asked nicely. Then again, something tells me Briar Sterling could have as many men's balls as she wants—a whole collection of them she could wear as earrings.

The thought makes me grin, but the grin fades as a voice inside my head says, *You practically offered yours up the other night.*

I clap the kid on the back—too hard, I guess, because he stumbles a step. "Let's get you that smile."

We spend the next forty minutes or so getting the barrel room set up. The table and chairs are heavy—mahogany, he says, from an estate sale—so I bring them downstairs myself, telling the kid he should get going with the flower shit.

"There are lanterns too," he says excitedly.

After I get the furniture set up in the dark, slightly dank room, I help him weave the flower garlands between the barrels. It feels counterproductive, given that we're eventually going to need to take those barrels down to use them for their intended purpose, but it does look better. Especially once we get the small copper lanterns hung, along with some twinkle lights that stream down the side of the brick wall opposite the barrels.

"She picked all this out herself?" I ask again as we get a thick purple tablecloth arranged over the table.

When I looked at this room, I only ever saw a dank space—a place that served a purpose but otherwise added nothing to the brewery.

Briar, though...she saw an opportunity.

The woman has vision.

I don't use this word lightly, but the barrel room looks fucking magical.

"Mostly," Otis says excitedly. "Sophie says she's 'got a good eye.' Briar's pretty great, right? You're so lucky you're working with her. God, you must get to spend, like, all day with her, right? That's the dream."

I give him a sidelong look. "You've got it bad for her, huh?"

He pulls off his knit cap, revealing a mass of messy dark hair. Wringing the hat between his hands, he says, "I know she's never going to go for me. Sophie tells me that all the time, but I was hoping I could at least change the way she looks at me. You know. So she doesn't think I'm, like, a little brother. I was kind of hoping you could help me with that."

"Me?" I point to my chest in bemusement. This is the first time anyone has ever asked me to play cupid. I hope to hell it will be the last.

"Hannah mentioned you go to this boxing gym." He wrings his hat in his hands. "I thought maybe if I could get swole, she'd see me as more of a man."

"You shouldn't get fit for someone else, kid. You do it for yourself." Or, in my case, because you need it. Because nothing else burns off the bad feelings.

"Then I'd like to do it for myself. Can you train me?"

"How do you know I'm any good at boxing?" I ask with a laugh.

"Look at you!" He gestures with the hat and nearly drops it. "You look like you could carry a house."

"Depends on how big it is."

"There you go." He slings the hat up again. "I couldn't even carry a henhouse."

"Sure, I'll bring you," I say, making a split-second decision. This kid's all right, but he needs confidence. Either boxing will help him, or he'll take one blow to the face and retreat to his smartphone. Might as well bring him once, introduce him to some of the guys. Maybe he'll surprise both of us. "But first you've got to help me with something. We're doing a beer tasting this afternoon to figure out what to make next. Let's set it up down here. Give Briar a real thrill."

She'll need it, because I have to tell her that the brewery isn't actually organic, and probably hasn't been since it earned its certification.

THE KID and I park ourselves at a table in the tasting room, waiting for Briar to arrive. He blathers on about some video game I've never heard about and couldn't care less about; I stew over how to solve this latest problem.

It's a pretty big blow, on top of the beer's failure to ferment quickly enough.

Another half hour passes before Briar arrives at the front door with Dottie and a dark-haired woman. Briar's hair is blowing in the wind, moving like a sinuous golden scarf.

It takes me a second to look away from her and identify her companion as Nora. Interesting. She didn't mention they were meeting, but Hannah's been all hot on the topic of Nora, so I'm not surprised.

"They're here," Otis exclaims unnecessarily as he leaps to his feet and bounds toward the door, opening it even as Briar pulls out her key.

"Otis," she says, surprised. Her gaze strays to me. "I didn't know you were coming over."

I cross my arms over my chest. "He's joining us for the tasting."

"Oh, lovely," Dottie says. "We'll have representatives from three generations. That's just as it should be."

Otis seems disgruntled at the reminder that he's a decade younger than Briar, but he accepts a hug from Dottie as all three women hurry into the tasting room, Nora shutting the cold out behind her.

"Nora, this is Otis," Briar says, gesturing to the kid. Her lips firm into a line as she flings a hand at me. "And Liam, our head brewer."

"Is that the royal we?" I ask.

Briar doesn't crack a smile, not that I'd expected differently.

Nora greets both Otis and me before telling me, "I tried your home brew at the last Brewfest. It was fantastic."

I nod, and give credit where it's due. "I like what you're doing down at The Ginger Station too. But I hear you ruined my buddy Cormac's science experiment."

She stares at me, obviously baffled.

"Cormac Peebles," I add. Lifting a hand up to his approximate height—six-two or maybe six-three—I say, "About yay high. Curly hair. Glasses. Talks like he was unpopular as a child."

Her eyes widen. "Are you kidding me? He still blames me for that?"

A laugh sneaks out of me. "Yeah, but he said you probably don't remember him from high school. He's obviously wrong."

"Oh, I remember him," she says in a pissed-off undertone.

"The universe works in such mysterious ways, doesn't it?" Dottie looks excited, like she thinks everyone's going to link hands and sing "Kumbaya." "How *remarkable*. And after all these years your parents have found new love together. I suspect you'll be seeing a lot of each other, and you'll have plenty of opportunities to put any past unpleasantness behind you. I've never met the young man, but his father tells such lovely, colorful stories about him and all of his inventions."

"It wasn't my fault," Nora snaps, clearly not ready to put

anything behind her. "Men love to blame women for the problems *they* create."

I laugh again, lifting my hands up. "Otis and I aren't touching that one with a ten-foot pole."

Briar fixes me with a piercing stare. "You and Otis are friends now, are you?"

"He's taking me boxing," Otis says, as if we're going on a date.

"Yeah, that's why he's here," I lie, wanting to keep the surprise a surprise. "But first we have something set up for y'all downstairs. We're doing the tasting in the barrel room."

Briar's brow pinches. "We should do it up here."

She thinks I'm trying to embarrass her by bringing her successful guest down to a dark, dank, shitty little room.

"Otis helped set it up," I say. "Took us a long time. Lots of glasses."

Truthfully, I had no idea how many people she was bringing, so the only thing we have set up are the beer bottles and a leaning tower of shot glasses, but I moved a couple of barrels over in case more seating was needed than the intimate duo of chairs Otis got from the estate sale.

"Fine," Briar says stiffly, still obviously as annoyed with me as Nora is with Cormac.

I let Otis lead the way, figuring the kid deserves some glory.

Dottie follows him through the door to the back, trailed by Nora, but Briar hangs back, giving me a look that nearly makes me laugh again, even though it would obviously piss her off if I did.

It's not my fault she's cute when she's mad.

When she's mad. When she's drunk. When she's boxing...

"Did you have to say that about Cormac?" she whisper-hisses.

"Sure. It's true, and I prefer for things to be out in the open."

"That's not why you did it," she accuses, her eyes fastened on mine. "You wanted to cause trouble. You love causing trouble."

I stare right back. "Maybe it's trouble that loves me."

I can almost feel the tension radiating between us, like heat shimmering over blacktop in the middle of summer. Without thinking, I reach over and smooth a mussed part of her hair.

Her lips part, and I'm sure she's going to blast into me. Remind me that I'm her employee, and I was the one who wrote those rules. She'd be right to do it.

But a voice drifts toward us through the wooden door. "Simply remarkable. Oh, Briar dear, come take a look. You must see this."

Briar's lips part further, and I let myself imagine what it would be like to say *fuck it* and kiss her. To suck that full bottom lip into my mouth and spear my hand into her soft hair.

My mouth goes dry as I watch her turn away and walk through the door without another word.

I want to go with her. I want to watch her take in the room— the manifestation of her vision. I'd love to soak in her sweet smile.

Which is exactly why I don't.

Let Otis keep her initial excitement for himself. He's done more to earn it.

Instead, I slip behind the bar and seize the photo of her father to take out our list of rules. I grab a pencil and add: *Don't touch your boss.*

CHAPTER THIRTEEN

BRIAR

I gape at the barrel room, taking in its complete transformation. The soft silk flowers. The warm lighting. The romantic purple velvet tablecloth, draped over the small antique table I spotted on the listing for the estate sale. The beers we'll be tasting are arranged on top of it, waiting for us.

Liam made it clear he didn't want to be any kind of partner in Silver Star, and yet he helped make this happen.

I'm glad he's not down here, because my breath catches in my throat, and I almost feel like...

Briar, you will not cry, for God's sake.

I may be too soft, but I won't let myself cry in front of Nora, who is clearly made of stronger stuff.

"Do you like it?" sweet Otis asks, as if anything else might be possible. I've wanted to transform this room for so long, but when I shared my idea with my father a couple of months ago, he harrumphed about time wasters and children who think money grows on trees.

It's everything I thought it could be, though, as if Liam and Otis plucked it from my dreams. Sophie, too, of course. Dear

Sophie, who always finds ways to help other people, even though she's plenty busy with her pop-up business.

My throat choked with emotion, I say, "It's perfect. Thank you."

Nora glances around the space with brisk efficiency. "I suppose you didn't set it up like this so the staff could use it as a break room?"

"I'm going to offer a dinner experience down here. Only one couple at a time. A local restaurant is partnering with me."

"Very nice," she says with a small smile.

Her approval feels like a lifeboat, carrying me along, even though I remember Liam's advice about not caring what anyone thinks. I don't think I'd like to be that way, though. I don't want to care what everyone thinks anymore, but that's not the same as not caring what *anyone* thinks.

I want the good opinion of the people I respect.

"It wasn't that hard," Otis says with a broadening grin as Dottie pats him on the back.

I can hear the squeaking of the stairs down the hall, and my heartbeat picks up before Liam fills the doorway. The entire space brims with his scent, his masculine energy, and the half smile on his face commands my focus. He's pleased with himself, but right now, at this moment, I know it's because he's pleased *me*.

"Ready for the tasting?" he asks.

"Oh, yes, please." Dottie smooths the front of her button-up sweater. "It's cold outside today, so I wouldn't mind a bit of a tipple." She takes a seat in one of the chairs. I offer the other to Nora, who lowers into it, but probably only to keep Dottie company.

I find Liam's gaze and hold it as if it's something precious. The intensity with which he stares back warms me from the inside out. "Thank you for helping."

He inclines his chin, acting as if it were nothing. "It's my job to help out around here."

"Please don't tell my business partner that," Nora says. "He might start thinking *I* should hang flower garlands."

"God forbid, but I think you could probably manage it," Liam replies with a completely straight face. "You'd just need a stepladder."

Otis snorts.

Nora rolls her eyes.

Dottie, who seems to have tuned out the teasing, picks up one of the labeled glass bottles on the table. "Oh, yes, I think I'd like to start with this one, if you wouldn't mind."

"Would you like to make an introduction?" I ask Liam as Dottie pours beer into four shot glasses. Everyone takes one except for Liam.

"That's my rosemary saison," he says. "Bottoms up."

So Liam. Short and to the point. Like it or you don't. Spit it out or swallow, he wouldn't care.

My mind abruptly goes to a very different place, and my cheeks burn as I lift the little glass for a sip. I feel Liam's eyes burrowing into me. He's waiting. But I don't let myself think he cares about my opinion.

The flavor is mild at first, but the herb hits on the back end. It's mellow but distinct.

"I love it," I gush.

He nods once, still standing by the door, as if he'd like to be as close as possible to an exit at all times.

The beer seems to sour in my mouth at the thought of him ducking out and leaving.

"You haven't tried it," I point out.

His smile is faint. "I remember what it tastes like."

"Sorry, man," Otis says, hacking, and I tear my gaze away from Liam to look at him. "Nope. Can't do it. It tastes like my grandmother's garden smells. This is an old-people beer." He darts a regretful glance at Dottie. "Sorry, Dottie."

"Why would you be sorry?" she asks, giving him her full attention.

I suspect she's teasing him, but from the panic in his eyes, he has no idea. "Because you're…I'm sorry, that's all."

"Well, I think it's *delightful*," she says. "It tastes like—"

"A garden," Otis mutters.

"*Exactly*."

Nora takes another sip of hers, then says, "It's good. Not for January, though."

"No," Liam agrees.

"It's a spring beer."

He gives her a knowing smile, as if they're sharing professional respect.

That must be why I feel my stomach tighten with something like jealousy.

"Let's keep going," I insist.

The next is an amber beer. Then a plum IPA, which Otis likes well enough to claim the bottle.

Then a fig spiced ale.

"This is it," I say, seeking out Liam's gaze again. "The next one we should make."

"You haven't tried them all," he says, but he gives me a slow, lazy smile that says more than words could: this is the beer he hoped I'd choose. If Nora's approval felt like a high five, his feels like a hug.

"When you know, you know."

"It'll take five weeks."

"We should still do it," I say with a nod, wishing it would take less time but knowing it's worth it. "We can make a faster beer for our third choice."

"Your wish is my command. You're the boss."

The tension between us feels like an unplucked guitar string, until Dottie cuts it, turning another bottle over in her hands and saying, "Oh goody. I was hoping you'd bring a lager. Can we try this one next?"

The moment has passed but not the feelings it stirred.

I like Liam more than I should, way more than I planned to.

CHAPTER FOURTEEN

BRIAR

After Nora, Dottie, and Otis leave, I expect Liam to retreat into himself again. I have calls to make, and the brewery is big enough that we don't need to be in each other's company. But he follows our guests to the door and stands beside me as they walk away. I feel him next to me, looming.

"Sit with me a minute," he says.

"That didn't sound like a question."

"Wasn't." He studies me before adding, "I'm going to pour you a drink before we talk."

Tension grips me. "So it's *that* kind of talk."

The grim line of his mouth confirms he's about to unleash bad news. "Let me get you that drink."

I grab his wrist before he can walk away. "I don't want to be that person," I explain, releasing him. "I don't need something to prop me up for bad news. I want to be able to handle it. I *can* handle it."

This time he gives me the same look he gave Nora earlier.

God, his respect feels good. I want to drink it down.

"Okay," he says, his Adam's apple bobbing in his throat. "Let's sit."

We settle across from each other at one of the tasting room tables, and as he gets settled, his leg glances against mine again. I know he didn't do it on purpose—he's a big man with long, thick legs—but it lends to the feeling of intimacy.

Outside, people keep bustling past the brewery, peering in through the window and pausing to read Liam's handwritten sign, but inside it's cozy and warm and still smells of sage. We're in a world all our own, tucked in together.

But I don't have long to savor the feeling.

He brushes a hand over his short beard. "I'm just going to come out and say it."

"I'd expect nothing less."

He smiles so briefly I could have imagined it, then gets to the point. "The brewery's not organic. Based on what I've seen in the stockroom, it hasn't been for a long while."

His words ripple over me before stabbing in. I swear and then press my face into my hands, which is as close to burying it in the sand as I can manage right now.

"Yeah, pretty much," he says.

I don't even know where to begin. Neither does he, apparently. We settle into a stark silence, during which I don't see anything except the orangish glow between my fingers. Then his chair screeches back, and his big, warm hand cups one of my shoulders.

He doesn't speak. He just keeps his hand there, his fingers rotating slightly, caressing me. His heat seeps into me, becoming my own.

"My father," I finally say. "He...do you think he knew?"

I certainly wouldn't put it past Bubba to cut corners and maybe pocket the difference between organic and regular supplies.

"I don't know. But I guess we'll have plenty to talk about at dinner with your parents next week."

I lift my face from my hands and peer up at him.

He slides his hand off my shoulder and caresses it down my upper arm, sending pulses of sensation through my sweater. His gaze holds me captive. His mouth, of course, lifts into a mischievous smile.

"You're trouble," I say softly, the word crackling between us. But the moment of levity vanishes as I'm hit with the weight of what that dinner with my father would actually be like. "He won't appreciate being ambushed in his own home."

He lifts his eyebrows. "If he's done nothing wrong, it won't be an ambush. Maybe he'll want to take legal action against Bubba or kick his ass."

I laugh at the image of my father trying to chase Bubba down. "That wouldn't go very well for him. Maybe he can go boxing with you and Otis to get some practice first."

"Yeah, I really cornered myself into that one," he says with a chuckle. "But the kid's got heart. He reminds me a little of my little brother."

I try to smile, but it slides off my face like melting ice cream. "This is bad, Liam. If people find out...our business partners..."

"The optics wouldn't be great. I figure we should just drop the messaging, and if anyone asks, we say we were having trouble sourcing all organic ingredients. We can always change course later. Were you planning on hiring someone to do PR?"

"I can't afford it right now, but Hannah's going to help me get the word out once we reopen. The band's performance should help promote the New Year's party. They have a lot of followers."

I think of Melly...

"And there's someone else," I say. "She has a pretty big social media following, and she's been freelancing for *The Asheville Gazette*. She's going to do some coverage of the brewery, although... I don't really trust her to be honest."

"So let's not talk to her. We shouldn't invite someone you don't trust to write about us," he says, shifting in his chair, his leg touching mine again.

"It's complicated."

He leans back. "Run it past me. Every now and then I manage to solve a problem without punching my way out of it."

A smile escapes me. "Let's just say my dad's making me give her access. It was one of the stipulations in his agreement for handing over the business."

"And is that guy John the one who put this agreement together?"

"Yeah." I rub my arms, suddenly cold. "He's my godfather."

"Condolences. That guy's a real shithead."

I let out a surprised laugh. "How do you know? You barely said anything to him. We were only there for five minutes."

"I knew after two."

"But *how*?"

"Will you believe me if I say it takes one to know one?"

"No, because you're an asshole, not a shithead. There's a difference."

He gives me a crooked grin. "Oh, so you have an encyclopedia of bad behavior?"

"If I did, I definitely wouldn't show it to you. You'd get ideas."

"I don't need any more ideas."

Neither do I.

I can't stop looking at him, soaking in the details of his smile and the way his eyes crinkle at the corners when he really gives into it. I want to trail my fingers across the solidity of his arm to the larger expanse of solidity that is his chest. But I can't. So I grip the edge of the table, hoping the solidity of the wood beneath my fingertips will wake me up, the way a lost dreamer might pinch themselves.

I clear my throat, but it's no more steadying than the table was. "Why'd you sign the contract so quickly if you don't trust him?"

He gives a lazy shrug. "*You* looked at it. I trust you."

"*You do?*"

A bigger smile spreads across his face. "Shit, did I make a mistake? Do you have designs on me, Briar?"

My heart beats a little faster, but I tell myself he's just passively flirting again. Courting trouble, the way he likes.

"Yes. I have plenty of designs on your big brain."

"Most women want me for my big—"

"*Liam.*"

"Just saying. It's about time someone tried to take advantage of me. Do you have any idea how boring life is when no one tries to cross you?"

"No," I say, my blood going cold. He's joking, obviously, but the truth is, I *don't* know. My whole life has been a carousel of different people who've used me and thrown me away.

"No, I don't know," I repeat, sadness humming through my words.

"That's because you're beautiful and kind." They're soft words, but he says them fiercely, his jaw tight. "There are people on this earth who take pleasure in controlling beautiful things. But beautiful doesn't mean delicate. Anyone stupid enough to try leashing a snow leopard deserves to lose a hand."

"You think I'm like a snow leopard?" I ask, stupefied.

"They were my favorite when I was a kid. I wanted to be a park ranger in Southeast Asia so I could watch them. I figured it would be the perfect job, not many people around, just animals. And animals are always honest, Briar. You do a dipshit thing, they give you a dipshit response. But if you put in the work and earn their respect, you'll have earned something worth having."

"You want an animal's respect, but you don't care about being respected by people?"

"I never said that." He reaches across the table, but his hand stops short in the center, lingering there, his fingertips tracing the veins of the wood. "I said I don't care about being liked. That doesn't mean I don't want respect from the people I respect."

"You're too late, you know. I like you."

He smiles softly. "You just got done telling me I'm an asshole."

"I guess I like assholes."

"Then you really need to have sharp teeth."

"The better to bite you with?"

"You might want to stick to biting other people. The kid who bit me in kindergarten told me I taste terrible."

I laugh, but it dries up in my throat. "Liam..." His name comes out quivery and wrong. "I'm *not* strong. I'm scared it's all going to fall apart, and it's going to be my fault. I don't want to let everyone down."

His hand finally finishes his journey across the table, and he takes my hand and layers our fingers together—each of his caressing each of mine. "You'd be stupid not to be scared. It's not going to be easy, Princess. I won't lie and tell you otherwise. You might lose. But if you do, you're going down with style. You're smart as hell, don't forget that."

I gasp at the feel of him, but he's not done yet. Flexing his fingers against mine, he says, "You made more sense drunk than most people do sober. And you're stronger than anyone gives you credit for. You're going to show them, Briar. You're going to show them, and they're never going to forget it."

"Liam," I say, my heart hurting. "Otis is bringing the new hires for the tasting room tomorrow. What am I supposed to say to them? They're giving up most of their holiday break to work for me, and I might only be able to employ them for a few weeks."

"Definitely don't tell them what you told me," he jokes.

I reach across the table and shove his arm, then regret it, because it's been so long since I've touched someone—really touched them—and he feels so good.

I expect him to get up, to walk away from me, because we both know he should, but instead he nods. "Come with me."

"Where?"

"There's a computer in your office, right?"

My office. It's *my* office now, not my dad's. Still, it'll always be the place where I did a remarkably bad job of firing Cleet and Ross. I've been avoiding it, but maybe it's time to reclaim it.

"Yeah," I say distantly.

"So come on."

Five minutes later, we're sitting in the office in front of the desktop—me in the desk chair, because Liam insisted, and him in a laughably small aluminum visitor's chair with a black plastic seat that groans every time he moves.

I glance at him as I log on to the computer. "Are you ready to tell me what we're doing in here? The suspense is driving me nuts."

"Good. Let's keep it rolling a little while longer. Turn your back while I get this set up."

I don't like turning my back. Not on most people. Not after what I've been through, but I don't feel anything but bubbling anticipation when I swivel my chair around. Liam slides his seat forward with a small scrape of metal against the linoleum flooring.

I hear the muted click-clack of keys, followed several moments later by what sounds like a church choir singing.

"You've taken my need for inspiration very literally," I say as I rotate the chair back around. I grin at him when I see the opening credits for a movie on my computer screen. "We're really watching *Rocky*?"

"Damn straight. You need a break, Briar. Let's take a break." He runs a hand across his stubbled jaw. "These movies are cliché at this point, but they meant something in the beginning. That was a lesson to me. Not everything that's popular is bad."

I stare at him in the harsh glow of the fluorescent lights overhead, at a loss for words.

"This means a lot to me," I say, the truth of it expanding inside of my chest like a new universe. No man has ever made me feel supported like this. Jonah's support had all been delivered in brittle promises, never in actions. "It's hard to put it into words."

He lifts a finger to his lips. "So you'd better not try. C'mon, Briar, we don't want to miss this part."

It's obvious he doesn't like to take compliments.

"Yeah, wouldn't want to miss all the singing," I say in a soft voice, as if we're in a movie theater and not huddled together in the office. It truly doesn't look like my space in any way. I haven't replaced the stern *I'm the boss* chair or put up any art prints on the walls. Part of me is afraid to, as if doing so will make my failure a certainty rather than just a possibility. "I know that's what Rocky's known for."

He brushes his knuckles softly against my arm. "Glad you see things my way."

His slightly rough skin sends a shiver through me, and I find myself wondering what it would feel like for him to touch me other places. Most of the men I've dated have been soft, suited, and civilized, like Jonah. Intimacy would be different with Liam, but I'll never experience it—a thought that makes my skin feel too tight.

"You got hurt," I say abruptly, lifting my fingers to the bruise on his cheek, skating lightly over the skin. "You were practicing?"

He captures my hand in his and holds on for a second—heat pouring between us—before lowering his arm.

"I was," he says, his voice a little rough. "I'm training for a local tournament at the end of January."

"I don't like the thought of someone hitting you."

He gives me a wicked grin that I feel in all the places I've declared closed for business.

"Who says I'll be the one who gets hit?" he asks, then nods to the screen. "Focus, Princess. There *will* be a quiz."

We watch the movie side by side in our chairs. It feels companionable, but there's something else hazing the air between us, the tension that's been there since Sunday night. It ebbs and flows, but it doesn't go away.

He works for you.

He's Hannah's brother, and she said to stay away.

He's never serious about women.

He'll break your heart, again.

But the pulsing awareness I have of him doesn't care about any of that. All it cares about is the strong arm that touches mine when he laughs and the sidelong looks he gives me at his favorite parts of the movie.

We've watched it for maybe forty minutes before I pause it and gesture to the small green, leather-upholstered loveseat positioned next to the office door. Sometimes Dad had meetings with multiple people, and he'd sit on the couch and position his visitors across from him on the tiny chairs.

"You must be uncomfortable in that chair," I say. "We could turn the screen around and sit there."

He glances at the couch and then at me. "We could."

"Should we?" I ask, feeling awash in self-consciousness.

It's his stare. It's soaking into my skin and spreading.

"We shouldn't, but I think we're going to anyway. This chair feels like it was constructed to torture people."

"It probably was." I reposition the monitor before pressing play again. "My dad didn't like to keep other people comfortable in meetings. He thought it gave him the upper hand."

He huffs, "Can't wait to meet him. I've heard such good things."

"You may like him," I say with a shrug as we head over to the couch. Our sides brush together as we move, but neither of us make any real effort to put distance between us. "A lot of people do."

"I doubt it," he says as he lowers onto the couch. "He hasn't been very nice to you, and I'm inclined to take that personally."

I flick off the overhead lights and sit next to him, feeling my body dip toward him. I know I should edge away, but I let my thigh and arm press against his as we tune into the movie.

Fifteen minutes later, he winds his arm around me and starts playing with my hair. I don't say anything as I sink further into him, every atom in my body focused on the places where we're pressed together. He doesn't acknowledge it either.

It's like we've silently agreed that if we avoid commenting on what's happening it won't be a big deal. We're just two colleagues sitting together, watching a movie as a much-needed break.

But when Rocky tells Adrian he can't win the fight—he just wants to go the distance—I shift to look at Liam. Our legs are still touching, and his face is closer than I'd realized, angled down toward me.

"You don't think I can win?" I ask in a small voice.

"I do," he insists. "But I don't think it's the winning that matters, Briar. Not with this. It's about going all in, even if you don't think you've got a shot."

"Is that how *you* fight?"

His smile is approving again, and I find myself tracing it with my finger, as if touch is a direct conduit to memory.

He watches me with a feral look in his eyes. "I thought we said *no touching the boss*," he says, his voice low and raspy. "I believe in following the rules."

"You're not my boss, and you're the one who wrote it."

"Good thing. Say...do you think a kiss qualifies as a touch?" he asks, reaching back to cup my head through my hair.

He's close enough for me to see the glints of gold and red in his short beard and the constellations of amber in his eyes. The bluish bruise above his right cheekbone.

My every nerve ending is drunk on him, but that doesn't stop me from remembering the way Hannah begged me to never, ever date Liam. I'm positive he has no interest in dating me, but I'm also sure she wouldn't want me to make out with him *at work*.

I edge away on the couch. "We can't do this."

"No," he says, wrapping his fingers around my wrist. "I think what you mean is that we *shouldn't* do this."

"We shouldn't," I repeat, my voice shaky. "You're right about that."

His focus is totally mine, as if I'm the only woman on Earth. The only one who matters.

"But I really want to," he admits gruffly. "Do you want me to kiss you, Briar Sterling? I'll know if you're lying. You're a terrible liar."

"You're a bully." But I stay put, his fingers still surrounding my wrist, caressing me with tiny movements.

"Some people have said so, but I think you know better."

I do. He's gruff and says what he pleases, but he's kind too. He was kind to Otis. He was kind to me that first night, bringing me to the boxing gym because he could tell what I needed even when I couldn't.

"We can't do this," I say again, more emphatically, for both of us. Rocky's fighting Apollo Creed now, and it's not going well for him. I gesture at the screen in desperation. "He's losing."

"Exactly," he says, tugging me a little closer. I slide toward him, needing the solid assurance of him. "When the chips are down, that's when you need to feel the most alive."

He reaches up to cup my chin, cradling it as he peers into my eyes. To my surprise, I'm the one who pushes up and kisses him.

CHAPTER FIFTEEN

LIAM

Some madness must have possessed me.

That's the only explanation I have for why I asked Briar if she wanted me to kiss her. The only explanation I have for why I'm kissing her now, even though I know what it could cost me.

But the price doesn't feel so urgent right now, with Briar's warm lips on mine and her fragrant hair gathered in my fist. The first kiss is soft, tentative, but I press in closer, needing to feel every inch of her mouth. I want her tongue, her taste. She gives it to me, slanting her head and making a needy little sound in the back of her throat. Like maybe she's been thinking of this too, ever since we were at the gym together and she threw her first punch.

It feels good in a way so few things do, and at this particular moment, I only care about getting closer.

With my free arm, I tug her into my lap, still kissing her. I sigh into her mouth at the sensation of her weight settling on my lap, her legs tucked on either side of me. Fuck, she's so perfect there, and I hope to hell she'll want to stay awhile, even though she must feel how I'm reacting to her. I'm prepared for it to wake her up, out of this haze of closeness that's descended around us.

But instead of getting up, she weaves her hands behind my neck and rocks closer to me, her tongue moving with mine. My hand finds her hip, and I pull her even closer, the feeling of her against me nearly annihilating my brain.

I suck on her bottom lip and then kiss my way down her cheek to her throat, sweet smelling and soft—and then shove her sweater down to kiss the swell of her breasts. God, they're pretty, and I'll bet they'd be even prettier if she threw off her sweater and bra to let me suck on her nipples. I want to know what shade of pink they are. I want to know what she'd taste like if she took off her pants and spread her legs for me.

I'd like it all to happen here, so she thinks of it every time she sits down in that rolling chair. So she can't catch a glimpse of this couch without remembering the things I did to her here.

"Liam," she says, her voice breathy as she writhes against my needy cock, every movement of her hips making me crazy. "The movie's over."

I press another kiss to the curve of her breast, then look up at her in disbelief. "I couldn't give a fuck. I'm right where I want to be, doing just what I want to be doing."

Her hips are still making tiny rotations she might not even be aware of, but I know from the look in her eyes that this is about to end.

"You're going to say this was a mistake," I muse. The thought makes my dick feel like it just got dunked in ice water, because she's right. What the fuck am I doing?

I wasn't supposed to touch her. That's not what this was about.

I put on the movie because she needed a boost, and I wanted to be the one who delivered it. While I couldn't give a shit what most people think of me, I'm starting to care a lot about what this one woman thinks of herself. But I knew the movie was a mistake the minute the opening credits started. Because she was just a whisper away from me, sitting in that office chair.

All I saw was her.

If I hadn't seen the movie before, I couldn't have told you a single thing that happened. I was only paying attention to her gasps, her sighs, and the way she leaned forward slightly when something intense was happening on screen.

So, yes, it was a mistake. A stolen moment that should never have happened, but I still don't move her off my lap. I can't make myself do something that's so counter to what I want.

Peering into my eyes, she asks, "Wasn't it a mistake?" She's looking at me with such earnestness. She's pretty when she's earnest, her eyes big and brown. I get suckered with the need to protect her whenever I look into those eyes, whether she needs or wants it or not.

I tuck her mussed hair behind her ear, then run my fingers along her delicate jaw before leaning in to kiss her sweet mouth one more time.

"Yeah," I say, inches away from her lips. "But I wouldn't mind making this particular mistake again."

"We can't," she says, her voice threaded with worry.

At least she sounds sad about it.

I think about Hannah, and how hard it was when the most important person in my life wouldn't talk to me for months. No, I can't let that happen again.

"No," I agree with a sigh. "I guess we can't."

Briar finally crawls off my lap, leaving me with a huge hard-on tenting the front of my athletic pants.

She looks at it like she thinks it's going to wave hello to her, which is actually exactly what it's doing. She bites her bottom lip, which felt plump and delectable in my mouth. "What are you going to do about that?"

I lift my eyebrows, amused. "Well, I'm glad you asked. You see, I was blessed with two hands—"

She gasps as if she wasn't riding my dick through a few layers of fabric ten seconds ago. "You're going to do that *in here?*"

Heat ripples through me. "Wasn't planning on it, but are you offering me the use of your office?"

She glances at the door again, and then she shocks the hell out of me by nodding. "I'm not going to be in here, though."

"You want me to?" I ask incredulously—and also because the thought makes me hot.

Her cheeks burn, but she nods before leaving, then closes the door with a click behind her.

I don't waste any time before I tug myself out and glide my palm over my flesh, thinking about the little noises Briar made and the way her lips and tongue felt. Thinking about those little rotations of her hips and how badly I wanted to tear her clothes off and take her here in her office.

Thinking about all the things I want but can't have.

I clean up afterward and leave the office.

There's no sign of her anywhere, only a little Post-It note affixed to one of the tables in the tasting room—

I'm going home. I'll see you tomorrow.

Before I leave, I look for our list of rules for success and write down a new one, the taste of her still in my mouth.

I'M on my way home when my sister calls me. A sick feeling creeps over my skin. I did exactly what she asked me not to do, and if she finds out I made out with her friend and then jacked it in her office...

She's not going to find out. Briar and I agreed it was a mistake that can't happen again, end of story. Plenty of people kiss without it meaning anything. Of all the kisses happening now, at this exact moment, at least eighty percent of them are meaningless. Sure, I pulled that statistic out of my ass, but that doesn't make me any different than most people.

There's only one problem: it was more than a few kisses.

I can still feel Briar's soft lips against mine and the brush of her hair on my neck. Her little moans are echoing in my chest.

The call cuts off, but my phone immediately starts ringing again, because my sister has never been patient.

On edge, I answer it on my Bluetooth.

"Hey!" Hannah says. "Want to grab dinner with Travis, Ollie, and me? We're going to that place in West Asheville where they let kids make their own pizzas. Ollie already sketched out the design for his."

"Yeah, sure," I say, well aware that I wouldn't be getting an upbeat dinner invitation if she knew how I'd spent my afternoon.

I'd tried to do what my sister had asked for. I'd done my best to ignore Briar. If she were only beautiful, it would have been easy enough, but she's interesting. She's got so many damn good ideas...

I head home before dinner and find an impossibly long golden hair attached to my shirt. Idiot that I am, I wind it around my finger. I leave it like that for a moment, smiling at the golden sheen. The soft perfection.

Yeah, no question. I'm in big trouble.

"That's it," I say out loud. "Quit it *now*."

I force myself to throw the hair away, instantly feeling a pang of loss in my chest.

Fifteen minutes later, I grab the Christmas gift I got for Travis's son, Ollie, because I'm not sure I'll see them again before they leave for New York next week. I'm about to exit the apartment when I pause and pull my phone out of my pocket.

It takes me approximately thirty seconds to reactivate Tinder.

Do I want to sleep with a random woman?

No. I don't have the slightest desire to even look at the app.

But it feels like I'm proving something to Hannah, and maybe myself, by having the app on my phone. If I'm on Tinder, then I'm definitely not interested in fucking my boss.

I GET to the pizza restaurant right on time—and I'm shocked to find Hannah, Travis, and Ollie actually beat me there. Hannah's giving me a smug little wave from the side of a booth across from the front door. My sister, who's so chronically late that everyone in our family always tells her to meet us fifteen minutes before we need her. Then again, Travis is an *on time is late* person, so maybe I shouldn't be surprised.

As I approach their booth, positioned beneath an oversized chalkboard listing the restaurant's draft beers, I grin at Ollie, who's wearing a Teenage Mutant Ninja Turtles sweatshirt, and hold up the present I brought for him.

"Is that for me?" he asks, his eyes fixed on the green-wrapped box as I sit down beside him and set it on the floor next to the booth.

I bump his small fist with mine, feeling a rush of warmth. Otis reminds me of my little brother when he was a teenager, but Ollie reminds me of him when he was this age, just seven—a kid old enough to want independence but too young to have much of it. "Nah, man, I just carry it around everywhere I go to confuse people."

"Really?" he asks with wide eyes. "It's a box for pranks?"

Hannah laughs. "Yeah, there's a teeny-tiny hole in it, because it's for his—"

"Hannah," Travis says in his *oh, Hannah* tone, fond and exasperated.

She laughs harder, pressing a hand to her mouth.

The familiar sight sends another wave of guilt through me, because there's no way she'd be this relaxed if she knew where I'd had my mouth an hour ago.

"What, Hannah?" Ollie asks. "What's the joke? You know I don't like not knowing."

"I'll tell you when you're eighteen," Travis says with an easy smile, then nods to me. "How's it going at the brewery?"

I glance at Hannah, who's studying the menu. "I think I'll take the Fifth."

"Well, thanks for setting us up with Mick, man. He's pretty good. It was more fun with you, but I get that you're too busy to make it work."

I nod. "Yeah. There's a lot to do. Going to be busy for a while."

My sister peers up at me. "I *seriously* hope you've been nice to Briar. But not *too* nice. I know how you feel about lazy dating."

"What's lazy dating?" Ollie asks before darting a glance at his father. "Come on, Dad, I don't have to wait until I'm eighteen for everything. I don't want to waste my whole life away waiting."

Travis smiles and tousles his son's hair. "Sure, but I don't think you're going to find it that interesting. What Hannah's saying is that Liam sometimes dates his coworkers because he doesn't want to go to the trouble of finding someone he actually likes."

I lean back in my chair, crossing my arms. "What does hypocrisy feel like? I've always wondered."

Travis gives me the sheepish grin of a man who started fucking my sister while she was, technically, working as his nanny. It's only because he's good to her that I let him get away with that.

"It tastes like ice cream," Hannah says with a grin. "That's why people indulge so often."

The server comes by. Ollie's the first to order, asking for the make-your-own-pizza option and showing the server his design. She pretends to be interested in his complicated drawing. He gets fidgety as the rest of us order our food, probably because Hannah goes last and takes her sweet time.

"Is that box really not for me?" Ollie whispers in a gush, no longer able to hold back.

"Oh, it's for you, all right," I say with a grin. "Promise to follow all the directions?"

He casts a sidelong glance at Hannah, his little face dead serious. "You know it's Hannah who needs help following directions."

"So definitely work on it with your dad instead of her."

It's a kombucha-making kit I got from a friend who runs a small local company. The closest I can get to introducing him to the art of making beer without Travis getting on my case.

"Are you talking about me?" Hannah asks, her eyes sparkling, as the server walks away.

"Yes," Ollie and I answer at the same time, and then we fist-bump each other again, laughing.

"Dad, can we try the claw machine?" Ollie asks. "I know they're designed to make people fail, but I think I figured out how to beat the system. I made a diagram."

He flashes the back of his pizza picture, and sure enough, there's a diagram of a claw machine.

Ollie's seven, doing academic work usually reserved for middle schoolers, but he's not going to beat that claw machine. No way, no how. From the defeated look on Travis's face, he knows he's about to lose twenty bucks to his kid's mission. But I'll give the guy this, he goes with grace. I pat him on the back as he leaves the booth with Ollie.

"Godspeed."

Hannah laughs, then whispers conspiratorially, "I called ahead and bribed the host twenty bucks to reposition the animals so Ollie has a better chance."

"So instead of Travis wasting twenty dollars on a shitty stuffed animal, you'll have wasted forty."

"The things you do for love." Then she tips her head, studying me. "Speaking of, maybe it's time for you to try dating again. I mean actually dating, not the lazy, getting-laid-by-whoever's-around approach. It's been, like, four years since you've been serious with anyone."

"Oh, for fuck's sake." I lean back on my side of the booth, tension thrumming through me as I run my finger under the band on my wrist. "First, it's *Liam, take this job.* Then *Liam, stay away from my friend.* Now you want to handpick a wife for me? Should I expect a shotgun wedding too?"

She lifts her eyes skyward. "Oh, I fully expect you're never getting married."

"Thanks."

She pauses, considering how far to go, and like usual, decides she might as well go all the way. "That shit with Julia went down ages ago. It wasn't your fault then, and it's not your fault now. You don't need to be alone."

I raise my eyebrows. "Maybe I want to be alone. When I told Margaret I didn't want her to leave a toothbrush at my apartment, she threw all of my shit into the beer I brewed. In front of everyone."

"So, you have questionable taste in women. I used to have questionable taste, too, and now look at me." She gestures to the claw machine, located in a cramped row of machines right next to the single-occupancy bathroom.

Travis looks like he's in a war zone, and Ollie has an expression of utmost concentration as he maneuvers the claw one last time before it lowers. It grips the stuffed toy, and Travis's whole face lights up. "You did it, Ollie!"

I'll be damned, it lifts the stuffie up, carting it toward the chute that'll give the tyke his treat. But it falls right before it gets there.

I turn to study my sister. "That's how things go for me, Han. Always will. No point in fighting fate."

She gives me a stern look that a little sister has no right to have in her repertoire. It's being around Ollie that's done it to her. "And yet, you seem very fond of putting on boxing gloves."

"I don't need a woman to be happy."

She waves a hand through the air like a tennis pro deflecting a ball. "So find a man. Find anyone. I'm sick of you moping around by yourself all the time. It's not healthy."

"But I have you, so obviously I never get to be alone."

This time her smile's sad and tired. "I love you, you big asshole."

"I regret to inform you that I love you too."

"I'm sorry you had to cancel your trip to see Connor and Dad so you could help Briar."

I'd had tickets to Boston for Christmas weekend, but I couldn't possibly take that trip. Not now. I would have missed Briar's family dinner, and I wouldn't have been around to babysit the beers.

"Don't tell her I did that," I interject. "She'll think it's her fault I had to cancel."

"Probably." She gives the table a knock with her knuckles, asking for luck. "But I'll make up for it."

Guilt tickles the back of my throat, because truth be told, I *want* to stay. "You owe me nothing. You know I like a challenge."

"Says the man who refuses to look for a real connection because he struck out once."

I decide to throw her a bone. "I reactivated Tinder before I came over here. You're welcome."

She doesn't seem ecstatic. "Great, now you can bone more strangers. I want you to *fall in love*. It's time. It's probably past time. You're getting old and set in your ways." She wags a finger at me. "I'm going to talk to Dottie about you."

"Why?"

I glance over at Travis and Ollie, and God love the guy, Travis is having a go at the machine now, his expression of anxious concentration both hilarious and touching.

"If anyone can trick you into falling in love, it's Dottie Hendrickson," Hannah says, making it sound like a curse.

I think about how I wrapped one of Briar's hairs around my finger earlier, like a lovesick teenager who needs some well-timed mockery to get his head on straight.

"No thanks," I say, to myself as much as Hannah. "I'm too busy to fall in love. I've got the brewery shit to deal with, and then I've got my fight at the end of January. I'll give the whole love thing a rain check."

She scrunches her nose in distaste but says, "I'm going to come to your fight."

"Why? You hate watching my matches."

"Sure, but if someone beats the shit out of you, I at least want the chance to heckle them."

"You're a good sister."

"I know," she agrees just as Travis and Ollie come back to the table.

They don't have any stuffed animals with them, but there's no defeat on the kid's face. Travis is the one who looks like someone gut-punched him.

"Your plan didn't work?" I ask Ollie.

"No," he says, "but that's okay. I just have to make a few extra calculations. I'll try again next time."

"How about I buy you a stuffed animal, short stuff?" I suggest, but he shakes his head.

"No, thank you. I have lots of stuffed animals. I like defeating the odds. That's most of the fun."

"Yes, by all means, let's make life more difficult for ourselves," Hannah says, watching me as she speaks.

I lift my glass to her in a toast. "Finally, some sense."

Sense is something I could use more of, myself. Because part of me wants to believe this means Hannah would be happy if I end up dating Briar. That thought is a lot like that hair wrapping around my finger—seductive at first, then too tight.

Because I'm being an idiot again.

Hannah might want me to date. She might want me to be happy. But she meant it when she told me to stay away from her friend. And Briar's not just my little sister's new best friend—she's my boss, the woman who holds my future in the palm of her hand.

That means I need to keep my distance, because obviously I'm incapable of controlling myself around her when I don't.

CHAPTER SIXTEEN

BRIAR

When my alarm goes off on my phone the next morning, my first waking thoughts are about Liam. No wonder. I've never done anything as dirty as asking a man to touch himself in my office before. I still can't believe I was so bold with him—or that I stood outside of the door, my ear pressed to the wood, hoping I could hear him running his palm over himself while he thought of me. That's something I'd prefer for no one to know, ever.

Oh, God...

Something is *definitely* wrong with me. I need to tell someone, but I can't talk to Hannah about this for obvious reasons, and it wouldn't be right to ask Sophie to keep it secret.

I set the phone down and settle for telling Karma the cat all about it while I do my morning yoga. He is nonjudgmental but seems disinterested and only wants his food. So I feed him and then get ready for the day and head into Silver Star, feeling a strange undercurrent of excitement and worry.

Will Liam mention what happened yesterday?

Should I?

It took me hours to fall asleep last night because I kept

running through what had happened in my head, along with every minute leading up to it.

When I get into the office, Liam hasn't arrived yet, but I find his new rule penciled onto our list—

Definitely don't kiss your boss. Especially if there's no HR rep.

A wrenching feeling nearly makes me stumble, but it's obviously for the best that we both think it's a mistake. Yes, it felt good to kiss him, but—

No, *good* is a word you'd assign to a movie or a perfectly in-season pear. A yoga session that leaves you feeling lithe.

Those kisses were *amazing*. Transcendent, even.

But what we did was also wrong, and I already know from experience that kissing the wrong man *always* has a price.

Kissing this man again could cost me my best friend. It could also cost me Liam himself, my main ally in running this business. I'd never be able to respect myself if I let another romantic mistake ruin my life.

So I straighten my spine, tell myself again that it's for the best, and add another rule beneath his:

Definitely don't kiss your employee. You might have to hire an HR rep.

While I'm writing, a knock lands on the front door, and I nearly drop the pencil. I'm trembling slightly, I realize.

It's the thought of seeing him again.

But it's not Liam at the door, it's Dottie Hendrickson, plus

Constance and Ann from her Wise Elders group. They were both part of the sage smudging of the shop a few days back.

"My dear girl," Dottie croons when I open the door, my hands still clumsy. "Good morning. We feel so blessed to be here."

I hug her as the other two women pass us and sweep into the tasting room. Constance has a crocheting project protruding out of her bag.

"Thank you so much for offering to help out," I tell them.

Constance gives my hand a hardy shake. "I'll do just about anything for entertainment. Since I retired, I've been a movie extra, a matchmaker, a crafter, you name it." She laughs, then steps aside to make way for Ann, who ignores my hand and goes in for a tight hug.

"Oh, aren't you a sight for sore eyes," she says. "You smell good too. Bless you."

I pull back. "Now, Dottie told me you two wanted to volunteer your time, but I insist on pay—"

"Oh no, baby girl," Ann says, already shaking her head. "We already discussed this. We'll only take payment in scratcher tickets. No other compensation will be accepted."

"Scratcher tickets?"

"Ann thinks she's going to win the lottery," Constance says with a snort, adjusting the bag on her shoulder, "and Dottie's been feeding her delusion."

"She had a lucid dream about it," Dottie says emphatically. "She even saw the type of ticket. Big Boy Bucks. They're real tickets, Constance. Mark my words, it was a premonition."

Constance clucks her tongue. "She probably knows the name of every scratcher brand in this country. Besides, I had a lucid dream about going to bed with that celebrity bad boy with all the abs, and that's not going to happen either." She pins her gaze on one of the front tables—the same one where Liam told me I was smart and beautiful. "Well, I don't know about you, but that chair right there is calling my ass's name."

"Oh, I butt-dial people all the time too," Ann says as she adjusts her hearing aid. "My son-in-law says it's because I have a big posterior, so I told him I'd rather have a big posterior any day than a skinny white butt like he has."

"Oh, for God's sake." Constance rolls her eyes as the two of them make their way to the table in question. "If you're gonna put that ugly thing in your ear, you might as well get some use out of it."

"He *is* ugly, bless his heart," Ann says, stuck on her son-in-law tangent. "Ugly as sin, if you ask me, but my daughter insists he has what it takes where it counts, and they've been married long enough that I have to assume she means it."

Dottie smiles and takes my hand, making no immediate move to join them. "You look radiant," she repeats. "Did something happen?"

For a second, I consider letting the truth spill out.

But I just shake my head. "No. I'm excited to get started. Otis and the new hires he found should be arriving any minute."

"Wonderful," she says with a beatific smile. "You know, I've been trying to convince Ann to try that online dating we were talking about the other day. What was it? Flint? Candle?"

"I think you mean Tinder."

She smiles. "Yes, that's the one. Have you given any further thought to dating again?"

"Oh no," I say, thinking of Liam's lips on my neck, my breasts, my face. I swallow against my suddenly dry mouth. "No, I'm still very much off it."

But I feel myself flushing.

Dottie gives me a knowing look and then surprises me by reaching out to touch my rose quartz necklace. Sophie, Hannah, and I all have them—Dottie supplied the rose quartz, which was supposed to help us be open to loving again, and I made the pendants.

Those three pieces are the last jewelry I made. I cried the entire time I worked on them, even before Karma scattered the jewelry wire all over floor.

Because jewelry and love were two things I felt had been torn away from me, and in my heart I believed neither would be the same again. Making jewelry, which had always been a creative escape for me, would forever remind me of feeling like a failure. And falling in love would make me feel stupid.

"*Of course* you're off dating, dear," Dottie says. "You've had some bad luck, no question about that. My first marriage was dull as dishwater, so I understand completely. I thought I was done with love, but love wasn't done with me. And it's not done with you either. It's like I've said—all signs point to you finding love right here at Silver Star. They have for months."

Worry swirls inside of me, small cyclones joining to make one massive mess. "No, Dottie, I don't—"

Someone knocks on the door, and I peer out of the glass and see Otis.

"Ooohoo, men are already showing up," Dottie says.

I open it too quickly, and Otis practically falls into my arms.

He grins at me and tugs off his stocking cap before turning and gesturing behind him to a group of five women in their early twenties. "They're all available to work in your tasting room next week."

A Japanese girl with an adorable pixie cut waves to me with a grin, and another woman, with long blond hair and a nose ring, gives me the stink eye. A third is on her phone, seemingly unaware that any of us exist, and the two others are studying their three elderly supervisors with suspicion. One of the newcomers finally peers at me and asks, "Is this, like, some kind of elderly outreach program?"

Constance, who's still comfortably seated, barks a laugh. "Yes, isn't it good of them to think of us? I needed a reason to get out of bed. Just wait, girls. Gravity kicks in when you turn forty, and it doesn't stop kicking."

"Come in," I say, giving them a warm smile, my heart beating fast. "I'm Briar. Welcome to Silver Star."

The women pour into the tasting room, and I direct them to sit at the table next to the one where Constance and Ann are seated.

Ideally, I'd interview each of them and ask about their service experience, but I'm not in any position to make demands. I need service staff, and if they're willing to put in the time next week, I'll give them a try.

Last night, I spent an hour writing a motivational speech about being underdogs, inspired by *Rocky*. I'm deep into it when Liam shows up at the front door with a couple of big sacks of grain slung over his shoulder, wearing no coat over the dark-green thermal shirt that hugs his straining muscles.

He opens the door one-handed, then steps into the room with a gush of cold wind.

Everyone in the tasting room except for Otis shifts in their seat to gawk at him, which is for the best, because I cut my motivational speech off midword.

I clear my throat. "This is Liam, our head brewer—"

We made out in my office last night, and I told him to touch himself in there. Would you like to see where I keep the coffee maker?

"Can I help you carry that?" one of the new hires says.

Liam chuckles, a deep sound that vibrates through the room and my body. "No, this is how I keep in shape. You tell them, Briar."

"Yeah, he's always carrying things around," I say, holding his gaze for a moment.

I can't tell what he's thinking, which is frustrating, but then again I can so rarely tell what he's thinking. He doesn't wear it, the way Hannah does.

"Can you carry me around?" Ann asks with a broad grin that dimples her wrinkled cheeks. "Sometimes my legs get tired, and my hip might as well be held together with glue sticks."

Constance mumbles something about selective hearing, and Liam laughs again as he continues on toward the back, giving me one final glance that makes my knees wobble.

I force myself to remember our list.

Kissing him was a mistake, but it's a mistake we can put behind us. We *need* to put it behind us—the sooner, the better.

MOST OF THE new hires don't even pretend to listen to the rest of my speech. They whisper under their breath and peer at the door leading to the back, probably hoping for another glimpse of Liam in that shirt. Afterward, they fill out the employment paperwork Uncle John put together, and I hand them over to the wise elders for training.

Dottie gives her sweetest smile as she stands next to their table. "Now, I'm about to teach you how to pour the perfect beer. Once we've mastered that, Constance will run you through a few scenarios about how to behave with difficult customers."

I'm smiling as I walk through the door to the back, but my smile fades when I reach my office.

Liam's waiting inside for me on the couch by the door. Yes, *that* couch. His legs are splayed in front of him, his hands woven together.

I swallow my gasp before it can leave my mouth.

"Rocky should get you for plagiarism," he says with a teasing smile, getting to his feet in a fluid motion. He's only inches from me now.

"None of it was word for word. I figured they'd be confused if I started talking about boxing."

He laughs, but it dies away as his gaze darts to my mouth. The way he's looking at me...

It makes my skin want to be touched and my fingers want to stroke.

I look away. "Well...thanks for checking in."

He wraps his hand around my chin, turning my face to him.

A gasp escapes me. "You're being rude."

"I know. I was rude last night too. It won't happen again."

"I know," I say tightly. "I saw your rule. I added one of my own."

"Did you?" he asks, his fingers still on my chin. "What did it say?"

I step back, my skin instantly missing the electric sensation of his fingers on me. "It said that I probably should hire someone in HR."

"Pick Dottie's friend with the glasses," he says. "She'd be a great fit. Good instincts."

"Everything's a joke with you."

"That's why I'd be terrible at HR."

I glance pointedly at the couch. "It's not the only reason."

His laughter fills the room, but I won't smile at him. Not now.

"It was a good speech, Briar. You're a natural leader."

I have to laugh at that. "I have it on good authority that I'm not."

"Whose?"

I swallow dryly. "My father's."

"No offense, but fuck your father."

A surprised laugh barks out of me.

"This is a clean slate. *Your* clean slate."

"This is starting to sound dangerously like a pep talk."

He smiles, but there's an edge of sadness to it. "Maybe I wanted my *Rocky* moment too." He shuffles on his feet a little, drawing my awareness to his body. I liked the way he felt against me yesterday. I enjoyed it so much it's filled my mind like a virus.

I don't mean to touch him. It's almost like someone else's hand is lifting to his arm, settling on his hard bicep. "Thank you for caring enough to try. You know...I've been thinking about that name tag you were wearing last weekend. You really have been my Mr. Miracle."

He flinches away as if I'd burned him.

He must see the hurt in my eyes, because he captures my hand in his and squeezes before releasing it. "I should tell you...I promised Hannah to keep my distance from you. I'm assuming you know why. I haven't been doing a good job of it, obviously, but I love my sister. She was there for me when I needed her. She's always been there for me."

Our eyes are glued together as I slowly nod. "Yeah. I...she asked me to make the same promise. It wasn't hard to make at the time."

He smiles wryly. "You didn't think I was capable of charming you?"

"I underestimated how good your beer was."

His smile grows wider, and although neither of us moves, we seem to get closer anyway. "So the beer is my only attraction, huh?"

"I'm not the one who said it."

His lips curl in a way that makes my chest tight. But he quickly sobers, his smile fading. "We should probably avoid being alone together."

"Yeah," I agree. "Feel free to add it to the rules."

The smile ghosts over his lips again. He turns toward the door, signaling that our conversation is over, which is probably for the best, but then he turns back around.

His mass seems to alter the gravitational pull in the room. Everything is leaning in toward him, including me. For a long moment, he just watches me, his eyes as hot and unavoidable as the sun. Then he says, "It's not only the way you look."

"What?"

"You're beautiful, Briar. Everyone knows that. But that's far from the only thing you have to offer. And even though that shouldn't have happened last night, I don't regret it. I'll remember it. I'll always fucking remember it. So it *was* worth it for me."

I stare at the door for a long time after he leaves through it.

CHAPTER SEVENTEEN

LIAM

<u>Briar and Liam's Rules for Success</u>

Don't be alone with your boss. You might just kiss her.

Don't allude to kissing your boss.

Don't let Ann get you alone in the storage room. She might pinch your butt.

Text conversation with Briar

OMG did she really pinch your butt? I'll have a talk with her.

I think the Tinder girls put her up to it. I saw one of them giving her a scratch-off ticket.

Definite payoff.

That's sexual harassment.

> I enjoyed every second. Feel free to pinch my butt anytime.

> New rule: don't encourage your boss to pinch your butt.

> You're no fun.

It's a Thursday evening at Silver Star, and I'm singing to my pale ale.

Yes, that's right. I'm serenading a beer.

This coming Monday is Christmas Day. That means the New Year's Eve party is next Saturday.

If this beer is going to be ready on time, I have to carbonate on Tuesday. Wednesday at the latest.

I'm not usually a superstitious man, but I will buy rabbits' feet by the bag and knock on every piece of wood I come across if it means this beer will be ready even a few minutes sooner.

I care about making Silver Star a success. I need it to happen for myself, because it feels good to make my own beer. I also need it for Briar, who's been working her cute butt off all week. Once we have a few of our new beers out, she'll be able to start booking high-dollar guests in that cozy little room we decked out.

She's got other ideas too, so many ideas my head is swimming with them. I see her enthusiasm infecting everyone else on staff too. Even the old-timers seem reluctant to accept that their employment is only temporary. I've caught Ann talking about what we should do for Valentine's Day—as if anyone with sense wants to do anything on Valentine's Day other than wait for it to be over. But the atmosphere all of Briar's big ideas has created is intoxicating.

I want to do my part. I want my beer to be ready to serve at midnight on New Year's Eve, just like she envisioned in that shitty diner. Unfortunately, its levels still aren't where they need to be.

I told my father as much on FaceTime last night, and he said, "Remember when we sang to that lager when you were a boy? Sing to it. The yeast is alive. You need its goodwill if you're going to make a beer worth drinking."

That got a smile out of me.

My old man taught me to brew when I was a kid. After our mother left, my grandmother encouraged him to share what he loved with us, and he took it literally.

I was too young to drink the beer, or so he said, but he was all too happy to take care of our "stock." He used to get trashed in the basement on weekends, watching old episodes of *M*A*S*H*. Sometimes that meant Hannah and I had to make mac and cheese for our brother Connor, or help him with his homework.

Still, we all love our dad. He's the kind of person you can't help but love—if you're not my mother, obviously. But she was cold and hard to love. Kind of like me.

Which is why I need to stop gravitating toward Briar like one of those dumbass moths who keeps swooping in for another go at a lightbulb, thinking this time might be different.

I frown as I press my palm against the vat and then sing the next verse of—

"Are you singing 'Champagne Supernova' to our beer?" Briar asks, walking into view with twinkling eyes.

"You told me what Dottie said about it being the champagne of beers, and I'm a desperate man."

I soak in the sight of her standing in front of me, so touchable, and become achingly aware of the fact that we are, however briefly, alone together.

We've avoided that this past week. It hasn't been hard, because the brewery's been busy.

Hannah and Sophie have been posting flyers about the New Year's party all around town, plus Travis and the guys have been doing publicity for the event. As a result, we've had curious people peeking in through the glass windows ever since we took down the cardboard CLOSED sign and flipped the official sign around to OPEN this past Monday. It didn't take long for the customers to start flowing in.

Doesn't hurt that it's gotten around that the new owner is the most beautiful woman alive and that we have a bunch of twenty-something women serving our beer. Someone caught wind that Otis met them all on an online dating site, and a local blog posted about it. The words "scrappy" and "innovative" were used, and it puffed Otis up something good. No doubt it's also boosted his confidence that a couple of the bartenders seem interested in him.

A few of them have approached me, too, but I made it clear I wasn't interested. They're too young, for one thing. For another...

I glance at Briar.

"The beer's not going to be ready?" she asks, her voice resigned.

"I'm singing to it," I say, my palm still pressed to the vat. "Women can't resist a good serenading. I bet it'll be popping off by morning."

She gives me a tired, *shut up, Liam* look, and I add, "My dad used to do it. He's the one who taught me how to brew."

"When you were a kid, right? Hannah told me."

"Sure. Kept me out of trouble until it got me into trouble."

She smiles. "I'll bet you were a hellion."

"Nah. I was a real stickler for the rules. I just didn't have any. My father believed in letting us learn from our mistakes."

"You have plenty of rules now," she points out, reminding me of that list we've been updating daily. It feels like flirting, writing back-and-forth messages to each other using the same pencil, its lead worn down.

"I suppose I do."

Brief silence descends between us, seeming to vibrate with unspoken words, before she says, "I need to know if it's going to be ready, Liam."

"I'm worried," I admit. "But I haven't given up. I'm not going to give up."

Her smile fills her whole face as she presses her hand to the side of the vat, next to mine, and starts singing the next verse of the song. Her voice washes over me. Soft and sweet but strong, like Briar herself.

"Well, damn, if it doesn't shape up now, it's a lost cause," I say, making her smile broaden as she continues to sing.

I start singing with her, edging my hand over so our fingers are touching as our voices harmonize.

I've never really noticed a woman's fingers unless they're wrapped around my cock. But right now, the slight pressure of her pinky against my index finger is the only thing that matters.

It's a stupid thought, but I've been having a lot of stupid thoughts about Briar lately. I tell myself it'll pass with time—an argument that was more convincing before she started harmonizing with me.

The door to the tasting room opens, and a few seconds later, one of the front-of-house twenty-somethings, a blond with a nose ring, steps into view from the other side of the vat. "You guys are singing loud. Like, it can be heard in the tasting room. Someone asked if it was karaoke night. Do we do karaoke?"

"No," I say, "and we never will. Karaoke should be recognized as a form of torture."

Briar laughs under her breath, then presses her hand more fully against mine. "Stop it." Turning to the girl, she says, "We're singing to the beer, Sorcha."

Of course she knows her name. She probably knows the name of everyone who works here, along with where they were born and what their favorite drink is.

"Old people are so weird," Sorcha mutters, rolling her eyes, just as the door to the tasting room opens again, admitting the sound of approaching footsteps.

"Dear, I've told you those words aren't allowed in this brewery," Dottie says as she comes into view. "We're only as old as we allow ourselves to be."

Categorically untrue, but Sorcha blushes and says, "Sorry, Dottie," looking like she might actually be sorry. Dottie has that effect on people.

"Now, what's all this fuss about?" Dottie asks.

The bubble Briar and I had formed is broken, but I remind myself it's better like this. I can't be alone with her without wanting to break every rule on that list and burn the paper.

"They were singing to the beer," Sorcha says as if she's accusing us of something.

"Delightful!" Dottie grins at us. "Should I ask everyone else to join in?"

I nudge Briar's foot with mine. "What do you think, boss? Should the whole staff sing 'Kumbaya' to the pale ale?"

When our gazes meet, it feels like a warm glow is transferring between us. "You know what? Yes."

"Uh...what about the customers in the tasting room?" Sorcha asks. It's obvious she thinks we've completely lost it.

"They can join in," Briar says.

"Uh...you guys know singing to the beer isn't going to make it ferment faster, right?"

"Well said," Dottie replies, patting her on the back. "Singing alone won't do the trick. I'll need to gather some crystals from home and place them strategically around the room to create an energy field. I only wish I'd thought of it sooner."

She hurries out of the brewing area, which is separated from the hallway by a short half wall. She's a woman on a mission, leaving behind Sorcha, who's gaping at us.

"Spread the message, Sorcha," Briar says, giving me a sidelong look. "We're all going to raise our voices."

Sorcha hurries away, turning into the hall and leaving us alone again.

There goes the most important rule on our shared piece of paper.

"You know she's never coming back, right?" I comment.

"She'll be back," Briar insists.

"If you say so, Princess. But I'm telling you right now, if the crystals and the singing actually work, it's going to break my brain."

"You said you weren't giving up."

"I'm not."

"Well, I'm not giving up either," she insists, eyes on mine. "I believe in you."

My heartbeat picks up pace, but I smirk at her. "That would probably mean more if you hadn't just told me you believe singing and crystals are going to mature this beer."

"You're the one who started it."

There's not much I can say to contest that. So I settle for brushing my hand against hers again, making it look like an accident.

"*Liam*," she says, her voice trembling with meaning.

I let myself remember what it felt like to have her in my lap. What a fucking decadence that was.

"*Briar*. We're breaking a very important rule."

"Let's not break any others," she says with a smile.

But her lips are trembling a little, and I feel like a dick for having pointed out the obvious. I feel like even more of a dick for making this so hard on both of us, constantly pushing the boundaries even though I know there's a line we cannot cross again, no matter how much I want to take her hand and vault over it.

The door to the tasting room creaks, and more footsteps approach us.

Briar perks up. She's obviously expecting Sorcha and a bunch of backup singers, but it's Otis, scratching his head.

"Uh, guys, I think Sorcha just quit. I'm sorry, Briar. I swear I didn't do anything. I offered her an Airhead, and she said it was the last straw and just walked out." He hesitates. "Actually, maybe she thought I was calling her an airhead."

I dart a look at Briar. "I should have put money on it."

"Are you sure she's gone for good?" she asks Otis, looking so sad about it, I'm tempted to run after Sorcha and convince her to come back.

He nods, obviously no happier about disappointing her than I am.

"All right." I clap my hands. "Let's get this going."

She gives me a disbelieving look. "You're going to lead this bar in song?"

A grin stretches across my face. "I'll have you know my father, Hannah, Connor, and I were in a family band together. We were the quadruple threat of the farmers' market. No one could go there without having to listen to us sing about dental hygiene and vegetables."

Her laughter spurs me on. "I know. Hannah showed us the videos."

"Then you know I was lead vocals for that one song about carrots. Do you doubt my ability to lead the crowd?"

"No, I really don't doubt you. Or the carrots." Her smile turns mischievous, as if she knows exactly what she's doing to me. "But please feel free to prove to Otis and me why we shouldn't."

"What are we singing?" Otis asks, always game to do anything for Briar. He's still got it bad for her.

Then again, I'm not one to talk.

I'm about to lead a bar full of half-drunk people in song to make a girl smile.

"Well?" Otis asks.

I evade his question by marching into the front room and coming to a stop next to the bar.

The tasting room is three-quarters full of people who seem to be in a competition to talk louder than one another. We're all losing, as far as I can tell.

Constance left for her family cruise yesterday, but Ann's here, happily wiping down the bar.

I glance back at Briar, who followed Otis and me out here, then give a wolf whistle.

Every eye in the place lands on me, except for Ann's—which means her hearing aid is switched off again.

I almost laugh at the realization that I did this to myself on purpose.

"Salutations," I say. "We'd like to invite you to join us in song. We're trying to help our new beer reach peak fermentation in time to serve at our New Year's Eve party next week. You all know about the New Year's Eve party, right?"

"Yeah!" Otis shouts, joined by no one.

"Fantastic," I continue. "So we're going to sing 'Champagne Supernova' to the beer."

People have started to chatter disinterestedly again, so I add, "And anyone who sings with us gets a free round of our delicious tropical IPA, on the house."

We've all agreed it's the least successful of Bubba's brews, and the one we'd like to offer up first at the drink-us-dry party. His pale ale is also on the list, since we'll hopefully have our own, as well as the overly sweet holiday ale.

Spontaneous applause erupts across the room.

I grin at Briar. "Two birds, one stone."

She surprises me by reaching out and squeezing my hand before walking behind the bar to get the song queued up on the sound system. We smile at each other as we sing along, our interwoven voices leading the charge. Everyone joins in—even Ann, who looked up in astonishment and then started humming along.

I don't hate it. Not even a little.

We're belting out the last lyrics when the front door swings open, and my sister, Sophie, and Nora walk in, all of them pink-cheeked from the cold.

Hannah comes up to me after the last strains play, her coat still on and cold air wafting from her. "What kind of pod person are you, and what did you do to my brother?"

Laughing, Briar circles the bar to greet them. "We were singing to the beer. Liam said your dad used to do it."

Hannah smiles at the memory, but I can see uneasiness in her eyes. I'm behaving like a lovesick schoolboy, and she knows it's unusual for me.

Turning back toward Briar, Hannah says, "If you've resorted to singing, it's a good thing Nora brought your backup plan, huh? We've got the kegs outside in her truck."

"Backup plan?" I repeat, glancing at Briar.

Briar bites her bottom lip—a nervous tell of hers.

People are already lining up at the bar for their free beers, and Otis, who was all about this plan five minutes ago, seems to have withered and has a fixed smile on his face as he starts to fill cups with the IPA.

"It's just in case," Briar says, commanding my attention. Her tone is apologetic, her eyes pools of emotion.

"Oh." I feel like she just dealt me a gut punch at the end of a boxing match. "You bought cider from Nora for the New Year's Eve party."

"We have to be prepared for anything."

I nod, knowing she's right. Briar's got business smarts, always. She has to look toward the future and do what's best for everyone. But it still burns. She told me she believed in me, and all along she had a backup plan lined up, which means she thinks I might fail. Maybe she's certain I will, and she's been feeding me a bunch of bullshit.

Briar reaches for my arm across the bar, her gaze seeking mine. "It's a good idea anyway. It's a new release for The Ginger Station. We're both going to have it on tap on New Year's Eve, but they're closing early."

Anger spikes through me, and I pull away. "And you didn't think that was relevant information for your brewer?"

My sister glares at me. "Maybe she thought you'd overreact for some mysterious reason."

"I'm fine," I say, sounding distinctly not fine. "You're leaving for New York tonight?"

Hannah's red curls bob with her nod. "I know you're the one who sent me this sweatshirt, by the way."

I force a smile. "It suits you."

It's a dark-green hoodie with *Worst. Nanny. Ever.* scrawled across the chest. We love giving each other a hard time, Hannah and I, but she knows how I feel. She was the best nanny ever to Ollie, same as she's been the best sister ever to Connor and me.

I'm annoyed at myself for breaking my promise to her. But, dammit, it sucks that Briar went behind my back. I can feel her staring at me, silently begging me not to be mad, because she can't stand it when people are upset with her.

Which really pisses me off, because part of me wants to make her feel better for having made me feel worse.

"I ordered your present," Hannah says, nudging me with her fingertips. "You're going to hate it."

I kiss the top of her head. "Merry Christmas. Say hey to Travis and Ollie for me."

"Don't forget to call Dad."

"I won't."

I know Hannah wants to say more. Maybe she's tempted to issue another warning about her friends being off-limits, but she lets me walk away so I can help Otis, thank God.

Probably because he just spilled an entire pint of beer on a guy who's almost as big as I am.

I slip behind the bar and take over for him, freeing him to run off to fetch the mop. I don't look back at Briar until after I've poured the first beer, but she's still staring at me, a worried expression on her face.

When I glance her way again a couple of minutes later, she's exiting the brewery with Nora, my sister, and Sophie. They gather near the front window, though, probably overseeing the unloading of those kegs. I keep glancing outside, unable to stop myself, hoping for a glimpse of golden hair.

Five minutes later, my phone buzzes in my pocket. I ignore it and keep pouring. It buzzes again.

Nope.

A few minutes later, Dottie bustles back into the brewery with a big duffel bag. She rushes up to the bar with the urgency of a doctor treating an emergency room patient.

"You sang to it, didn't you?" she asks, her voice full of excitement. "The energy in here has shifted. I can *feel* it."

"So we don't need the crystals?"

"Oh, crystals are always helpful, dear boy." She pats my hand and then hurries into the back to get them positioned.

The line for free beer eventually peters out, and once everyone's settled with their drinks, Otis gives a theatrical shudder. "Let's never do that again."

Ann pats him on the back. "I say that every time I go to Texas Roadhouse, honey, and I keep going back. I bet you'll be singing your booty off again by the New Year, and if the good lord smiles on me, I'll be singing with you. The energy of this place is making me feel young again."

Otis and I both smile at her.

The elderly managers are, in their way, as much of a draw as the young women serving the beer.

But the real magnet is Briar.

I glance out the front windows again, but she's long gone.

Dottie hasn't come back either. I'm guessing the whole brewing area is going to be covered with those crystals, like little grenades waiting to break our feet or tumble down from shelves and hit us on the head.

But I'm just superstitious enough not to try and stop her. I need that beer to be ready in time, even more than I did earlier tonight. I told Briar I don't care what anyone thinks, and usually that's true, but I want to prove that I can deliver results.

Otis releases a long sigh. "I'm gonna go smoke a blunt," he tells me. "Want to come?"

"No, man. I'm heading home in a minute, if y'all are good with handling this."

"I'll join you, sweetheart," Ann tells Otis, and I laugh at the shocked look on his face.

"Miss Ann, I said I was going to—"

"Oh, I heard you. I had to turn my hearing aid on so I could hear those hooligans. I couldn't believe my ears when I heard them saying you'd promised them free beer."

She gives me a censuring look that has no place on the face of a woman who works for scratch-off tickets and beer.

"We want to get rid of the tropical IPA," I point out.

"It's not so bad," she says. "I mix it with pineapple juice in the evenings." She nods at Otis. "Shall we?"

"But, Miss Ann—"

"I enjoy a little grass sometimes. Your grandma does too. You can tell me all about that dating app you kids are on."

I huff a laugh. "He's only interested in our dear leader."

He shoots me a look of betrayal that makes me feel like an asshole—and, worse, a hypocrite.

"Oh, baby," Ann says, smoothing a hand down his arm. "You got to change that tune. That woman's looking for a wolf, not a lamb. But don't you get down on yourself. There are plenty of women who'll go for a full-grown sheep. My Rufus was a sheep everywhere but in the bedroom."

The look on the kid's face nearly makes me laugh, but then I check my phone and find a string of messages from Briar:

> Please don't be upset.
>
> I was going to tell you.
>
> I just didn't want to mess with your focus. I know how hard you've been working.

I ignore them, not ready to answer her.

There are also a couple of texts from an unknown number:

> Hello, Liam. This is Don Sterling. I do hope Briar passed along my invitation to dinner tomorrow evening.
>
> What can I do to convince you to come?

I pause, staring at the messages, wondering what this jack-off's game is. He's going behind Briar's back, obviously. Undermining her. Again.

I'm still pissed about the ginger beer, but there's only one answer I can give him.

I won't let her face him alone.

CHAPTER EIGHTEEN

BRIAR

"Oh my God, please don't stress about my brother," Hannah says as I tuck my phone back into my pocket after texting Liam. "He'll get over it."

We're outside, watching the delivery drivers as they finish unloading the kegs of ginger beer. They're bringing them around the back, thank God, not through the tasting room. Liam would only get more pissed off if he had to watch them get shuttled past him.

"He's always been a big baby about his beer," Hannah continues, zipping her coat up over her sweatshirt. "But you made a wise decision. He'll realize that as soon as he gets his head out of his ass."

Nora nods. "Never let a man talk you out of a sound business decision. I say this as someone who let José name one of our ginger beers after his ex."

"Was it you?" Hannah nudges her arm. "Were you the ex?"

Nora laughs, but Sophie's watching me closely. "Are you okay, Briar?"

No. I can't stop thinking about the look of betrayal in Liam's eyes. It feels very important for him to forgive me, and

I know it has nothing to do with preserving a comfortable work environment. He's important to me, and not only because he's the genius I need to make this place work. I care about him.

"I'm fine," I say with a forced smile, watching as the delivery guys disappear around the corner and through the back door. "He was right, though. I should have told him."

"Well, he knows now," Nora says practically.

Sophie checks her watch. "Are we going to have a drink? I need to get to the airport in a couple of hours."

"Me too," Hannah says with a sigh. "I don't have high hopes for Travis's mother. She calls everyone *dah-ling* and tried to book me Botox for Christmas."

Nora laughs. "At least she's generous. I'd go for it if I were you. You'd have a built-in excuse for not smiling. Maybe I'll start pretending I just had Botox."

I lead them into the back, making sure the kegs were dropped off in the right place, and then into the barrel room. The soft lighting and beautiful garland-draped barrels remind me of the effort Liam went to the day he and Otis set this up, and guilt sneaks into my veins as my friends get settled—Sophie and Hannah on the chairs, Nora on a barrel.

I sigh as I pour them glasses of the latest beer Liam brought in for me to try—a delicious spring beer with a hint of elderberry and lemon verbena. After handing them out, I take a seat on another of the empty barrels.

"So what are you doing for the holidays, Nora?" Hannah asks. "Let us live vicariously."

Nora takes a swig from her drink. "I'm sorry to report that my mom and I are having the Peebles men over for Christmas dinner."

"You're complaining about dinner with Eugene?" Hannah asks. "How *dare* you. I love that salty bastard."

"Well, you're more than welcome to cancel your trip and join us. Mom's making meatloaf."

I sigh. "That sounds nice. I hate spending Christmas with my parents. They always invite some investor or someone they want to impress and dress me up like a doll."

"Ugh, I'm adding another plate for you." Nora waves her glass at me. "I'm not joking. You'll be saving me, and I'll be saving you. You heard what Liam said about Cormac. He's going to spend all night talking about his high school science project. I'll need to get hammered just to get through it alive."

"I might actually take you up on that."

"Good," she says, smiling, then gestures her glass toward the door. "You can ask Liam to come if you want. I'll even let him give me a hard time about my ginger beer. Brewers love to gab about how their stuff is better."

"He probably would too," Hannah grumbles. "But I'll tell you right now, he won't come. He hates Christmas."

"Yes, damn all those happy people with their presents and smiles," Sophie says with an easy grin.

But suddenly my heart is beating hard. My intuition tells me this is significant for some reason.

"Why?" I ask, my gaze on Hannah.

She shrugs. "His ex-girlfriend's birthday was on Christmas. It reminds him of her. He always gets tanked. Even when he's around family. He was supposed—" She cuts herself off.

"He has an ex-girlfriend?" I ask, dumbfounded. "But you said..."

She waves a hand. "Yeah, I know, but this was a long time ago. It's been years since he's dated anyone for longer than a month. He doesn't like it when I talk about his ex, though, so I've probably said too much."

The conversation moves on, but I don't...

Liam has an ex-girlfriend.

He cared about her enough that he hates Christmas because it reminds him of her.

He hasn't dated anyone seriously since they broke up, which means he hasn't moved on.

Nausea twists my stomach, putting me in danger of a Code V.

Stupid girl.

I thought something special was building between us, but maybe that's just the way it feels when you spend every day with someone, working toward the same goal. For all I know, I'm no more important to him than any other part of Silver Star. The paint. The mortar. The—

The twinkling lights arranged over the barrels catch my eye. He didn't need to help Otis put this room together for me. It was nowhere in his job description. He also didn't need to watch *Rocky* with me or sing to the beer.

Working on this room was like giving me a big bear hug. Maybe I don't mean as much to him as this Christmas girl, but I mean something. We're friends, at least.

But the way he kissed me...

That wasn't the way you kiss a friend.

I wrap my arms around my chest, which doesn't ease the confused ache in my chest.

Hannah and Sophie leave—Hannah with an *oh shit*, because she's running late—but Nora hasn't finished her beer yet, so she agrees to stay for another five minutes.

My mind dips back to what she told us about dating her business partner.

"Can I ask you a personal question?" I ask hesitantly.

A smile drifts across her face. "Aren't we past all that? We all slept with the same loser."

"The reason it didn't work with you and José...was it because you worked together?"

A speculative look enters her eyes. She knows I'm talking about Liam but doesn't call it out. "No, Briar, but I'm not going to sugarcoat it. It sure made shit awkward afterward."

I feel like I just tried to swallow a tennis ball, but I manage a stiff nod.

She finishes her beer, then says, "I hope you come on Monday. I'm not the kind of person who makes invitations without meaning it. I'd like it if you were there."

"Thank you."

When she gets up, I lean in to hug her, and she smiles. "I'm not much of a hugger."

"I respect that."

"Now, I suspect there's a huge man sulking somewhere out there. Good luck."

She leaves, and I check my phone.

Nothing from Liam.

I take a deep breath and head over to the vats, feeling like a mother hen checking on her egg.

I turn the corner at the edge of the half wall, hoping I won't see him. Also wanting desperately for him to be there.

Instead, I see Dottie's butt lifted up in the air next to the vat containing the pale ale. She's doubled over in the corner.

"Dottie!" I shout. Oh God, she's in her eighties, and I've let her do too much, and now—

She flinches and then stands up straight, turning toward me. "Briar," she chides, clucking her tongue. "You shouldn't sneak up on elderly people like that. Why, you nearly gave me a heart attack."

I place a hand over my racing heart. "What on earth are you doing?"

"I created a network of crystals to speed up the fermentation. I only wish I'd thought to do it sooner."

"It can't hurt," I say. "Thank you."

I head into the tasting room, which has cleared out a lot, and find Otis and Ann behind the bar. Both of them smell like pot, but I don't want to point it out in front of customers.

"Do you know where Liam is?"

"Uh...he just left for home," Otis says, watching me closely.

"*Oh.*" I reach reflexively for my rose quartz necklace and start fidgeting with it, my mind spinning. I'm not going to see him until morning. I won't be able to tell him I'm sorry. I—

I bolt out of the front door of the brewery, searching the salted sidewalks for him. It's not hard to spot him. He's heads taller than most of the people around him, his hair looking like burnished copper under the streetlights.

"Liam!" I run to him, nearly slipping on an icy patch of side-walk. Someone yells at me to be careful, but my ears are filled with static buzz. The only thing I can concentrate on is reaching him.

He turns to me with a look of shock. I'm almost proud of myself, because he's not a man who's startled often.

"I should have told you about the ginger beer," I say, panting as I reach him. "But I didn't want you to think it's because I don't believe in you. I *do* believe in you."

He studies me for a moment before sighing and taking off his coat, which he drapes over my shoulders. This is becoming a habit. The coat is warm and smells like him. I barely took notice of it the last time he made me borrow it, but this time I instantly fall in love with it.

My inner critic whispers, *This is the problem with you, Briar. You walk around falling in love with coats and men who don't want you...*

"Go home," Liam says, his voice gravelly.

"You're mad at me."

"Doesn't matter."

I reach for his arm. He's only in a long-sleeved shirt now, but he's warm beneath it, and my fingers curl around him. "It matters to me."

Emotion flickers through his eyes, but then his jaw hardens. "Of course. Because you want everyone to like you."

"I want *you* to like me."

He holds my gaze for a long moment, my hand still wrapped around his forearm, as if he might slip away if I let him go. I have the urge to pull him closer. To wrap us both up in the coat as if it has the power to hide us from the world.

"I wouldn't say liking you is the problem, Princess," he finally says. "I like you just fine."

"I have faith in you," I say. "Please believe me. *Please.*"

He takes a step toward me, and my whole body reorients itself, tipping toward him. My breath freezes in my lungs. It's the way he's looking at me...

"I like hearing you say please," he finally says, his voice thick with meaning.

"*Please.*"

His hand lifts to my face, his rough fingers tracing my jawline. For a moment, I'm sure he's going to do it—he's going to kiss me right here, out on the street where anyone can see us— but he lowers his hand. I see it ball at his side, and then he steps back.

My gaze tracks his Adam's apple as it bobs in his throat. "You were making the best decision for the brewery. I get that. I shouldn't have taken it personally." He pauses. "Your father issued me my very own invitation to your family dinner tomorrow night."

"He did?" I ask, feeling raw. Not surprised, though. My father has always preferred dealing with men.

"He did. I assume he got my information from your godfather. You know, I thought lawyers were supposed to keep things confidential, but not good old *Uncle* John."

"I'll talk to my dad about the organic certification. You don't have to come," I say, full of nervous energy at the thought. I don't like that Liam's upset with me, but pity is so much worse than anger. "I'd prefer it if you didn't."

He gives me a slow perusal, ending on my eyes. His voice hoarse, he says, "There are a lot of things I want but can't have too."

"I'm not going with you," I insist. "I don't want them to think—"

"Oh, it wouldn't cross their minds that you'd slum it with someone like me," he says with a harsh laugh.

"You know that's not what I meant." I'm proud of how detached I sound, particularly since my heart is practically beating its way out of my chest. "They won't take me seriously if...I won't go over there with you."

"That's okay," he says with a bemused smile. "I can make my own way. Maybe I'll take my bicycle."

I clench my jaw. "You do that."

He turns to walk away, and I remember with a start that I'm still wearing his coat. He must be freezing in that shirt.

"Liam, your coat!"

He peers back at me, his lips quirked up. "Keep it. It looks better on you." His lips inch up further. "In fact, wear it tomorrow night if you'd like. We'll give them something to talk about."

CHAPTER NINETEEN

LIAM

I'm not going to admit this to anyone, particularly not Dottie, but when I check the beer's gravity in the morning, and it's exactly where it needs to be, I decide there's something to be said for singing and crystals and chasing luck like it's a leprechaun.

I tell Briar we're on track. Her relief seems on par with mine, but she barely says a word to me afterward. She's angry at me for accepting her father's dinner invitation. I get that. I have a parent who isn't likeable either, and I'd break time and space to keep Briar from having dinner with her. Doesn't mean I'm going to respect Briar's wishes. I'm going as her backup tonight, with one mission.

I don't care who Daddy Sterling is, I don't care how much he's worth—he's not going to make his daughter feel like shit tonight.

Even if she made me feel like shit yesterday.

The day passes quickly, and before I know it, I'm riding my bike toward Sterling Manor.

The air is so crisp it hurts, but it feels good too—like a slap in the face when you need to focus.

When I get to the address Don provided, I roll to a stop in front of the gate and press the call button.

Of course there's a gate. God forbid anyone uninvited should get in—or anyone invited should have an easy escape. It strikes me as ironic that the Sterlings' gate is painted gold rather than silver.

A woman's voice answers over the intercom, "Sterling Manor," and after I provide my name, she buzzes me through. That's a nice surprise—I figured I'd be asked for my social security number, birthdate, and a government-issued ID. Actually, I'm kind of sorry they didn't ask, because I would have enjoyed denying them.

A long, black-paved, circular drive leads to a tall, bland white house with pillars supporting a front porch decked out with white rockers and built-in ceiling fans. I park my bike facing the gate, behind two back-to-back black town cars, before heading to the front door. There's no sign of Briar's little car, so presumably she was picked up.

The door opens before I get there, and Briar steps into the entrance, golden light spilling out around her. She's a vision in a green floor-length dress, her golden hair cascading around her shoulders, but she's dressed for a fancy dinner, not Friday night at the folks'.

"I asked you not to come," she says in an undertone when I reach her.

"That's some dress." I gesture to my old jeans and black thermal shirt. "Does this mean I'm underdressed?"

She bites her bottom lip. "*Yes*."

Oh well. I have a feeling I won't be making a good impression tonight, no matter what I do. She peers over my shoulder, her eyes catching on my Triumph. "You really brought your motorcycle."

"I'll give you a ride if you ask nicely," I say, then grin at the scorching look on her face. "Let's go in. I also brought a six-pack."

"A six-pack?"

"I thought your old man would like to taste the goods."

A cold wind billows across the porch, so I wrap an arm around her and lead her back inside, closing the door behind us.

There's no one waiting in the foyer, which has a mottled marble floor leading to a curving staircase, beside which stands a large, obviously fake silver tree covered in white lights and bulb ornaments. It would only look impressive to someone who enjoys hotel lobbies, but maybe that's my childhood talking.

My mom took off when I was ten—Hannah was seven, and my brother was only a few months old. Our dad claimed he couldn't keep all of those cleaning sprays and brushes straight, so our house was always disorganized chaos. Dirty but comfortable. Less stressful than when my mother was there, watching us with thinly masked disapproval.

"They're in the sitting room," Briar says, tugging on a lock of her hair.

"Great. Lead the way."

She glances at me nervously. "I'll take your coat."

"You want this one too?" I tease, trying to get her to relax.

Her answering smile is weak as she takes it from me.

I watch her hang it up, and when she returns, I whisper, "Don't worry, Princess. I'm not going to tell your daddy what happened in his old office last week. Not even if he asks nicely."

She scowls and stands up straighter, which is exactly what I was aiming for—so I'm smiling as I follow her to the left of the stairway and around the corner, into a room with deep-maroon walls, oversized paintings that look like a toddler water-gunned paint onto the canvases, and dark, velvet-upholstered furniture.

Briar clearly didn't inherit her exquisite taste from her parents.

A squat man in dress pants and a collared shirt stands from the couch and holds out his hand. There's nothing of Briar in him except for the amber of his small, squinty eyes, but they lack her warmth. I take his sweaty palm and pump it once before nodding to the woman who just entered from the other doorway —a blonde in a red dress. Her hair is the same honeyed color as Briar's, but her eyes are a cold saltwater blue.

We exchange polite introductions. Me, Liam. Him, Don. Her, Alicia. Briar's parents make the kind of light, meaningless conversation that strangers might exchange in an elevator.

"I presume Briar didn't tell you about the dress code," Alicia says after a minute, tutting her tongue.

"Actually, Don here is the one who invited me. Briar's always very good about communicating the rules. We keep a whole list of them at the brewery."

Briar shoots me a surprised look. Probably because no one's ever stood up for her in this depressing-ass place. I don't need her to tell me that. The writing is on the wall.

Don gives a low laugh. "Well, she always was a rule follower. Not much of a leader, no matter how hard we've tried."

"The person who creates the rules *is* the leader, Don, wouldn't you say?" I give him a smile that says *fuck you* as clearly as if the words ripped out of my mouth. I didn't like him before I met him. I definitely don't like him now. Briar's mother is no better, simpering and agreeing with his every word. Barely even bothering to look at her daughter.

He laughs as if I'd made a joke. "Well, I'm not surprised she's had to make some rules for *you*." Shifting his attention to Briar, he adds, "I'm glad you're finding your backbone, sweetheart. I guess Briar Boot Camp was a success."

"Briar Boot Camp?"

"Let's not do this, Dad," Briar says tightly.

Ignoring her, he tells me, "Just my nickname for the program I started a few months ago to toughen up my girl. I don't know if she told you, but her last business was a failure. Success takes work."

Briar's cheeks go pink, and anger buckets into my bloodstream. I snap the band at my wrist so hard it nearly breaks.

"She's lucky she's got so many people rooting for her," I say dryly. "What kind of program was this, exactly?"

"Let's sit down at the dining room table," Briar suggests, already walking as she says it.

Don throws a hand toward the door in a show of exasperation. "What my daughter doesn't understand is that feelings have no place in business, but you get it, Liam. I can tell you do."

I don't respond. But only because Briar would probably prefer it if I don't say the words I'm choking back.

We follow her down a hall lit with antique fixtures, to a butter-yellow dining room with an oversized rectangular mahogany table at the center, surrounded by chairs upholstered in leather with brass fixings.

But my gaze isn't on the furnishings—it's on the heavy wooden plaque bracketed to the wall, right above one of the five chairs with place settings.

Don's Recipe for Success, it reads.

Briar resignedly sits in the chair beneath it.

"Ah," the big guy says, patting his chest as he lowers into the chair at the head of the table. "I see you've noticed my wife's little gift to me."

"Nothing little about it." It could definitely brain someone if it fell. Brain Briar, to be specific. "Is there assigned seating?"

"Yes," Alicia says, beaming. "You'll sit opposite Briar, between Don and me, so the girls can get cozy across from us."

"Girls?" Briar asks with a frown, eyeing the setting next to hers with suspicion.

Her parents sit down, so I round the table and do the same.

"We have another guest joining us for dessert this evening," Don says. "Didn't I mention it?"

"No," she objects emphatically, "you didn't. Who's coming?"

"Your friend Melly."

Briar instantly turns to me, her back stiff. "I think I'd like to have one of those beers now, Liam."

"You brought beer?" Alicia asks with a sour look. "I selected wines to accompany the courses."

"No problem. I'm sure she'll have some of that too," I say, pulling the six-pack out of my backpack and handing Briar the one she likes best, the spiced fig ale.

"We don't have a bottle opener," Alicia says stiffly—an obvious lie. In a house like this, where wealth is flaunted, they probably have five of everything.

"No need." I pull the bottle back, then press the cap against the lip of the table and tap it open.

"The wood..." her mother gasps.

I hand the beer across the table to Briar, who's watching me closely, a smile playing on her lips.

After she takes it, I lift up the rest of the six-pack by the cardboard holder. "Anyone else in the mood to indulge? We're going to be brewing all of these at Silver Star, eventually. We figured you'd be interested. Family business and all that."

Don, who's been studying me with the fascination of a tourist on safari, nods. "Yes. I think I will."

I hold out the six-pack so he can choose which one he wants. The bottles are labeled with masking tape—a classy little touch I thought he'd enjoy.

"Dealer's choice," he decides.

"Oh, wait one second," Alicia says, losing her cool. "Wait just one second." She rushes out of the room.

"Did she leave something in the oven?" I ask as I open another of the beers on the table.

Then a third.

I hand one of them to Don, who's chuckling. He wags a finger at me. "I heard you were trouble."

"Glad Briar speaks so fondly of me." I let myself admire her as she takes a long sip of her beer.

"Not from Briar," Don says dismissively in a way that instantly raises my hackles. "Briar's bleeding heart always gets her into trouble." He flicks a finger at the recipe for success. "*Look beyond others' feelings.* She can't. Bleeding heart, like I said. But *I* can. So I asked around about you, sure. It's a man's right to look out for his family." He has a *gotcha* smirk on his face when he says, "I heard about the fight at Mountain Morning."

"It's not exactly a secret, and I wouldn't call it a fight. The only injury I had was to my knuckles, so I guess you'd say it was more of a beatdown. But you don't need to worry about that. I graduated from anger management. They even gave me a silver star."

Briar coughs, suppressing a laugh, and I grin at her before focusing on Don.

He runs a hand across his smooth jaw. "I also heard you got fired from Big Catch."

"Aw, but that was a misunderstanding. I had every intention of quitting. My boss beat me to it."

He narrows his eyes at Briar. "John says you've hired other people."

"I have." She straightens her back.

"And do *they* have checkered work histories?"

I snort. "Maybe so. From my understanding, the majority of them were recruited off dating apps."

"Dating apps?" he sputters, his face reddening. He thinks I'm screwing with him but doesn't understand how.

"Sure. Who else would have been available in the time frame you gave her?"

"We've been open since Monday," Briar says, ignoring me.

"Pretty incredible, don't you think?" I ask her shithead father. "Not many people could manage a thing like that. I'm surprised you haven't stopped by."

"I'll be sure to put in an appearance after the holidays," he replies with a wolfish smile. No doubt he'll put together a whole smorgasbord of complaints to bring up at these enjoyable dinners.

"We're only pouring Bubba's beer right now," I say, "so you might want to wait until our big party if you're looking for something different."

"You're trying to put out a new beer by New Year's?" he asks with interest.

"It was your daughter's idea. She's got a helluva lot of good ones. You must think so too if you made the whole brewery organic on her say-so."

Don's expression sharpens, and I know—I fucking know— this asshole was in on the grift.

"Did you know Bubba wasn't using organic ingredients, Dad?" Briar asks directly, her face pale but determined.

She's not mine to be proud of, but I *am* proud.

Before he can answer, Alicia power-walks back into the dining room, a bottle opener in each hand, followed by a woman carrying white wine in a wine chiller.

Alicia's lips tremble when she sees the other open beers. "Oh dear."

"Would you like one too?" I ask, grabbing another beer from the holder.

"No." She gives a sharp nod to the woman with the wine, then shoves the bottle openers at her. "We'll all have wine," she says imperiously. "And you can bring out the salad course."

Within thirty seconds, she has an overfull glass of white in front of her.

Don, who has been holding Briar's gaze this whole time, finally says, "Well, I don't have the first clue what you're talking about, Briar. We told Bubba to brew them organic, so I assume that's what he did. Bubba's a man who can take instruction."

"Yeah, I'll just bet he is," I put in as the rest of us are served wine I definitely don't want. "And I've got no problem taking *her* instructions."

"Oh, no more business talk," Alicia says, waving around her wine glass after taking a swig that roughly halved the liquid. "I'm sick to death of hearing about that brewery. I thought we were finally done with it. It was my least favorite of all your businesses."

I let myself laugh. "Really, I figured it would have been the gummy candy shaped like tits."

She gasps, and the server hurries away.

Don, however, smiles. "Touché. Well, no worries, honey. The brewery is Briar's problem now."

He takes the first sip of his beer, and then his gaze narrows on me. "You made this, son?"

"I did."

He glances at Briar, sitting under that self-indulgent sign, her expression strained, and nods. "Good work."

I nearly laugh, because he's talking about me, in front of me, as if I'm some bargain-basement find. But the hopeful look on her face stops me.

I'm destroyed by the realization that she still wants this asshole's praise.

"Well, I, for one, would much rather talk about pleasant things," Alicia says, and takes another long sip from her wine glass. "What are you doing for the holidays, Liam?"

It feels plenty natural to smile. "Making beer."

The server returns with a tray of salads, which she passes out, and a short, blessed period of silence follows while everyone embraces the excuse of eating to shut the fuck up. Then Alicia leads a shallow conversation about the holiday events around Asheville, which isn't particularly interesting, given I don't plan on attending any of them.

My eyes keep straying to Briar.

She doesn't like being here, but I don't think it's just that contract she signed that keeps her coming back. She still wants approval from these people, and I know in my gut she's never going to get it. Because if they ever gave it to her, she'd have no reason to come back.

As we're finishing up the main course, the buzzer for the gate rings, and Alicia perks up. "That must be Melly."

Briar takes another sip of her beer. "By all means, we wouldn't want to keep *Melly* waiting."

CHAPTER TWENTY

BRIAR

In, hold, out. In, hold, out.

I'm hardly doing well, but at least I haven't needed to run to the kitchen to search for a paper bag. Being in this house always makes me feel like a child lost in a labyrinth. Never alone, but always alone.

I don't like that Liam is across the table from me, seeing me like this. Meek. Quiet. Accepting. I transform every time I step through that door, turning back into Briar the Doll. Briar, the seen but not heard.

Briar, the obedient daughter.

And now I'm going to have to sit down next to *Melly* and pretend she isn't the one person I truly hate.

I lift Liam's beer for another sip, find the bottle empty, and glance at him across the table. He must see the need in my eyes, because without a word, he takes another beer out of the six-pack, ignores the two bottle openers my mother set down beside him, and opens it on the edge of the table.

I smile as he hands the bottle to me. Part of me is glad he's here. He's made it clear he's on my team. Before I met my new friends, I didn't even have a team. No one had ever really stood up for me.

At the same time, Liam wouldn't be here if not for Hannah —Hannah, who made her boundaries very clear.

The smile ghosts off my face as heels click-clack toward the dining room, and my mother emerges with Melly, who is dressed in a black floor-length dress with lacy three-quarter-length sleeves. Her auburn hair is chin length and perfectly curled around her sweetheart face.

"Well, *hello*," she says.

She's not talking to me. Her eyes slid right past me as if I were wallpaper, finding Liam. His muscles are straining against that black shirt, which brings out the red in his hair.

"Who are *you*?" Melly continues.

A horrible feeling creeps through me, like black mold spreading under my skin.

She obviously wants him, just like all the women at the brewery, and she usually gets what she wants...

But instead of getting up to greet her, Liam leans back in his chair and crosses his arms over his chest. "I'm Liam. I work with Briar."

It's obviously his turn to ask who she is, but he doesn't.

Undaunted, she hugs my father, calling him "Uncle Don," and then sashays around to Liam, holding out her hand.

He shakes it with a flat expression.

"I'm Melly. I'm Briar's best friend from boarding school."

I drop my beer bottle.

It cracks on the floor and sprays fizzy liquid. My dress is mostly unscathed, but the wood flooring under the table gets doused.

"Briar!" my mother practically screams.

Blood is beating in my ears. I can feel everyone staring at me, just like they did the night the whole staff of Silver Star quit. I hear my mother leaving the room, heading toward the kitchen. I can feel Liam taking in my shame and lack of grace.

"Still such a butterfingers," Melly says as she helps herself to my mother's chair.

"My mom's sitting there."

"I'll move when she gets back," she says, her arm brushing against Liam's. Her features scrunch. "I don't want to sit in beer."

Liam gets up, surprisingly graceful for such a big man. "I'll sit in it. I prefer smelling like beer." As he passes me, he skims his fingers across my shoulder, giving it a quick squeeze. It happens so quickly, I might have questioned whether it really happened if not for the heat trailing from that spot.

Emotion clogs my throat as I watch him collect the bigger pieces of glass on the floor into a pile. Then he takes the napkin from the unused place setting and swipes the chair and sits down next to me.

"So, Melly," my father says, not remotely interested in the seating arrangements or the mess. "Your father's told me all about your success. He says it's not easy to break into social influencing. That's what you call it, right?"

"Yes, I'm an influencer," she says, smirking at me. Reminding me that she played that role before, and that she was good at it then too.

My hands fist beneath the table.

"What, exactly, do you influence?" Liam asks.

"People," she says with a wide, red-lipped smile. "People who want to look like me, or have a similar lifestyle."

"So you're an advertiser."

"It's more like a public service."

He wings his eyebrows up. "Oh? In what way?"

My mother rushes in with her housekeeper, Martha, who has a massive stack of towels, a trash bag, a mop, and a bottle of multi-purpose cleaner. The chef who cooked our dinner is following them, holding a tray with five dessert plates containing some kind of fruit tart I don't want to eat.

"Let me clean it up," I say as Liam gets up. "Please. I'm the one who made the mess."

I don't know Martha well—my mother always has a new housekeeper—but the woman must be at least sixty-five, and I don't want her getting down on her knees to clean up after me.

"Honestly," my mother says, rolling her eyes, "that's what she's here for."

I ignore my mother. "I'm not trying to do your job, Martha, but it was my mess. I'd like to clean it."

She silently checks in with my mom, who rolls her eyes again for posterity before nodding. Martha hands over the cleaning supplies, and Liam holds a trash bag open for me so I can pick up the rest of the glass. He helps mop up the floor, too, but Martha insists on bringing everything back to the kitchen herself.

My father chuckles to himself as Liam and I return to our seats.

"It's like I told you, son." He points a finger at the wooden plaque hanging over my head. "My daughter will never get anywhere because she cares too much about other people's feelings. Make sure you don't keep making the same mistake."

I take a bite of the tart, which is probably delicious but tastes flavorless in my mouth.

"She's always been like that," Melly says, cutting into her fruit tart with the side of her fork. "Too sensitive." Giving me a sly smile, she says, "Remember that time I borrowed your doll?"

My heart seizes in my chest. I can't believe she's actually admitting to it, talking about it as if it were nothing. As if it were *funny*.

"Yes," I say after a moment. "*I remember.*"

She flourishes her fork at me. "You know, your dad actually gave me twenty bucks to do that. He wanted to see how you'd react."

My father shakes his head. "And of course she let you keep it for a whole week."

The floor falls away beneath my feet. My father has always loved "throwing down the gauntlet," as he likes to say, but I was six years old and homesick and *scared*. Losing that doll to someone I'd been told would be my friend had chipped away at the one solid piece in my foundation.

I get to my feet.

Liam stands up beside me, stepping closer so his side touches mine. Strength laps off of him, bolstering me. I can feel him telling me I can do this—I can finally take a stand.

Still staring at my father, I ask, "Did you tell her to chop off all my hair too?"

He looks surprised, thank God, but my rage doesn't care. I've never been this angry before. I've always turned my fury on myself, but now I know my father has never been on my side. Never. I was just a game to him. A gamble. He never wanted me to succeed for *my* sake.

"I think your recipe for success is bullshit and always has been," I say.

My mother gasps. "Language, Briar."

"Everyone thinks so." I dart a look at Melly, who has whipped cream on the corner of her mouth. I wish I could take a photo. "And you're not a real influencer, *Melly*. You only have eleven thousand followers on Instagram, and you live off your trust fund. I can only imagine you got connected to the paper through someone your father cut a deal with."

Her pointed stare is probably supposed to be scathing. It probably would be if I cared what she thought of me anymore.

"Your father just gave you a brewery, Briar. You're hardly in a position to judge."

"Yeah," I say, "but I don't try to pretend to be something I'm not. Let's go, Liam."

He strolls around the table and grabs what's left of the six-pack, shoving it into his rucksack before saluting my parents and Melly. "I wish I could say it's been a pleasure, but I don't lie for other people's benefit if I don't like them."

He returns to me, pressing a steadying palm to the small of my back as we walk out of the room, heading toward the foyer. I can feel the support radiating from him. It's the only thing saving me from hyperventilating.

When we reach the cold marble entryway, I realize there's a flaw in my escape plan.

"I don't have my car." Defeat slumps my shoulders. I couldn't bear to ask my father to give me a lift, and I don't want to wait in their yard for an Uber. I'd feel like a child sitting at a bus stop, waiting for a school bus.

"Won't be a problem," Liam says.

I open the coat closet, and he darts a wolfish grin at me when he sees it: his two coats, hanging side by side.

"You actually wore it," he says with a grin.

"I wanted to see if they'd say anything."

"Did they?" he asks, pulling it off the hanger. He holds the coat open for me, and my throat clogs with emotion. It's such a simple thing, but so few people have wanted to take care of me.

"My mother said she was buying me a new coat. So I have that to look forward to." I slide my arms into the sleeves, feeling the soft glide of his fingers through the fabric. "Why isn't it a problem that I don't have my car?"

"Because we're taking my bicycle," he says wryly.

My pulse kicks up at the thought of riding his motorcycle with him. "But you must only have one helmet."

"And you'll be wearing it."

"What about your head?" I ask as he gets his coat on.

Am I really going to leave with him?

"I've been told it's harder than dried cement," he says. "But I'll try extra hard not to get into an accident."

He pauses after opening the door—waiting for me to decide—and that's what does it. I step out into the night with him. The cold wraps around me, but I barely feel it. My pulse is still racing, my blood heated, and that awful anger is thrumming through me, needing to be released.

I tug Liam's arm, and he halts, turning toward me. He towers over me, but no part of me is intimidated by him anymore. I feel protected when I'm with him.

"Liam, I want you to take me to the boxing gym. Please. I need it."

CHAPTER TWENTY-ONE

LIAM

I can't deny her, even if the ground beneath me feels like the thin ice I crawled across to rescue our dog, Bets, when I was a kid. I fell into the pond and nearly drowned.

Don't regret it, even though Bets fell in with me. I kept an iron grip on her, and when I was saved, so was she.

I won't regret this, either. Or at least I won't regret helping Briar. She just proved she's capable of standing up for herself, but she deserves someone else to stand up for her too.

Besides, if I don't do as she asks, I'll probably do something rash. I've already had at least a dozen intrusive thoughts about beating Don Sterling bloody and burning Sterling Manor to the ground.

"You got it, Princess," I say. "We'll go now."

When we get to the bike, I hand her the helmet from the top box, expecting she'll make a fuss about accepting it. I'll have to put it on her myself if she tries to object, but she doesn't. She slips it on her head, then adjusts the strap until it's as tight as it goes. Still too big for her but better than nothing, because we have to get out. Now. The need to get away thrums off her like a low chord from Cormac's bass.

I gesture to Briar's long dress. "How attached are you to that dress?"

"My mother bought it for me. I hate it."

I grab the utility knife out of my backpack and hand it to her. "We don't want it getting caught in the wheel."

Eyes shining, she opens the knife and slices half her skirt off, revealing her legs, encased in black stockings that hug her every dip and curve.

"God, that felt good," she says, handing the knife back to me. I return it to my bag without looking, my gaze on her legs. The loose green fabric flutters down from her fingers and gets caught by the wind. Before either of us can grab it, it ripples up and into a tree and snags on a branch. It looks like a flag, and I'll be damned if I wouldn't pledge allegiance to Briar's flag.

She's laughing, her eyes gleaming, as she climbs onto the bike after me and clings to my waist. She nestles her head into my shoulder, and an unfamiliar feeling unfurls in my chest.

I want her, obviously, but I'm used to that by now. This is a bristly, protective feeling that's usually reserved for my sister and brother.

Those fuckers at that table hurt her. They all hurt her, and they should pay.

"I've never been on a motorcycle before," she whispers in my ear.

"All you need to remember is to hang on tight, Princess. Don't ever let go."

The front door of Sterling Manor bursts open.

"Briar?" her father bellows.

"Does the gate open automatically when people are leaving?" I ask Briar.

If not, I'll have to try pushing it open manually while her father shouts at me. Not ideal, but I bet I can do it. Bonus points if I break it.

"Yes." Her arms squeeze around me, a tendril of her hair tickling my neck. "Let's go."

"Briar, get back here right this moment," her father snaps. "You're acting like a child."

We're facing the gate, but I reach back and give him the finger. I figure the anger management classes must have worked after all, because I settle for doing no more than that.

I rev up the bike, getting a gasp from Briar, and then we're on the move. The gate opens before us like a promise. *You CAN get the fuck out of here, congratulations.*

Truthfully, it feels good not having the helmet on. The air is whistling in my ears and blowing my hair back from my face. Danger dances through my veins.

Nah, it's her that's got me feeling like my blood is dancing.

The whole way to the gym, Briar holds me tightly, her arms wrapped around my waist, her whole body arced into mine. Probably because she's scared she's going to fall off, but I like the way it feels.

My dick likes it too. It gets a little harder every second.

This trip to the gym isn't about me, though. Briar's got some shit to exorcise. Been there, needed that. Better for her to do it with me than to blow up her life.

When we get to the gym, all the lights are out, not that I expected anything different. It must be past nine, which means the place is ours. Mick gave me a key last year when he needed someone to stick around late on the weekend to receive a package, and he's never asked for it back. I think he understands that I sometimes need to work out when no one else is around—when it's only me and my demons. And he's a good enough friend to support me without being asked.

After I park the bike, I wait for Briar to get off, and then I climb off myself, watching as she removes the helmet. Her fingers are shaking a little, so I take over and then return the helmet to its spot on the bike.

I can't resist running a hand through her hair to smooth it. Her beauty strums another chord inside of me.

"Liam," she whispers, her soft eyes holding mine.

So much sadness and need are carried on my name. I want to drown in those deep waters, but I also want to survive, so I start walking toward the front door of Bell's.

She follows me but waits a few steps away while I unlock the door. Probably because she's feeling it too—the potential for everything to shift in a way we shouldn't allow.

The familiar scents of the gym wash over me. Sweat and dust. I take off my coat and hang it, and in my peripheral vision I watch Briar do the same. She pauses before removing her high-heeled shoes as well.

I lock the door behind us and head onto the main floor of the gym.

I don't look back as she trails me inside. I can't. The sound of her padding in after me is enough to sharpen my awareness of her.

I make my way to the rack of gloves, finding the pair that's too big. I make a mental note to get this woman some gloves that fit. If she's going to make this brewery work despite everything stacked against her, she's going to need them.

I can do that for her.

At least I can do that.

She pauses beside me, and I let myself soak her in. She looks so sad it makes me want to kill someone, to be perfectly honest. The anger is hot and brutal and familiar, and it feels good.

Anger is never confusing. It doesn't make you feel helpless. It demands.

"You *should* be angry," I tell her, the words coming out like sandpaper. "I'm fucking angry."

She surprises me by smiling. "Why?"

"No one gets to treat you that way. Especially not them."

I've been watching her for weeks. Trying to come up with ways to make this brewery work for her sake as much as mine. Because she's the kind of woman who makes a man want to believe.

"Put them on," I say, handing the gloves to her.

I watch as she does, her hands still trembling.

"That woman at your parents' house. You said she cut your hair?"

She pulls the gloves on. She should look ridiculous in that ruined green dress and the boxing gloves, but she doesn't. She's a vision. A fucking goddess. An angel.

Mine, a voice in my head whispers. And I practically claw the back of my head to shut it up.

Briar meets my gaze, and I'm grateful to see the spark of determination in her eyes.

"The boy she had a crush on liked me."

"Of course he fucking did. Who would settle for her if they thought they might have a shot with you?"

She gives me a trembling smile. "I've always kept my hair long. I like it this way. It makes me feel..." She shrugs. "It's stupid."

"It makes you feel safe." I let my fingers trace the length of one of the locks. "Nothing stupid about wanting to feel safe."

She turns to me with a gleam in her eyes. "How did you know?"

"Takes one to know one, Princess. Now, what did that cunt do to you?"

"You sound like Hannah."

"We were raised by the same asshole. There was no hope for either of us."

"You met my father," she says softly, the words knifing through me.

"Yes, that was my displeasure. Now, what did she do to you? You might as well tell me now. If you don't, I'm going to take it upon myself to find out."

She glances down, and without thinking, I reach over and tip her chin up—tension flash-frying me when our eyes meet.

She's quiet for a moment, and I don't think she's going to confide in me. None of my business, really, so I should back the fuck off. But for once in my life, I want to know something I've got no right knowing.

She parts her lips. "She..." Pain fills her eyes, and I stroke her chin with my fingers. "She and her friends...they had this dumb club. They invited me to join them, and I was so excited, even though she'd always been kind of mean to me. Melly said I had to meet them in this old cabin in the woods..." She takes a break, working up to it. "They tied me to a chair and chopped my hair off. All of it. It wasn't this long back then, but it was way past my shoulders. There were..." She swallows, her eyes full of tears. "There were some patches that were practically bald in the back. They left me out there in the cabin, and no one found me until the next morning."

"I see," I say, already calculating what I could do to ruin this woman's life. I'd never hurt her physically, but there are many ways you can ruin a person. Sure, the assault happened years ago, but it's obvious Melly feels as much remorse over what she did as I feel about hitting the owner of Mountain Morning. "And I suppose they warned you not to tell anyone."

Briar nods, her chin moving in my hand, which is still cupping it. "I said I'd decided to cut my hair. My parents and the teachers thought...they thought I'd had some kind of episode. Melly got all of the other kids to call me Batshit Briar."

"And you still didn't tell."

"No one…"

"You don't think anyone would have done anything," I say woodenly, feeling like I probably should have turned pyro and set that mansion on fire after all.

The look on her face says it all.

I run my hands through her gorgeous hair. "You don't cut it much."

"I trim it myself," she says in a voice that's thin but strong. "I don't want to let anyone else do it."

I take a moment to try to choke down the feelings rising up in my chest. Anger, of course. Always anger. But also a softer feeling—the kind that can crush a man if he's not careful.

"The doll," I say, barely able to get the words through my clenched jaw. "How old were you?"

"Six."

I release her and grab another pair of gloves—not mine, but I don't have any patience for retrieving mine right now. In all honesty, I don't want to wear any. I'd like to feel the give of my flesh when the punches land on the bag, but I also have that fight coming up, not to mention all the challenges at the brewery. It's no time to break myself.

I put the gloves on while I prowl over to the heavy bags, leaving Briar to her bag as I pour my rage into mine. A growl tears out of me as I beat it with my fists, hitting as hard as I can. Needing to get the worst of the rage out.

But I keep seeing the way Briar recoiled from me the first time we were at this gym. It was because of that woman. *Melly*. That woman's got no sweetness and light, but she might not have felt bold enough to try anything if Briar's asshole father hadn't encouraged her.

They hurt her. They all hurt her and stole from her—her hair, her strength, her safety—and I want to *destroy* them. The dark need consumes me.

I throw punch after punch, sensing Briar doing the same beside me, and then the seam splits on the old bag I'm going at, and stuffing explodes into the air.

I laugh and edge back, finally looking directly at Briar, who's staring at me with wide eyes. Her pink lips are parted, and her hair's a sweaty mess around her shoulders because I forgot to give her the elastic.

"Are you afraid of me?" I ask hesitantly. I don't want that. That's the last thing I want. I would die before I hurt her.

"No." She drops her gloves, which she must have removed at some point. "I'm afraid for you."

What a Briar answer.

"You think the bag's going to take revenge?"

She takes a step toward me. Then another, spanning the space between us.

"I don't like that you didn't wear a helmet earlier. I hope you don't do that a lot."

"Only when I have to save a lady in distress."

"You save a lot of ladies?" she asks, her voice hardening.

"Most of the women I've spent time with lately don't need saving."

Her expression falls, and I realize that for the first time in a long, long time, I care what someone thinks of me—and right now, she's not thinking anything good.

"You don't either," I say quickly, tearing the gloves off and letting them drop. "But you make me want to rescue you."

She reaches for my hands and runs her fingers over them before lifting one of them to her lips. She watches me as she kisses the knuckles. I've lost some sensation across my knuckles —too many hits—but I feel every millimeter of her sweet, soft mouth.

I wrap the other arm around her, feeling an impossible need pulse through me.

"You're not going there for Christmas," I say. It doesn't come out as a question.

Surprise fills her eyes. "Why do you care?"

"I just do."

"I'd be alone."

"You won't be alone. I'll make sure of it."

She licks her lips, and suddenly I can't take it anymore. I can't wait. I can't hold her at arm's length, when that's the last thing I want to do.

"Fuck it." I weave my hand through her hair, gripping it, and lower my mouth to hers, the way I've been dreaming about ever since I kissed her in her office.

She kisses me back, thank Christ, pushing up into me like she wants our mouths to fuse together.

I can't have her. She's not mine. But I don't pull away. I need the feeling of her lips against mine, and the little moans she's making in the back of her throat. She weaves her arms around the back of my neck and pulls me down to her like she wants to consume me.

She could if she wanted to. I'd let her swallow me whole.

I suck in her bottom lip, then pull away just enough to say, "The bench," my voice so ragged with need I barely recognize it.

She leans in and kisses me again. I lift her up by the hips, and she laughs into my mouth as she wraps her long legs around my waist. I'm still kissing her as I move blindly toward the bench, sucking on her lips and her tongue. When I finally reach it, I sit back, lowering her with me, and she's straddling my dick again, just like the other night.

Her hair is everywhere, and I grab a fistful and tug it lightly as I kiss her, moaning when she presses her hips into me. I break away, my face still inches from hers, and say, "You're beautiful and strong. They don't deserve you."

Wonder is written across her face, and it kills me. I tug her closer, wanting to absorb her pain and kiss every delicious inch of her.

She pulls away slightly, doubt flickering in her eyes. "We shouldn't be doing this."

"Oh, I fucking know it. Right now, I don't care."

Resolve hardens in her gaze. "This is what I want. This is what is going to make me feel better tonight. We don't have to make a big deal out of it at work, and..." She sucks her lower lip between her teeth. "It would be better if Hannah never knows."

"That's for damn sure." I pause, studying her, my hand lowering from her hair to her perfectly sculpted ass. Her legs are still wrapped around me, as if she wants to keep me here and mistakenly thinks there's even chance in hell I'd willingly leave. It makes me feel wanted in the best kind of way, even though there's a warning siren blaring in the back of my head. The knowledge that this shouldn't be happening, and there will be a price I might not want to pay.

She said she needs me, though, and I'm not backing away.

My body is the only thing I know how to give people anyway, and if she wants it, it's hers. For tonight.

"Are you saying what I think you're saying?" I ask.

I already know the answer, but I'd like to hear the words in her sweet voice.

She takes a slow, deep breath, her whole body shuddering against me, then nods. "I want to be with you tonight." She glances at the door. "Is there...is there any chance someone else will come in?"

My dick instantly gets harder. I didn't think she meant she wanted to do it *in here*.

CHAPTER TWENTY-TWO

BRIAR

The look on Liam's face sends panic skating through me, even though I can feel how much he wants me. It's literally pressing into me, making me dirty promises.

Big promises.

"You want it here?" he asks.

"Oh my God," I say, alarmed. "You think I'm a slut. I mean, here I am, practically begging you to—"

I try to get up, but he firms his grip on my butt.

"I don't think you're a slut, but I'm not about to complain if you want me to fuck you." His voice is a lustful growl, and I'm so turned on by the way he says *fuck*—confidently, with zero, well, fucks. He pulls me closer, his next words practically whispered against my lips. "But I figured you'd take me back to your apartment."

"I don't do this sort of thing. I'm usually in relationships, but after I found out about Jonah—"

The sound he makes now is definitely a growl.

"You don't like talking about Jonah," I say. "I remember. I don't like talking about him either, but he's the last man I—"

He stops me with a hard kiss, lifting his hips as his mouth claims mine. He kisses me like he wants to suck my soul out of my body. I can feel him beneath me, straining for me, and I'm sure I'm sopping wet. It'll be embarrassing when he feels it.

He pulls back, his eyes glimmering, his jaw a hard, severe line. "I want to make you forget that asshole's name for good."

"You're jealous?" I ask.

The possibility had never occurred to me. Hannah made it clear that Liam doesn't date. He hooks up with women. He gets them hooked on *him*.

I feel a pulse of anxiety, worried that that's exactly where I'm headed, but then he looks me over with hooded eyes and says, "I don't like to think about him being within fifty feet of you. So, yes, I guess you could say I'm fucking jealous."

"You're the only person who does this to me," I admit. "I've never asked anyone else to touch me in a public place."

"Good."

This time I kiss him, pushing down with my hips so I can feel him right where I need him. Oh God. It's been so long since anyone has touched me like this, and I'm feverish for him. I want all of him. I need to feel *alive* after being trapped in that mausoleum tonight, and I know he's the man who can give me that. The only man who can make me feel good right now.

"You didn't answer me," I whisper against his lips, hovering less than an inch from him.

"I've forgotten every question anyone's ever asked me," he says, his lips curving into a grin.

"Will anyone show up?"

"No. I'm the only one who has a key other than the owner and the cleaning service. And the cleaning service only comes in the afternoon, just after closing."

My answer is to get up and pull the dress up over my head. I go for the clasp of my bra, but he stops me, his eyes shining with admiration. "I'd like to do that myself in a minute."

My mouth goes dry as he gets to his feet, every action fluid, because even though he's a big man, he's an athlete. Then he tugs his shirt over his head, and it feels like all the blood in my body is suddenly pounding between my legs.

His body is a sculpted work of art, and he has a Celtic tattoo that weaves around his right bicep. I've never noticed it before now. I've only really spent time with him in winter, and long-sleeved shirts have hidden it from view.

He also has a few scars, including one that's a few inches wide on his upper chest.

"Liam..." I trace his tattoo with my fingers, wanting to learn every dip and swirl, and the hot, hard muscle under my fingers fills me with longing.

Usually with men, I'm concerned about where sex might lead. I already know it's a dead-end road for the two of us, which is surprisingly freeing. I'm analyzing myself less, and feel completely in the moment.

He shoves my stockings and underwear down one-handed, then reaches for me, his hand finding my wetness. His pupils consume his eyes as he works me with his fingers, the sound of it making me blush even as I'm consumed with the pleasure from what he's doing to me.

"This is for me," he says in a commanding tone.

I find myself nodding.

His lips skate across my collarbone, dropping kisses as he moves his fingers, and then he leans in and softly bites my neck. That sensation, paired with what he's doing with his fingers, makes my knees weak.

"Liam..."

"Wait here for a second."

He pushes the bench we were on up against a wall made of old white concrete blocks. There's some kind of schedule taped to it, but Liam wrenches it off the wall and tosses it aside before turning toward me, hand outstretched.

"I want you to take your stockings off and stand on this."

I'm so mesmerized that I don't even ask why. I pull them off the rest of the way, and then I let him give me a boost I don't need. Peering at me with an intense gaze, he gets down on his knees in front of me. "Wrap your leg around my shoulder."

"I usually can't come that way," I tell him, my knees practically buckling at the thought of him burying his head there while I'm so exposed. "It's okay. You can—"

"Any man who doesn't work for it doesn't deserve it. Wrap your leg around my shoulder." He runs his hands down my calf as he says so, the feeling surprisingly sensual.

So I do as he said, my whole body quivering with how much I want him to touch me, but also now with worry. He's going to think it takes too long. That it's too much to ask, and I'll feel like I have to pretend...

His mouth moves up my slick inner thigh, and soon every worry leaves my head as he kisses my leg, inching up slowly. He's acting as if he'd happily sacrifice everything for the opportunity to lick and suck and taste me until morning.

A shudder of pleasure works through me as he reaches my center, his tongue moving over me without hesitation. He traces the area where I'm so sensitive that every brush of his lips and tongue makes my body quake. He barely pauses to breathe as he throws himself into it, giving it everything. The same way he gave that bag his all, his muscles flexing and bunching as he beat his fists into it.

I'd stopped punching my own bag so I could devour the sight.

He's so *physical*...and it makes me want to exist in my own body more. I'd like to enjoy it with someone else. With *him*. I've been thinking about that possibility ever since that night in my office.

No, that's not totally true.

I've been thinking about it since our first day at Silver Star, when we started that list together. But something inside of me ignited when his lips touched mine. I feel it every time he looks at me, every time his fingers brush mine—and the sound of my name in his voice sends shudders of need through me.

It's also been so long since anyone has lavished attention on me and cared about my pleasure.

My body is starving for it.

Just for tonight. He can be yours tonight.

He surprises me by wrapping a hand around my hip, burying his face between my legs as he continues to suck and stroke me with his tongue. A tingling sensation washes through me, and I lean my head back into the wall, suddenly afraid I won't be able to keep my feet.

What if I tumble off the bench and onto the floor?

What if he gets tired of kneeling there?

What if putting his mouth on me secretly disgusts him?

"You don't have to do this, Liam, you—"

"Do you want me to stop?" he asks, lifting his head but taking over with his hand. He makes delicate circles and thrusts a thick finger inside.

"I'm going to fall."

"I'll catch you."

"I'm worried it's too much for you." I pant as he moves his finger inside of me.

"Then you're worried about the wrong thing, Princess," he says, his pupils still dilated. "Because it's not nearly enough."

He stares up at me as he presses his mouth to me again, sucking in and swirling with his tongue—and I reach down and grip his hair. That anchor to him calms me and allows me to lose myself to him.

I let the sensations take over, and it's barely a minute later that I feel a gush of deep, overwhelming pleasure that has my mouth falling open and inhuman sounds tumbling out. I press into his mouth rather than worry I'm going to smother him. When the quaking finally passes, he gently guides my leg down and then lays one final kiss before getting to his feet.

His smile is smug as he leans forward and kisses me.

I thought I'd be disgusted. No one has ever kissed me after doing *that* before. But it makes the need inside of me burn hotter.

"I thought you should know how good you taste," he says in a fevered whisper as he gathers my hair in his hand and kisses me more deeply, pulling me against his body with a command that makes my knees go weak again. He lifts me off the bench easily, our mouths still connected, and sets me on my feet.

I reach down for the button of his pants, and he smiles against my mouth as I fumble with it before getting it loose.

I tug down the zipper, and seconds later he has his pants and underwear pushed down. He springs into my hand, already so hard it takes my breath away. He's big, not that I'm surprised. Everything about him is big, and I've felt him against me, nudging me, telling me without words how much he wants me.

"I have an IUD," I whisper, "and I got tested after..." His jaw clenches. "Well, you know. But you...maybe we shouldn't."

"I haven't been with anyone for months," he says. My breath catches. From the way Hannah talked, I thought he was sexing women up left and right, but I've never known Liam to be anything but honest.

"Does this mean you want me to fuck you, Briar?" he continues. "I need to hear you say it."

"I...want you to fuck me."

His mouth closes over mine, and I whimper into it when he finally unclasps my bra, on the first try.

He pulls back and just looks at me for a long moment.

"What are you doing?" I ask softly.

"If I only get to see you like this once, I want to remember. You're the most beautiful woman I've ever known. You light up every room you're in, but not only because of the way you look. There's something inside of you that does it."

Hundreds of men have told me I'm beautiful. Tonight, I actually believe it.

He steps forward again and gathers me in his arms. I melt into him, not even wondering where we're going. It doesn't matter, really. I'd go anywhere with him.

He carries me over to the boxing ring before setting me down beside it.

"Here?" I ask with a smile as he sets me down.

"Yes. If I have this mental image, no one's going to be able to stop me. I'll win every match."

He pushes his pants down further.

"Take them off," I say, my mouth dry. "I want to see everything."

He grins as he does what he's told, revealing his muscular thighs. Oh God, he's so beautiful. There's another Celtic tattoo on his thigh, and his thick cock juts up toward me, making me promises.

My whole life has been a string of broken promises, but not tonight. Please not tonight.

I want this to be my last memory of when I was with a man —not my final time with Jonah. Quick and unsatisfying and... sad. Because I always felt so alone when I was with him.

Sex should never be sad.

Liam may not love me, but he's already shown up for me more than any other man ever has. It's a thought that should be depressing, but right now, it's not. It feels like a revelation. This is how relationships should be. In the past, I just accepted what others gave me, not realizing I could ask for more.

This man has done so much for me.

The way he's stood up for me over the past two weeks has helped me start to make my vision a reality. Even though he keeps insisting the brewery's only mine, we're building something together.

Liam lifts me up by the hips, his big hands spanning across my flesh. My legs wrap around him as he backs up, pressing my back to the insulated ropes around the ring. One of his hands cups my butt, holding me close.

"I'm going to think about you every time I'm in this ring," he says, leaning in and burying his face in my neck. His teeth graze my skin, and I buck against him, needing more. I want every last inch of him. Every beat of his heart. Every gusting breath. Every curl of ink on his body.

Tonight, just tonight.

"Now, Liam. *Please.* I need you."

"Hold onto the ropes like a good princess," he says, and I grip the top rope with both hands as he reaches down to adjust himself.

He rubs the tip against me, sending a shock wave of pleasure through me that renders me breathless. Then he slowly pushes in, the pressure catching me by surprise. He's bigger than anyone else I've been with. But I'm also wetter than I've ever been in my life, so turned on that I already feel on the cusp of coming again.

He moves slowly, getting me used to him, and my body stretches to take all of him. He's filling me up, and we're in his gym, and *we shouldn't be doing this*. But even though I've always tried to follow the rules, it feels so, so good. Better, even, because it shouldn't be happening.

Tears burn in my eyes, and horror ripples through me, because I can't let him see me cry. I can't. So I bury my face in his hard chest, kissing him there as he starts moving inside me, the friction of him delicious.

He groans, deep in his throat, and thrusts in hard, making the ropes shake behind me. "God, I'm not going to last long. This is...fuck, you feel so good, Briar. This is like every fantasy rolled into one."

Something about the way he says it—*fantasy*—sends spiderweb cracks through my enjoyment.

Fantasy.

Because it's not supposed to happen, and it won't happen again. It's a blip in reality. A mistake even as it's happening.

But the next time he thrusts in, he reaches for my face and kisses me deeply—and he keeps kissing me as he slows his thrusts, each one so deep I gasp into his mouth. He stares into my eyes as he takes me, my body going liquid with pleasure. It feels like *his*. And then he stuns me by pulling out.

"Turn around and hold the ropes," he says gruffly before leaning in and teasing one of my nipples with his teeth. "I need to be able to touch you."

I turn and do as I'm told, and he leans over me, his big, beautiful body cupping mine. Seconds later, he's inside me again, only his hand slides between my legs. He gently rubs me there as his thrusts turn harder and more possessive, his other hand wrapped around my hip. His grip is firm, and I know he'd never let me fall. He'd protect me from anything.

I feel myself coming apart, my breath turning loud, embarrassing sounds gusting from me as I tumble closer to the edge.

"Are you going to come for me?" he whispers, his fingers

toying with me as he thrusts in again, so big and wide and deep and—

Another strangled sound escapes me as the pleasure takes over, painting over all the dark feelings I've had tonight with pure joy.

I clench around him, and he groans, kissing my neck as he thrusts in again, and again, and then harder. But just when I'm sure he's going to pulse inside of me, he pulls out.

Confused, I turn around and see him moving his hand over himself, his arm flexing. Then he groans as he comes...into his hand.

I know without asking that he purposefully put that distance between us, and suddenly I feel very naked. I also feel like an idiot.

The emotion clogging my throat says this was more than a one-time release for me, but it's very clear that's all it was for him.

I force a smile, and he laughs and kisses the side of my mouth.

"Fuck, that was..." He trails off, the smile ghosting off his face, and then nods toward the locker room. "I'll be right back."

When he returns, I'm fully clothed.

A FEW MINUTES LATER, I'm clinging to Liam on the bike, feeling like I want to cry. Despite what just happened in the gym, there's more space between us than ever.

When he parks in the lot outside my building, I half-expect him to take off as soon as I clear the bike, but instead he gives me a severe nod and says, "I'll see you upstairs."

"You don't have to," I reply, heat burning behind my eyes. I didn't want it to be like this with him. He's one of my safe spaces—a person I've learned to rely on.

"I know," he says, some warmth returning to his face. "But if you don't let me walk with you, I'll have to follow you to make sure you get in safely. You'll be saving me from stalking you."

It's a lukewarm joke, his attempt to paper over this awkwardness that's grown between us, but I nod. I don't want him to go. Not yet. I know that once he does, this divide between us will only crack wider.

"Just be forewarned that my cat hates other men."

He smiles at me, his eyes twinkling. "No worries. *Cats* love me."

I shove his arm, but his double entendre feels like a salt-filled scratch. I'm sure it's true, and I'm just one in a long line of women who've wanted to sleep with him.

I lead the way up the steps, surprised when he settles his hand on my lower back in front of the door. I don't mean to lean into him, but I feel myself doing it as I unlock the door.

Before I walk in, I peer up at him and find him staring at me, his eyes full of...

I'm projecting.

Liam doesn't feel longing for anything but solitude. He's said so on many occasions.

I clear my throat and enter the apartment, caught off guard again when he follows me.

"So this is where Briar Sterling lives," he says, glancing around.

"Would you like to look through all my drawers like Hannah did?"

He smiles. "Maybe."

Karma emerges from the bedroom. I'm prepared to grab him when he inevitably starts hissing. But then my cat, who has hated every man I've ever brought home and once scratched

Jonah's bare bottom, starts to do figure eights around Liam's legs as he releases a deep, low purr.

"He likes you," I murmur in shock.

He huffs a laugh as he reaches down to run his palm over Karma's soft back. "I told you cats like me."

When Liam rises, his eyes are fixed on me. I know he's about to leave, and suddenly my throat feels thick. I don't want him to go.

So I blurt, "Will you...you said you didn't want me to go home for Christmas. Did you want to spend it together?"

I know what I'm asking. Hannah said it was his ex-girl-friend's birthday, and he always gets drunk.

If he spends it with me, then maybe it will mean...

I'm not even sure what I *want* it to mean.

He works for me, and he's my best friend's brother. Trying to date him would be another fatal mistake. It would prove that I don't have what it takes to succeed.

Worse, I don't think I could bear to be around him if we tried dating and the relationship failed. I'd have to watch other women flirting with him and know he might choose to go home with one of them.

My tender heart couldn't take that, so it would be better for him to say no. I'm almost entirely sure I want him to say no.

But when he finally shakes his head, I feel my cheeks burn.

"No, Briar," he says. "I don't think that's a good idea. But I meant what I said. I'll take care of it for you."

"I wasn't suggesting we do *this* again. I meant we could hang out as friends."

"It's still not a good idea."

So am I nothing to him now that we've slept together? Has everything we've been building burned to soot?

I want to ask, but I've already bared too much of myself tonight.

"What do you intend to do?" I ask. "Hire me a fake family?" I could make him feel better by telling him about Nora's invitation, but I don't *want* him to feel better. I want him to want me more than he wants to be alone.

He lifts my chin so our eyes meet. "Let me handle this."

"It's not necessary. I won't go to my parents' place for Christmas. You're right—it would be terrible. But it'll only be a temporary escape. I can't avoid my father forever."

"Why not?" he asks, his eyes flat. "He makes you feel bad. Seems to delight in it."

I barely hold back from saying that Liam's making me feel pretty shitty right now, too, after making me feel really, really good. The whiplash hurts so much more than expecting nothing and getting less.

I break eye contact and admit, "I need to have a family dinner with them every week. It's in the agreement I signed to take over Silver Star. If I start not showing up, he'll probably sue me for breach of contract." I force myself to meet his gaze again. "He'd really do it, Liam. I know he would."

He nods, a hot, angry look on his face. "Okay. I'll go with you."

"What?" I stammer.

"The next time you go, I'm coming with you. Every time you have to go, so will I."

"But you said..."

"I'll text you about your Christmas plans," he says, then runs his fingers in a rough caress over my jaw.

I back away. "You don't need to treat me like I'm a child. I told you I don't need your help."

"I'm not being condescending." His brow furrows. "You deserve to have other people stand up for you, whether you need it or not. That's all. You're someone worth fighting for."

I almost laugh, even though I've never been less amused in

my life. "Let me get this straight. I'm worth fighting for, but not for you?"

His expression turns agonized, and he fists and then flexes his hands. "Oh, Briar, no. I'm not good for anyone. I don't know how to care about someone like that anymore. It's better if we're just...friends."

Then he turns and leaves me alone with Karma, and the fear that I ruined everything in my life. Again.

CHAPTER TWENTY-THREE

LIAM

I try to sleep, but I keep seeing Briar's face. The way she looked at me when I was inside of her, warm and trusting—and the way she looked at me before I walked out of her door last night, like I'd stabbed her in the heart.

Yeah, I messed up good. But in my defense, I didn't know what to do. I'd given her what she said she wanted. I'm not capable of giving her more.

It's obvious sleep isn't coming, so I decide to do the smart thing and stop trying. I head to the brewery and test the gravity of the pale ale.

And I'll be damned. It's coming through like a real slugger. After everything we've been through, it's actually going to be ready in time.

Maybe I have Dottie's crystals to thank for that, or it's possible the singing did it. Whatever fucked-up miracle won the day, I'm going to pull this off after all.

My first thought is that I need to call Briar, but I can't casually call her after what happened last night.

Guilt sinks its teeth into me. I'm no better than Briar's

asshole parents and that insufferable bitch from her boarding school.

I hurt her.

I should have stayed away, but I was weak, and now I've screwed up everything.

At least I haven't broken her heart. Not yet. That's what Hannah was really afraid of, and it's one thing I can still prevent myself from doing.

I spend the rest of the morning pacing between the vats, my mind lurking in the dark places it has mostly stayed out of during the uneventful years I spent at Big Catch under the not-so-watchful eyes of Frodo.

I have no idea what time it is when I head into the tasting room and take a seat at one of the tables, nesting my head between my hands. All I know is that the sun is out—good enough for me. After a few minutes of sitting there, feeling like shit, I pour myself some of the tropical IPA.

I need a drink, and right now, I don't feel like I deserve a good one.

I'm still sitting there, nursing the crappy beer, when the door creaks open. I don't turn to look, because I want it to be her...and I also don't. I still don't know what to say. No waves of brilliance have lapped over me.

We're in an impossible situation, Briar and I. I like her. I like her *a lot*. I'm a little obsessed with her, to be honest. But I haven't forgotten my sister's warning.

If I mess this up badly enough, I could lose my sister, my job, *and* the woman I want. In other words: I could lose everything, and so could Briar.

I don't place great odds on me not messing up.

"Oh, dear. Did I leave too much moldavite here last night?"

It's Dottie Hendrickson.

I need to have a conversation with Dottie, but I don't have a single clue what she's talking about, nor do I have the patience to find out.

She sits down beside me, giving me a sidelong look as she pulls off a crocheted hat and fluffs her dyed purple hair. "Something very interesting happened to you last night."

I bark a laugh, barely holding back the *no shit*. "I suppose you could say that."

I glance at the clock mounted on the wall. It has somehow slipped from early morning to ten. Still a couple of hours before opening, which means Dottie's here earlier than she should be.

I shift to get a better look at her. "Why are you here so early?"

She gives me a prim look. "My intuition told me I was needed."

"I'm surprised you didn't say the web of crystals spoke to you."

"Would that be more believable?"

"No."

"Someone dear to me saw you sitting in the window, looking mournful."

"Mournful, huh?" I throw back the rest of the beer. "I'm feeling just fine. Couldn't sleep is all. There's something I was hoping to talk to you about, though."

She pats my hand. "Good. Let's go do that, dear."

"Go?" I repeat, my mind working slowly. Barely working at all, to be honest.

But the idea of going doesn't seem so good. Briar will be here soon, probably. I shouldn't miss Briar. Maybe when I see her, the words that will make it all better will magically come to me.

"Oh, indeed," Dottie says, with another hand pat. "You don't want her to see you looking like this."

"Who?" I ask.

"Your boss, dear. No one wants their boss to see them while they're red-eyed and smelling of beer at ten in the morning."

I manage a half-ass smile. "You think she'd fire me?"

"We'll never know, because we'll be at my tea shop enjoying a nice cup of tea and some deep conversation."

You know what? Dottie's a sweet little old lady who's doing a shitload of free work to help Silver Star pick itself up and dust off its boots. She's also been good to Briar and Hannah. I won't deny her the joy of getting her own way.

HALF AN HOUR LATER, I'm sitting across from Dottie at one of the little tables in her tea shop, a white metal chair groaning beneath my weight.

The server, who seemed a little in awe to be waiting on *the* Dottie Hendrickson, has already filled our cups with tea.

Dottie, who usually has a lot to say, has been surprisingly quiet.

"So, you're probably wondering what I wanted to talk to you about," I start, but she's already shaking her head, throwing me off.

"Oh no, I *know* you want advice about Briar. That much is obvious."

I consider her words. "What kind of advice?"

She points to the steaming teacup waiting in front of me. "Drink up, dear boy. The caffeine will do you good. Green tea only has about a fourth as much caffeine as coffee, so you'll need plenty of it."

I eye the spindly handle. When you're a big man, you get used to breaking things without meaning to. But breaking this cup in my big mitt would be a pretty shitty cherry on top of my bad day.

"No, thanks. I didn't come for advice. I was hoping you might be willing to include Briar in your Christmas plans."

"She asked you to make plans for her?" she questions. "How extraordinary." Her expression is full of an innocence I'm starting to question.

"Not exactly, but I didn't think she would. She'd probably spend the day alone or go to her parents' house out of duty."

Her gaze drills into me. "And how will *you* be spending the day, my dear?"

"I'll be at the brewery, where I need to be. Doing my job."

"Everyone needs a day off."

"And yet, here you are, two days before Christmas."

She smiles at me. "I'm mostly retired, dear. I'm here because it's where I choose to be."

"And the brewery is where I choose to be. But Briar needs to be around people."

"We *all* need to be around people."

"Christ, I hope not."

I expect her to act offended, but she laughs.

"Oh, you *do* remind me of Beau."

"Beau Buchanan?" I ask.

Because, yeah, I'm a brewer who grew up in Asheville. I know all about Beau Buchanan.

He started Buchanan Brewery back when Asheville was a place that didn't show up on travel websites' top ten lists. Back in his day, there weren't breweries around every corner, a new one every day. There was just Buchanan Brewery. Beau Buchanan paved the road we're all walking along now.

My dad knew and admired Beau, and his legacy means something to me.

Hannah told me that Beau and Dottie were a thing for decades. He passed away several years back, though, and Dottie's now seeing the guy who runs the bakery next door, a man who always has a smile on his face yet is surprisingly not obnoxious.

"The very same," she says. "He was a god-awful grump too."

A laugh bursts out of me. "Thank you. I think."

"It's a compliment. You know, Beau and I worked together for years. It's a beautiful collaboration, working with someone you care about. Building something together."

"I see where you're going with this." So does the ache brewing in my chest. "But it's not like that with me and Briar."

It feels like that, though.

Which is exactly why I need to back off.

I always failed group projects at school. The only collaboration I didn't totally screw up was helping my dad and sister raise my little brother—and that was done out of necessity. We'd been thrown into the deep end and needed to learn to swim or drown.

Dottie hums through her teeth. "No, of course not. You're not at all her kind of man. I was thinking she might be a better match for Otis."

"The kid?" I ask in disbelief.

"He *is* a sweet boy, but don't let his age fool you. He's matured in all the ways that matter over the last few months. We're all so proud of him. Why, he staffed the whole tasting room!"

"He's a child," I practically growl, my blood starting to simmer. "Briar needs—"

"Yes, Briar needs a man," Dottie says firmly. "Are you a man, Liam, or are you a child? I'm afraid the passing of years is not the deciding factor there."

I stare at her, dumbfounded. "Come on. You're close with Hannah..."

"I am." She smiles beatifically. "She's such a lovely girl."

"Yeah, she's a peach, all right. You'll excuse my language

when I ask if you're also aware that she'll cut my balls off if she finds out—if she thinks anything is going on between Briar and me."

She lifts a finger. "She did say she would do that, yes."

"Hannah doesn't make idle threats." It fucking sucks that my sister doesn't trust me with her friends—and the worst part is that she's right to doubt me. Sighing, I add, "Look, I'm not going to lie and say I don't...admire Briar. Anyone would. But Hannah has good reasons for thinking I'm not worthy."

Dottie sighs as if she's almost all out of patience. Leave it to me to be the man who breaks her legendary calm. She pulls a hunk of stone out of her pocket and clunks it down in front of me.

"That's not much to look at," I comment. "Is it supposed to mean something?"

"It's more moldavite. It'll help you see things as they truly are, my dear. You need a lot of it, I'm afraid."

I raise my eyebrows. "I thought you said you left too much at the brewery."

"I was wrong. I should have stuffed it into your pockets." She takes a ladylike sip of tea. "Do you truly believe your sister asked you to stay away because she thinks you're unworthy?"

"She thinks I'd hurt Briar, and she's probably right. But that's not the only reason I should stay away. I really need this job. I was going crazy at Big Catch. Working with Briar is..." I rub a hand over my chest, trying to ease the ache. But it's a bitch of a feeling that won't go away. "If this works out, it'll be every-thing I've ever wanted. A dream job. A creative outlet. I can't throw that away."

She plays that silent game of hers again for a moment. Then she says, "You didn't strike me as a man who'd admit defeat before he even plays the game."

I give her an incredulous look. "And you didn't strike me as the kind of person who'd think any of this was a game."

"Life is a game, Liam. Winning and losing are part of it, and they can both hurt. But we don't get to experience any of it if we refuse to play."

Her words are a sucker punch to the soul, but I lean back on the seat and say, "I'm a sore loser."

"So perhaps I should be sitting here with Otis."

I have to laugh at her boldness. "You're threatening me?"

"I'm speaking factually. Our dear Briar deserves to be loved. I've made it my mission to find her a partner." She smiles at me, her whole face leaning into it. All of her wrinkles, I realize, are from forming this smile. Decades' worth of smiles live on this woman's face. "I think you'll find that I am also a sore loser."

I swear under my breath, pushing the tea away.

"Does it vex you to think about her with another man?"

Vex me? It makes me want to flip the table.

"Sure," I respond tightly. "But I've got no right. She's not mine."

She gives me another long look. "Drink your tea, dear."

"Is this where you drug me, and I wake up in some kind of rehab community for assholes?" I glance down into the teacup. "Because I already tried that. Turns out anger management classes are just full of other angry people."

"There's nothing but love and tea leaves in that cup."

"So you *did* drug it," I say with a reluctant smile.

"If you choose to see it that way."

I ignore the tea, my hand tapping the tabletop. "Look. I'm not going out with Briar. I like my balls where they are, and she's my boss. It's not happening. But I do want to make sure she has somewhere to go on Christmas. Can you help me with that?"

"*Of course* she'd be welcome to join my partner and me. But, as it happens, I know she already has other plans."

"Oh?" I ask, feeling like an opponent in the ring has a one-up on me.

"Indeed. I'm sure she'd tell you all about what she's doing if you were to ask."

"She's not going to her parents' house?"

"No, thank goodness."

So where *is* she going? Hannah's gone, and Sophie left for the holidays too.

Otis.

He and his grandmother will probably be in town.

Dottie has been hinting that she thinks Briar might eventually come around to the kid's obsession with her.

Could she possibly be right?

My mind skips back to the past—to a shitty groove I've worn into the record of my life.

Me screwing up with a woman. Another man stepping in with sympathy when it was most needed...

It's happened before.

I can feel my mouth settling into a severe line, and even though my temples are aching, I want to hit the gym to release the awful feelings flooding me.

"Well, this was a lovely talk, my dear." Dottie sips her tea as if she didn't just throw me for a massive loop. She's not done yet, though. She skewers me with a look and says, "But I'd be doing you a disservice if I didn't tell you that your life will still feel too small unless you let more people into it."

I almost tell her that I *have* let other people in. I've buddied up with Mick, I like Travis well enough, Cormac wanted to get that drink, and I told the kid I'd give him boxing lessons. But even as I open my mouth to say the words, I remember that I quit Travis's band, I still haven't followed up on Cormac's invitation, and I haven't asked the kid when he's free. Given what she just told me, I doubt I will.

I don't really believe Briar has any romantic interest in Otis, but if I had to watch him twirl her around and kiss her and run his fingers through her hair...

Well, I think I'd fucking die. It wouldn't be a good death, either, the kind that goes down in history books. It would be a pathetic, wasting-away kind of death.

I go to pick up the teacup, and yep, there goes the handle, snapping under my grip like it's a toothpick.

"Shit, sorry."

She shrugs. "It's been known to happen."

"Not everyone needs a big life, you know."

She gives me a sad smile. "Maybe not, my dear. But *you* do. You deserve to take up every bit of space your body requires. Now, finish that tea."

"So you can try to read the leaves? Hannah warned me about that."

She winks at me. "I imagine she also warned you that it's your quickest way out of here."

I could just get up and leave. She'd be hard-pressed to stop me. But being rude to her would be different than being rude to my ex-boss or Briar's horror-show parents. She's a tough lady, a straight shooter, but she's also good people.

So I lift the cup up, the jagged handle digging into my skin, and drain it.

Dottie smiles as she accepts the cup from me. She tips it over onto its saucer, rotates it a few times, and then turns it over.

"So what does fate have in store for me?" I ask after a moment.

She looks up at me, her eyes lively. "Oh, you mistake me, dear. I wasn't looking at the leaves so I could tell you your future. I wanted guidance for my own path."

"You're seriously not going to tell me what you think is in there?" I ask, bemused.

"There's no point in speaking the words if you're not ready to listen to them."

It's as good as a dismissal, which I've been waiting for, but I don't get up. Because there's something else that's been nagging at me.

"There's this woman," I say.

"I very much hope you're not seeing other women," Dottie says, a little tartly. "That would be foolish for—"

"No. There's no one else."

The satisfied look on her face says I've finally given something away without intending to, but I don't backtrack from the truth. "It's someone who's been giving Briar a hard time her whole life. I think she might cause some trouble for us."

CHAPTER TWENTY-FOUR

BRIAR

I'm self-conscious when I walk into the brewery on Saturday, worried that everyone will take one look at me and know there's a delicious ache of soreness between my legs from what Liam and I did together. But no one seems to notice the change in me, and there's no sign of Liam.

After the way he left me last night, pathetic and alone, I dreaded seeing him, so his absence should be good news. No Liam means I'll have time to pull myself together. Instead, his absence sends me into a panic. Where is he? Is he coming back? Did I ruin everything by asking him to break our rules?

I finally break and ask Otis if he has any idea where Liam might be. He doesn't. So I ask Dottie, who nods. "I had a lovely chat with him this morning."

"You did?" I ask, glancing around. Otis is close enough to overhear us.

"Oh, yes." Dottie pats my arm. "He was in quite a state. It was obvious he'd lost sleep over something. But he *did* give me some excellent news at the end of our talk. The pale ale will be ready in time for our celebration."

That *is* good news, but I don't care the way I should.

Liam's not here. He's upset because of me. It suggests he cares more than I thought he did last night...

"He went home?" I ask.

"Yes. I could tell he needed the sleep."

The brewery's closed tomorrow and on Christmas, so the earliest I'll see him is on Tuesday.

Again, that should be a relief. A few days might be long enough for us to remember our list of rules. We can reset and be friends again—friends with an inconvenient attraction that will hopefully fade over time.

But the tight feeling in my chest is more like panic than relief.

"You're still having Christmas dinner with Nora, aren't you?" Dottie asks.

"Yeah," I say distractedly, running my fingers over my lips.

"Liam was very concerned about making sure you had plans."

I smile despite the pain ribboning through my chest. "Of course he asked you."

"I didn't tell him where you were going, of course." She hesitates before adding, "Will you come to my Christmas Eve dinner tomorrow night, dear? I'd like it if you would. You'll fit right in, and my granddaughter will talk your ear off about running a brewery."

"I'd like nothing better," I say honestly, feeling a rush of heat behind my eyes. I mean it, of course. Dottie is the sweetest person I know, and the rebranding of Buchanan Brewery after the younger generation took over from the older was a runaway success. I'd love to talk the Buchanans' ears off, but that's not why I'm so grateful for the invitation. Dottie is accepting me as family. Treating me like I matter in a way my own family never has.

My mind tilts toward Liam.

He's alone, and his only plan is to stay that way. That makes me sad down to my bones.

THE DAY PASSES SLOWLY, and all of it feels dull.

Is Liam drinking already? Will he spend the next two days drinking? Will he go to the gym and break another heavy bag?

I'd like to think he's upset because of what happened between us, but it seems just as likely this is something he goes through every year because of her, whoever she is.

I want to go to him, but I won't.

Liam said he couldn't be with me, and I should take him at his word.

I've always been the one to give people second and third and fourth chances. I gave Jonah the benefit of the doubt when he told me he was really busy with work. And I bought my business partner, Theresa, new accounting software when she insisted her outdated software was the cause for our "missing" money.

But no more. I'm not going to run toward more rejection with my arms open wide, hoping the void will hug me back.

It's probably better this way, anyway. While there's obviously a spark between us, there's Hannah to think of, plus the good of the brewery.

Before I leave for the night, I gather the staff together and hand out scratch-off tickets as bonuses, telling everyone we'll have real bonuses next year.

If we're still here, it goes without saying.

"I think it's gonna be my lucky day," Ann says, laughing as she flips through her stack of tickets.

"Miss Ann, there are terrible odds of winning," Otis tells her.

"Someone's gotta win, honey. Someday it's gonna be me."

Everyone gives her knowing smiles, but I admire her willingness to see possibilities where others see improbabilities.

I want to hope too.

I slide Liam's tickets behind our list of rules, telling myself I'll give them to him later. *He's not gone. He didn't leave. He's coming back, and it hasn't all been ruined.* The words feel like a winning lottery ticket, too dear to be hoped for.

MY FATHER TEXTS me that night, asking if I'm coming over for Christmas Eve or Christmas dinner, as if I didn't flee his house on a motorcycle and lose half my dress in the process.

I respond with a simple, *No*, and he replies,

> I look forward to your party, sweetheart. Mom asks if it's okay to bring outside alcohol.

No, I respond again, my heart beating faster at the defiance.

I spend the next evening at Dottie's little purple house. It's tiny, especially given the number of people packed inside and spilling out into the frostbitten yard. But the gathering is warm and full of laughter. Otis and his grandmother come over, and all of Dottie's grandchildren stop by, including the ones who run Buchanan Brewery. Small children fill the cottage with laughter, especially when Dottie's partner comes out in a Santa suit.

I still haven't heard from Liam. Not a word.

It's his silence that hurts most of all, I decide. I'd started to get lulled into thinking we were rebuilding the brewery together, and this is presumably his way of reminding me that there is no us.

I go home, feeling emotionally drained, and find a poorly wrapped package waiting on the stoop of my building.

My hands tremble as I lift it up. The gift tag is addressed to me in Liam's sloppy handwriting.

I glance around, worried someone might witness me taking the gift, which is absurd, since it's for me.

When did he stop by?

The disappointment of having missed him lodges in my throat, but I let myself in and carry the gift to my kitchen table. I'm very aware that his hands touched it, just like they've touched me.

Karma hops onto the tabletop, gives me a dubious look, and meows loudly.

"Exactly," I say.

I tear a corner of the wrapping paper before ripping off the rest. My heart goes gooey in my chest as I study the brand-new boxing gloves.

There's a sticky note resting on top of them.

Every boxer needs their own gloves. And you, Briar, are a prizefighter. Never forget that.
Dottie probably already told you, but the beer is going to be ready on time.
Merry Christmas,
Liam

I go to sleep with the gloves clutched to my chest.

CHAPTER TWENTY-FIVE

BRIAR

"Oh, thank God you're here," Nora mutters when she answers the door to her mother's house the next afternoon. It's a tidy white Arts and Crafts bungalow with a bright-red door decked out with a fresh evergreen wreath.

Nora tugs me inside the house, which smells like warm spiced wine.

"Cormac is insufferable," she hisses as she leads me past the beige couch, where her mother and Cormac's father are cuddled together, whispering in undertones. They don't seem to notice we exist, let alone that we're in the same room as them, but I slow my pace. What is the etiquette for greeting someone who looks like they're about to get ravaged?

"Oh, don't mind them," Nora continues as if I'd spoken. "They do that a lot. My mom will come up for air soon. We're going to make gingerbread cookies before dinner, and Mom gets really into it. But first let's grab some mulled wine. Everything's better with mulled wine."

"Yes, please."

But when she leads me into the kitchen, a warm, cozy space painted sage green with a white-and-gray tile backsplash, she sighs heavily. Cormac is standing at the stove in a Rudolph sweater, pouring himself mulled wine from an enormous pot. He's tall and lanky, with curly light-brown hair, glasses, and gray eyes.

Nora's sigh turns to outrage when we reach the stove and she sees the container is nearly empty. "Cormac, if you finish it, you need to make more. It's a house rule, even for guests."

He huffs, adjusting his glasses, and takes a calculated sip of the wine. "Your mom offered it to me. We don't have any more bottles of red."

"You knew Briar was coming."

"So take it." He shoves the glass at her just as she extends her hand in a warding-off gesture, and the warm red wine splatters all over both of them.

Nora's eyes widen. "You did that on purpose."

"I don't think he did," I say. "It got on him too."

There's mulled wine spatter on his glasses, and he looks horrified.

"Don't try reasoning with Nora," he says darkly, grabbing a dish towel and swiping at the stains on his sweater, which have made it look like someone ax-murdered Rudolph. "She's incapable of reason."

Nora looks like she's about to explode, so I lead her over to the marble counter and grab the roll of paper towels off its holder. "Do you know where your mom keeps the cleanser?"

She silently retrieves it from under the sink, handing it to me.

"Oh no," Cormac says, still swiping ineffectually at his sweater. "That's not the right cleanser for this mess at all."

"Says the man who's rubbing wine *into* his sweater," Nora points out.

His eyes widen for a second, as if he didn't realize what he was doing, but then he shrugs and uses the edge of the sweater to wipe off his glasses. "I must have been doing it subconsciously. I hate this sweater."

"My mother gave it to you," she hisses. "Have some respect."

"And it was very sweet of her, but I don't like it. I'm only wearing it because my dad said it would be nice."

"Saying that takes away from the gesture." She shakes the roll of paper towels at him. "Look, we'll clean this up. Go do... whatever. Hang out with our parents while they make out."

He gives her a sour look. "It's my mess. Let me clean it the way it should be cleaned."

"Fine," she snaps, throwing the roll at him, and he fumbles it before wrapping his fingers firmly around the cylinder. She grabs a growler from the fridge while he lowers down to search the cabinet beneath the sink for something that might or might not be there.

Nora commandeers two glasses, then gestures for me to follow her. "Let's hang out in my room."

But before I can leave, Cormac calls out to me. "Hey, you're running that brewery Liam Moroney works for, right?"

My heart throbs in my chest at the mention of Liam's name, and I wonder for the thousandth time what he's doing today. Drinking probably. Thinking of *her*.

I won't lie. I spent an hour on social media this morning, trying to find his profiles (nonexistent) and then scrolling back through Hannah's timeline in search of any photos of Liam and a mystery woman.

If there were, Hannah has deleted them.

I clear my throat. "Yup, that's me."

"We're playing at your New Year's party. Nora's going to be there too. I'm looking forward to it, but it'll be my first live performance, so I'm kind of nervous."

"Don't expect me to ask for an autograph," she says with an eye roll.

"Autographs don't make any sense," he scoffs, still kneeling in front of the cabinet. "Who cares about having something with someone else's name signed on it? I don't like flowers either."

"Wasn't going to bring you any."

He ignores her, keeping his focus on me. "Anyway, I actually just got a text from Liam."

"You did?" I blurt.

"I'd asked him if he wanted to grab a drink, like, weeks ago, and he just now texted me back. I thought I was the only person who forgets about texts. Anyway, Liam's cool. He offered to teach me how to make beer. I love learning how to do new things."

"Consider some etiquette lessons," Nora mutters.

"Did he sound drunk?" I ask before I can think better of it.

Cormac's brow furrows. "How can a person sound drunk on a text?"

"I don't know, forget it," I say as Nora gives me a speculative look. "I was only curious."

Nora angles her head toward the hallway. "Let's go have that drink. Cormac has some work to do."

"Oh, we won't be brewing the beer today," he replies. "It's going to happen in a week or two, probably, because he says he has a lot of stuff leading up to—"

"I was talking about cleaning the kitchen," Nora clarifies.

"Oh, right," he says, and his head disappears back under the sink.

Nora tugs me out of the room, down the small, creaky hallway, past a bathroom, and to and through a door with a crystal doorknob. The room beyond it is small but neat, with a double bed covered by a purple comforter, a rolltop desk with a chair, and a beanbag chair.

"Let me just change my shirt," she says and disappears into the closet, reemerging in a plain red sweater.

"Did you get a reindeer one too?" I ask.

"Yes, but I'm not a masochist. Cormac didn't have to put it on." She blows hair off her face with a puff of air. "I always feel like I'm walking back in time when I'm over here."

I smile ruefully. "I know what you mean. I become a child as soon as I step into my parents' house."

"I claim the beanbag chair," she says with a return smile, then plops down onto it and pours ginger beer into each of the glasses. One of them goes to me.

"Soooo..." she starts.

I get settled in the chair at the desk and take a sip of the ginger beer—the holiday variation we'll have at the New Year's party—because I have a feeling I might need it for whatever's coming next.

"Why did you go out with Jonah?" she asks.

Not what I was expecting...

I study the glass in my hand, taking in the lovely caramel hue and the bubbles fizzing to the top. It smells like caramelized fruit. I take a sip, steeling myself for the Jonah talk, and nearly hum at the taste.

God, I love the transformation that's at the center of brewing—how you can start with a few disparate ingredients and end up with something ambrosial. "This is delicious."

"It is," she agrees. "So is my question."

"I think Jonah could tell I was lonely, and he took advantage of it," I say, feeling the familiar weight of self-recrimination in my chest. But I fight it. I'm sick of feeling guilty for wanting the world to be kinder than it is. "He knew my dad had promised to give me the brewery. He said he'd help, and it made me feel less alone. I..." The ache in my chest seems to speak the next words. "I've *always* felt alone, for as long as I can remember."

She gives me a sad smile. "Guys like him look for weak spots to burrow into. Like worms. You shouldn't blame yourself. Manipulation is literally their thing."

"Why did *you* go for him? You're not weak."

She points a finger at my chest. "Neither are you. You thought you needed him, but you didn't. Look at you, running off, making A-plans, B-plans, all kinds of plans. I don't know many people who've done as much in as little time. You didn't need Jonah to do any of that. You just thought you did."

My grip on the cup tightens. "But I *do* need Liam."

"You don't need him any more than he needs you," she says archly.

"Are you kidding? Anyone would be glad to have him. He's insanely talented. You tasted his beer the other day."

"I've tasted it at competitions too. He *is* crazy talented, but that's not the only thing people care about." She picks at the laundry tag on the beanbag chair. "Everyone knows he got arrested after beating up the owner of Mountain Morning so bad he had to be hospitalized overnight."

Something sours in my stomach. I hadn't realized it was that bad. "That happened a long time ago."

"People remember. That's one thing you can be sure of in places like this." She glowers at the door. "Like Cormac with his science project. It doesn't matter that I knocked it over by accident, or that Liam had a good reason for what he did. Those things still happened, and people still remember. They always remember the bad stuff."

"He had a good reason?" I nearly fall off my chair in my eagerness to hear it.

"Look," she says, setting her glass down. "Gossip is like that telephone game. You never know how much of the truth you're getting."

I should probably pretend my interest is solely professional —that I want to make sure Liam isn't some raging psychopath who's going to start punching rude tourists in the tasting room or drowning employees in our pale ale. But Nora has been good to me, and honesty should never be met with a lie.

"I really need to know."

She nods. "Look, like I said, I don't know the whole story, but it was over a woman. He was serious with someone, but then his boss hooked up with her at the brewery's holiday party. Everyone found out, because the fire alarm went off and the building had to be evacuated. They were both only half dressed."

"She cheated on Liam?" I blurt. I can't imagine ever cheating on anyone—a betrayal like that would eat a hole right through me—but to cheat on *Liam?* Unthinkable.

"That's what people say. But it went deeper. I guess Liam didn't go after the guy until later. I think maybe you should ask him about all of this, though." She laughs. "Or we could bribe Cormac to do it."

I take a sip of my drink, buying some time. I want to confide in Nora, but it feels like a betrayal of Hannah and Sophie to share something so personal with a new friend first. At the same time, I can hardly call Hannah to complain that I asked her brother for sex and he gave it to me.

Even in my own head, it sounds stupid.

I *asked* for this.

I knew he wasn't interested in a relationship. It's irrational to be angry with him because he made me want one.

"Nora?" a woman's voice calls. "Nora, where are you? We're about to start the cookies."

Nora leans over to open the door, calling into the hallway, "I'm in my room with Briar. We're having a private conversation."

"Oh, did Briar arrive?"

She rolls her eyes at me. "Yes. We'll be out in a minute. Go ahead and get started without us." She shuts the door again and plops back down. "See? They always get lost in this dreamy realm where they don't remember other people exist. Did you know Mr. Peebles was my elementary school principal? It's super weird, but I *am* happy for them. My mom deserves a good guy, and God knows if she would have ever even tried dating again if not for Hannah."

"Please don't tell Hannah I asked about Liam," I say, my chest tight. "I don't want her to think I have...you know, inappropriate feelings for him."

Her stare is pointed. "But do you?"

I take a deep breath, hold it, then let it out. "Yes. But I need to get over them. You'd think I'd learn."

She laughs, deep and throaty, and lifts her glass to clink it to mine. "I hear you there. My dad was a dirty cheater, so you'd think I'd have recognized all the tricks when Jonah came sauntering in and asked me out. But it's always different when you're in the thick of it." She's silent for a second before asking, "You think maybe you're displacing your feelings onto Liam because he's helping you like you thought Jonah was going to do?"

It hadn't occurred to me, so I sit with the idea for a moment.

"Maybe partly," I say, "but he's also..."

"A hot, sexy asshole who rides a motorcycle and gets into trouble?"

"He has a tattoo that winds around his leg," I gush. "And one on his arm too. I can't stop thinking about it."

I also can't stop thinking about how he stood up for me at my parents' dinner, and his insane offer to keep going there with me even though he clearly hates my parents, and vice versa. Or his encouragement of my dream. Or the excitement I feel every time I check our list of rules. But the way those things make me feel is a lot more dangerous than the pure lust I experience every time he touches me.

"You slept with him?"

I sigh and nod before burying my face in my hands.

"It was good, wasn't it?" she presses. "You wouldn't be this wound up over bad sex."

"It was the best I've ever had. If it was just sex, though, there wouldn't be a problem. I like him...a lot, but I don't think he's interested in me like that. Even if he was, I'd be worried about ruining our dynamic. You told me it was awkward when things didn't work out with you and José. I'm...oversensitive. If we tried dating, and it blew up, I don't think I could be around him every day. I couldn't do it."

"So unfuck the situation, my friend. You think he can forget about what happened? You both need to be on the same page for that to happen."

"I think he wants to. He told me he can't care about anyone like that. It must be because of the woman the Mountain Morning fight was about. He's probably still in love with her."

The words feel painful coming out, as if each of them is covered in shattered glass.

"I doubt that very much," Nora says, adjusting her position in the beanbag chair. "I saw you and Liam together. There's definitely something there. But my advice is to give him what he says he wants. You'll see soon enough whether he meant it."

"He gave me boxing gloves for Christmas," I confess.

"Good," she says with a grin. "So you won't hurt your hands if you need to hit him."

Shouts erupt outside the room, and Nora springs up from her beanbag chair. Worry written all over her face, she hurries out the door, and I follow her.

"Nora? Nora!" her mother is shouting from the kitchen.

We burst into the room, which smells like gingerbread and is no longer spattered with wine. Cormac is in the corner, guzzling his mulled wine and shaking his head, while his father and Nora's mother are embracing over a sheet full of cookies.

"What is it?" Nora asks, stopping so abruptly I almost bump into her. "I thought you were dying."

Cormac finishes the wine and sets the cup on the counter with a smack. He mumbles something like "close enough."

Then Nora's mom, whom I still haven't properly greeted, gestures her over to the cookie sheet.

"Just look at what this beautiful man did for me. Just look."

Eugene is watching her like she's every dream he ever had pressed into one person. "It's the first cookie I ever decorated," he says proudly.

I walk over and see one of the cookies on the sheet has a crown—a diamond ring.

"Oh shit," Nora says, her expression full of shock. But then she forces an incredibly fake smile. "Congratulations."

"Let's all have a congratulatory drink," I say, because she deserves a moment to gather herself.

Nora's mother gasps. "Who *are* you?"

CHAPTER TWENTY-SIX

LIAM

I get drunk every year on Julia's birthday. It's something I've done for so long, I'm accustomed to it. It's built into my muscle memory to get blackout drunk on Christmas, when little tykes are opening their plastic junk and their parents are downing buckets of coffee. Sometimes I do it with my dad and brother, or Hannah. Sometimes I'm alone.

But today, I'm standing outside Otis's grandmother's house with a six-pack, wondering what the fuck is wrong with me.

It's Dottie. She put this picture in my head of Otis getting through to Briar, and now I can't unsee it.

I'm here because I want to see if *she's* here.

I want to see her, period.

I know that's a bad idea, but I can't summon the energy to care. Not today.

I knock, and an older woman answers the door with a surly look on her face. The smell of cooking turkey wafts out, making me realize I haven't eaten for a while. I can't remember how long.

The older lady instantly waves her cane at me. "Is there no

decency left in this world? You'd try to swindle money out of me on Christmas day? Who sent you, boy? What do they know?"

I pause for long enough that she beans me with the cane. "Well?"

Otis appears behind her while I'm still rubbing my head. "Liam?" he asks, as stunned as if Santa Claus had dropped by for a hang. "Holy shit, are you here to have dinner with us?"

"*Language,*" the woman says.

"Sorry, Grandma."

"Do you know this large man?"

"Yeah," he says. "This is Liam. We work together." His eyes widen. "Wait. Is there, like, an emergency at the brewery? Did the vats explode?"

"No explosion," I say, feeling like an idiot. "I...thought maybe Briar might be here."

"Uh, no," he says, his eyes full of confusion, "but—"

"Come in, come in," his grandmother says in a weary voice. "You're letting all the cold air inside."

I follow her into the house, now certain I'm an idiot. Dottie tricked me somehow, but I can't think how or why she would have, since she didn't know how I'd react to her hint.

"Would you like a drink?" Otis asks. "Or are you looking for Briar because of the emergency?"

"No emergency," I say.

"So what are you doing here, son?" the woman says gruffly.

It's a question for the ages.

I hoist up the six-pack. "I brought beer."

She glances at the beer. "Is it good beer?"

"His beer's always the best," Otis says. "That's why Briar hired him."

Turning back toward me, she asks, "And do you like light or dark meat?"

"I'm not fussy."

She studies me for a long moment, as if judging my truthfulness. "You can stay, but there'll be no funny business."

"Yeah, stay for dinner, Liam," Otis says eagerly. "You can help me decorate more posters for the New Year's Eve party. Sophie and your sister want to put up fifty more when they get back. It's going to be epic."

I'm about to say, *No, I definitely don't want to do that. I have a date with a bottle and my bed and a very, very bad mood.*

But the words don't come out. I keep thinking about what Dottie said about needing other people.

Hell, maybe there *was* something in that tea, because I'm actually thinking about staying.

"Yeah, okay," I say, feeling sweat bead on my forehead and the back of my neck.

HALF AN HOUR LATER, I'm sitting at an old work table next to Otis, putting stickers on a poster covered with exclamation marks.

My brother would give himself an ulcer laughing if he could see me now. Hannah too.

"I don't like spending the holidays alone either," Otis remarks out of nowhere as he adds yet another exclamation point to his poster. "I'm glad you think we're friends. I wasn't sure you liked me. I got the impression I talked too much when we were getting the barrel room decorated for Briar."

"You did," I say, smiling, "but that was a nice idea. I wish I'd thought of it."

He sets down his neon marker to get a better look at me. "What are your intentions toward Briar?"

Talk about a turnaround. I'd come here to figure out *his*

intentions—and, honestly, to get in the way of them if at all possible.

I take a sip of my beer, trying to figure out what to say. Finally, I land on, "I think a lot of her...and I think about her a lot."

"Obviously," he says. "Who wouldn't?"

"So we understand each other. I know you feel the same way."

He lifts his beer up as if toasting me. "But you're the lucky one, because she wants *you*."

"Why do you say that?"

He laughs. "Look...Ann and I might have been high the other night, but Briar ran outside without a coat to look for you." He sounds wistful as he adds, "I always knew it was a long shot. She's...*her*. And I know I'm a lot younger. But I thought at least I could be around her. Help her out. I still want that."

"I want that too."

"So?" He gestures toward the front of the house. "Why don't you go find her? Doesn't seem like you to give up after one try. We've all seen what you've done to get that beer ready on time."

"My sister made me promise not to date any of her friends. I screwed up pretty badly in the past, so she had her reasons. I wasn't expecting that anything would happen between Briar and me, so it was an easy promise to make."

He stares off in thought, then pops yet another exclamation point onto the poster. "Sophie likes them," he explains offhandedly, then adds, "You know, *I'm* afraid of Hannah. Most people are, but I didn't think *you'd* be afraid of her."

"I'm not afraid of her. I'm afraid of disappointing her. She's my little sister. She used to look up to me. It's not a good feeling having your little sister think you're a jackass. I'm the one who taught her how to read. I played dolls with her, for fuck's sake."

Otis nods in understanding, and I remember what Dottie said about how much he's grown. I didn't know the kid before, but I see it. He's on that cusp between being a boy and being a man.

"Look, I shouldn't have agreed to take you boxing and flaked out. That was shitty. We'll figure out a time to go. Just be ready for all the guys to give you a hard time. They do that with fresh meat."

He hesitates, eyeing me. "Do they all look like you?"

"A few of them. But you know what? Maybe they used to look like you. We all start somewhere."

After giving this some thought, he nods again. "I'll do it. Would you like another beer?"

Yes.

We have another. And then one each with dinner. And then five more.

CHAPTER TWENTY-SEVEN

BRIAR

I'm sleeping with the gloves again when I'm awoken by a heavy knock on the door. Karma yowls and jumps onto my face, and another knock lands before I manage to peel him off.

It's pitch dark outside.

Why would someone be at my door at this hour?

I tiptoe out of my bedroom and through the living room, dodging the sectional in the dark. When I reach the door, I stand still for a second, worrying my lip.

I won't open it. I'll see who it is, that's all. And if they won't leave, I'll call the police.

I peek through the peephole, my heart racing, and see... nothing.

"Oh, that's not creepy at all," I mutter to Karma, who has settled at my feet and is giving the door a death stare. Unfortunately, it works better on people than on possible ghosts.

No sooner does that thought cross my mind than a figure sways into view. The breath escapes my lungs as I throw the door open without a second thought.

It's *Liam*. He came. He came to me after all.

Karma bounds outside, and I nearly scream, worried he'll be lost in the cold.

But he starts weaving around Liam's legs like he belongs to him. Liam crouches to pat the cat's head, and the sight of his big hand nuzzling Karma's fur makes my heart melt. Even though it's freezing outside, Liam isn't wearing a hat or gloves. I want to wrap him up in a hug and give him my warmth.

He put someone in the hospital, I remind myself.

He slept with you and left without a backward glance.

He hasn't dated a woman seriously for years.

But I know he's not dangerous to me. His energy has always felt protective.

"Come inside," I say.

He walks in, Karma trailing after him like a lovesick cat. Oh, of course he's crazy about him too.

I shut the door after him, biting my lip as I watch him sit on the sectional and bury his head in his hands, his reddish hair tufting between his strong, scarred fingers.

It's only when I sit down next to him and get a whiff of alcohol that I realize he's been drinking.

Disappointment seeps into me. He's here, but he spent this day the way he always does—thinking about another woman.

"How'd you get here?" I ask, my voice choked. "I hope you didn't drive."

"I walked."

"From where?"

"Montford."

Several miles in the dark. In the freezing cold.

"Oh, Liam."

He glances up at me, his eyes bloodshot. "I let you think the other night didn't mean anything to me, but it did."

I set my hand on his leg, needing to touch him. "It meant something to me too. We were both confused."

"No. I wasn't confused. I don't want you thinking that. I knew I wanted you. It would be impossible not to want you."

"But we both know it's more complicated than that."

"Not just because of Hannah or the brewery." The sadness in his gaze floors me. "I...Julia told me there was something missing in me, and I think maybe she was right. I don't want to hurt you."

I lift my fingers to his face, feeling the cold he carried in on his skin and his beard. Maybe I can seep warmth and light into him. He needs it, and my heart aches to do for him what he's done for me over these past weeks—to be strong so he can be vulnerable.

"What, exactly, do you think you're missing?" My voice comes out as a whisper as my cat leaps onto the couch and curls up next to him.

"If I knew that, Princess, I'd be halfway toward finding it," he says with a gruff laugh, then shakes his head, his short beard brushing against my hand.

"Tell me about Julia."

"I'd rather not."

"You know everything about Jonah. The rule about not oversharing came after I'd already told you about him."

"I don't want to talk about that prick either."

I tip my head up and brush a quick kiss across his lips. "Tell me, Liam. You need to get it off your chest. I can tell. You spent hours walking here because of it."

He swears under his breath. "What do you want to know?"

"Everything. I want to know you."

His smile is wry and full of self-deprecation. "Most people who do are sorry for it."

"You want them to be. You push them away on purpose so they can't get close."

"Let's not get hasty," he replies with dark amusement. "I don't like most people. I don't let them get close because I don't *want* them close."

"But you liked Julia," I say, my words arrowing into my own heart.

He shrugs. "Sure. For a while."

He's quiet for a long moment, and I'm sure he's done sharing. I'm trying to resign myself to that and respect his boundaries when he surprises me by continuing.

"We were together for two years, but she fucked my boss at the holiday party I refused to go to, and everyone found out. I think she wanted me to challenge Steve to a fight or some shit, but I didn't. I quit, obviously, but I figured there was no point fighting for her. Why fight for someone who doesn't want you? If she wanted to be with him, let her be with him. Maybe she'd finally be happy. But Steve had a coke habit, and a few weeks after she got with him, she overdosed on his drugs. She almost died."

"That's when you attacked him?"

He hangs his head. "I should regret that, but I don't. He didn't take care of her. But neither did I. It was my fault."

"That's a stretch. Why would you think it was *your* fault?"

He gives a humorless laugh, and his gaze seems haunted when it meets mine again. "Because she told me so when I visited her in the hospital. She was in tears. She said she'd only slept with him because I hadn't paid her any attention in months. After it happened, she'd prayed I'd step up and tell Steve to go fuck himself, but I didn't do anything. She was trying to overdose, Briar. Because of me. She loved me, and I destroyed her."

My heart is fracturing inside of my chest. I'm tempted to ask whether Hannah knows about all of this, but I know better. He wouldn't have told her this part. This is something he's carried alone, and what a heavy load to carry.

The weight of his memories must have been slowly breaking him.

I know what that's like.

My hair is down to my waist now, but I still play with it constantly to reassure myself it's there. That I won't reach back and feel the shorn spots my mind still fears exist.

I nuzzle closer to him, running my hands over his face, his hair. Giving him the soft benediction he needs. My heart is so full of him. "She was struggling with her mental health, Liam. That's not your fault. You didn't do that to her. You can't protect people from their own brains."

"I should have seen it. I should have been there for her, but I didn't even notice she was struggling. Briar, I get so wrapped up in what I'm doing, I don't notice whether I've eaten. A lot of times, I don't remember I haven't called someone back until it's been months. I can't be responsible for someone else's happiness. I can't even..." He swears, pulling away. "I can't even casually sleep with someone without messing everything up. You know all about Margaret, obviously."

"She wanted more than you were willing to give."

"What do *you* want?" he asks, staring at me intently.

The question engulfs me, and all I can do is shake my head, feeling the inadequacy of the gesture. What *do* I want?

No one has really ever asked me before.

I want the brewery.

I want my friends.

I want to believe in happy endings, and winning scratch-off tickets, and happily ever after.

I want *Liam*, but I'm terrified it would be another mistake for both of us—one that might break us.

Hannah doesn't want us together.

The brewing world is cautious of him.

There's so much on the line...and neither of us has a history of healthy relationships.

"I don't know," I whisper, my voice ragged and full of anguish. "*I don't know.*"

He gives me a smile filled with so much pain I almost burst into tears. "I shouldn't have come here, Briar. I just wanted you to know that the other night meant something to me."

He pulls away and gets to his feet, turning toward the door. But he only makes it one step away before I quite literally throw myself at him.

"You can't walk home from here. No way."

He smiles as if I'd said something cute. "No one's going to mess with me. The walk will sober me up the rest of the way. I drank too much with Otis."

"You drank with Otis?" I ask, stunned. "Is he still alive?"

He barks a laugh. "I didn't say we went drink for drink."

"What were you doing with Otis? I thought..."

I thought he'd holed up to brood about Julia, and that coming here was an afterthought.

"I was looking for you. Dottie said something that made me think you'd be there. You weren't, obviously, but he and his grandmother asked me to stay, and I figured..." He lifts one big shoulder. "Maybe it was worth trying to be a guy who says yes to things like that."

My confused and broken heart tries to make sense of this.

He went there looking for me. He wanted *me*. Maybe he even got drunk because of me instead of Julia.

"Otis is crazy about you too, you know," Liam says. "You're not alone, Briar. We're all behind you. We're all invested in making the brewery work. You've made us want it as much as you do."

My eyes fill with tears. All my life, I've longed to hear those words. It's still hard to trust them, but I want to stuff them into my soul and keep them forever. I want to keep *him*.

"And I've got your back," I insist. "You're not leaving." I position myself firmly between him and the door.

He gives me the wry look of a man who could move me as easily as most people could move a barking Chihuahua.

"Don't make me put my new gloves on," I warn. "I had a pretty good boxing teacher."

He smiles then—a real smile. "You got them?"

"I've been sleeping with them," I admit, feeling those hot tears still pressing at my eyes.

"I should've gotten you a stuffed animal instead."

"No." I plant my palm on his warm, hard chest. "I love them. I'm just upset because I didn't get you anything."

He tips my chin up. "You honestly think you didn't get me anything? You gave me *everything*. Before you burst into my life, I was stuck in a dead-end job, just surviving. You've made me feel alive again."

I place my other palm beside the first. I can't let him leave. I can't. It feels like my world will end if he walks out that door. "You're staying here tonight. I want you to hold me."

"The gloves weren't doing the trick?"

"No. I need you."

Those words are so hard for me to say to anyone, especially to a man. Jonah took my need and twisted it against me, but I know Liam would never do that purposefully. Liam is good and loyal and strong, and everything Jonah only pretended to be.

"We should stay away from each other until we decide what to do," he says, his eyes conflicted.

"I won't let you get past me. I'm unrelenting when I have a goal. Ask anyone."

"I don't need to ask anyone." He holds my gaze, and the warmth I see in his eyes fills me with wonder. "I've watched you. I've seen the way you've stepped up. You're fucking remarkable in every way."

"*Stay*," I say again, one more time, my voice cracking.

His face softens, and he leans down and scoops me into his arms. The tears finally track down my cheeks as he holds me close, and even through his shirt and coat I can feel his heart beating hard too. He holds me close for a long moment, like he can't bear to let me go, then kisses my forehead and carries me into my bedroom. He lays me down in the bed like I'm something precious, then pulls the covers up to my chin. But he makes no move to get down beside me.

"You're not leaving," I say, starting to sit up, worry pumping through me.

A ghost of a smile passes over his handsome face. "Am I allowed to take my coat off? Or is getting comfortable out of the question?"

"I'll allow it." I smile, but tears are still sliding down my cheeks. I won't feel settled until he's in the bed with me.

He removes his cell phone from his coat pocket, setting it on the bedside table, then shrugs off the coat. Sits down on the edge of the mattress and takes off his shoes.

"You can take your pants off too."

He gives me a regretful smile, then reaches over to wipe away my tears. "No. I think I'd better keep my chastity belt on."

I laugh in surprise as he slides under the covers next to me, my body naturally tilting toward him because he's so big.

"Do your feet slide over the end of the bed?" I ask, fascinated.

"I'm not Bigfoot, Briar," he responds, looking amused.

"But you *are* big everywhere."

He groans as he reclines on his side and pulls me to him, my back to his front, my body fitting perfectly against him.

A deep sense of peace fills me as he wraps his arms around me, holding me close and enveloping me in his scent.

He might think he's incapable of protecting people, but I've never felt this safe with anyone else.

CHAPTER TWENTY-EIGHT

LIAM

I'm sure this makes me sound like the asshole I am, but in the past, it's always felt like torture to stay over at a casual fling's house after sex. Like the opportunity cost for fooling around is hours of lying in the dark next to a near stranger. But lying next to Briar feels so different.

I'm not going to lie—I obviously want her again. But I also want to hold her, to listen to the way her breathing evens out once she's found the peace of sleep. I'd like to memorize the way it sounds and the feeling of her tucked up against me. It might never happen again, so it would be foolish not to soak it up.

Which is why I vow not to waste a minute of the night on sleep.

But sleep must have pulled me under after all, because I'm awoken by Briar whimpering in my arms.

Adrenaline rushes into my system, and I look around for threats, seeing only Karma's yellow eyes glowing in the dark and the digital face of a clock. My gaze lowers to Briar, snuggled up against me. She whimpers again, her body trembling.

I stroke her hair and whisper, "Wake up, Briar, you're having a nightmare."

She continues to tremble, so I turn her in my arms. Her eyes open with a far-off look, and I know she's still caught in it. So I stroke her hair again, murmuring to her. Seconds later, recognition fills her eyes.

"*Liam.*"

"What were you dreaming about?"

"I'm glad you're here," she says, sounding on the verge of tears again.

I hadn't liked seeing her cry earlier. It felt like a stain on my permanent record. A verification that I'm pretty good at making people sad without even trying, which isn't the kind of talent anyone gives out medals for.

But she asked me to stay, and she fell asleep in my arms.

"What was it about, Princess?" I ask, the nickname coming out softer now than it had in the beginning.

"They were cutting my hair," she says in a small voice. "But it wasn't just Melly. My father and mother were with her."

I tense up, my jaw clenching. "They're not going to touch a hair on your head ever again. I'll see to that, no matter what happens between us. I won't let them hurt you."

"It's not your job to protect me, Liam. I need to learn to stand on my own."

"Not my job, no. Consider me a permanent volunteer."

She smiles up at me, even more beautiful mussed and tired than she is usually.

I have to admit to myself that I could fall in love with this woman. It's not rational to love a woman you've only known well for a couple of weeks, but I've always had big feelings. My mother used to shake her head about my rages, telling my father it must be from his side of the family, because all of the other kids in her family were quiet and well-behaved. I figured that was why she left—because Hannah and I had been too much for her, Connor, too colicky. Three courses of parenthood, when she'd only wanted a taste.

Sometimes life gives you more than you want.

Other times it feels like it will always be less.

I'd loved Julia, but not in the way she'd wanted to be loved, with flowers and anniversaries and parties. My love wasn't loud —it was steady.

I asked Briar what she wanted earlier because I want to give it to her. Even if what she wants is for us to be friends and coworkers, and for everything else to fade away.

The way I feel about her won't fade, but I'll pretend if that's what she needs, even though I hate pretending.

"You stayed," she whispers to me.

"I was given little choice. I couldn't risk being attacked by a featherweight woman. You were very intimidating."

She snuggles in closer, wrapping an arm around my back. "Thank you."

"You don't have to thank me for doing exactly what I wanted. It was self-serving."

"Yes, you're incredibly selfish." She tips her head up, her lips only a couple of inches from mine, and by God, I'd like to be selfish. I'd like to take exactly what I need, but I won't do anything that might cause her more pain.

So I just continue to hold her, my fingers drifting up and down her back.

"You want me," she says. It's not a question, nor is it a guess. Lying in my arms right now, she can feel how much I want her.

"Obviously."

She shifts and presses her hips forward, making me groan. "I want you too. Maybe we're overcomplicating this."

"Oh, I think it's pretty damn complicated."

Her gaze beats into me. "So why does everything feel less complicated when we're together?"

I'm not supposed to kiss her again. That's not why I came here. I was going to tell her she meant something to me and leave everything in her hands. But I'm in her bed, and she's rubbing up against me, telling me she wants me—and I've never wanted anyone or anything more than I want her. Everything *does* feel less heavy when we're together. Her smiles can carry me for hours. Her ideas always light answering fires inside of me. And the way she feels against me...

The way she feels against me defies words. It can only be described as transcendent. It's the feeling of a dream sliding into reality, of hope swelling after years of darkness.

I lower my head to her, brushing our lips together—just a little taste of what's been forbidden to me—but the moan she makes has me deepening the kiss. Her hair falls around me like a curtain blocking out the world apart from us as she kisses me back, and she's right. Everything *is* okay right now. It doesn't matter that we weren't supposed to do this again. All that matters is the two of us on this bed. She starts moving her hips as she kisses me, and I make a fist in her lush hair, tugging on it. My other hand finds her hip and guides her movements, because I enjoy torturing myself.

I'm so hard I might actually die if I don't fuck her—and wouldn't that be an interesting trip to the emergency room? But I don't want to rush through this.

She pulls back slightly, her lips pink and inviting, glistening slightly. "Liam..."

I squeeze my fist in her hair. "You can say my name all you want, but don't you dare say please like you did last time. I'm writing it on the list."

She laughs. "Why not?"

"Because I'm not ready to come, and if I hear you begging me to fuck you, it's going to put me right over the edge."

Her eyes widen. "Really?"

I pull her on top of me so she's straddling me, one leg on either side. "Can't you feel what you're doing to me?"

The pleased look on her face nearly tears another groan out of me. I like being the reason for that look on her face. I'd like to please her in other ways, always.

"I'm so glad you're here," she says in a quick rush of words, and I lift my hand to her cheek, cradling it. Feeling...

I've never been good at knowing what I'm feeling, but I'm glad I'm here too. There's nowhere else I'd rather be, no one I'd rather be with.

No matter what trouble it causes for both of us, I'm glad I came—and not just because she's on top of me. It's the way she's looking at me mostly, like I could be good news for her. I want to earn that look. I want to help her make Silver Star into the best fucking brewery in Asheville.

I'd want that anyway—it's been so long since I've believed in my work—but I want it specifically *for her*.

I want Briar Sterling to have everything she's ever dreamed of. I want to do stupid shit, like reach into the sky and pluck out a star for her, and throw the best New Year's Eve party in the history of Asheville, even though I've always thought New Year's Eve parties were a joke.

Dammit. She's still looking at me like that, and the words spill out. "I'm glad I'm here too," I admit. "I've missed you."

It's true. I'm usually not aware of missing people until I see them and figure out the void inside of me was shaped like them. But with her...

I've felt her absence like a broken tooth (yes, I'd fucking know). Always there, always hurting, particularly since I knew *she* was hurting.

"I don't know what's going to happen," she says, her expression tentative, "but I want you tonight."

I kiss her again and then reach for the hem of her red sleep shirt, pulling it up over her head and tossing it. She's still straddling me, her golden hair loose, framing her pink-tipped breasts. An angel, down to her soul.

Fuck me, I'm a lucky man. Come what may, I can't regret stumbling down dozens of wrong paths if they led me to this time and place and *her*.

"You are the most beautiful thing I've ever seen," I murmur as I trace her with my hands, following my touch with my lips. I kiss her breasts, taste her nipples, and she holds the back of my head, clutching me to her like she doesn't ever want me to stop.

Fine by me. I'm a man who knows how to focus when the situation calls for it.

She's the one who eventually pulls back, but only to say, "I want your shirt off too."

I grin, because why *wouldn't* I be grinning? "You liked what you saw last time?"

"Obviously," she says with a soft smile, echoing what I said earlier.

I sit up, Briar still on my lap, and tug it off in a quick movement, tossing it. Her palms skim over my chest, trailing fingers across a couple of scars I've picked up.

"How'd you get these?" she asks softly.

"By being a dumbass." I kiss the side of her face, then the little beauty mark beneath her eye. "I got into some fights when I was a kid. Nothing too serious."

"And this?" Her fingers roam over my tattoo.

"Also by being a dumbass," I say with a snort. "But if you like it, I'll be a dumbass again and get another one."

In response, she leans in and runs her tongue lightly over it. More tattoos it is.

I slide my hand down her thigh, her leg still wrapped around me, then my fingers trail inward. God, I need to feel her slick heat. Her hand instantly descends to my belt, and I take over, suddenly eager to get my damn pants off.

"Take your shorts and pants off," I say, my voice hoarse, as I set her down on the bed so I can finish undressing.

I watch as she complies, my throat dry as I take in the sight of her—a fucking vision—and then I sit down and pull her back onto my lap, wanting it like this so I can touch every inch of her.

"Liam...I don't want to wait anymore."

Neither do I.

I adjust myself, and she sinks down on me slowly, the sensation unreal. My eyes feast on her. I can't look away from her face, from her needy expression as she takes me, every inch of me burying into her tight, wet heat. A desperate growl escapes me as I grip her hair again and kiss her deeply.

Something inside of me needs this—my mouth on her while I'm so deep inside of her.

She gasps when I'm all the way in and then starts to rock again in a steady cadence that drives me around-the-bend crazy. The caveman in me wants to pound into her. To take her. To lay claim to this woman. But I have a more powerful need to give her pleasure and make this a memory she'll want to return to once she's found someone more appropriate, someone who wouldn't blow her life apart...

I don't like that thought one bit, so I focus on what's happening between us to blur it out. Our bodies, rocking together; her lips, seeking out mine again and again. I reach between her legs as we move in sync, finding that perfect spot where we're joined, making her tremble against me.

Then I rock her all the way back onto the mattress, her legs still wrapped around me, and thrust in deep—again, and again, feeling her rise to meet me, needing this more than I've ever let myself need anything.

This feels right in a way that goes beyond the base needs of sex, but it feels fucking dirty too, the way it should. I could be inside of her all day and night, and it wouldn't be enough. I want to lose myself in her and never find my way out. I want the little sounds she's making in the back of her throat to be the last sounds I ever hear—and the first sounds I hear every morning.

Her lips find my neck, kissing and sucking, and I hope it leaves a mark. I want to leave my mark on her too, so people look at us and know.

I *want* them to know.

I especially want anyone who'd be stupid enough to hurt her to know that if they mess with her, they very much mess with me. And they'd be foolish to mess with either of us.

I bury my face in her neck, licking and sucking as I thrust in.

"Liam," she whispers. "I'm so close."

So am I. The last time we were together, I pulled out at the end. Not because I didn't trust her, but because it felt like I'd be making a claim I had no right to make. Today, I'm ready to make that claim.

I shift my head to kiss her as I thrust in deep, and I feel her clench around me—the sensation instantly triggering my own orgasm. Pleasure cascades through me, changing my body chemistry, as I empty into her. Still kissing her. Still sucking in her sweet sounds.

I'll be damned if it doesn't feel like something that was broken inside of me is shifting back into alignment.

Earlier, I realized I could fall in love with her, but here's the truth: I'm already falling.

CHAPTER TWENTY-NINE

LIAM

Briar falls back to sleep before I do, her breathing turning slow and even, and the peace I feel with her asleep in my arms is enough to put me to sleep too. The next thing I'm aware of is a ringing phone.

Briar's still in my arms, but she sits up, blindly reaching for the bedside table to *make it stop*.

She throws me a wild look when she sees the screen. "It's Hannah."

I brush a soothing hand down her bare back. "She doesn't know I'm in your bed, Briar. She's not psychic. You can answer." I glance out of her window, taking in the dim glow of predawn light, and feel a tickle of anxiety. I'm used to watching out for my family, especially for Hannah. "She's not a morning person. If she's calling this early, it must be important."

She bites her lip and answers the phone.

A second later, she says, "Yes, that's what happened, but honestly, Hannah, it's barely seven." She pauses. "No, I didn't take pictures. It seemed like it would be rude."

Since I'm mostly sure the call is not related to an emergency or the fact that I'm here, I breathe a sigh of relief. Hannah's okay.

I head into the bathroom to take a leak and then start the shower, figuring Briar can join me there once she's off the call. The water feels like it's purging the worst of my hangover and mostly sleepless night, so I stay in there awhile, laughing to myself at the sweet, fruity smell of her soap.

I'm still washing when she walks in, dressed in her sleep shirt and panties. She smiles at the sight of me using the soap. "You're going to smell like me."

"Good."

She takes a step toward the shower door, but then pauses, her expression uncertain. "Hannah called because she wanted to know about Nora's mom and Eugene. I forgot to tell you that he proposed to her yesterday. We were all really surprised."

"Why don't you come in here and tell me all about it. I'll pretend to be interested in Eugene's love life while I finger-fuck you."

"*Liam*," she gasps.

I laugh. "Who are you worried is going to hear me? Karma? Now, are you going to come in, or do I have to get out and carry you in?"

Her eyes light up with mischief, and she runs out of the bathroom, leaving me with no choice but to follow her—soaking wet and buck naked.

She shrieks with laughter when I catch up with her in the hallway just beyond the bedroom and wrap my soaked arms around her. "You're all wet!"

"Now you are too," I say, slinging her over my shoulder. "Hopefully in lots of interesting places."

She slaps my shoulder as I march us back to the bedroom. "You're horrible."

"I am, but you seem to like it, so I don't have any motivation to change."

I slide into the en suite bathroom and set her down next to the shower, grinning like a total idiot—feeling like one, too, but not caring much. "I think you should take those clothes off, Briar. They're soaked."

She smiles playfully as she slowly pulls her loose top over her head, letting her hair fall in a wild riot around her bare chest.

Damn, she's a sight for sore eyes. I could stare at her for the rest of my life, and it wouldn't be long enough, but why settle for staring when you can touch?

I grab a fistful of her hair and use it to tug her closer. "Come into the shower with me. I want to do dirty things to you."

"My hair will get wet," she objects.

"I want to wash it for you."

She grins at me. "You promised to do dirty things to me."

"Oh, it'll be fucking dirty. You haven't seen me do it yet."

I kiss her while she's still laughing.

She pulls back and steps out of her underwear, leaving her entirely bare for me. She's a goddess, framed in gold.

I open the shower door and tug her in with me.

The hot water beats down on us as I kiss her slowly, losing myself in the moment. She's warm and safe, and right now she's mine. She kisses me back with the same slow reverence.

I run my hands through her hair and pull back. "Where's your shampoo?"

She points to a wire rack built into the corner of the over-sized shower stall. "You're really going to wash it?"

"I want to take care of you. But don't worry, I haven't forgotten that I made other promises too." I turn her in my arms and reach between her legs as the water continues to pound down on us.

"Does this mean I have to talk about Eugene's engagement?" she says in a breathy voice. "Because I don't think I want to anymore."

I lean in, rubbing her slickness with my fingers. "Please don't."

She hums and backs into me, my dick hard as hell as I thrust my fingers into her, hungry for the way she's responding to my touch.

"I wish I had more hands," I mutter as I run my other hand over her slick body, palming her breasts as she grinds into me.

My mind starts wandering—*When will this end? How will it end? Does it need to end?*—but I corral it back to the present moment. I want to enjoy her while I have her. I can only hope that she might want to keep me too, that we'll figure out a way to make it work.

Briar moans as I curl my fingers inside her, finding a spot she likes, and suddenly the only thing that matters is giving her pleasure.

"Bend over for me, Princess," I whisper in her ear. "Hold onto that wall and lift your ass up."

She glances over her shoulder at me as she plants her hands on the wall and pushes her waist out.

Fuck me, I want to slam into her—I want it so badly my body is nearly trembling with need. But promises were made. I run my hands over her sopping-wet hair again, then grab the shampoo from the rack and squeeze some into my hand.

"You're washing my hair right now?" she whispers as if scandalized.

"I'm taking care of you," I reply, using one hand to start rubbing the shampoo in while I return the other to its rightful spot between her legs. "All the way."

"Oh my God," she whispers, arcing into my touch.

But I can't rinse the shampoo out with only one hand, and

there's something else I want to see—another sight to memorize in case she's taken from me.

"I need both of my hands to finish up your hair, Princess," I whisper into her ear. "You'd better take care of yourself while I finish."

She looks back at me, her eyes full of desire, and I get a little bit harder. Something that shouldn't be possible. She keeps her gaze locked on mine as she removes one hand from the wall and reaches between her legs.

I do the only thing I can and lean in and kiss her wet lips before rinsing the rest of the shampoo from her hair and massaging the conditioner in. All the while, she continues to pleasure herself, her body responding with small gasps and shudders, and finally I can't take it anymore. I fist a hand in her slick hair and bend my knees enough that I'm level.

"You can stop fucking yourself, Princess," I say. "I'm going to take over."

A glorious sound escapes her, and she pulls her hand away, slapping it against the wall.

I don't wait. I can't—

I'm already lined up, and I thrust into her in one long stroke.

It feels so good, I nearly lose my balance and wipe out on the wet tiles. She pushes back, deepening our contact, and I use my hand in her hair to turn her head enough so I can press another desperate kiss to her mouth as I pull out and, using my grip on her hip, press back in. Then I do it again, still kissing her, because I want nothing more than to lose myself in her again.

We keep moving together, the water spraying down on us, and again, I feel something inside of me, slumbering for too long, awakening.

She breaks her mouth away from mine for just a moment, to say, "I'm so close, Liam. I'm—"

She doesn't need to say another word. I feel her clenching

around me, and the sensation is so overwhelmingly good that I lose myself with her. Maybe I find myself too, because right now —still buried inside her, our bodies pressed together—I feel at peace.

It's possible she feels it too, because when I finally start to pull out, she reaches around and coaxes me back. "Just for another second."

I squeeze her close, and after I finally pull away, I help her rinse her hair.

We dry off and pull on our clothes—silent but in an almost worshipful way, not uncomfortable at all. When we're dressed, Briar takes her brush out to the living area and sits down at the small table.

"Will you let me braid it?" I ask.

It's not the sort of thing I'd say at the boxing gym, definitely not in front of Mick, but I've been thinking about it for a while now.

Her brows knit together. "Most men don't know how to take care of long hair."

"I'm not most men."

She hands the brush over.

I section her golden hair and slowly pull the brush through each part, careful not to tug against her scalp.

She peers back at me as I start to weave her long tresses into a braid.

"No, Briar," I say, deciding to answer the unasked question. "I don't know how to do this because I'm a man-whore or because I used to work in a hair salon. You know our mother left when we were little, and Hannah was a few years younger than me. I learned how from the internet so I could help her."

I pull the elastic from my wrist and use it to tie the end of the braid. Maybe she'll give it back to me, and it will smell like her for another few days.

She turns in the chair, her eyes full of worry. "I don't want to get between you and Hannah. I love Hannah too."

"I know you do," I say, brushing my fingers across her cheek. "Thank you for that. I like knowing she's got other people looking out for her. But we're not going to worry about Hannah right now. Not today. I think we should just spend time together. We'll figure the rest out later. Now, what do you usually do at this time of morning? Walk me through your day."

Worry still shines in her eyes, but she smiles. "I usually do some yoga before I head to work."

"Okay, let's do yoga."

She gives me an incredulous look, and I shrug. "You boxed with me. I'll do your weird woo-woo stretches and pretend they're exercise."

"You're going to like it," she insists, sunshine flooding her expression. "It feels amazing."

"If you say so, boss."

And what do you know? She's right. Even if most of my enjoyment comes from the excitement she seems to get out of leading me through her pretzel maneuvers and occasionally collapsing on the floor, plus the sight of her body curved into the different forms.

Afterward, we eat granola together—the next step in Briar's routine—and she tells me all about "Great-Aunt Sky," who taught her yoga and drew pictures with her. I'm glad not everyone in her childhood was an asshole, not that I'm surprised. Someone good had to be involved in the making of this woman.

"Where does Great-Aunt Sky live?" I ask as we clean the dishes in her kitchen sink.

"In the mountains in Georgia." A frown creases her beautiful face. "I was hoping she'd come visit this month, but it didn't work out this year."

"I think I'd like to meet your aunt someday."

She gives me a look of skepticism that's not flattering to my ego. "You don't need to say that."

"Obviously not, but I mean it."

With her hands still submerged in the dishwater, she tips up on her toes and kisses me.

We go to the brewery together, and I help her take down the tinsel tree, then convince her we should donate it and get ourselves a real one next year.

"I didn't think you'd care about Christmas trees," she comments, giving me a sidelong glance.

"I definitely don't care about fake ones. Real ones smell nice."

"There are a lot of hidden depths to you, Liam."

Ann, who came in to escape her son-in-law (her words), says, "You got debts? You should consolidate those, son. The interest payments will do a number on you."

As the day winds down, Briar and I exchange a look, and she says, "Maybe you could stop by later. If you want to."

Oh, I want.

IT'S late evening by the time we get back to Briar's place. I'm surprised by the need I feel to learn more about her through her things. While she changes in the bedroom, I stroll around the living room, studying the framed art prints on the wall, and then pause by the wooden chest next to the sectional. It looks almost like a decorative piece, but it's heavy and there's nothing on top.

"What's in this?" I ask as she emerges from the room in some flowing blue pants and a clingy white T-shirt I instantly appreciate.

"Oh, it's nothing." The panicked look on her face says differently.

"You secretly a drug dealer?" I tease.

She opens the lid, showing me the collection of stones, crystals, and metal wire inside.

"So you and Dottie have a secret side business peddling rocks?"

"Very funny." She looks away. "I…I used to make a lot of jewelry. I loved it. That was my last business."

"You kept this," I comment, studying her. "Do you still love it?"

She rubs the spot between her eyebrows, her gaze still on the crystals. "I don't know," she says after a long moment. "I stopped. Or mostly stopped. It made me feel like a failure."

"Because the business didn't do as well as you wanted?"

She looks conflicted for a moment, but then she says, "It *was* doing well. The woman I worked with…I thought we were a team. Turns out she was embezzling money, and then she ran off with everything in our bank account. I didn't even try to recover the business after that. That's why my dad doesn't trust my judgment. I should have known better than to trust her, but I *wanted* to trust her."

"So he figures you should have known she'd run off with all your money?"

"Yeah."

"And now you're worried that I'll take off into the night with a sack of hops."

"No," she says with a soft smile. "Should I be?"

I know what she's really asking. She wants to know if I'm going to fuck her over, like so many other people have.

I wrap my hand around her chin and lift it slightly, needing her eyes to meet mine. "I wouldn't intentionally hurt you. I'm on your side, no matter what. I want to protect you and your interests. And I have to tell you, you had no way of knowing that woman had bad intentions. You're not psychic, and thank God. You're already a triple threat."

She lifts her eyebrows, a smile spreading across her face. "Oh, yeah?"

I run a finger across her lips. "Beautiful. Smart. And kind."

She leans into my touch and says, "Considering other people's feelings is a weakness. I didn't make the rules."

"But we make our own rules, remember?"

"We're not very good at following them."

I smile as I lean in and kiss her. "Maybe not, but I'll bet you're good at making jewelry, and it just so happens I got my sister a spectacularly shitty Christmas present. Maybe you can help me not embarrass myself. Teach me how to make something for her."

"You don't actually want to learn," she quips, smiling as she says it.

"Like hell. I've been waiting my whole life for a beautiful woman to teach me how to do something useful."

Her smile stretches wider. "Okay, but remember you said you wanted to learn. You have no one to blame but yourself if you don't like it."

"I will." I steal another kiss. "But let's put on *Rocky II* so I feel extra manly while we make jewelry."

We watch *Rocky II* while Briar shows me how to wrap wire around the stones. She makes it look easy, but it is *not* fucking easy, and mine looks like a Macaroni Picasso a toddler would take home.

"That's really good," Briar says, tracing her finger over the pendant I'm trying to make.

"Look at you, lying to my face."

She laughs. "It *is* good. You just got started."

"My hands are too big for this."

"We can fix it."

And no shit, she gets right in and makes it look like I made something worth keeping.

"Only with a great stretch of the imagination can I say I made that," I point out.

"We made it together," she replies, and a warm feeling spreads through my chest. I never thought much of group projects. But maybe all those teachers who assigned them to us were onto something, because it feels good, building things with Briar.

Or maybe that's just *Briar*. She's a natural leader. A person who builds people up rather than tearing them down. The true opposite of her shithead father.

I lean in and kiss the side of her face. "You're a good teacher. Maybe this will butter Hannah up enough that she won't kill me."

"We're going to tell her about us?" she asks, her voice tremulous. "Does this mean you want to keep doing this?"

"I don't want it to be the end of something when she gets back. I want it to be the beginning."

"Me too," she says with a smile that wrecks me.

She wants me too. I take a moment to revel in that before continuing:"And it may not be my place, but I don't think you should give up something you love because you had the shit luck of having a bad friend. As you know, I've had some bad friends too."

"Sure," she says, looking pointedly at me, "and I wouldn't give up trying to make friends because one of them wasn't good."

She surprises a laugh out of me. "Look at you calling me out. But you're right. I think maybe we're both right."

We pack up the jewelry supplies and fall asleep on the couch together. I wake up past midnight, and she's asleep beside me, tousled and cute. I gather her in my arms and carry her to the bed.

I'm tucking her in when her eyes flutter open. "You're still here."

"Is this my cue to leave?" I ask, grinning.

"No. I want you to stay. If you want—"

"I want."

I climb into bed beside her and pull her close, my head buried into her hair and my arms wrapped around her.

"Liam, what are we doing?" she whispers, gripping my arms as if she's afraid I'll leave her.

"I don't know, but I like it." The dark interior of the apartment emboldens me to admit, "I like *you*, Briar Sterling."

"I like you too," she says, nestling closer. "So much." And I fall asleep, feeling completely happy for the first time in a long, long while.

CHAPTER THIRTY

BRIAR

I wake up in the middle of the night, my heart pounding.

In my dreams, my father destroyed my Felicity doll, tearing the limbs off as he repeated over and over again, "It's for your own good."

This time Liam doesn't wake up, but he pulls me closer reflexively, his arm wrapped possessively around me, and rests his chin on top of my head. My breathing evens out, and I relax into his warmth and protection.

I wish Hannah weren't coming back this week—a thought that floods me with guilt.

I promised her I would never date her brother. I'd made that promise easily, as if it meant nothing. Because at the time it *did* mean nothing. I only wanted Liam because he was the best at what he did. Not because he was funny and loyal and...well... *Liam.* But then I got to know him.

I tried to stay away, but we were always together, always within a few feet of each other, it seemed. And he's been supporting my dream in a way I never thought possible.

He taught me to throw a punch.

He let me assist him in making the New Year's beer.

And he's made me feel like my knowledge is valuable. No other man has ever shown any interest in my jewelry wrapping. Certainly no one else has asked to learn it.

Making jewelry with him last night restored some of the simple joy it used to bring me.

No one else has ever made me feel like Liam does. Valued and seen. Understood. Wanted.

Is it possible Hannah will understand?

Or will she look at me the way my father has so many times—

Oh, Briar, you sweet little fool. You didn't listen to reason, and this is what happens.

Hannah loves Liam to death, but she warned me to stay away from him. She told me he wasn't serious with women and always kept them at a distance.

I know for a fact that he broke things off with Margaret because she wanted to move a toothbrush into his apartment. What would he do if he knew that I want to weave him into even more of my life, not just for a stolen weekend, but permanently? All day, I've been imagining what it would be like for us to live together and work together, and maybe even go on double dates with Hannah and Travis.

Oh, he'd probably hate that.

And yet...

I could see him enjoying it. He'd give me one of his *here we fucking go* smiles, and then he'd lean into the experience—just like he did with making jewelry.

He's right. The situation we're in is complicated, but it has never felt that way when we're together. It feels right.

I fall back into a fretful sleep, until I'm awoken by the buzzing of Liam's phone on the side table. It's early, before six, so I glance at the screen, worried something might be wrong.

Seconds later, the phone clatters down from my shaking

fingers. I squeeze my eyes shut. If only I could unsee what I just saw. It feels like the floor has fallen out from underneath me, again. I'm that naïve girl who believed in Jonah. The fool who kept looking the other way when the numbers weren't adding up.

I'm the girl who was born with an overly soft heart tailor-made to be broken.

CHAPTER THIRTY-ONE

LIAM

When I wake up on Tuesday morning, I reach for Briar but find the bed empty. I pull on my pants and leave the bedroom. The place is small enough that it only takes me seconds to find her. She's already dressed and is sitting at the little kitchen table with Karma curled up on her lap. A mug of coffee sits forgotten in front of her as she stares off at nothing.

Something has changed. Something all the way bad.

"What's wrong?" I ask, striding toward her.

Her gaze shifts sharply to me. "Don't come any closer."

Alarm pulses through me, and I stop in my tracks and look around, half-expecting to find someone else in the apartment. Yesterday, it felt like we were perfectly in tune. How could that have slipped away in a single night?

"What happened?"

"Your...your phone buzzed, and I thought something might be wrong because it was so early. So I checked the screen, but..." She pauses and swallows. "It was an update for a dating app."

It takes me a few seconds to understand what she means, because I haven't been using any dating app. Haven't had a millisecond's thought about being with another woman since I got to know her. Then it hits me...

I downloaded that app to get Hannah off my back.

"Briar—" I take another step closer, but she's still got that wild look, almost like she's afraid of me, so I stagger to a stop. "It's not—"

"I know we're not together. You've got every right." She looks down into her coffee mug. "But this is just so much like what happened with Jonah. Sophie found out what he was up to when he left his phone at her place. After everything, I...I can't do this. I'm not ready. I should have known I wasn't ready."

"It's not what you think," I say, my heart racing, blood pounding in my ears.

She gives me a sad smile. "That's what he said to Sophie too."

Jesus Fucking Christ.

"I am *not* Jonah. I downloaded that damn thing after we kissed the first time, because I wanted to be able to look my sister in the face and tell her I was trying to date other women. I didn't want to lie to her. *Or* you. But, yeah, at the time I figured it might be better if both of us found someone else. You seemed to think the same."

"Liam, I don't need to know this," she says, tears forming in her eyes.

Feverish desperation flashes through me, frying my nerve endings. I have to fix this. I have to make it right, but I'm not sure how. Maybe it's too late to make anything right. Maybe there was never a real chance of making anything work between us.

But I can't let her misread this situation.

"I haven't messaged a single person on there since reactivating it. I couldn't bring myself to even look at it. You can check. I *want* you to check."

Tears are streaming down her face now. The need to make it better is so overpowering it nearly topples me, but I don't go to her. I need to respect her boundary.

"*Please.*"

"Liam," she says again, a different kind of plea. Like she's saying, *Please, stop, you're hurting me more.*

But I can't. Not yet. She needs to know the truth, dammit.

"I care about you, Briar. I tried not to want you, but some forces are too powerful to be denied. If you're done with me, I understand—it's a fucked-up situation, no doubt—but I can't have you thinking I've been talking to other women. You're the only woman who's been on my mind. You're *always* on my mind."

She swipes tears off her cheeks—tears I put there—and it feels like someone has wrenched my heart out of my chest with their bare hand.

"Please, Briar. Please just let me comfort you."

"Put on some clothes," she says, her expression hardening, as if I'd offered to fuck her on the kitchen table.

I promised myself not to care what anyone thought of me anymore after I was arrested, but I care what she thinks. I care a lot.

I nod woodenly, then head into the bedroom and tug on the rest of my clothes, my heart beating unevenly in my chest.

She's going to send me away. Maybe she'll fire me while she's at it, not that I give much of a shit about my job at the moment.

She watches me as I emerge from the bedroom, her arms folded. Karma has his paws up on the table so he can get a good look at me too.

I lift my phone out of my pocket. "I want to show you my phone."

She waves me off when I approach the table.

"Please be fair about this," I say. "I know you're fair."

"*Liam,*" she says sharply. "It doesn't matter."

"It *does* matter."

"No, I believe you about the app. Mostly. I know you wouldn't offer to show me if you were lying."

I like that first part, the second part less. "So?"

"It just...helped me realize." She pauses to take a deep breath. "This was a mistake. I'm not ready, and it would be so messy for us to get involved."

"Doesn't feel like a mistake," I say, a contrarian born and bred. "I want to be with you, Briar."

She takes a second to digest this, then says, "What about Hannah? What about the brewery?"

"What about it? Don't you like working together? Because I fucking love it."

"We should *only* be working together," she says firmly, crossing her arms tighter, as if she's shielding herself from me. "And you and Hannah are so important to each other. I don't want to ruin your relationship. I'd hate myself if I did."

"She *is* important to me, but so are you. Please believe me, Briar. I need you to believe in me."

Her eyes soften for a moment, but then fresh tears drip down her cheeks. Silent tears. "You should leave."

Hopelessness swallows me. She's not going to change her mind. Not now. Probably not ever. The last couple of days have felt like a pocket out of time because that's exactly what they were. I'll have to return to the life I had before, only now I realize how empty my existence was.

"So you took what you wanted, and now I'm dismissed?" I snap, undoubtedly making shit worse. I'm like a wolf caught in a trap who immediately starts gnawing on his own leg. Except I'm also hurting her.

God, I'm being an asshole. I know what it must have felt like for her to see that stupid app on my phone after what Jonah did to her. I haven't opened it even once since downloading it. It was my attempt at a safety net—and now it's my downfall.

But if it wasn't this, maybe it would have been something else. Maybe my best will never be good enough for anyone.

Hurt ripples across her face. "You *know* it's not like that. It's just...it's better if we stick to the rules."

"All right." I back up toward the door. "No hard feelings. You can ask for a fuck anytime you feel like it. Goodbye, *boss*. I'll see you at work."

CHAPTER THIRTY-TWO

BRIAR

My heart has been ripped to little shreds.

I felt so safe with Liam—as if he could cocoon me from the world. But when I saw that app on his phone, that feeling of security evaporated, revealing a raw wound that's never healed.

Before Liam came out of the bedroom, I spent hours chastising myself for being a woman who wants to be loved so badly she keeps imagining it happening over and over again. A woman so desperate for affection she'll eat every sweet lie that's fed to her.

Now, I'm more confused but no less broken.

I start pacing the wood floors of my apartment while crying, feeling restless and broken. Karma trails me.

I'm desperate to talk to someone, but I don't want to call Nora when I'm like this. She's been so helpful, and all I've done is complain.

My great-aunt Sky has been my champion for years, but she's already said she can't travel to Asheville this winter. I don't want her to feel pressured to do something she can't or shouldn't.

I pull out my phone and tap my chin with it, my heart

breaking a little more with each passing second, and then call the person I feel most guided to.

"Briar," Dottie says urgently. "I was just thinking about you. Do you need me to come in early?"

"Oh, Dottie," I say, crying again. "I think I messed everything up."

"I very much doubt that. But come to the tea shop and have tea with me. There's nothing a good cup of tea can't cure. We'll work through all of this together."

"I don't think tea can cure what's wrong with me," I say through a sob.

"Maybe not, my dear, but tea and sympathy are the best treatment for any ailment. I'll be waiting for you."

I end the call and try to gather myself before leaving.

"Do I look as bad as I feel?" I whisper to Karma, who gives me a very telling meow as he surveys my Silver Star sweatshirt and old yoga pants. He's always been a tough critic. But I know this is the best I can do right now, so I put on a coat—not Liam's —and head out the door and drive downtown.

As soon as I open the door to the tea shop, Dottie pops up from her chair and hurries over, pulling me into a warm hug. I press my face into her shoulder, not even caring that one of the sequined stars on her shoulder is digging into my face. It's all I can do to swallow the sob building in my throat.

I'm so messed up I don't even know what I'm most upset about—Liam having that app on his phone, or my decision to send him away for it. His explanation made sense, and I do mostly believe him, but doubt is still knifing into me. I hate thinking of other women messaging Liam, wanting him. *Dating* him.

A voice in my head whispers, *Then how much worse will it be if you have to stand by and watch him parade them through the brewery?*

I burrow in closer to Dottie, needing her comfort, which is an anchor in my sea of confusion.

"Oh, it'll all work out, my dear," she says, rubbing my back. "I wore this silver star sweater today as a sign of solidarity. In fact, I ordered them for the whole staff. You know, Liam told me all about the woman who wrote that article. I'd already picked out a corrective profile of crystals for her, but I don't hold out high hopes for a full healing. Some people aren't willing to change. And your parents...honestly, dear, I have no words. Truly, I do not. But if you'd like, we can try to coax them into accepting some crystals too. I was thinking if you made them into jewelry, then perhaps they wouldn't realize—"

I pull back, alarmed. "Dottie, what on earth are you talking about?"

For a moment we just stare at each other, Dottie taking in my red eyes and dishevelment. "My dear girl, if you're not upset about the article, then what happened to upset you so?"

"What article?" I ask as adrenaline dumps into my veins.

"Oh, goodness. Oh, my. Come, come, my girl." She leads me to the table where she was sitting. After I've basically collapsed into the white chair, she shoves an open copy of *The Asheville Gazette* toward me.

"At least it's only on page five. Most people don't read real newspapers anymore anyway." She pats my hand as I start reading.

The headline is "Big Trouble at the Little Brewery," by Melanie Harris. Otherwise known as Melly.

Fuck.

I speed-read it, my pulse racing the whole time.

Melly paints Liam as a thug, and me as a weak link—the unremarkable child of a remarkable father, a woman who's been brainwashed by a handsome face. She implies that I let Liam talk me into losing the organic status my father fought for. She even quotes Bubba, saying he "can't believe" I threw away everything they'd built in such record time.

There's also a quote from Steve, Liam's former boss at Mountain Morning, who describes Liam as "unhinged and dangerous."

"This is full of lies." I peer at Dottie, my voice trembling with rage. I'm still upset by what happened between Liam and me, but the way Melly wrote about him...

It makes me want to retroactively steal all of her favorite toys and destroy them in front of her. It makes me want to shave her head. It makes me want to punch her, to be perfectly honest. How dare she...how *dare* she...

She looked at him, she wanted him, and when he chose me instead of her, she did this.

Of course, I see my father's Machiavellian hand behind all of it. He probably cut Bubba a fat check for his role in this mess.

"Dottie, what are we going to do? I think...I think maybe my dad's trying to pressure me into firing Liam. Liam embarrassed him last week, and my dad doesn't like being embarrassed."

She sits up a little straighter. "Well, there *is* the jewelry idea. Crystals can be very transformative—"

"I'm not making them any jewelry. I already got them what they wanted for the holidays."

My family has the ridiculous tradition of making wish lists for items we could easily afford ourselves. It makes gift-giving easy—and joyless.

She taps the paper with her finger. "Did this woman talk to you, or anyone else who currently works at Silver Star, about the brewery?"

"No. I don't think so."

"Then we'll be getting a retraction *and* an apology. Perhaps another writer at the paper would be inclined to tell the true story of the brewery. A *fair* story."

"You think we can convince them?"

She gives me a level look. "My dear Briar, we won't give them a choice."

"But, Dottie..." I take in a deep breath and say, "The truth is that the beer wasn't organic. Ever. My father and Bubba were lying. That's the truth, and if it gets out, our clients might demand restitution."

She pushes her lips out in thought. "It's always better to align yourself with the truth, my dear. It'll come out anyway. You might as well get ahead of it and play a part in the telling."

I nod, even though the thought sends chills through me. The cost might be enough to put us under...

"Now, why don't you tell me all about what had you looking so blue when you walked in here."

I'm tempted to keep my relationship problems to myself. We have more immediate hurdles to deal with than my love life. But I know it would be safe to spill my soul to her.

So I explain what happened over the last few days, leaving out the details that feel too personal.

Maybe I was expecting her to push me toward Liam, to tell me that I need to give it a shot because he and I are meant for each other.

Maybe that's what I *wanted*.

But she doesn't do that.

She just gives me a level look and says, "Yes, of course you know what's best. Love isn't easy, my dear, and both people need to be ready for the timing to be right."

WHEN DOTTIE and I get to the brewery, Liam's sitting in the tasting room, drinking a beer at one of the wooden guest tables. My pulse escalates at the sight of him. He lifts his chin to greet us as we walk in. He looks tired and wrung out, and his eyes are bloodshot.

He'd started to feel like the antidote to all of my bad dreams, and now we're here. It seems incredibly unfair, even if it's partly my own decisions that landed us here. I want to wrap my arms around him, and I also want to hit him. Both desires are equally strong. I've never felt this way about *anyone* before.

"I came to turn in my notice, boss," he says, not meeting my eyes. He lifts the beer, which I can tell from the scent is a tropical IPA. He *hates* Bubba's tropical IPA. We all do, honestly. That's why it's on our *drink-us-dry* list for the New Year's party. "I saw the article. I'm even more of a liability than I was a few weeks ago. You should get rid of me."

"You are *not* quitting," I say tartly, pushing the beer away.

His eyebrows wing up. "I was drinking that."

"You were feeling sorry for yourself."

The look on his face says I've officially gotten his attention, and also that he's kind of pissed at me. "So what if I was?"

"You can feel sorry for yourself later. The article is bullshit, as you know. My father's giving me another test, but I'm sick of playing his games. Dottie has a plan for dealing with the fallout. We're not giving them what they want."

"You're not giving me up, Princess?" His mouth turns up in a sardonic smile. "Because you could, you know. I figured you wouldn't be upset to get rid of me right now. I might be good, but there are plenty of good brewers out there who don't have arrest records or baggage. Ones your daddy might like a little better."

My heart lurches. His words are razor-edged, but I can feel the hurt flowing off him.

"Well, you figured wrong. Now, do we have a pale ale to carbonate or not? Because Dottie and I are ready. She even ordered matching silver sequined sweaters for everyone at the brewery, like the one she's wearing. I assume you got bigger sizes for Liam and Otis?" I ask, glancing at Dottie.

"Of course," she says with a smile. "Liam's might be a little small, but there's nothing wrong with a snug fit. I thought we could all wear them for the New Year's party."

"You heard her." I shift my gaze back to Liam, meeting the challenging look he's giving me. "We're all going to have festive sweaters, so we definitely need to have a beer better than this one." I gesture to the crappy IPA that I shoved away from him.

"*Yes, ma'am,*" he says, saluting me, his words sending an electric charge through me.

"We'll be fine as long as we stick to the rules," I lie in an undertone, telling myself it's true. "We've done it before."

He raises his eyebrows again, and I have the foolish urge to trace them with my fingers. To kiss him and forget the rules and also the sight of that app on his phone. I want to go back to the feeling of lying in his arms. But it's not that simple. My wariness has been reignited, and it's had plenty of practice over the last several years.

"Maybe I'll tattoo them onto my body." The way he says it is sinuous, invoking memories of that tattoo winding around his arm and the one on his thick, muscular thigh.

"Oh, that would be quite painful," Dottie says, tsking. "It might be easier to just memorize them. I could make a mnemonic for you, if you'd like to show them to me."

"Nah," he says, getting to his feet. "It's not remembering them that's the problem." He meets my gaze again, his eyes bottomless. "It's following them."

CHAPTER THIRTY-THREE

BRIAR

It's Friday, two days before the New Year's Eve party. My father has already confirmed that he and my mother are coming—and also that he expects me to attend the weekly Sterling family dinner tonight.

He didn't acknowledge Melly's article, or the role he clearly played in it, not that I'd expected differently. Accountability is not his thing—hence the way he made it our fault that he and Bubba flubbed the brewery's organic status.

He also has not acknowledged the retraction the paper printed, or the statement from Liam, reporting that he took over the brewing at the beginning of the month and has seen no evidence that the brewery was producing organic beer before the change in management.

We told the truth, which is exactly what was needed, but the truth is always a double-edged sword.

Because even if my father won't acknowledge our statement, other people have. Several of the bars and local grocers that stock our beer have called up threatening to cut ties over it. I've had to make several restitution payments, and I'm sure more requests will come. Maybe enough to sink us for good.

Everything had been shaping up so well, but now our path is full of stumbling blocks.

I haven't told anyone other than Dottie about the blowback yet, and all she's done is pat my hand and assure me that it's all going to be okay and that the truth is always a worthy cause.

Though Liam and I worked on writing his response together, and the words flowed like magic, he's barely said a word to me since.

He looks at me though.

He looks at me a lot, and every time he does, it feels like my heart is being ripped into smaller pieces.

It wants to love him. It wants to trust him. It wants to believe it's possible for us to have some kind of future together, even though publicly acknowledging our relationship is even riskier now. It might convince people that Melly had a point—that Liam has been steering the ship solo, and I'm a no one at my own brewery.

I don't want that, but I *do* want him. I've struggled to sleep at night, because I keep waking up, half-expecting him to be there, only to discover that the warm paw striking me in the face belongs to Karma. I want *everything*—Liam and the brewery and my friends—and each morning I wake up with the sinking feeling that I might end up getting nothing in the end. Just like last time, and the time before.

Maybe I really am doomed to be a failure, but I won't accept that fate without putting up a fight.

In honor of my new determination, I got a punching bag and set it up in my apartment. Karma watches me apathetically every night as I practice boxing with my new gloves. I haven't told Liam about it, but Hannah and Sophie know.

Now that they're both back from their respective trips, I've had a chance to catch them up on things. We haven't seen each other yet, but they've been supportive. Nora, too. Of course they don't know everything. All they know is that someone printed shitty lies about the brewery and we had to bite back.

I leave the brewery at noon to have lunch with my friends at Tea of Fortune. It feels good to see them, to *hug* them, and after Hannah commands an exhaustive report on the engagement of Eugene and Mrs. Applebaum, I find myself telling them the full story about Melly, from Felicity to the hair shearing.

"I'm going to fucking kill her," Hannah says.

"Liam doesn't seem to like her much either," I reply without thought.

"Of course he doesn't. I'm surprised he didn't tell me so I could punch her." She casts a sideways glance at Sophie and Nora. "Women can punch other women, you know. That's totally within the realm of fairness."

"Still assault," Nora comments, popping one of Dottie's special sandwiches into her mouth. The ones with the red pepper paste are so hot they burned the roof of my mouth permanently, but Nora claims she's immune to spicy food.

"We don't want to have to bail you out of jail," Sophie adds.

"We have to do something." Hannah lifts her chin, caught up in the tide of possible vengeance. "This isn't the kind of thing we can let go, especially after she wrote that shitty article. I mean, honestly, Liam can be a pain in the ass, but what she said about him is basically slander."

I shrug, trying to swallow my own feelings about Melly. "I can't imagine the retraction they printed will be good for her freelancing career."

"Still not enough," Hannah insists.

Nora gives us a wicked grin. "What if we buy a Felicity doll, shear off all the hair, and send it to her anonymously with a note saying, *I know what you did.* That'll probably fuck up a few sleep cycles."

A laugh bursts out of me.

"Hey," Hannah says, pepping up and giving Nora a high five. "That's diabolical."

"Those dolls are super expensive," I point out.

"Can't put a price tag on revenge," Hannah says. "Besides, it's doubly appropriate since everyone freaked out when Felicity cut her hair on that old TV show."

"Which TV show?" Sophie asks.

Both Nora and I shrug, at a loss.

"Philistines, all of you," Hannah mutters.

"What if Melly reports it to the police?" I ask.

"We'll just say we sent her a shitty gift because we thought she liked that doll...on account of she stole yours."

"We can even gift wrap it," Nora adds.

I look to Sophie, who's the most kindhearted and forgiving of all of us. "This is a bad idea, isn't it?"

"No, I think it's actually a pretty good idea. We can even stick some crystals in there for her betterment. I'm sure Dottie's picked some out."

The conversation shifts, and we talk for a few more minutes before we head back to our respective responsibilities, but Hannah insists she's going to walk to Silver Star with me. It seems...unusual, and my nerve endings prickle as we step out into the cold. She couldn't possibly know about Liam and me, right? He never would have told her, and even though Dottie knows, I don't think she would tattle on me either. Not about that.

"Did you like Travis's mom?" I ask, hoping to keep the conversation off Liam.

Hannah laughs. "I don't even think Travis likes his mom, but we had a good time. His sister's pretty cool. But, hey..." She stops walking and tugs me to the inner edge of the sidewalk, close to a brick building. "I was wondering if you've noticed how Liam's doing. I think he's avoiding me. I thought it might be because of that article. He's pretty sensitive about what happened at Mountain Morning. You know, he and that asshole Steve used to be friends."

"I know," I say, my heart lodging in my throat. "Liam's just been working a lot."

Has he been avoiding Hannah because of *me*?

I hate the thought.

"Yeah, that's a given," she says, shoving a lump of ice across the sidewalk with her foot. "But he hasn't been answering my calls. He *always* answers my calls. It's something we make a point of doing for each other because of what we went through after our mom left us."

Oh God...

I knew their mom left them, obviously, but I haven't given it much thought since getting close to Liam. He's such a big man, so confident in his body and his abilities, that it's hard to think about him as a little boy—a boy who was abandoned, just like my sweet, fierce friend.

And now he's not communicating with the one person who could comfort him...

"I'll talk to him," I choke out as a few tourists pass us. One of them glances back, either curious or lost.

"Oh God no, don't do that," Hannah says with a bark of laughter. "He'll know I told you, and then he'll get stubborn, and God forbid anyone cares about him." She rolls her eyes. "He's such a pain in the ass. But thank you for standing by him. That means a lot."

"Of course I did," I say through my hoarse, heart-choked throat. Guilt swallows me whole, because I *haven't* stood by him.

I remind myself of the awful feeling I had when I saw that app on his phone, but as the days pass, I feel increasingly sure he wasn't using it. The truth was written on his face that day, and I see it in the glances he's been giving me. Rueful. Full of need.

Still...he's kept to our rules. He hasn't even tried to talk to me for the last several days outside of our writing session. So maybe he changed his mind about me or decided I was too much effort, especially after that article my father masterminded.

I should forget what happened between us, or at least stop thinking about it constantly. Of course, it doesn't help that I'm always around him, seeing him but not interacting with him. It's as if the beautiful thing we were building has been hidden behind a sheet of unbreakable glass. I can remember it but not touch it. I can watch it but not feel it.

"He's been doing a good job, though?" Hannah pushes, leaning against the brick building we stopped beside. It smells a little like urine, so I pull her away from it.

"A great job. He's a genius."

He already has our next three beers fermenting, a job that's getting easier as we keg and bottle the rest of Bubba's brews.

She smiles, nodding. "Yeah, I think maybe he is. But I wish he'd let himself be happy. Every time he finds something that might make him happy, he withdraws. Like with the band. He could have had a really good thing going with them. That agent who was interested in them a couple of months ago already has a meeting set up with them for the New Year. He's ready to sign them after listening to a few of the recordings they did with Cormac and Mick. Liam could have been a part of that."

"I don't think he's interested in that kind of attention," I say without thinking. "Not for music."

She pauses, studying me. "You know...he told me he was on a dating app a couple of weeks ago, but I know for a fact he's not using it."

"How?" The word comes out hungry. Crap. Backtracking, I

say, "I'm only curious because the girls at work are always talking about it."

"What about you?" she asks. "Are you ready to start dating again?"

I shrug noncommittally, grateful she can't hear the voices shouting inside of me.

"Well, don't tell Liam." She raises a finger. "But I created a fake profile of a stupidly hot person and messaged him. I wanted to see what he'd do, because I had this theory that he was trying to pull one over on me with the whole dating app thing..."

"You catfished your brother?" I ask in disbelief.

"He didn't even read the message," she says, watching me closely. "And then he must have blocked my stupidly hot avatar or deleted the app, because his profile disappeared."

"Oh," I say, trying to sound like I couldn't care less about Liam and his dating life. "Well...I guess he wasn't ready."

"I guess not. Or maybe he's with someone, and he's trying to keep it from me. Have you seen him with any ladies at the brewery?"

"No." My pulse jumps. Is she trying to get a read on me? Or is she serious? "But I try to stay out of his personal business."

That much is sort of true. Now.

"Okay, I can see you're not going to gossip." She averts her eyes to the sky as if she just can't even with me. "We better get you back, you girl boss, you. I still can't believe you witnessed the engagement to end all engagements. Nora didn't seem as excited about it as I am. Say, do you think Eugene will let me be his maid of honor?"

"He'll probably ask Cormac," I point out as we start walking again.

"Yeah, that's true. You think I can be a groomsman? I'd wear a suit and everything."

"Eugene would probably do just about anything for you," I

venture, feeling an ache in my chest, because I know Liam would do just about anything for her too. And yet...

She'd asked him to stay away from me, and he'd been willing to break his word for *me*.

We make idle chatter all the way to the brewery. When we reach the edifice of Silver Star, she hugs me and takes off for Big Catch.

I head down to my office, and flinch at the sight inside. Liam's waiting for me on the couch. *Our* couch. He's wearing a black, long-sleeved T-shirt that makes his hair look especially coppery today, and it's been a few days since he trimmed his beard. He looks almost wild—and God, I want to touch him. I want to climb into his lap and forget the last week happened.

Does he want the same thing?

I shut the door, feeling so full of hope and anxiety that I can barely function. I walk over and stand in front of him, waiting for him to speak. Because I can't find any words yet.

"Is dinner at the same time tonight?" he finally asks.

I wince. "What are you talking about?"

"Dinner," he repeats. "At your parents' place. Every Friday, you said. Is it at the same time? It would work better if we go together. They might not let me in otherwise."

"You're not coming with me," I insist. My father already wants to destroy him. I doubt he'll be feeling more friendly tonight.

Liam lifts his eyebrows, his expression suggesting he doesn't have a single care in the world. "I think you'll find that I am."

I glance at the closed door. "You can't seriously expect me to take you. My father's got it in for you, and..." My throat catches. "You've barely said a word to me for days."

"I'm not intimidated by him." He hesitates, his jaw working. "And you made it clear you wanted to keep things professional.

This is me, doing that to the best of my ability. That means trying to stay away from you while we're at the brewery."

I search his gaze as he stands up, and see nothing but the truth. I want to reach for him, but I'm frozen. I want to know if he's been ignoring Hannah because of me, and to tell him to stop. I want to know if he still cares about me, and if he's still willing to put it all on the line...

Because I'm starting to think that I might be. Especially if I was right about Hannah, and she was implying she'd be okay with us seeing each other after all.

I want to touch him, something I've been missing all week. I want to tell him that I'm still scared, so scared, but I want to stop being afraid and keep taking chances. I've felt more alive in the past few weeks than I ever have, and I'm hungry for more of it.

But the only words that come out are, "We can't go together."

My breath freezes in my lungs as he reaches a hand toward my face, but he only tucks my hair behind my ear, his fingers lingering for half a second before dropping.

"I'll pick you up at seven fifteen on my bicycle. Probably wouldn't do for us to be late. We won't want to miss anything. Wear that jacket you had on last time."

"They'll think we're a couple," I say. "My dad already probably does."

"Good." He smiles at me, and the memory of his lips on me nearly breaks me.

CHAPTER THIRTY-FOUR

LIAM

A man who brews beer learns how to be patient. It takes time for things to become more than just the components you've put in.

Briar could have easily turned her back on me. Her father gave her an easy out, but she didn't take it.

I might have fought my feelings for her in the beginning, but I'm not fighting anymore. Instead, I'm going to fight *for* her—just like she fought for me after that article was published.

So, yeah, I *will* be going to dinner with her tonight, and every single night her parents demand her presence. Even if she decides not to give me another chance, and I'm reduced to following her around like a lovesick idiot, I'm going to show up at their place every week. I will not let her feel alone in that house ever again.

After I carry a keg into the tasting room, Otis waves me over. He's tending bar with one of the Tinder girls while Ann carries on a conversation with a customer. Knowing her, she's only hearing half of it.

"Did you tell Briar you were going to dinner?" Otis whispers conspiratorially as I set the keg down.

"Yup, and she was thrilled," I tell him with a wink.

"She doesn't know about our plans, does she?"

I lift a finger to my lips, warning him not to let it slip now.

The kid and I have become...friends, I guess you'd call it. I took him to the boxing gym with me earlier in the week, and even though he got the newcomer treatment, i.e. plenty of teasing, he liked it. So we're going back next week.

I met up with Cormac last night, too, my unusual need for socialization driven by both my determination to stop obsessing about Briar and my fear of being around Hannah.

Because my sister knows me. She'll take one look at my face and know that I've fucked her best friend. Hopefully, it will soften her to know that I'm also in love with Briar, but I'd prefer to tell her after I have a better idea of whether I still have a shot.

It's a mark of my desperation that I actually told Cormac about the whole sorry situation—in two sentences, which is the extent of my ability to talk about this kind of shit with another man.

"I'm no good with women," he responded. "I never know what to say. It's always too much or not enough. The last woman I dated...I told her she was talking too loudly, and she threw a drink at me. But we were at an event at the library. She *was* talking too loudly."

"What was she doing drinking in the library?" I asked.

He shrugged. "I don't know. I never got a chance to ask follow-up questions."

We both had a good laugh at that. He went on to admit he was uneasy about performing live with the band. While he's had to present at a bunch of amateur inventor conventions, in those situations the focus was always on what he'd made, not on him.

I'm a little rusty with this friend business, but I patted him on the back and assured him he didn't have much to worry about. He's the bass player, after all, and the audience doesn't usually laser-focus on the bass. I suggested he could just pretend he was still alone in his room, playing along to a recording. Surprisingly, he seemed to find that comforting.

Like Otis, he offered to help me prove myself to Briar. He told me he has a "particular set of skills," either purposefully or accidentally quoting Liam Neeson in *Taken*. Most of those skills are irrelevant to wooing a woman, but some of them will come in handy with my special project.

The other person I've spent time with over this past week is Dottie, mostly because she's made it impossible to avoid her. She started bringing in a special blend of tea for me every morning. I could tell her until I'm blue in the face that I don't actually like tea, and that any sane person prefers coffee as a caffeine agent, but she'll still keep bringing it.

Every day, she sits me down and asks me how I'm feeling, as if she isn't perfectly well aware that I'm not a person who enjoys talking about my feelings.

She's also told me more about her relationship with Beau Buchanan. I haven't asked any questions, but every time we sit down together, she slides the conversation in that direction. I might be hardheaded, but I'm not stupid. I know what she's not saying: it's perfectly possible for two people to be together *and* work together.

I'm hoping she's right.

With any luck, she's been buttering up Briar too, because even though I'm a patient man, I'd prefer not to wait forever.

It's a hard thing to miss a person who's right in front of you, but here we are, and *I do*. Still...she needs time to decide if I'm worth taking a leap for. I know what that feels like too much to resent it. I've spent years not wanting anyone to look twice at me. Hell, I didn't even want anyone to be nice to me.

Evening comes soon enough, and before I know it, I'm

packing up my bag—this time I've got a six-pack of Bubba's tropical IPA for the big man—and getting on my bike.

I'm on edge as I ride toward Briar's place, recognizing that there's a good chance she'll already be gone. She could have had one of her old man's town cars pick her up. Or driven there herself.

But when I reach her building, she's waiting for me outside, and fuck me, I'm pleased to see she's wearing my other coat against the chill. She's also wearing pants tonight—dressy pants, but it seems like a middle finger to the dress code. I can get behind that all the way.

Neither of us says anything at first. We just exchange one of those looks that talks louder than words. I tell her with my look that I want her; she tells me with hers that she knows but she's still not ready. As if we've settled something between us, she climbs onto my bike, and I hand her a second helmet from the case on the back.

"You have two?" she asks in an undertone, and I can practically hear her thinking I had to get one for all of the women I've given rides to.

I want there to be no misunderstandings, so I say, "I got it for you."

"You didn't have to do that."

"I know."

She puts it on and then grasps my waist. I can feel her hands trembling slightly, so I settle my hand over one of hers for just a second—reassuring her that she's not in this alone—and then start the bike up again.

When we get to the golden gates of Sterling Manor, Briar leans forward to announce herself over the intercom. I smile to myself, thinking it'll be a fun surprise for her parents to see me walk in with her.

I park the bike in the drive, facing outward again in case we need a quick getaway. As we get off, I point up into the skeletal tree by the house. The lower half of the green dress she wore on the night of our last delightful family dinner is still billowing from the branch it got snagged on.

"Want me to get that for you?" I ask.

She smiles wryly. "You'd climb that tree if I asked you to?"

"I was the kid who always picked 'dare' in truth or dare."

"Of course you were," she says, leaning her shoulder against me slightly.

"Offer stands. If you want, I'll get the bottom half of your dress back and wear it into dinner like a bandana."

She pauses, studying me with a half-smile that looks more genuine, and that's all the motivation I need to set off for the tree. I hear her calling my name through laughter as I stride up to the oak and start climbing.

I'm halfway up, the limbs straining under my weight, when I hear the front door opening. Alicia appears in the doorway, a look of horror written on her face. She's wearing a light-blue dress covered in tiny stitched snowflakes. It's probably high fashion, but the pattern is familiar.

I wave to her from my position in the tree. "Good evening. You look lovely, Mrs. Sterling. My nephew has those same pajamas."

Briar's nearly bent over with laughter, and I'll be damned if I wouldn't climb half a dozen trees to see her like this.

I glance up and, spotting my quarry, climb a little higher before I reach up and wrench the cloth free. After climbing back down a few feet, I jump the rest of the way, landing cleanly in a pile of leaves.

Alicia watches in unconcealed horror as I wrap the green fabric around my head like one of the kerchiefs I sometimes put on before working out. Honestly, I'd rather not wear it, but I'm committed to the bit.

"So, who's hungry?" I say, joining Briar on the pathway leading to the door. "I could eat a truckload of chicken nuggets."

Alicia slams the door in our faces, and a second later, I hear her shouting, "Don? Don! *Don!*"

"Huh." I turn to Briar, rocking on my heels. "I don't think she appreciated my help cleaning the tree. Maybe she liked it the way it was. It *was* kind of festive. People also like a little mystery, you know? Maybe your mom enjoyed answering questions about it."

Briar's still laughing, tears pooling in her eyes as she looks at me. "You...look...ridiculous."

"Thank you." I grin at her. "It looked better on you, though. Would you like to wear it instead?"

"No," she says through laughter. "Take it off. They'll—"

The door opens again, this time revealing both Briar's parents, overdressed like last time. Don's wearing a pair of dress pants and a blue button-down that matches the shade of Alicia's pajamas dress.

"He's a madman, Don," Alicia says, pointing a quivering finger at me. "Look at him. He's wearing a piece of Briar's dress like some kind of cannibal."

"Oh." I tear it off and extend it toward her. "Did you want to keep it? I should have offered."

She squeals and takes a step back.

"Okay, finders keepers." I stuff it into my pocket and turn to Don. "Hey, good to see you again, man."

He regards me impassively before turning to Briar. "You didn't say you'd be bringing anyone."

She stops laughing, which is a sin he'll hopefully have to atone for in the afterlife. "I didn't need to tell you. It's in the contract. I'm allowed to invite a guest, and you're allowed to do the same. Like you did last time."

"That was generous of you," I say, wanting very badly to

punch him in the face. "Most guys don't think to add a guest clause when they contractually obligate their kids to attend family dinners every Friday. But not you, Don, you're a two-steps-ahead kind of guy."

"You'd do well to remember that," he warns, making it clear that while I might have been a source of amusement, I am now a pain in his ass.

"Cool. Well, unless we're waiting for that woman you paid to torment Briar, we might as well go inside and eat. I doubt any of us will enjoy ourselves. I did bring beer, but the only 'organic' kind I had was Bubba's, so that won't be much of a bonus."

"Get out of here, you punk," Don says, his cheeks turning rosy. "You're not welcome." He turns to face Briar. "And you're an even bigger fool than I thought. Didn't you do enough to embarrass the family name when you were running around with that boy with all the girlfriends?"

Her face loses color. "Liam is here as my friend. He's also the best brewer in town, and I'm lucky he agreed to work with me."

Her father laughs humorlessly, resting his hands on his stomach. "You think I don't know how people work? I know *everything*. The only reason he'd care this much is if he's getting something out of it."

I step between them, my blood boiling. "You heard your wife. And I'm guessing you also proofread the story that got retracted. *I'm a madman*."

"Are you threatening me, boy?"

"No, sir. Wouldn't dream of it. All I'm doing is stating facts. I'm a madman, and I think very highly of your daughter. So naturally, I'd be compelled to do whatever it takes to protect her. From anyone."

He snorts in derision, looking past me. "I'll give you one

more chance, Briar. Come in to dinner and send your attack dog home."

"I'm allowed to bring a guest," she insists. "If you don't want us here, then we'll leave, but we're either staying or going together."

He glances at the metal gate protecting Sterling Manor from the riffraff, and it hits me.

"So you *did* invite her bully. Again," I say.

His gaze snaps back to me as Briar breathes in a sharp inhale.

"Melanie and her father will be coming to dinner," he says tightly, shifting his attention back to her. "There's some business to discuss, Briar, business that involves you, so you can understand why your friend here isn't a good fit for this conversation."

She gives him a look brimming with betrayal. "Melly's father, the real estate developer?"

The truth hits me as if it just ricocheted off her. All of this—Briar Boot Camp, giving her the brewery but only a few weeks' worth of budget, asking Melly to write about it...

He hasn't been testing her. He's been trying to push her toward failure.

CHAPTER THIRTY-FIVE

BRIAR

I thought my father was only testing me because I'd shown him I was weak. If I passed the tests, if the brewery was successful, he'd be proud of me. Finally, he'd be proud.

But that was never going to happen.

Sometime over the past year, Melly's father must have brought him an offer he didn't want to refuse...but it happened too late. My dad had already made someone else a different offer. Namely, me.

He'd convinced me to come home by offering me a signed-and-sealed promise to take over the brewery—a decision he'd surely regretted after Melly's father came to him with a deal. So my dad had tried every manipulative tactic in his personal toolbox to get me to give up. And, when that didn't work, he'd tried to make me outright fail—so when I did, he could sweep in with his friend's offer and convince me to sell. My dad would take a "fair" cut, no doubt, along with whatever golden prize he'd been offered in exchange for making the deal happen.

I'm tempted to walk back to Liam's bike. To let him take over and lead me away from this awful tomb of a house. But I'm not the weak woman my father thinks I am. Maybe I never was. And right now, I'm angry.

Liam helped me understand that anger doesn't always have to be a bad thing, something to stuff down until you can scream into a pillow. Anger can be powerful.

"You set me up," I say coldly. "All this time...you weren't trying to help me. You were trying to make me fail and trick me into thinking it was my fault."

Liam presses his palm to my lower back, and I nearly cry. He's being present in exactly the way I need—showing me he's my backup but not trying to take over. He knows I have to handle this myself, and he cares about giving that to me.

He cares about me, full stop.

My mother retreats into the house. She won't want to be part of this conversation, not that she minds my father's cutthroat nature. After all, she immortalized it in wood and hung it on the wall.

"Of course not." My father wraps his arms across his chest. "Look, it's cold out there. Why don't you come inside, and we'll talk all this over in a civilized way. Your...your friend can come in too."

"Great," Liam says, shoving in past him.

I stare at his back in confusion for a second.

"I need to take a leak," Liam adds. "I assume Alicia wouldn't want me to go on the bushes."

"Go, go." My father waves him away with an expression of total disdain that Liam probably loves.

Speaking of which...

What the hell is Liam up to?

Maybe he actually needs to use the bathroom, but it seems unlikely.

My father and I stand silently staring at each other until

Liam emerges a couple of minutes later. He heads toward us with easy grace, like he's completely oblivious to any tension.

I'm sure he knows it's exactly the sort of thing my father finds most aggravating.

"Just stay inside," my father hisses. "Come in too, Briar. You might as well come in."

"No. I'm not going in there. We came here, and you refused to feed us. You invited two guests instead of the agreed-upon one. I've fulfilled my end of the contract. We'll be back next week at the same time...until you tell us you don't want us to come. But this brewery *will* be successful, Dad. There's a ton of interest in the New Year's party, and we have distributors who are coming just to try Liam's beer at midnight. The waitlist for our dining experience is two pages long. Silver Star isn't going anywhere."

He pouches his lips. "Now, I wasn't going to put you out in the cold, sweetheart. The property is yours, if you continue to abide by the terms of the contract. You'd get most of the profits from this exchange, and there'll be a job for you once I get my next venture up and running." He shoots a hateful glance at Liam. "Hell, we could even find a janitorial position for your—"

"I haven't reneged on our contract," I say tightly, calmly, in the only tone my father will listen to. "Will you?"

"You haven't even heard what our friend has to offer."

"And I won't. Because the property isn't yours anymore, and it's not for sale."

"Now, Briar."

"You heard her," Liam says, his hand once again on my back. "And if you knew about even half of the work she's put in —oh, hell, what am I saying. You wouldn't be ashamed of yourself. You just should be. Your daughter is worth more than you could ever understand, and you don't deserve her."

"And you do?" my father sputters.

"No, I don't, sir. But that doesn't mean I have to stop trying. I think we'll be leaving now. Isn't that right, Briar?"

"Yes," I say, heat filling my eyes. But I won't let my father see me cry. If he does, he'll assume my tears are for him and not for Liam.

The truth is, I don't have any tears left for my parents. They were cried out years ago, into a pillow that didn't care about me either.

"Goodbye, Dad. Don't feel like you have to come to the New Year's party. And definitely—"

My words are cut off by a silver car pulling up to the gate.

Melly. I can see her in the driver's seat.

"Stay, Briar." My father reaches out and wraps his hand around my wrist. He's squeezing too hard. Liam sees me wince and tugs my father's hand off.

"Don't you ever grab her like that again," Liam says, his tone hard. Like he'd definitely have more to say with his fists if I weren't here beside him. My father seems to recognize it too, because he steps back, his face ashen.

"Let's go." I take Liam's hand and turn my back on my childhood home and the old dream of belonging there.

By the time we reach the bike, the gates have opened for the car. My mother must have buzzed them in from the interior of the house.

Liam gets on the bike, and I cling to him, needing to be close to him right now.

The car parks, and Melly gets out. Just Melly.

"You ready?" Liam asks, handing me the helmet he bought for me, but I hand it back.

"There's something I need to do first."

I stalk up to Melly, who's watching me with a wary expression.

"You got me into trouble, you know," she says in an undertone, glancing at the front door of the house.

"Good."

She shifts her attention more fully to me, her lips parting in surprise. "*Good?*"

"You deserved it. It was about time someone called you out for lying."

"It wasn't all—"

"All I ever wanted was to be your friend," I say, giving a voice to that hurt little girl who never had one. "And you never missed a single opportunity to hurt me. Maybe you think they're all just funny stories, but they're not. I still have nightmares about you holding me down and cutting off my hair. You may think that's funny too. But you want to know something? I'm happy with who I am as a person. I'm *happy*. Can you say the same?"

She doesn't say anything. She simply stares at me. Finally, I've made Melanie Harris wordless.

I go back to Liam and reclaim my helmet, hooking it on as he turns to study me over his shoulder, his eyes full of admiration. "You're not a princess anymore, Briar. You're the motherfucking queen."

And what do you know, I'm smiling as he revs up his bike and drives us out of the gates of Sterling Manor. I have no idea where we're going, and right now, I don't care.

I LAUGH as he parks his bike next to Sunshine Diner. "Really, Liam?"

"I have fond memories of this place. It's where I first realized you were a genius."

"I was drunk." I take off my helmet, and he returns it to the top box on his bike.

"And you still made more sense than most people. Let's have some food and a shitty whiskey, and then I'll take you home."

I catch his arm before he can take a single step toward the diner. He turns to me, his eyes full of a yearning that makes my heart quicken—and topples the last of the walls I've tried to build to keep him out.

"Thank you." I feel the words deep in my soul. "You've been there for me through all of this. You said the brewery wasn't ours, that it was just mine, but it *feels* like ours."

"I'm glad I'm earning my ten percent," he says, tucking my hair behind my ear. "I take it very seriously."

"You take *me* very seriously."

"I do," he agrees, his gaze burning into me. "You deserve more than what you've been given, and I aim to see that you get it. Now, let's get our whiskey and make Sharon's night."

"You honestly think she'd remember me?"

He reaches for me. My whole body begs for his touch, but he only tips my head up slightly so his eyes can fully search my face. "No one who's ever met you has ever forgotten you. That woman back there...Ellie—"

"Melly." I smile, certain he knows exactly what her name is.

"She's jealous of you. She wants to *be* you, but she knows she could never compare. So her best bet was to try destroying you. As if she could hope to take down a queen."

"*Liam*," I say in wonder.

"I know." He grins as he runs his fingers down the side of my face and then releases me. "I'm supposed to be a grumpy asshole. Don't worry. As soon as I get in there and taste that whiskey, I'll be grumpy as hell."

"You wanted to hit my father," I comment, barely noticing the brush of coat against coat as someone presses past me on the sidewalk. All my attention is on this big, beautiful man in front of me, capable of such stunning ferocity and gentleness at once.

"You'll never know how badly. Who knows what would have happened if I hadn't had one of those dumb elastic bands on my wrist. I mean, I broke it, obviously, but it helped. Let it never be said that a Moroney can't learn from past mistakes."

"Liam, I..."

I don't know how to say the words—to tell him I'm still so scared of being with him, especially knowing what failure would cost us both, but that I want to try anyway.

"Liam...I don't know if we're going to be able to keep the brewery open."

"I'm not going to let him take this from you, Briar," he says fiercely. "It's not happening. If your father or his friends try anything, every single person on staff, not to mention the guys in the band, will stand behind you and fight. We're your army. Use us."

"It still might not be enough," I admit. "Those restitution payments we've had to make... I don't know how long we can stay open. I've applied for a few loans, but my jewelry business tanked. I don't think they're going to approve them. This might all be for nothing."

"No," he says forcefully. "No. It won't have been for nothing."

"I believe you about the app. I mostly believed you before, but—"

"But you're still wary." He runs a hand over my hair. "I don't blame you. I'm not a safe bet. I'm...what did Melly call me in that article? A loose cannon. Or we can go with your mother's word for me."

"You are a madman," I say with a small smile. I'd like him to be *my* madman.

"I aim to prove myself to you."

My heart swells until it feels like my body is all heart, no room for bones. "You have. You already have."

His eyes glimmer with pleasure, but he shakes his head. "Not yet. I want to woo you, Briar. Don't you think a queen deserves to be wooed? That's what I did wrong from the beginning. I should have wooed you."

"No, I think you've done a pretty good job of it. Right now, you could woo me in the bathroom of Sunshine Diner if you wanted to."

He laughs. "Oh, I think we can do better than that. Have dinner with me tomorrow night."

We're closing early tomorrow so the staff has time to rest up before the long New Year's party. I figured I'd spend the time at the brewery, preparing, or at home, worrying. But this? This is the dream I didn't want to risk having.

Tears press against my eyes as I say, "*Yes*. But what about Hannah...?"

"I'll talk to Hannah," he says, his expression turning grim. "But if you're willing to give us a real chance, I'll be telling her, Briar, not asking her."

And that's it.

I grab the lapels of his coat and pull him down for a kiss. He groans into my mouth, his hand instantly lifting into my hair.

It's so easy to get lost in Liam. It has been from the beginning. At first I thought it was another sign that I was overly sensitive and letting my feelings about him get in the way of my better judgment. But maybe this is how it's supposed to be. Maybe getting lost in someone is a sign that you feel totally safe with them.

He pulls back, grinning at me like a wolf. "Come inside with me. Let's see if their food is as bad as their whiskey."

"Oh, it is," I say, but I follow him in, because I have a special fondness for this place too.

I fell into his arms for the first time just outside of it.

CHAPTER THIRTY-SIX

LIAM

It should be impossible to get fried food wrong, but I'll give Sunshine Diner this: they don't believe in the word impossible. Sharon isn't here, but Briar leaves a holiday card for her.

Yes. I've fallen for a woman who carries blank cards in her purse in case she wants to make someone's day.

I drop her off at her apartment after we eat and order symbolic whiskeys neither of us wants to drink. She invites me upstairs, but I'm fixed on doing this the right way from now on.

"Not tonight. I have plans for tomorrow. Let me do this."

She nods, and the hope in her eyes is nearly my undoing.

"We're going to be okay." It's the only promise I can make, since I know it's far from a sure thing that the brewery will survive the year.

"Is that a promise?" she asks.

"Damn straight."

I ride back to my apartment, tempted to turn around and say *fuck it* to my big wooing plan—why bother having plans other than being with the person you want? But I stay the course, since I've roped Otis and Cormac into helping me too.

When I open the door to my apartment and step into the

dark interior, a small flame flares to life in the corner, illuminating the face of the person sitting in my green armchair.

"Jesus fucking Christ, Hannah." My heart does its best to thump out of my chest as the tiny flame illuminates my sister's face. "Do you want to kill me?"

"Jury's out on that," she responds.

"I'm taking your key back." I flip on the overhead light.

Hannah hisses like a vampire and covers her eyes.

"How long have you been sitting in the dark?" I'd laugh, because it's fucking funny, but I know why she's here.

"It was worth it," she says, getting up from the chair and opening the globe-shaped bar sitting beside it. "I'm going to drink your best whiskey, and then I'm bringing the rest of the bottle home for Travis."

"I have a feeling I know what this is about," I say, closing the door behind me. It's a natural escape route, true, but I suspect my little sister is going to yell at me. No way do I want to get verbal smackdown from the half-pint. My weed-dealing neighbor is just the right amount of scared of me, and I'd like to keep it that way.

"Aren't *you* a genius?" Hannah murmurs, filling one of the glasses stored in the spherical mini bar nearly to the brim.

"Are you going to pour one for me too?"

"As if." She glares at me. "You've been avoiding me."

"I have."

She takes a long sip of her drink, shrugs, then says, "Asking you to leave your job felt like the bigger request, but you barely flinched. You seemed *excited* to get yourself fired. But you only waited a few weeks before trampling all over your promise to leave Briar alone."

I don't deny it. Instead, I sit on the couch and pat the cushion beside me, reminded of when she was a little kid and we'd watch cartoons together.

"Nope," she says, coming over to stand in front of me. "But I'm good with looming over you."

"Only with a lot of imagination could you call that looming."

She stomps her foot, and I sigh.

"Yeah, I'm a bad brother, but there's a lot you don't know."

"You're sleeping with her," she says, putting it out there, the way she likes to do. "I've seen the way you look at each other, and there's no way you wouldn't have gone for BabeinBoots999 unless you were getting it on with someone better. She was a total hottie with a body."

"What the fuck are you talking about?"

She admits to her catfishing scheme, and I shake my head ruefully, because if I'm a madman, my sister's a madwoman. Our baby brother's probably in some deep shit if he ever falls in love.

"Admit it," she says, nearly sloshing her drink with an exaggerated hand gesture. "You didn't answer her because you were already sleeping with Briar. I told you not to. You promised me. *On pain of death.*"

"Don't kill me just yet." I rub my forehead before looking up and meeting her eyes. "I...I didn't mean for any of this to happen, but we've been working together, spending a lot of time together, and she's..."

"Yes, she's gorgeous," Hannah fumes. "I knew that all along, hence why I asked you to make me that very important promise."

"It's not like that." My voice rises with every word. "I'm in love with her, dammit. I didn't try to be. It just...happened. It was inevitable."

A moment of silence lingers between us, full of unspoken words that could ruin or save everything. Then Hannah throws back half of the whiskey in a single gulp, sets her glass on the coffee table, and sinks into the chair. Frowning, she says, "You got drunk on Christmas again. I called you. I could tell you'd been drinking."

"It wasn't about Julia. I feel more at peace about what happened with her. I was with Otis. He gave me his blessing."

"Jesus Christ." She shakes her head, her red curls flying. "I was gone for less than a week."

"Maybe you should leave town more often," I quip.

"Does Briar love you back?"

I sink back into the couch cushions and run a hand over my beard. "I really fucking hope so. I kind of screwed up."

She groans. "I probably shouldn't have mentioned the whole Tinder thing to her this afternoon, huh? In my defense, I only had a suspicion. I was trying to pump her for information."

I have to laugh, but then I confess what happened earlier this week and tonight. I tell her about the problems with the brewery and Don Sterling's hope that Briar will fail. By the time I'm finished, her glass is empty.

"I'm not happy about this," she tells me, triggering a sinking feeling inside of me. I meant what I said to Briar earlier: I want Hannah's blessing, not her permission—but I want it bad.

"But I hope I will be," she finishes, her gaze hooked on mine. "I hope it's going to be the best thing in the world, and you'll have a dozen babies—"

"Yeah, that's a big nope."

She laughs. "And that you'll continue to be a grumpy bastard for your whole life, but a happy *grumpy* bastard. You're much more fun when that part's on lock. But you're on probation. I'm going to ask Briar for regular reports on how you're treating her."

I grumble. Hannah throws a pillow at me. And even though everything's still so uncertain with the brewery, I feel like it's going to be okay after all, the way Dottie has been telling me.

Hannah rises unsteadily from the chair.

"Yeah, you're not driving," I say. "I'll take you home." Unlike Hannah, I haven't been drinking, other than a few sips of bad whiskey at the diner.

My sister takes a step, shrugs, and grabs the bottle containing the rest of the good whiskey. "That's fair. You can tell Travis everything too. I know how you boys like to gossip."

I laugh. "You know what? Maybe I will tell him someday."

When we get to the door, though, I pause. "Say, Hannah, did you have any idea this would happen?"

She gives me a wry look. "Not really, no. But did I think it was possible?" She shrugs. "I've known Briar for months. She's gorgeous, she's funny, and she loves beer. Yes, I thought it was possible, and I figured I'd make it crystal clear that if you were going there, you were going to be very damn serious about it."

She taps my nose with the tip of her finger. "You're welcome."

AN HOUR LATER, I'm back at Sterling Manor, the green fabric wrapped around my head like I'm Rambo.

"Oats in position, over and out," Otis says into the radio. Sophie would probably slap me, but he needed a call sign, and he made the mistake of asking me to assign one to him.

I shouldn't have let him help. Cormac, either. I don't like the thought of either of them getting into trouble on my account. They both insisted, though, and I eventually agreed since I'll be the only one breaking and entering.

The plan?

I'm getting that "recipe" for Briar. Obviously, Don Sterling can have another one made—he could probably afford to have thousands of them made—but that won't matter, because we will have stolen this one from him. I figure she can chop it into firewood. Or have it whittled down to a crown and dipped in gold. Whatever she wants, but it *will* be hers.

When I went into their house earlier, I opened a hallway window. The alarm system was already glitching, thanks to Cormac, who created a device with a very different purpose that also creates interference for alarm systems.

I'll have to climb the fence, but that's nothing I haven't done dozens of times as a teenager. Thankfully, Ole Don doesn't have any cameras set up. I made a point of looking earlier, and to be honest, also kept an eye out on my first visit.

Otis is my getaway driver, parked down the street from Sterling Manor.

Cormac placed a call to the Sterlings an hour ago, informing them of a gas leak. He also confirmed they're currently at a hotel, far away from the scene of the about-to-be crime.

I slide into the evergreen trees at the side of the fence, out of sight of the Sterlings' nearest neighbors. The air is crisp with the scent of broken pine needles.

I'm about to start climbing when I hear a nearby rustling, followed by the sound of someone cursing.

I pop out of my cover and see Cormac, dressed all in black, heading toward me, his curly hair blowing around in the icy breeze. He waves at me, then trips over a root and almost face-plants in the brush.

Jesus fucking Christ. He's supposed to be safely at home now that he's successfully confirmed the Sterlings' location.

"What are you doing here?" I hiss as he reaches me, adjusting his glasses, which have fogged up.

"I wanted to help. I've never been invited to commit a crime before."

All the more reason for him not to join me for this one, but there's a determined look on his face. I weigh my options and decide to let him come. The Sterlings aren't likely to come back tonight, so it's probably safe enough.

I'll let him come for his own sake, so he can feel like a badass.

"All right. You ever scaled a fence before?"

"Uh...no. Is that a problem?"

Yes. "It's like a ladder. You climb it."

"Okay, sure..." He takes a black beanie out of his back pocket and pulls it over his curly hair. "I had to do that in gym class once."

Again...Jesus fucking Christ.

"Here goes nothing," I mutter.

We both start climbing, Cormac next to me. Thirty seconds later, I'm breaking his fall on the other side of the fence. He's got a wild grin on his face, like he thinks we've already gotten away with something.

"All right, let's go." I nod at him. "The window's back here."

I creep slowly toward the side of the house, Cormac following close behind me—his progress marked by the snapping of twigs. I pause beneath the window. Then I weave my hands together, creating a foothold.

"Do the honors, RoboCop."

I smile despite myself because he looks excited as he steps into my joined palms. The window slides open easily, and Cormac wiggles through, no problem. I pull myself up and climb through after him—a tighter squeeze, but it's a large picture window.

Once we're inside, I lead the way to the dining room, where the plaque hangs on the wall, gaudy and proud.

"Oh, I can see why you want to destroy it," Cormac comments in an undertone. "That's a really disgusting waste of good wood."

I grin as I lift it off the wall. It's made of heavy maple, and it weighs about fifty pounds.

"You need help with that?"

"That's okay, man. I got it."

We head back into the hallway, and he pauses in front of an alcove in the wall, sectioned off by fancy metal scrollwork. A small, framed print is tucked inside of it. "Is that an original Picasso print?"

He reaches through to touch it, then goes to pull his hand back and gasps, a look of panic on his face. "I'm stuck."

"Nah, you can't be." I set down the plaque, and give his arm a yank. But damn straight, it won't come out, no matter how he angles his hand. It's as if physics is bent in this one small portion of the house.

"Mayday, mayday," Otis exclaims into the walkie-talkie. "Wait. This is Oats. Mayday!"

I pull the walkie-talkie out of my coat pocket.

"What is it, Oats?" I ask, sweat beading on my brow.

"There's a car coming. It's not the Sterlings' car, but it's at the gate. The driver's a woman. She has blue hair, but she's pretty old. I know Dottie prefers it when we say 'prime of her life,' but this woman's face is all wrinkled and—"

"*Oats.*"

"She has some kind of card, it looks like, and she's swiping..." He gulps audibly. "The gate's *opening.*"

I stow the radio in my pocket.

"What are we going to do?" Cormac says, his face losing color.

"I could chop your hand off."

"Do you really think we need to?" he asks, totally serious.

I'd smile if I weren't worried there could be jail time in our future.

"I'm going to go look for some oil in the kitchen."

"But someone's coming," he hisses, giving his hand another ineffectual yank.

"So we better get out before they show up."

I hurry off, remembering the vague direction of the kitchen from when Briar's mom fucked off to it a couple of times during dinner. It takes me about five minutes, but I find it, locate a bottle of expensive-looking olive oil, and hurry back with it.

The walkie squeaks: "She's inside the house. I repeat: she's inside the house. I'm moving the car closer. Oats, over and out."

I spew half a dozen colorful curses as I slather the oil over Cormac's hand.

In the distance, I hear a door open and shut, but it's a huge house, and she's an elderly woman. Maybe she won't notice us. She might go about her business, completely oblivious to the intruders.

We're still at the alcove, the bottle of oil at our feet, the plaque of rules propped against the wall next to us, when a little old woman turns the corner with a small duffel bag. Her hair matches her light-blue sweatsuit.

She pauses, blinking at us. "What are you doing in here, boys?"

"Uh...yeah," I say. "We're..."

No innocent explanation comes to mind.

She glances at the bottle of olive oil at our feet.

"Did you kids break in here on some kind of dare? I heard all about this on *Dateline*. You might think risk-taking is worthwhile when you're a teenager, but when you're my age you'll realize this one life is all you've got."

"Uh...no," I say, since Cormac no longer seems capable of speech. "I'm thirty-three. I think Cormac's at least thirty."

"Last June," he says in a quiet voice.

"Are you okay?" Otis hisses on the walkie-talkie. "The prime-of-her-life woman is inside. I repeat: she's inside."

She purses her lips and squints at us. "I have pepper spray in my purse, boys. Do I need to make a mad dash for it?"

"No, ma'am," I say. "We were just..."

Her gaze lands on the wooden plaque angled against the wall. "You were taking *that*? Why in tarnation would you want that piece of garbage? The only person who'd want that is my niece's fool husband."

"You're Great-Aunt Sky," I say in wonder.

Her expression shifts, becoming more thoughtful than alarmed. "Only my Briar calls me that. My name's Zephyr."

Balls to the wall, I guess.

I rap my knuckles against the maple plaque. "We're taking this *for* Briar. But my friend here—"

Cormac raises his free hand.

"—got his hand stuck."

"I wanted to know if this was really a Picasso print."

"It is," she says, smiling now. "I've touched it too." She glances back and forth between us. "One of you must be in love with my niece. Or is it both of you? God love her, she's a beautiful girl."

"She seems very nice, but no, I can't say I'm in love with her," Cormac says.

Great-Aunt Sky's gaze stays on me.

"She's more than a beautiful face," I say. "And, yeah, I care about her."

"And are *you* more than a nice ass?" she asks.

Surprised laughter gushes from Cormac.

"I sure hope so," I say.

She nods a few times. "Good. I came here to go to Briar's New Year's party. I suppose you'll be there."

"We will indeed," I confirm. "I work at the brewery with her."

"Liam," she says, surprising me. "Yes, she's told me about

you. Now, you two had better make yourself scarce. Peanut butter should work if the oil doesn't." She starts padding away with her bag.

"Ma'am, do you need help with your bag?"

She waves me off without turning around.

I pour more oil over Cormac's hand, and this time he manages to tug it free.

We exchange a look, and then I heft up the plaque. "Let's get the hell out of here."

"Do you think we really need to climb through the window again?" he asks, eyeing the hallway. "She's already seen us."

"No, let's leave through the front."

There's a chance a neighbor's watching, but hopefully Great-Aunt Sky will cover for us if it comes up. She can tell them she hired a couple of gigolos.

We hurry toward the front door, and just as we're about to exit, a wolf whistle fills the air behind us.

"Even better than I thought," announces Briar's great aunt.

CHAPTER THIRTY-SEVEN

BRIAR

The next morning, I get more calls from unhappy clients. I'm able to talk a few of them around, but a couple demand their money back. I'm trying not to panic. We have the New Year's party coming up, and once people have tried Liam's beer, they'll want it on tap.

So I focus on the good things:

My great-aunt texted me this morning to say she will be coming to our New Year's party after all. She's staying at my parents' house, which isn't great news, but I doubt they'll want to join her at the party after our argument last night.

Liam is carbonating our second beer, and he says the third will be ready to carbonate by the middle of the week. We're moving right along. Our plan is *working*. We just need more time.

And we're going on a date tonight.

Before long, it's early afternoon. Liam and I are standing side by side in the tasting room. He gives me a sidelong look that fills my soul with buttery yellow light and then tugs out his phone. A second later, my cell buzzes in my pocket.

I check it, holding back a smile.

Meet me at the brewery at 7

I'll be waiting on our couch

I raise my eyebrows at him, then respond:

What'll you be doing?

I hear his intake of breath, a cough suppressing a laugh. Then he responds:

Just waiting. You're worth waiting for.

I hate myself a little for saying that, and more for meaning it.

[Kiss emoji]

He glances at me, then types:

This is ridiculous.

"My lord." Ann clucks her tongue. "You young people and your phones." She gestures to Otis, who has his phone out too. "This boy's hardly ever off his. Always swiping left, right, up, and down."

Otis's ears go red. "I offered to teach you," he mutters.

"Ain't no real men on there," Ann says, shaking her head. "All the old men on there are looking for twenty-year-old women to fool into their beds. You saw it as well as I did, son."

"There are other apps," Otis says, glancing down the length of the bar to make sure no one's waiting on the drink. It's a thin crowd today. "I found one called Golden Companions that I thought you might like. We can take a look now, while things are slow."

I smile at Liam, overcome by the sweetness of this community we've created.

Smiling back, he says, "Say, boss, can you help me with something in the back? I need a hand."

"No problem."

He leads the way into the back. I follow him through the door, then down the steps and behind the vat that held the pale ale, which is now being prepped to brew a new beer.

As soon as we're hidden, he takes my hand. "I have some good news. Hannah knows about us, and she didn't cut my balls off. She did, however, ambush me in my apartment with all the lights off and scare the shit out of me."

I laugh, but it feels like a hand is squeezing my heart. "And she's really okay with us? She thinks I'm good enough for you?"

"Oh, Princess," he says with a crooked smile. "That was never her worry."

I give him a gentle push. "You promoted me to queen. You can't un-promote me."

He grins and kisses me, right there in our brewery, and I like it. I like it so much.

"I have to go get some more supplies," he says, running his fingers across my cheek. "I'll be back soon. I'm looking forward to tonight."

"Me too."

He leaves through the back door, and I duck into my office to make a few phone calls. After the last one, I head into the tasting room to check on everything—and nearly bump directly into Hannah, who's trying to squeeze past Otis.

"I wouldn't let her through," Otis tells me.

Hannah rolls her eyes. "You're lucky I like your cousin. I told you. Briar is expecting me." She gives me a significant look. "Or she should have been."

"Do you...uh...want to go for a walk?" I ask, fidgeting with my hair. I've never felt uncomfortable around Hannah before, but I do now. She might be mostly okay with me dating Liam, but I still broke my word to her. I lied. I was a shitty friend.

"Sure."

I grab my coat, and we step out into the chill day. We walk a block without either of us saying anything, and then I pull her toward the building beside us so we're not blocking the sidewalk.

"I...Liam told me you know about us."

She nods dramatically. "Of course I do. Do you honestly think you could hide this from me? I mean...I had my suspicions weeks ago, when he practically vaulted into the bathroom so he could hold your hair while you vomited. I mean, who the fuck does that?"

Surprised laughter bursts from me. "I don't think he did that because he liked me."

"Uh. Huh. Sure. And he up and cancelled his plans to visit our dad and brother in Boston for Christmas."

I gasp. *Oh Liam.* Of course he did it without saying anything.

"I didn't know he did that."

"Of course you didn't. He tried to play it off like it was nothing, but he can't fool me." She runs a finger across the concrete siding, hesitating, then says, "Look...I was still a bit upset when I got home last night, but Travis reminded me that Liam would never have broken his promise to me if he wasn't really serious about it. So...what I have to know is whether you're really serious too."

I don't have to do any self-searching to answer her. Not anymore.

"*Yes.* We really tried to stay away from each other."

"Yeah, I know all about that." She sighs. "You're aware of how Travis and I met. Do you want to get a drink so you can tell me everything?" She lifts her hands. "Not the sex stuff. I'm open-minded, but not *that* open-minded. I'm just going to assume every Moroney is a tornado in the sack and leave it at that."

That's so Hannah. My cheeks are burning, but I can only smile at her. "Yeah, I'd like to have that drink."

HOURS LATER, I let myself back in through the front door of the brewery, buzzing with the need to see Liam.

Talking to Hannah felt…God, it felt so good to be fully honest with her after weeks of lying by omission. She actually teared up when I told her that Liam had told me about Julia—and then punched me in the arm for making her cry.

After we hugged it out and went our separate ways, I went home and got dressed for my dinner with Liam. A green sweater dress, since green feels like a significant color for us now, and thick black stockings to keep me from freezing. I wore his coat over it, because I like it better than mine. It still smells like him, and every time I put it on, it's like I'm getting a big Liam hug.

Despite everything that's still standing in our way, I feel… giddy and happy. Just happy.

When I reach the office, he's waiting for me on our couch, his arm slung across the back. He's wearing a green sweater that matches my dress, a coincidence that nearly makes me laugh with pleasure. The color brings out the gorgeous color of his hair, and he's wearing a pair of worn jeans that fits him so well poems should be written about it. I want to climb onto him. I want to sink into him.

From the way he's looking at me, taking in my dress and his jacket, he feels the same way.

"You ready to step away, boss?" he asks, lifting his eyebrows.

"I think I'd go anywhere with you."

"That's good, because we're going back to Sunshine Diner."

"Very funny," I say as he rises to his feet.

"We still haven't tried everything on their dinner menu. Maybe they have one perfect dish."

"I doubt it." I wrap a hand around his arm and hold his gaze. "Hannah and I talked."

"Was she rude to you?" he grumbles.

"No. I think she just wants us both to be happy."

He layers his hand over mine and smiles. "Then she should be thrilled. Come with me."

I expect him to lead me outside, but he takes me down the hall to the barrel room.

I open the door, and the magical sight inside makes me gasp. The table is set for two, and there's a charcuterie board set on top of it. Also two champagne glasses and a carafe full of—

"Our beer," I say in wonder.

He and Otis kegged it earlier today.

"*Our* beer." He grins. "But first I have an offering for you."

He leads me to the side of the room, where one barrel sits against the wall. It has a huge square topper, as if someone decided to turn it into a table, covered with a red velvet cloth.

He tugs off the covering, smiling at me like a magician revealing a rabbit.

A gasp rips from my lungs.

I'm very familiar with this particular piece of wood, having sat beneath it, under threat of squashing, for years.

"*Liam*. The rules. How...?"

"Probably exactly how you'd think."

"But that's so dangerous." I step forward and put both of my hands on his chest, needing to touch him and reassure myself that he's whole. "They have an alarm system, and—"

He wraps an arm around me. "Cormac's a genius, it turns

out. He disabled it temporarily and helped me get the plaque out of the house. The kid was our getaway driver. Your great-aunt Sky says hi, by the way. She showed up while Cormac's hand was caught in this metal scrollwork in the hallway. She gave us her blessing. I wanted to tell you earlier, but I didn't want to ruin the surprise."

"You met my aunt?" Tears form in my eyes. "She didn't mention anything earlier."

"I think she knew it was supposed to be a surprise. She told me I have a cute butt."

"You do." I hug him closer. "But I wish you hadn't done something so dangerous for me."

He pulls back slightly, looking me in the eye. "I'd do more for you. I had to do *something*."

I can hear the meaning behind his words. He'd needed to make a move against my father after what my dad had done to me—what he was still doing to me. And Liam had made a calculated risk instead of acting off the cuff.

This was a statement. *No, we will not be playing by his rules.*

"What are we going to do with it?" I ask.

"Whatever you want. Burn it. Make a crown out of it." His mouth lifts higher on one side. "I kind of like that idea. We could crown you at midnight tomorrow."

The world is full of possibilities suddenly. It's Liam. When we're together, I feel like we can lift this brewery up out of its troubles and shake them off as easily as if they were cobwebs.

My gaze lowers to the plaque that has hung over my head for as long as I can remember. Those awful, cruel words, telling me that I wasn't enough.

"I want to chop it into firewood," I say. "I want to feel it breaking. But first..."

I release him and approach the barrel. Holding his gaze, I

step out of my shoes, then slowly strip off my stockings and panties and climb onto the plaque-topped barrel.

"I want you to fuck me while I'm sitting on top of it."

"You have a thing for criminals?" he asks as he stalks closer, one corner of his mouth lifting higher than the other in a positively wicked smile. He captures each of my thighs with his hands.

"I have a thing for *you*. I want you, Liam. I want the man who cares enough to take a very stupid risk to make me feel better." I grip the collar of his shirt and pull him in for a kiss. "And you better never, *ever* do something that stupid again."

"Yes, boss."

He grins at me as he spreads my thighs wide, his fingers pressing into my flesh in a way that adds to my excitement. One of his hands drifts up, caressing, and settles at my center, rubbing rough circles that send pleasure coursing through me.

I'm so ready for him, so needy. It's only been a few days since he was last inside me, but it feels like a year.

"Now, Liam. Now," I whisper. "I need you inside me."

He reaches down, and the sight of him unbuckling his belt with his big, callused hands is nearly enough to make me come in anticipation.

When he steps toward me, I scoot to the very edge of the plaque and wrap my legs around him.

He takes my mouth in a kiss as he thrusts into me, the back of the plaque banging sharply against the wall. An almost feral sense of pleasure floods me as I cling to him, pushing up to meet his thrusts. He keeps kissing me as he moves inside me, and I suck on his lips and tongue. I want all of him, everywhere. I want to paint my name on his body with my lips.

We're both wild with need, and it doesn't take us long to finish. Me first, taking him over the edge. He finishes inside me, his face buried in my hair, but keeps his arms wrapped around me like he doesn't want to let me go.

"I don't want to lose you," he whispers into my hair. "I can't lose you again."

When he finally lifts me up off the plaque and sets me on my feet, I kiss him before looking back at it.

It's cracked right down the middle, and I feel an effervescent sense of joy.

We're breaking all the rules.

In fact...

"I don't want to hide this," I say as he zips up his pants. "I don't want us to be together in secret. If we're going to try this, I want it to be out in the open. Even if people talk."

He lifts my hand and kisses it, his gaze holding mine. "People are going to talk anyway. It's impossible to keep them from talking. Believe me when I say I've tried."

"So you're okay with openly dating your boss?" I ask doubtfully. I know people will have plenty to say about each of us—me, the naïve woman being influenced by a stronger man; him, screwing his way to the top.

"I told you, Princess, I don't care what most people think. People can gossip all they want. All the better if it drives customers through our doors. I don't care about that. I want to be with you."

"Good. Because..." Heart pounding, I admit, "I'm falling in love with you. Does that freak you out?"

"Yes," he says, but he's smiling. His whole face is lit up from within, and he lifts a hand up to cradle my chin. "I still feel like I'm going to mess everything up. But I'm glad you feel that way, because I'm desperately in love with you."

He kisses me, his hand still possessively cupped around my chin, and I kiss him back again and again.

After we clean up in the staff bathroom, Liam fills both of our flutes with the beer, and we settle into the chairs.

"Have you tried it yet?" I ask, smiling.

"No. We'll know at the same time if it's complete shit. Seemed only right. But please, for the love of God, don't pretend for my sake."

"I don't think I'll have to." I pick up my flute and lift it into the air. "To Silver Star." I hesitate, then speak my heart. "To being a team."

"You've brought me around to the idea."

We stare into each other's eyes as we lift our flutes for the first sip.

Relief washes over me, because I won't have to decide whether or not to pretend.

"It's delicious," I say, still tasting the crisp bright pop of the bubbles. "It's perfect, Liam. It *feels* like New Year's."

"Thank Christ," he says with a snort, but I see the light in his eyes. He knows it's good too, and he's proud of himself, as he should be. "Now can I take you home? Because I'd really like to take you back to my place. Maybe I'll keep you there."

I smile at him, feeling perfectly happy. "Karma wouldn't like it."

He nudges my foot under the table. "You're welcome to bring your pussy."

I laugh, shaking my head ruefully. "She'll be delighted to hear it. But I want to go to the boxing gym first. I think it would do us good to throw some punches." I gesture to the broken plaque. "And we need to make firewood. I think we should have a bonfire at the party."

His lips curl into a half smile. "We can toast marshmallows."

We stop at my apartment first. I can't go anywhere for the night without feeding Karma, but Liam also insists those gloves he gave me weren't meant to be cuddled but to be used. Once we've collected them, we head straight to the gym.

The first time we went there, it felt like I was intruding on some macho man's world. The second…I was only paying attention to Liam. Now, it feels like it's become another place that's ours.

He shows me the new heavy bag Mick acquired, and we practice for fifteen minutes or so, listening to "Eye of the Tiger" at my request. Then we head out to the parking lot with the axe Mick keeps inside for fire emergency preparedness to chop the plaque into tiny little pieces. I shout out a war cry before dealing my first blow. Which makes it more embarrassing when I barely dent it.

Liam smiles at me before easily delivering a blow that severs it. But he hands it back over. "Try it again."

And I do. Again and again, until my arms ache, getting a few pieces cut off before he does the rest of the work. We stuff the chopped wood into the back of his truck and put a tarp over it.

He takes me to his apartment, which is small but tidy, with a brew room larger than his bedroom and a guitar mounted on the wall in the living room. It feels good to be with him in his space, in his bed. Neither of us can sleep, so we stay up late talking. Plotting for Silver Star as if its future isn't still uncertain.

But we don't have to wait for the party to get answers to all our unvoiced questions. Because when we come in the next morning, there's a couple of inches of standing water on the tasting room floor and another six in the back.

My dream is underwater, and I have a pretty good idea who put it there.

CHAPTER THIRTY-EIGHT

LIAM

"It's over," Briar says, sitting on the curb outside the brewery, an expression of helplessness on her face. "We weren't looking too good before this happened, but I thought we were going to make it. I hoped the party would be enough to tide us over. But now..."

It was a plumbing "malfunction," according to the utilities company. I'm guessing it had a human source—one with deep pockets—but that doesn't matter right now.

What does?

No way will this place be dried out before the party.

But I'm not going to leave that water in there. I don't care that everyone's busy or that it's New Year's Eve. I'm calling in all my favors.

After I text a few people about the situation, I make myself sit on the frozen curb beside Briar. She needs my stillness right now more than my strength. Still, I can't help but say, "I could find and kill everyone behind this, and then it really would be over. For them."

"And for you." She places her hand on my thigh. "I'm not letting you go to jail."

I nearly smile. "Is that your only objection to my plan?"

"We know my father was behind it."

I wrap my arm around her. "Probably."

The defeat Briar obviously feels lights a fire inside of me, though, because no, this will not be the end of what we've been building.

"We're not giving up," I insist, standing and pulling her up alongside me. "We can't. Your great-aunt came all the way here for a party. We promised her some action."

A smile drifts across her face, but she glances back at the brewery, and her bottom lip trembles. "It's over. We don't have enough money for the repairs. We wouldn't even if the party went well, and now..."

"We're not letting your father sell this place to that douchebag. We broke his rules, remember?"

She gives me a sad smile. "I'd sooner let it become another Hot Spot. But I *will* have to sell it. I..." Her eyes tear up. "I didn't want to have to do that. I really thought we were going to make it..."

I pull her close. "It's not over yet. It's not over until we say it is, and we don't. Your ten-percent shareholder is holding out."

I've obviously been hanging out with Dottie too much, but I think Briar's spirit requires optimism right now. I'll deliver— for her.

She kisses me, but I can tell she's not convinced.

"You're not giving up either," I insist, holding her close enough that I hope she can feel the steady beat of my heart.

"I don't want to."

"So don't. I've messaged some friends about helping us get the water up."

I pull my phone out of my pocket to check for responses. "Mick's on his way with his shop vac. Travis has one too. Rob doesn't, but he's coming. So is Otis. And Cormac says he has a shop vac he retrofitted himself, so it's probably ten times better than the others, knowing him. They'll all be here within the hour. My sister and the rest of your friends know what's up, and they're coming too."

"They are?" she asks, as if she can't imagine all those people would want to help her.

I hear someone approaching us, but I don't take my eyes off her. "They're your friends. Your family. And they're coming to help us, Briar. We'll have the water up today."

She presses a hand to her throat, and I can see it. She's trying not to hope. She's afraid of it. "We still can't have the party inside."

"No, dear," says a voice from the sidewalk. I finally look away from my girl and see Dottie Hendrickson, dressed in one of those silver star sweaters and a gray overcoat. "That's why we're going to have it outside."

"Outside?" I'm as fond of Dottie as the next person, but I'm not convinced she can change the weather. It's dry and cold. Not the kind of night people want to be gathered outside in while wearing party clothes.

"You have a lovely little beer garden in the back. We'll need lots of space heaters," she mutters. "And a tarp. Of course, we know people who have everything we need. It's only a matter of putting it all together."

Briar bites her lip. "But the noise ordinances..."

"It's New Year's Eve." Dottie's expression is full of righteous conviction. "If anyone wants to complain, they can complain to *me*. Now, come with me, Briar. We're meeting at the tea shop straightaway. It's all been arranged."

I glance at the road as a few cars roll past. "The guys—"

"Will take care of the standing water. I know all about it. But they don't need you to oversee them." She touches my hand, which is still wrapped around Briar's waist. "*She* needs you, my boy. You need each other, and I'm so glad you've risen to the occasion."

It's going to hurt to walk away from a job half done—almost as much as it does not to say *that's what she said*—but Dottie has a point. I nod in agreement. "Yeah." Glancing at Briar, I say, "We've got a party to throw, and a queen to crown."

"Indeed," Dottie says, beaming. "Now, come with me."

"We'll be right behind you." I squeeze Briar's waist. "There's something I gotta say to my boss."

"Oh, yes, I wouldn't want to get in the way of a business meeting," Dottie replies with a bold smile. "I'll be just ahead of you, my dears." She takes several steps down the sidewalk, pretending to be interested in sights she's seen a hundred times.

I take Briar's hand and lift it to my lips. "Even if we don't raise enough money to fix the damage and stay open, it's worth a try. If nothing else, we'll have a hell of a going-out-of-business party with our friends."

She nods fiercely. "If we have to sell, we'll just start up again smaller. I want to do this with you. I won't give up the way I did with the jewelry." Her jaw trembles as she looks back at the brewery. "But I wanted it to be here, dammit. I wanted it to be this place."

I bend down to give her a soft kiss. "Remember, I'm Mr. Miracle. Don't discount the possibility that we might get another one tonight."

"You don't believe in miracles."

I smile against her lips. "I got you to give me the time of day. I have new appreciation for them."

CHAPTER THIRTY-NINE

BRIAR

Text conversation with Dad

My rules have gone missing. Do you know anything about that?

I don't know what you're talking about. Do YOU happen to know why the brewery flooded last night?

Of course not.

Maybe a pipe burst. It WAS cold last night.

But even if there's damage, it won't impact the deal.

They'll be renovating the whole building.

It's a good time to sell.

Goodbye, Dad. Feel free to come by later. We're having a bonfire. We have plenty of firewood. ;-)

The sight of all that standing water broke something inside of me. I still don't believe the party is going to happen. I'm pretending for Liam's sake. But when we arrive at Tea of Fortune, I'm shocked by all the people who've gathered to help us—even Nora's mom is present, along with Eugene and a few people I don't recognize.

Hannah, Sophie, and Nora get up as soon as we come in, hurrying forward and gathering around us.

"The doll situation has been taken care of," Nora says, exchanging conspiratorial smiles with Hannah and Sophie.

"You guys really did it?"

"We can neither confirm nor deny that," Hannah replies.

Maybe I should feel guilty, but I don't. I'm grateful they care enough about me to want to defend me—and I'm proud that I finally defended *myself* the other night.

"What doll situation?" Liam asks.

Hannah bumps him with her shoulder. "Just because you're dating my friend doesn't mean you get to know everything. The doll situation is privileged information."

"Well, all right. Don't get your panties in a twist. I don't actually care."

"Do you care that we ruined that woman Melly's day?" Hannah asks, putting a hand on her hip.

He glances at me with a grin. "I definitely don't give a shit if her day is ruined, but Briar already ripped her a new one last night. Anything else is icing on the cake."

"You did?" Sophie clasps my arm. "Oh my gosh, that's great, Briar! It felt good, didn't it?"

"It did." I look at each of my friends in turn. "But thank you. It means a lot to me that you want to stand up for me. I can't believe everyone here wants to help us."

"Well, believe it," Hannah says. "Plus you have Travis and the guys out there dealing with the standing water. You have no idea how much Travis hates messes. He'll blast that water away, no problem."

Dottie, who has stopped in the center of the room, wolf-whistles.

"Now, dears. We have a lot of work today, but we're going to help Silver Star put on a *monumental* New Year's party tonight. A party this town will be talking about for years to come."

The tea room erupts in a chorus of wolf whistles, and Liam hugs me close and kisses the top of my head...which leads to another round of wolf whistles.

He grins at everyone. "Yes, I know. I'm a lucky man. Now, let's get to work."

NORA HOLDS a lot of outdoor events at The Ginger Station, so she has a tarp for us, plus lots of twinkle lights that we use to blanket the outdoor space, making it look like it's speckled with stars.

Liam brings out the kegs, including the rapidly diminishing supply of Bubba's beers, our new pale ale, which we decided to call Champbier, and Nora's ginger beer. We set up the outdoor bar, with Ann and Otis as our bartenders, and an enormous sign, made by Sophie, advertising our "drink us dry" campaign.

My sweet aunt joins us later in the afternoon after texting me about the "Man with the Nice ASS." She also asked if she could stay with me, since my parents have been even less fun than usual, and my father kept talking about his stolen rules until she had "no choice" but to tell him to stick them up his ass.

The answer was yes, obviously.

When she arrives at the brewery, I hug her for a good five minutes before she pulls away and asks me to show her around. I do, even though the damp floors squeak under our shoes and the interior already smells like mildew. We end the tour at the back, where everyone is hard at work transforming the beer garden.

"You're going to do just fine, my sweet Briar Rose," my aunt says, tapping my hand. "You've done a beautiful job here."

I laugh. The brewery's floors are all water damaged, and it's definitely not looking its best.

"You've barely seen it."

"But I know there's no one better suited to run this place than you." She surveys the work in progress in the beer garden before pointing to Liam's backside. "And I'm glad you have that man. I'd recognize his backside anywhere. He's very handsome, my dear, and surprisingly polite for an intruder."

I smile at his butt, which *is* very nice, and then at her. "Me too. I love him, Great-Aunt Sky."

"I can tell." She smiles at me. "You're glowing, my dear. None of your other beaus have made you glow like that. Now, what can I do to help?"

I introduce her to Dottie, and twenty minutes later, my aunt is setting up a fortune-telling table with one of Dottie's friends in the corner of the tented area.

There's so much to do, so many things to set up, that the time melts away. We've barely finished when eight o'clock hits and customers start showing up.

Hannah and Nora put out social media blasts about the change in plans, but several people find it surprising upon arrival that our big party is being held outdoors on a day with a low of thirty degrees. A lot of them leave, but plenty choose to stay and enjoy the *drink us dry* specials, especially once the band goes on at nine. Rob, Travis, Cormac, and Mick have only been playing together for a few weeks, but they're in perfect rhythm, and they draw people in off the street.

Liam and I take over the bar service to give Otis and Ann a

break, and I keep stealing glances at him, wondering if he wishes he were on stage with the band.

"Nope," he finally says, the second or third time I look at him. "Not even a little."

I laugh. "How'd you know what I was thinking?"

"It was written all over your face. But I don't understand how you could think I'd want to be up there with them if I could be doing this with you." He gestures to the crowd gathered around us, laughing and talking. "They're happy because of you. Because they're excited about Silver Star. *This* is what I want. *You're* what I want."

"You're what I want too."

But there's something else I want for us too—something I'm worried we won't get to keep.

IT'S NEARLY MIDNIGHT. Great-Aunt Sky is deep in conversation with Dottie and the rest of the Wise Elders Group, and my friends are dancing around the space heaters.

We're down to only a dollar for Bubba's beers, and everyone is at least a little tipsy, except for Liam and me. We've tasted the pale ale, and we know it's worth waiting for. A couple of other tasting room employees are manning the bar now, and Liam and I are standing at the edge of the tarp, holding hands as we watch the bonfire we started just beyond it in the firepit.

"It's almost a shame my dad didn't come to see it burn," I tell him, snuggling into his shoulder.

We're both dressed in the sparkly star sweaters Dottie got for everyone on staff. We all put them on a few hours ago, but Liam's is one of the only sweaters that's visible—because he never gets cold and isn't wearing a coat. Dottie was right about how it would fit. The sweater is at least one size too small for him, but Liam is probably the least self-conscious person I've ever met. He tugged it on, shrugged when he realized it clung to every single ridge of his chest, and then continued to wear it. He also has a name tag on—almost everyone does. They're leftovers from the Big Catch party.

Liam's says, *Hi! My name is* MR. MIRACLE, *and I like to* BREW BEER. The first name tag he filled out was immediately balled up (by me), because it said, *and I like to* FUCK MY BOSS.

He pulls me into his warmth, his arm wrapped around me like he's never going to let go. "We can take a picture of the fire for him and bring it to dinner next week. Were you thinking he'd appreciate the symbolism? Or did you hope he'd run in there to save his *precious?*"

"Very funny." I pause, watching the flames consume the wood. "Do you think my father will ever change?"

He peers down at me. "Do you want me to be honest?"

"Always."

He hugs me closer. "No, Princess, I don't. But we'll keep showing up every Friday until he changes that agreement. And, who knows, maybe someday they'll surprise us and suggest going out for burgers instead of staring uncomfortably at each other across the table. But if not, who cares. These are the people who've shown up for us."

I lean up on my toes and kiss him. "You've shown up for me from the beginning, even when you kept trying to act like an asshole."

"It's not my fault you're so good at getting people to see your way of thinking. I'd stopped wanting much of anything before you came along, but you made short work of that."

I kiss him again, then press my cheek against his intensely shiny sweater. "I love you."

"I love you too." He checks his phone, then says gently, "It's time, Briar."

Seconds before midnight, we begin the countdown side by side. Then cheers ring out as we announce the new year. We weave our way through the throng of partygoers and start passing out the free samples of our Champbier.

Most people are a little drunk already, but everyone seems to love the new ale. At least five people pull me aside and say they'd like to place orders. I'm proud of us, and I want to celebrate, but my heart is also stuck in my throat.

It's our first beer, and I'm worried it'll be the last one we produce at Silver Star.

🍺

"IT WAS A BEAUTIFUL PARTY," I tell Liam, nuzzling into him as we sneak into the deserted tasting room.

He seeks out my gaze. "But it still wasn't enough."

The party was about a fourth as big as it should have been, given the unconventional location, and we didn't just miss out on the people drinking. We missed out on the merch they might have bought. The six-packs.

And even though the guys saved us from a substantial water removal bill, the floors and drywall are noticeably damaged. That won't be a small expense...

"I don't think so," I say softly. "I estimate we'd need at least thirty thousand dollars to fix everything, beyond what I can contribute from my savings. And that's not even factoring in the amount of time we'll need to be closed."

"So what you're saying is that we still need twenty grand, plus salary for the staff and enough money to cover a few zero-income weeks," he says. "I guess it's a good thing we have so few employees."

"You're going to put your own savings into this?"

"Of course," he says, cupping my cheek. "I take my ten percent stake very seriously." He smiles. "And my girlfriend."

My gaze catches on the photo that's still propped up behind the bar. My father's image has no place here.

"There's something I need to do," I say, then slide behind the bar to take the photo down.

"More fuel for the fire?"

I smile, but get distracted when I notice the list of rules that was wedged behind it. I'm hit with a swell of nostalgia, but it's time to destroy our old rules, just like we destroyed my father's in the fire.

I glance at Liam, and he gives me a knowing nod. "Yep, those have to go too. Into the fire, or you could shred the list in a fit of rage. That'd do too."

Smiling, I tug the paper toward me, but when I do, a little collection of scratch-off tickets is revealed behind it.

"More of Ann's scratchers?" Liam asks.

"No, actually." I hand them to him. "They're yours. I got them for everyone as holiday bonuses. But you left early that night."

"Seems to me I got a special bonus." His lips quirk upward. "Maybe I should give them to Ann."

I'm hit with a strange feeling of déjà-vu. Ann had that dream about landing a winning ticket, and it was a Big Boy Bucks, like the ones he's holding.

"Liam," I say, excitement catching in my voice. "What if...?"

"Oh, Briar." His expression is full of fond disbelief. "No one ever wins with these things."

"Please." I take a penny from the give-a-penny, take-a-penny dish. "Maybe it'll be..."

A karmic intervention, but I can't bear to say the words. I named my cat Karma because I wanted to believe in it, and yet...

Standing here, with him, I can't let the dream go.

He takes the penny from me, squeezing my hand. "There might be another way."

I nod at the tickets, my hopeful heart lodged in my throat.

"All right." He scratches through the first four without winning anything. There's one left, and he turns to me. "I'm not giving up. It doesn't matter if we don't get the money."

"Scratch the ticket." I clutch his arm, anchoring myself.

He scratches the coating away and looks up sharply. "We actually won something."

Wonder seeps into me, but then I look at the total prize. It's a thousand bucks. It's welcome and needed, but it's not enough to save us.

I smile at him, but there's a sob caught in my chest. "I knew it was a long shot. It's nice that we won something, though."

He kisses me as my eyes begin to well, but I hold back the tears. It feels wrong to cry when I have so much of what I wanted.

Dottie pushes through the front door, but she stays put in the entryway. "Oh dear, am I interrupting a private celebration?" Her brow furrows when she sees my face. "Shouldn't this be a happy occasion?"

I force a smile. "I'm so grateful to you, Dottie. You and Ann have done so much for us. This place has been as much yours as ours these last few weeks, and Otis and Constance—"

"This is not a *funeral*, Briar," Dottie says. "It's a celebration of life."

"That *is* a nicer way of looking at it," I agree, my throat catching as I survey the damp room.

"A celebration of life and of rebirth, because you're making a completely new version of Silver Star."

"We..." I will myself not to cry. "We're not going to be able to stay open any longer, after the organic issue and now the flooding. I'm going to have to close the brewery."

Before I finish, Dottie's already shaking her head. She walks toward us with purpose. "Now, my dears, I know you're anxious to do this all yourself, and I admire that. Of course I do. I'm an independent woman myself. I also know you won't take charity."

The door opens again, admitting Ann, who's wearing one of the star sweaters under her fuzzy, faux-fur coat. She has on a teetering six-inch-tall silver New Year's headband.

"But would you accept an investment?" Dottie continues. "I, for one, would very much like to invest in Silver Star, and I know I'm not alone in that."

"Are we doing the hat thing now?" Ann asks.

"Yes," Dottie says, still staring at us. "I think it's time for the hat."

Ann opens the door again and shouts, "Eugene, Dottie needs your hat!"

"Good gracious." Eugene steps inside, takes off his newsboy cap, and holds it out to Dottie. "You don't need to shout in my face."

"What's all this about?" I ask as the door opens again and my great-aunt comes in, followed by Hannah and Travis, Sophie and Rob, Otis, and Nora. Cormac enters last, alone.

"Well," Dottie says, puckering her lips. "I had a talk with a few parties I thought might also be interested in investing in your business. You know, we've all tried the beer. It's simply divine, and we love your ideas about using the barrel room and releasing future beers on a weekly basis."

"I'm not about to stop working here," Ann puts in. "I'm having the time of my life, and Otis only just started showing me how to use that Golden app thing. It's only been a few days, but I already met a hunky silver fox."

"And I'm so proud of you and your man with the nice ass," Great-Aunt Sky says, beaming at me.

"I'm very invested in keeping my brother employed," Hannah adds with a smile.

"I'd like to keep working here for now, too," Otis says. He nudges Sophie's shoulder, adding, "and I had this idea that maybe Soph and I could do some pop-up crafting events here."

"So it makes sense for our crafting business to invest," Sophie says in a no-nonsense tone.

"And I'm going to twist your arm to put my ginger beer on tap," Nora says before glancing at Liam. "Because I sure as hell want your beer permanently on tap at The Ginger Station."

"We *all* want to invest," Cormac blurts, then frowns at the hat his father is still holding out. "But what are we supposed to do with the hat, Dad? No one uses paper money these days. I figured we'd be Venmo-ing."

"It's symbolic." Eugene murmurs something about kids these days and then shrugs. "And Dottie printed out the brewery's Venmo code and put it inside. But we should hurry this up. My woman's out there with a bunch of young single men. She might rethink everything if I'm not careful."

Nora gives him an approving look; Cormac says, "They're probably looking for *young* single women, Dad."

My eyes fill with tears as Eugene starts to pass the hat around. "You guys...I can't believe this. You don't have to—"

"No," Dottie says firmly. "But we *want* to. We believe in you. We all want a part in what you're building."

I nod, the tears falling down my cheeks. I have to hug all of them. I have to make them cookies and light candles for them and lift them up, because of everything they've done for me. They've become the family I never thought I could have. But first...

I turn to Liam, peering up at him, and he grins down at me.

"They're our miracle, Briar."

Then he picks me up, twirls me around, and kisses me in front of everyone.

And I let myself believe again, fully, that I can be truly happy—that I can have the man I love *and* my dream.

"Oh my God, now you're *kissing* in front of me too?" Hannah moans.

Liam laughs. "Yeah, and I'm going to do it again too."

He tips me backward and kisses me again, and I really do feel like a princess.

EPILOGUE
BRIAR

Six months later

I smile at Liam. "You ready for this?"

"As ready as I am every week," he replies with a grin as he climbs off his bike.

I stow my helmet and do the same.

Stubborn man that my father is, he hasn't yet agreed to remove the clause in our original contract that says I have to attend family dinner every Friday. And, unfortunately, they have been insisting that we actually stay for dinner lately.

When we arrived at Sterling Manor on the first Friday after the New Year's party, my father had emerged by himself, in his *pajamas*, and shouted, "I know it was you!"

I nearly shouted it back, but Liam placed his hand on my arm and said, "Does that mean we can go?"

"Leave!" he'd shouted.

We had, happily.

A similar scenario had played out the following week, but then my father's strategy shifted. The week after that, we started getting invited inside.

The first dinner we had with them in the new year was completely silent, although yellow crime scene tape had been adhered to the wall where the plaque of rules used to hang. I was reasonably sure my father had done that, not the police. The tape looked almost sulky.

The next week, my dad couldn't help himself. He started bragging about the progress he was making with his new business—a shared office space for writers my mother had high-handedly named The Writers' Salon.

"We'll have a new James Joyce on our hands, you watch," he'd said.

"Jesus, I hope not," Liam had muttered.

My parents were basically insufferable, and they only got worse once Silver Star reopened and started doing well. My father, of course, took credit for our success. He said things like, "I always knew you'd blow it out of the park" and "Liam's unconventional, and that's good, because there's nothing conventional about successful people." He'd say these things with a straight face, while serving up the most conventional dinner in the most conventional house.

Liam and I have formed a weekly tradition of following up the Friday dinners with a trip to the boxing gym.

For obvious reasons.

The truth is our brewery never would have survived January without our investors. Dottie's partner's son is a trained contractor. He handled the repairs for us at a bargain-basement price, but we were still closed for almost three weeks. A brutal blow. We reopened with a huge party, though, and then had weekly release parties for the beers Liam had been working on in the interim.

February was a good month. March was a great month, and we were able to pay our investors back with interest by April.

But my father played zero role in it.

Liam and I have tried everything we can think of to get my parents to ban us from Friday dinners for good. We wear Halloween costumes. Sometimes, we study knock-knock jokes so we can annoy them all night. Always, we bring beer and refuse their wine. But my father has yet to set us free.

Liam grins at me, tapping his chest. "I think tonight's gonna be our lucky night. I'm wearing a Mr. Miracle name tag. Strange and wonderful things happen when I wear these name tags."

Liam enjoyed joking around with them so much Cormac had given him a thick stack of them as a birthday gift.

I layer my hand over his. "You should have saved it for tomorrow."

We'll be attending a wedding in the afternoon—Eugene and Nora's mom are tying the knot at The Ginger Station. Hannah is absolutely blissful that she was asked to be one of the grooms-men. Nora is the maid of honor, Cormac is the best man, and Ollie gets to be a ring bearer. It's going to be a huge blowout. Garbage Fire will be playing, and the staff is serving one of our summer beers—Zephyr, named after my great-aunt, who helped us come up with the flavor profile.

Nora is currently out with Hannah, trying to find a last-minute date for the wedding after the guy she'd been seeing ghosted her. She's adamant about bringing someone, because even though the relationship was super casual, she's been playing it up as something serious at work. José's long-time girl-friend is now his fiancée, and she's gotten even weirder about the two of them working together.

I sigh, running my hand along Liam's jaw. "Just think. We could be out with Hannah and Nora right now, trying to find Nora a wedding date."

He grimaces. "Yes, I'm sure they would have welcomed my presence."

"So you could have found Cormac a date."

"Guys only play matchmaker when their women make them, and your closest friends are all taken."

"Not Ann."

"Ann's only single because she's enjoying that Golden app Otis got her hooked on."

I shrug. "So you could have stayed home with Travis, invited the rest of the guys over, and jammed."

He nods and flicks the Mr. Miracle name tag with his middle finger. "You raise a good point. That does sound a lot fucking better than this. So much for miracles."

I shove him playfully, and he sweeps me off my feet, carrying me up the path in his arms. "We make our own fun," he says.

I press my cheek to his chest, feeling impossibly lucky. Yes, we still have to spend an hour or so a week with my insufferable parents, but it's so much easier with him. It's almost enjoyable, exchanging glances over the table. Thinking of new ways to hopefully get released from the agreement.

It's not that I never want to see my parents again. I don't know if I have it in me to say words like "never" and mean them, which is probably evidence of that soft heart my father holds in such disdain. But I don't want to be compelled to be here.

When we reach the door, Liam sets me down. "My turn," he says with a grin. "I'm deeply motivated today. I've got plans for us, and they don't involve sitting around and being talked at for hours."

Meaning it's his turn to try to end dinner before it begins.

He knocks. "The madman and madwoman are here!"

I lean against him, and he wraps his arm around me. He's obviously in good spirits, despite what's sure to be another aggravating conversation.

The door opens, and my father appears. Much to my mother's horror, my dad has started wearing more casual clothes for our family dinners. Tonight, he's wearing a shirt with the logo for our local minor league baseball team, the Asheville Tourists, paired with athletic shorts. There's no sign of my mother, which means she's probably already drinking a martini to drown her sorrows about my dad's new wardrobe. I think it's part of a strategy he's formed to bond with Liam so he can then use Liam to influence me. It's not going to work, of course, but I've come to realize this is as close to caring as my father gets.

"Lovely to see you both," he says. "Come on. We got some beautiful steaks tonight. Biggest steaks you've ever seen."

"Oh, too bad." Liam snaps his fingers. "Maybe we should reconnect next week. I just became a vegan. It was those fake chicken nuggets your old company makes, sir. I tried them once, and now it's an addiction."

My father glances at Liam's thick biceps. "There's no way you can maintain your physique on a vegan diet, son."

"Oh, sure I can. I just need about ten avocados and a pound or two of potatoes, and I'll be good as gold. I can help Alicia prepare them. There's a specific method."

My dad glances over his shoulder. "Well, I did want to talk to you kids about a pretty big opportunity for our little brewery, but I'm not sure Alicia will—"

"Oh, I wouldn't want to put her out," Liam says. "No problem at all. I can bring my own dinner next week."

My father flinches. My mother would hate it if a guest brought their own food, and we all know it. "No need for that. Just send...maybe send an example of what you can eat."

"You got it, *Dad*," he says. "Coming right up. We'll see you next week."

Before my father can say anything else, Liam sweeps me back into his arms and struts toward his bike.

"I can walk," I say, trying not to laugh as he hurries down the path. I can hear the front door closing.

"No time for walking. We don't want to give them a chance to figure out a workaround." He sets me down next to the bike. "How'd I do?"

"I think it's a record," I say with a grin.

"Good, because we've got plans."

"Are we getting steak?"

"Even better," he says as he puts my helmet on me and buckles it.

SEVERAL MINUTES LATER, he pulls up in front of the boxing gym.

"It's open," I tell him, almost scandalized.

"You see, businesses have to stay open for a certain number of hours a day to stay successful, Briar."

I raise my eyebrows. "This place is almost never open."

He unclasps my helmet. "Because Mick is lazy, and we usually come after hours. I like to take full advantage of the privacy."

I lean in and kiss him before climbing off the bike. My pulse is racing, because I sense he's up to something, and I don't know what it means yet.

He joins me on the sidewalk, and we walk in together, hand in hand.

When we enter the reception area, we find Mick sitting behind the desk, his legs propped up. He's a big guy, like Liam, with dark hair cut short and a scar across his jaw. He's a bit rough around the edges, but he's always been nice to me.

"Aw, fuck," he says, glancing at his watch. "You're, like, two hours early, man."

"We got out of dinner." Liam raises his eyebrows. "I told you I was going to try to get out of dinner."

"It was the Mr. Miracle name tag," I feel compelled to add. "We think it has magical properties."

"Hello, Briar," Mick says with bemusement. "Well, all right."

He gets to his feet, then strolls into the gym, cupping his hands to his mouth. "Everyone out. It's an emergency. Something to do with the electrical system. We'll be open tomorrow. Out you go."

Mick's orders are met with a few groans from the guys working out. Still, everyone starts to pack up and clear the gym.

I give Liam a confused look and whisper, "Why are we kicking these people out?"

Mick pats Liam on the back. "That's for hooking me up with the band. I'll see you tomorrow."

Liam gives him a brusque nod as he walks off.

Once he's gone, Liam leans in close. "Be patient, Princess. We just got at least an hour of our lives handed back to us. We can afford a few minutes."

But my racing heart tells me otherwise. What does he have planned?

The few guys who ducked into the changing room to get their stuff filter out and exit the gym, and then "Eye of the Tiger" starts streaming over the loudspeaker.

I laugh with delight, pulling away from Liam. "Are we going to act out a training montage?"

"Something like that," he says as he reaches into his backpack.

"Are you giving me a beer?"

"If you want one. But I thought I'd give you these." He hands me my slightly scuffed gloves.

"I'm not sure I feel like boxing right now. Maybe after a drink."

"Come on, Briar. Just a couple of rounds."

There's something urgent in his tone. Almost...nervous.

Frowning at him, I put on one glove. I try to put on the other one, but there's something inside of it.

A gasp escapes me as I pull out the little black box.

"Liam," I say, my voice shaking. "The other glove. Help me get it off."

He smiles as he pulls it off, and then he lowers to one knee.

My whole body trembles as I open the box. The ring is gorgeous. It's antique, white gold, with a princess-cut light-blue stone.

Tears flood my eyes as I look at him.

His smile is warm and so full of love. "Great-Aunt Sky and Dottie helped me pick it out. Dottie said this particular stone has better resonance than a diamond. I don't know what that means, but I figure she's right about an awful lot of things."

I weave my hand into his hair, because he's still down on one knee, and I need to touch him.

"Briar...this was where I first took notice of you. Obviously, I'd noticed you before. It would be impossible not to, but the joy you felt when you made that first punch...it was like watching a fire light inside of you. I fell a little in love with you, and now I'm so deeply in love with you it makes me sick of myself." He reaches up to wipe the tears off my cheek. "So, please, will you do me the honor of being my wife?"

I slide the ring on and tackle him back onto the mats. He takes the fall easy, letting me sprawl on top of him, my arms around his neck.

"Yes, yes, *yes*," I cry out.

"Thank God," he says, grinning as he kisses me. "That name tag really is something."

I lay a path of kisses down his face. "You definitely should have saved the name tag for the wedding tomorrow, because you wasted its power. You could have written anything on there, and I would have said yes. I love you so much."

"I love you too," he says with a broad grin. "And I'm relieved. It would have been really embarrassing if Mick had kicked everyone out and you'd said no. Would you like that beer now? I made a new one for you. Dottie told me the meaning of all the herbs. It probably tastes like shit, but it's heavily symbolic."

I laugh, so full of joy I feel like I could float away, but I'm anchored by the very large man I'm wrapped around. "That sounds delightful, but there's something else I'd like to do first."

Because everyone knows the first step toward happily ever after is enjoying your man in a boxing gym.

ABOUT THE AUTHOR

ANGELA CASELLA is a romcom fanatic. Writing them, reading them, watching them—she's greedy, and she does it all. In addition to her solo releases, she was lucky enough to collaborate with Denise Grover Swank on three complete series.

She lives in Asheville, NC. Her hobbies include herding her daughter toward less dangerous activities, the aforementioned romcom addiction, and dreaming of a self-cleaning house.

Visit her website at www.angelacasella.com